CICADA SPRING

CHRISTIAN GALACAR

CICADA SPRING

A NOVEL

Book design by Maureen Cutajar
www.gopublished.com

ISBN-13: 978-1508616696
ISBN-10: 1508616698

As adults, we find solace in the knowledge that monsters do not exist. This is true because it's what we choose to believe. That is the privilege of the practiced mind. But the terrifying reality is that monsters are real. They do exist. They are us. And that is more horrifying than anything I ever imagined as a child.

CHAPTER 1

The girl stopped at the creek and looked down at the blood. Some of it was from the cut on her lip, but most of it—the darker blood—came from between her legs. She tried to wipe it away with her hands, only smearing it into broad red streaks across her fair skin. Bending at the water's edge, she regarded her rippled reflection: bruised flesh and wild hair. A tear welled in her eye and broke free. It traced her nostril, caught for a moment, then fell from the tip of her nose into the water. She looked away, her heart dropping from the sight of her face.

The sky through the canopy of trees was an overcast, ashen plate, the color of a moth's wings. A premature New England summer on the heels of an early heat wave had turned the evening into a solid thing. Humid, earthy scents hung heavy in the air, and in the woods where she found herself now, the ones that separated downtown Heartsridge and Durham Street, the crickets began to sing their lonely songs of approaching night.

It was May 7, 1979, a Saturday, and Kara Price was fifteen years old.

She glanced up and down the trail cautiously, looking left, in the direction of town, and then right, toward home. When she was certain she was alone, Kara removed her sandals, her shirt, and her underwear. She folded them neatly on a flat rock beside the creek, save for the underwear, which she crumpled and threw into a bush. She left her bra and skirt on, rolling the skirt up at the bottom to spare it from the water. Her hands trembled as she picked up her purse. They felt like clumsy, impersonal appendages that belonged to someone else. She fumbled with the zipper for a moment, eventually sliding it open, and removed a small packet of tissues which she placed on top of her stack of clothes.

The water was unsympathetic—it stole her breath. She waded into it, determined, watching for anyone coming up the path. Cupping her hands, she leaned forward and christened her face. Her lip caught fire in a flash of needling pain and she winced, turning her head as the sting fell off into a low whimper. She ran her tongue over the spot, finding an awkward, cumbersome lump. Then she tasted the sick metallic saltiness of blood. Clenching her jaw, she brought another splash of water to her face, washing away the tinge. She hated that taste; it was something like old pennies.

Next she splashed water on her legs, her arms, and her stomach, and began running her hands over her body in slow circular motions. She just wanted him off of her. She wanted to be clean. He had done terrible things to her in the backseat of his car, and she was certain she could still smell him. It was as if he were still on top of her, breathing and sweating. She just wanted to forget him, to put what had happened behind her.

Five minutes passed, and by the time her skin was free of blood she was nearly numb from the cold. When she was finished, Kara stepped out of the creek and blotted herself dry with the tissues. She put her sandals and shirt back on. The shirt was a pink top, and on the straps were small specks of blood. She would throw it away when she got home, but for now, she needed to slide back into that sordid skin.

Kara could not allow anyone to find out what had happened. She was ashamed and embarrassed about the whole thing. *Maybe I deserved it,* she thought. And for the first time in a long while, Kara found herself longing for her mother's touch, wanting to feel that safety a child can only find in a parent's embrace. But she couldn't tell her mother. This could very well have been her own fault. How could she look her in the eyes? Her mother had expressed her disapproval for the outfit she was wearing that morning, telling her it was not professional for a first day of work. Kara had scoffed and told her she was being too old-fashioned. "Get with the times, Mom!" she'd said. Maybe her mother had been right all along, though. And maybe Kara had brought this on herself.

Even if she did tell someone, who would believe her? This notion, this feeling of helplessness, gripped her stomach and filled her with a dreadful hollowness. She was alone, and somewhere inside, in the badlands of her consciousness, she knew that her life had just significantly changed, that her course had shifted, and now she was heading toward some dark horizon where storm clouds were stacking, promising to bring hard times. Kara sat down at the edge of the water, brought her knees to her chest and started to cry into her arms. Time elapsed in an incoherent daze.

Why did he do this to me? Did I do something wrong?

The questions rolled through her mind, repeating like some sort of awful scrolling text, the words bright and red against a black abyss. But no answers came. There was only a strange, far-off guilt to greet her, a feeling that she had done something terrible and that no one could know. It was a secret she must keep. So that was what she would do.

Once she'd cried herself out, Kara stood and headed down the trail in the direction of home. The hard orange glow of the streetlights along Durham Street silhouetted the new-budded branches of the trees ahead, turning them a seasick green. When she reached the road, she turned left. Her house was only a quarter mile ahead on the corner of Durham and Columbus. Walking briskly in the cover of twilight, Kara stuck to the shadows below the low corridor of branches overhanging the sidewalk. But she ached and burned between her legs, and this eventually slowed her. She reached down and touched where it hurt. Pulling her hand away, she looked at it. Clean. The bleeding had stopped; all that remained was the pain. It was like some kind of sick, unwanted legacy he'd passed on to her.

There was a small playground in front of the Clarke Middle School a few hundred yards before her house. Kara stopped, taking a seat on one of the half-buried tires cresting out of the ground. Only the year before, she'd attended this school and played on these tires with her friends, hopping from one to the next, but it felt like such an impossibly distant place now. She would've given anything to be back in that earlier version of her life—young, innocent, carefree, no knowledge about the sad truth of the world—but the harder she reached for it in her mind, the farther it receded, slipping through her fingers as she tried to grasp it.

Toughen up, Kara, an internal voice said. This was something her field hockey coach used to yell at her from the sidelines. She recognized the words, but this wasn't her coach's voice—it was her own. *Toughen up, Kara.*

So she toughened up as well as she could, stiffening her posture, throwing back her shoulders, choking back tears. In this moment, her mind forged a distorted lens, and through it Kara viewed the rape as something that sometimes people just had to endure. Plain old bad luck. Something that needed to be gotten over and moved past. The facts of life, kiddo. She would never tell anyone that she'd been raped. This was her decision. This was her choice.

Then Kara remembered her face. How would she explain it? People would ask questions. If she had learned anything growing up in a small town, it was that curiosity was a powerful drug, and it demanded answers. She needed a story, something believable, something she could retell over and over again when people asked, cracking a counterfeit smile to sell the lie, maybe laughing a little at her own expense.

Kara recalled the path she'd taken through the woods. At the start of it there was a two-foot drop where the asphalt of the parking lot in back of the Saver Mart met the beginning of the trail. It was a place people could easily fall if they weren't careful, just a silly mistake. If she rubbed a little dirt on her palms and knees, she could really sell the story. It was decided. The cliché of the assaulted woman explaining away her bruises by saying she'd fallen was something that Kara did not yet understand. In her mind, the lie had no holes, no cracks in its veneer to be pried open by doubtful eyes. It was time to go home now, time to get gone and get on.

She stood and left the park.

The front lights were already on when Kara got to her house. She stopped at the granite walkway step and rehearsed her story one more time. While she ran through it in her head (Mom: *Kara, sweetie, what happened to your face?* Kara: *Oh Mom, I'm such a klutz...*) her eyes fell on the features of her house. It was a picture she'd seen a million times before, but now what she saw looked different and somehow sinister.

The windows were dark and stared back at her like large, sunken, accusing eyes. The red front door resembled a jackal's mouth ripped open wide, howling with laughter. To the far left, the large bay window revealed the kitchen. Kara saw her mother pouring a glass of wine at the counter. Her father wasn't there, and then he was. He walked in behind Kara's mother, wrapped his arms around her waist, and kissed her neck. Her mother smiled, turning her head to meet his cheek. They rocked from side to side for a moment in a lovers' slow dance. Then her father backed away, picked a magazine up off the kitchen table, and disappeared into the house. The smile remained on her mother's face long after her husband had left the room. It was all framed so serenely in the yellow glow of that window, like a silent home movie from a time before Kara had been born. Young love not yet pressed with the task of raising a daughter. Watching her mother and her father brought a thickness to the back of Kara's throat, an achy feeling, the feeling of holding back the tears that so desperately wanted out. But Kara remained strong. She would not cry. *Toughen up, Kara.*

Looking left, Kara gazed mindlessly down the sidewalk, searching for something she could hardly define. Perhaps a last bit of calm before everything crystallized. Four houses away, Mrs. Twomey stood in her front yard, watering her prized tulips— brilliant reds and yellows that cut the haze of the settling evening. The woman's silver hair cinched tight in a bun resembled a shimmering coin in the distance. Underscored by a blue gardening apron and white cotton gloves, she almost looked cartoonish, drawn into the scene by some unseen hand of God—the Almighty Animator. Then Kara's eyes moved from Mrs. Twomey, looking hard down the center of Durham Street. The streetlights on either side had the illusion of bending inward as she focused on the distant vantage point. She stared with a purpose, trying to see beyond the limits of her vision, trying to find some new place beyond reality—salvation—until the road fell away into a gray and orange haze and her awareness harmonized with the moment. But what she found was not deliverance. She found a place where past, present, and future—the primary colors of being—all overlapped like sheets of transparent film, existing all at once in a deep, dark, dreadful fourth color.

In her mind she saw herself, an eight-year-old girl, wearing a purple snowsuit, being towed up Durham Street in a wooden toboggan. Her father had the yellow rope wrapped around his hand and taut over his shoulder, his feet sliding on packed snow as he leaned his weight forward, trying to find purchase and pull her along. He stopped, turning back to smile at her. The scene shifted to August of that same year. She sat on the hatch of the family station wagon, swinging her legs, waiting for her parents to take her to Crane's Beach for the first time. They drove in the heat, eventually breaking to cool, salty air. Marsh all around, sand dunes and blue skies. That day she spent nearly two hours in the surf and earned her first sunburn. Her mother had to stop for burn cream on the way home. Kara remembered this. She remembered the smell of her toasted skin and then, later, the smell and cool feel of the Lidocaine. It was seven years behind her, half a lifetime ago, but she remembered. Here the images were clear, but yet they were also tainted, viewed through the filter of that fourth, dark color where everything existed all at once.

Kara brought her hand to her face and touched her lip. It stung fiercely, the sweat on her fingers bringing the pain to a point again, dousing her recollections of childhood. She clenched her jaw, inhaling long, thin breaths through her teeth. *Toughen up, Kara.*

She walked up the brick walkway to the front door. Through it, Kara could hear her mother talking. "I think she said she was out at six so she should be home soon. You could probably light the coals now." There was a beat of silence. Then: "And did you get the mail today? We still haven't received our invite to your cousin's wedding." The voice soothed her. It was the sound of home, the sound of family and comfort and rescue. Somehow it touched her heart. Squeezed it. And then broke it.

Home, Kara thought distantly. Her lips parted, and she whispered a word to herself as if she didn't believe it: "Mom." At that, the world around her blurred gray and white and every color at once and then fell into a dizzying darkness. Her knees became rubber. The strength, the toughness, the walls, the barriers, the story about how she'd tripped and went face first into the ground all fell with it. And when it did, Kara's mother opened the door and saw her daughter standing there. Toughen up. But how?

"Oh my God!" her mother yelled, and Kara Price, the fifteen-year-old who was afraid that everyone would find out, afraid that she had done something wrong, fell into her mother's arms and wept.

She was eight again. And it was spring.

Harry Bennett pulled his Eldorado into the junkyard, the car dipping and diving through a landscape of dried-up puddles and washed-out potholes. He accelerated and peeled through the entrance gate, past a faded sign that read HEARTSRIDGE TRANSFER STATION in big orange letters. In the distance, at the far end of the rolling mounds of garbage, a black pickup truck sat parked. Harry sped toward it. When he was close, he brought his car to a skidding stop. The tires of his Cadillac belched out plumes of pale dust as they crunched over the baked gravel. Harry turned off the ignition and stepped out, waving vaguely at the truck as he opened the back door of his Cadillac.

Eddie Corbett hopped out of his pickup, wearing khaki slacks and a denim shirt. He was a short, balding man in his mid-fifties, with glasses sitting atop a small upturned nose. There was something very pathetic about him, the way he stood: hands in his pockets, shoulders slouched. Desperate.

"Why the hell did you want to meet me all the way out here on a Saturday?" Eddie asked, folding his arms. "I could've met you at your office."

Harry was leaning into the backseat of his car. When he straightened and turned around, he was holding two one-gallon jugs of water in each hand. "Evenin' to you too, Eddie," he said. "Had an errand to run out here, thought I'd kill two birds."

"What errand does the mayor of Heartsridge have at the dump?" Eddie moved toward Harry.

"Need to ask you a favor," Harry said. He turned and placed the two jugs on top of his car. Then he bent back down, grabbed another two, and put them beside the others. "We're friends, right? I was hoping you'll be able to help me out. Who knows, maybe help each other."

They weren't friends. If it weren't for the fact that their wives were cousins, they might never have known each other at all. Save for the occasional run-in around town, the only time the two men ever spoke was at holidays and birthday parties. Even then the conversation was stilted and forced.

Eddie wrinkled his brow, running a hand through what remained of his thinning hair. "A favor? What could I possibly have that you want?"

Harry removed his gray sports coat, folded it over his arm and put it in the backseat of his car. He rolled up the sleeves of his shirt, stopping midway up his forearms when the muscle grew too thick. "It's the thirtieth anniversary of the Heartsridge Spring Festival, starting this coming Thursday, so we're expecting it to be a big one." Harry removed his tie, tucking it into his breast pocket. "Do me a favor, Eddie, and grab me that bucket over there." Harry pointed behind Eddie to an old rusty bucket sitting next to a toppled-over ice chest.

"What the hell you need that for—"

"Christ! Just get it!" Harry snapped, his face darkening. "I've had a shit day, and I got things to do."

Eddie flinched and jumped back, his glasses sliding to the end of his nose.

Harry was in his fifties, the same as Eddie, but he was in far better shape. Standing almost six feet, two hundred pounds and built of solid blue-collar muscle, intimidation came naturally to him. He grew up working at the Bentley Warren gravel pit over in West Elm, running the rock crusher for almost twenty years before starting his own trucking business and then parlaying that into politics. His mix of street smarts and common-man work ethic had made him a shoo-in when he finally decided to run for mayor of Heartsridge. He was a man of the people, for the people. He reminded folks that hard work paid off. In a way, he represented hope. And for that, he was loved.

"Okay, don't blow a gasket," Eddie said, pushing his glasses back up. He walked over and grabbed the bucket.

Harry brought his hand up to his head, clamping his middle finger and thumb over his temples. The veins throbbed beneath the surface, his head flaring behind the eyes. "This fucking heat," he muttered.

"What'd you say?" Eddie placed the bucket in front of Harry. "You okay? You look a little worse for wear."

Harry looked up, his eyes sunken and dark. "Yes. I'm fine." He dropped his hand away from his head and turned back to his car, grabbing two of the jugs off the roof. He pulled their caps off with his teeth and proceeded to dump the water into the bucket. "Now, where were we?"

Eddie eyed the bucket. "You were talking about the festival," he said, distracted.

"Right, yes, Spring Festival. It's going to be big this year, real big. It should bring us a good haul in tourist dollars, too." Harry grabbed the other two containers of water and emptied them in with the rest. He tossed the jugs aside.

"Okay, but how can I help with that?" Eddie pulled a pack of Salems from his pocket, lit one and inhaled deep, blowing jets of smoke through his nose.

"We need your lot," Harry said, walking up to Eddie and standing only a few feet away. Harry dwarfed him.

He was referring to the parking lot attached to the strip mall Eddie owned in West Elm, the next town over. The property sat directly at the intersection of Route 6 and Route 1A, which made it a straight two-mile shot from West Elm to Heartsridge. Eddie had bought the place ten years back using his retirement savings—his wife Jeannie had just about lost her head when he told her what he'd done—but in the end it had proven to be a sound investment, so transgressions were forgiven. With all the properties rented, it generated a sizable monthly income, enough for Jeannie and Eddie to retire early.

"My lot?"

"Yes, we need your parking lot for extra parking. Tourists are easily spooked, and if they show up in Heartsridge and there isn't anywhere to park, they'll just leave and say better luck next time. Especially the ones who are just passing through, and they're a good portion of it. But if we have your lot we can run a free shuttle between West Elm and Heartsridge. I figure if we advertise off the highway it'll work out just fine. Gives us the extra space, and we can put a little coin in your pocket for your troubles. It'll only be for the weekend, of course. We shouldn't need it Thursday. Usually it's only locals on opening night." He slapped Eddie hard on the shoulder, a thick politician's smile set across his face.

"Aw, Jesus, I can't do that." Eddie threw his cigarette to the ground and crushed it under his boot. "I have rental agreements with my tenants. I can't just tell them their customers can't park there for three days. They could sue me."

"Oh come on, show a little spine." Harry turned away, shaking his head and setting his hands on his hips. "Can't let your tenants run your life. You'll get three thousand dollars, a grand a day to do nothing. Hell, half the businesses in that mall have booths at our fair this year. It'll be just as good for them. Besides, we're family, Eddie. That's the kind of thing you do for family. Am I right?"

"I'm sorry. I can't do that, family or not. This is my livelihood. If my tenants leave or sue me, I won't be able to pay the bills. I'll be screwed. I got two mortgages to think about."

Harry gazed off into the distance to where the sun dipped below the horizon, splashing its fading firelight skyward onto what remained of the disappearing world. He brought a hand back to his temples. His jaw muscles bulged and rippled as he clenched his teeth. He was starting to hate Eddie Corbett. He'd always thought the man was a coward, but he was offering money now, *real* money, and Eddie was turning it down. This disappointed Harry but didn't necessarily surprise him. If it had been a surprise, Harry wouldn't have made sure he had a Plan B. He always had a second course of action ready. His ability to see all the angles was, perhaps, second only to his ability to exploit them. It was what made him such a successful politician. He'd offered Eddie the easy way; now it was time for the unpleasant.

Eddie continued. "If I could help you, I would—"

"Bullshit!" Harry spun around, pointing a rigid finger at Eddie. Strands of his dark hair broke loose from their slick hold, falling in sweaty bands across his forehead and around his eyes. "You're a chicken-shit, Eddie. You always have been and always will be," he said in a low, hard voice.

Eddie bent backwards as Harry pushed his finger into his face, almost so far back that he looked as though he might stumble and fall on the seat of his pants. "Harry, please... I..." He trailed off.

And then as quickly as Harry Bennett had changed into the wild-haired lunatic, he broke a smile, pulled his hand back, and brushed his hair away from his face. Calmly, he said: "You know what the problem is with cowardly chicken-shits, Eddie? 'Cause I do. They're weak. Every... last... one of 'em. Weak as sugar-glass. Pathetic."

"Fuck this and fuck you," Eddie said. He started to turn back to his truck. "I'm outta here, you prick."

Harry straightened. "Eddie, family or not, if you turn your back on me I'll crush your goddamn skull." The threat was sincere.

Eddie stopped and looked Harry in the eyes. Neither spoke for a few seconds in the hostile silence; they only looked at one another. Harry kept his smile wide.

Eddie broke first. "What do you expect me to do? You drag me all the way out here, ask me to do you one hell of a favor, and then talk to me like that. How would you react?"

"I'm sure I don't know. No one would ever talk to me like that. I'm not weak like you." Harry turned away and went back to his car, leaning once more into the backseat. When he turned back around, he was holding two things: a brown burlap sack and a manila envelope. The burlap sack was tied at the top with baler twine. Something inside yowled thinly and tried to push its way out—a hopeless attempt. Harry tossed the sack forward. It landed with a soft thud beside the rusty bucket of water. The thing inside continued to try to escape.

Eddie didn't move. "What the hell's in there?" he asked, looking down at the sack. Most of the color had drained from his face as if he were coming to grips with the realization that he might be in trouble.

"I tell you, Eddie, women only want things for the sake of having them. They say they want something, but they don't want to take care of it. They can be so ungrateful and irresponsible. That's why I never gave Ali kids, you know that?" Harry said implacably. He moved a few steps closer, but Eddie didn't seem to notice him. He was still watching, with increasing revulsion on his face, the twitching burlap bag on the ground. "I told you, Ed…" Harry slammed the envelope he was holding in his hand against Eddie's chest. "Weak." He laughed. "She's cute, though. Maybe Jeannie would think so too."

Eddie's attention shifted back to himself. He looked down at the envelope pressed against his chest, held in place by the mayor's burly hand. "What… what is this?"

Harry relaxed his arm, letting the envelope slide. "Open it and find out. But I think by the look on your face right now you already know."

Eddie caught the package before it fell.

Harry turned his attention to the sack on the ground, kneeling beside it. "I tried to be nice, Eddie." He pulled a small knife from his back pocket, grabbed the twisted neck of the burlap bag, and cut the twine. "Just try and remember that come the Christmas party. No need to make things awkward in the family. This is just between you and me... for now."

While Eddie fumbled with the envelope, trying to open it, Harry reached his hand into the bag, grabbed something furry, and pulled it out. "There you are, my little princess. Just couldn't keep your legs shut, huh?" He was talking playfully to the white cat as he held it up by the skin of its neck. It twisted lazily in his hand as he brought it near his face and spoke mischievously to it in a strange sort of sick baby-talk. "You were supposed to stay inside, yes you were, but you didn't, no, you didn't. No, you went out and screwed some other pussy and got knocked up." Harry laughed and stood up, cat still in hand. "Looks like you and Lilly here aren't so different."

Eddie's neck was bent down as he shuffled through the stack of pictures he'd pulled from the envelope. He no longer looked scared; he looked guilty. "How did you get these?" he asked, the defeat thick in his voice. When he looked up, Harry was standing beside the rusty bucket of water with a cat clutched in his hand. It made a low, distressed, growling sound as its limbs dangled helplessly paralyzed from its body.

"You don't get to the Mayor's Office without having an ear to the ground and an eye in the sky. I've known about you and that little piece of ass right there for months now, just never thought I'd ever need anything from you. To be straight with you, I really didn't want to have to ever use those pictures. A man's business is his business. It just so happens that my business is more important than you getting your rocks off every Thursday night at eight. If you'd just cooperated it never would've come to this."

The pictures Eddie Corbett held so anxiously in his hands were of him and a young woman, Wynona "Nona" Finn, having a romp in the back room of her hair salon, High Wave. She'd started the business two years before, renting one of the vacant spaces in Eddie's strip mall. It was a year after her grand opening that Nona's boyfriend, Glen, cheated on her and ran off with a twenty-something waitress from West Elm. Then it was Eddie who took the vacant space in Nona.

Most of the pictures didn't show Eddie's face. But how could they? It was buried between her legs, only black-and-white shots of the back of a bald head. The last three photographs, the ones where Nona was bent over the manicure table and he was pulling at her hair, face turned up in ecstasy, were undeniably Eddie Corbett, though. No getting around that.

"I've seen enough. You're one sick son of a bitch, you know that?" Eddie said, sliding the pictures back into the envelope. "What are you going to do with these?"

"Well," Harry said, still holding the cat, "that depends entirely on you." Then in one quick motion he turned, bent to one knee, and plunged the animal toward the bucket of water. Its hind legs kicked for the rim as its tail submerged, but Harry grabbed it tight with his other hand and pushed it under. The cat let out one final yowl, and then it was completely under. The only noise was the occasional clatter of the metal bucket's handle banging off the side of the container.

Eddie looked on, his face twisted into a look of horror and disgust. "You're... you're insane," he whispered. Not so much to Harry but to himself, as though he were coming to terms with the fact.

"Ohhhh, I don't think so. I just know how to get what I want. Weak people like you only make it that much easier. Just think, if you could've kept your dick in your pants, you wouldn't be in this mess." Harry pushed down harder on the cat, the water coming up almost to the folds of his cuffs, small splashes slopping out onto the ground.

"So what are you going to do with these?" Eddie took a cautious step toward Harry.

Harry didn't respond, only continued to press down on the pregnant cat in the bucket, his body hunched over, bobbing up and down as he mumbled to himself: "I don't get it. Why doesn't she ever listen to me? I knew a pet was a bad idea."

"Harry?" Eddie repeated.

Again, Harry didn't answer. Then: "Well, what the hell do you think I'm going to do with those pictures? You too stupid to figure out how blackmail works?" He glared up at Eddie, who stumbled backwards a few steps as if shoved.

Harry stood up, shaking his hands off before wiping the remaining water on the seat of his pants. "I want your lot, Eddie. We need it. Now, you can let Heartsridge use it for the festival, or I can leave an envelope like that one on your doorstep for Jeannie to find."

"I... I—"

"Yeah, yeah, you'll do it. You're a coward, not dumb."

Eddie looked down at his feet. "What about the negatives? I want those destroyed. I'm assuming these aren't the only copies."

"Correct you are, my friend," Harry said. "And those are safe with me. You can have them after the festival's over. I have no use for them or you after that." He reached down and grabbed the cat by the neck, tossing its limp body underneath an old refrigerator beside them. He sighed and kicked the bucket over, spilling the water into the dirt. "I'm telling you, pets are a waste of money."

Eddie stood there silent.

Harry turned and went back to his car, reaching into the backseat and grabbing one last thing. It was a black bag of trash, closed at the top with a blue rubber band. "Almost forgot the reason I came here," he said.

Eddie still said nothing, only watched, his face pale.

Harry walked the bag to the mountainous pile of garbage and dropped it gently at the edge. He walked back to his car, got in, and fired up the Eldorado. As he was backing out, he said, "C'mon, Ed, everything will be fine. Cheer up." Then he laughed and sped off.

Driving toward the exit, plumes of dust twisting up behind his car, he could just barely see the silhouette of Eddie Corbett in his rearview mirror, standing there, slouching, and slowly moping back to his truck. Then the dust closed in like a curtain, and Eddie was gone.

CHAPTER 2

The killer drove a truck, a '71 Ford he'd stolen up north. It was a hard-lived machine—sun-cracked red paint, rust-spotted chrome bumpers, bald tires. The cab had the baked-in smell of vinyl rubber and motor oil. Raw smells of sweat and grit. He sat parked in the back of the empty truck stop with the engine off, smoking a Marlboro. It was night, and rain poured down in fat droplets, sheeting his windshield like crystal syrup, beating hard off the truck's roof in drunken time. He was waiting for the man who was going to exit the bathroom at the far end of the lot.

He'd followed him south since the gas station in Hanover, New Hampshire, pulling to the side of the road and dousing his lights when the man turned into the rest stop. He'd watched through the sparse divide of pines that separated the highway from the parking lot as the man exited the blue Pinto and walked into the bathrooms of the building lettered MASSACHUSETTS STATE HIGHWAY INFORMATION.

Once the man had gone inside, the killer brought his truck into the rest area and drove to the back of the lot, shutting off the engine. After making sure there weren't any other cars, he pulled a small switchblade from his pocket and hopped out of the truck. Sticking to the tree line, eyes monitoring the bathroom door, he made his way to the man's car. Sticking the blade in the tread, he flattened the front right tire. Puncturing the side would look too suspicious, too intentional, and it might spook the guy too much. *No mistakes,* he reminded himself.

Going back to the tree line, he returned to his truck, lit a cigarette and waited. The Pinto had immediately started to lean on its crippled leg. Less than a minute later, the tire had gone completely flat. Now the killer continued to watch, whistling softly to take his mind off his hammering heart, flicking the blade of the knife open and closed, open and closed, over and over again. *Click-click, click-click, click-click.* He loved that sound.

This would be his fourth time, and he was finally starting to rid his craft of the sloppiness that'd plagued his first three outings. The times before had gone reasonably well but not perfectly. There had been little things he'd forgotten, small oversights that left a lingering bitterness in the back of his mind: the gun getting caught in his coat pocket as he'd tried to pull it, leaving cigarette butts behind, standing too close and getting blood spray on his clothes. He tried to forget about those things, promising to learn from his mistakes, apply the lesson and move forward. Growth. Progress. But many nights the mistakes found him startled awake in a cold sweat, claustrophobic thoughts of cement walls and cold steel bars racing through his head. That was no good. It was a cancerous, slow rot from the inside out. The memories of his kills were infected with these small degrees of incompetence, thwarting any attempts to fully enjoy his work. And what was the point of it all if he couldn't even enjoy it?

It'd been almost two months since he'd shot Stephen, the

hitchhiker from Vermont, and according to the news, the case remained open without a single lead. The same went for the other two. That had to mean something. He couldn't be all that incompetent if he'd managed to go this long without so much as a sniff in his direction. It'd been almost a year since he started killing. With three victims under his belt, he was moving beyond amateur, and so far, the police hadn't even connected the murders. Or if they had, they were keeping silent about it, which more than likely meant they didn't know much of anything. So why couldn't he enjoy his work? Why the sour aftertaste when he was so sure it should taste sweet? It didn't seem fair.

Perhaps it was the possibility of getting caught, the possibility that deep down he knew his urges were becoming more powerful than any logic or rules he could put in place. No matter how many lessons he applied, his poor impulse control led to hastily made decisions. No one could cover every minute detail. Eventually he might slip up. That remained the eventual truth. He could feel his handle on the darkness inside him slipping. Like a wild horse spooked and charging, the illusion of control was quickly disappearing.

There had been a time when he actually could stop himself, though. He'd fought the urges all through college. It wasn't until nine years after he'd graduated that the long, aimless drives around New England started. Sometimes he would just get in his car and drive north. Six hours would pass in what seemed like the blink of an eye, and he would be at the Canadian border. Then he would turn around, head home, and do it again the next day. Soon he began looking for hitchhikers, not really planning on going through with anything but seeing how close he could bring himself to that point of no return, sometimes just playing through scenarios in his mind, sometimes actually picking up strangers, driving them ten or fifteen miles, and then dropping them off, the whole time feeling the cold steel of his gun pressed against his stomach or sitting in his pocket. Eventually he got bored though, and the urges, like any compulsion, demanded harder stimulation—the good stuff, the real stuff. He finally saw no good reason he should have to hold back any longer. But he was certain this was his choice. He didn't *have* to start killing. He just didn't see why he shouldn't. He could control it if he wanted to, sure.

His hope was that if things went right this time, in his periphery there would be no lingering bitterness to spoil anything. The idea of a perfect kill made him almost giddy. *No mistakes.*

He tamped out his cigarette and was about to light another when the door to the men's room swung open. His breathing became shallow and steady. He slunk back in his seat, pressed flat into the darkness of his truck.

The man exited the bathroom, wiping his hands on the seat of his pants. He walked a few feet and stopped at one of the vending machines outside the information booth. He fished through his pockets for a few seconds but seemed to find no change and gave up the idea. He continued back to his car, halting in his tracks about ten feet from the Pinto when he noticed his tire was flat. He brought both of his hands to the top of his head and bent his neck back, yelling an assortment of expletives into the night that fell flat against the rain. The man covered the remaining distance to his car with an irritated, concerned gait, kneeling down by the tire and inspecting the damage.

The killer continued to watch. It might just have been his favorite part, the watching. It was when he felt most powerful, as though the situation were his and only he knew it. It was his secret knowledge that they were not long for this world, his secret power over them. And he liked to hold onto it as long as he could to prolong this control, to savor the rawness of it all.

Keeping his eyes on the man, he leaned over to his glove box and opened it, pulling out an old 9mm Luger. Besides a small pension inheritance, the pistol was about the only thing his father had really given up in death. And it wasn't so much that he'd left it to him as it was he'd helped himself to all his father's belongings, including his bank accounts, before anyone knew the old man was dead.

The killer tucked the Luger into the pocket of his coat, an old Army jacket with a faded peace sign duct-taped on the back. It had been his father's as well (the jacket, not the peace sign; he'd added that himself). He'd never liked the man, especially after his mother left and his father *really* started to drink, but he did like some of the old war memorabilia his father collected. He'd wanted him to go into the service after high school, thought it would make a man out of him, but much to the old bastard's dismay, he chose the college route instead of being sent off to Vietnam to die in a rice field. He wasn't sure, but sometimes he wondered if that made him a coward. *Click-click, click-click.*

The man hurried to the back of his car, opening the rear door and pulling out a green slicker. The rain had let up slightly but still continued to come down at a steady spit. After he rushed into his raincoat, the man unlatched the trunk, bent down, and began rummaging through it.

The killer continued to watch. *Click-click, click-click, click-click.* Then he stopped with the knife, sliding it back into his pocket and breathed deep and slow through his nose. He turned the key to the ignition and started the truck. The engine growled to life. His lights flicked on, slicing the dark. They caught the man and his maimed vehicle in their beams. The man straightened, leaning back out of the trunk. He cupped a hand over his brow, shielding his eyes. The killer put the truck in gear and slowly drove forward.

The man raised his hand, waving at the truck as it came closer. "I got a flat here," the man yelled, hardly audible. His wave turned into a swooping, beckoning gesture. "A flat. You got a jack?" He pointed excitedly to his tire.

The killer pulled up alongside the man and his car, rolling down the window. "Car trouble?" he asked, grinning.

The man walked up to the truck and wiped his hand over his face, clearing away the rain. "Yeah, looks like I must've run over something on the highway. My tire's completely pancaked. I guess it's my lucky day."

The killer laughed. "Yeah, I guess so. I was just sleeping back there. Woke up to see some fool running around in the rain. Thought I'd offer a hand if you needed it."

"I suppose that makes me the fool, huh?" the man asked.

The killer had known the guy was young when he'd first spotted him back at the Gas n' Guzzle in New Hampshire, but now that the fellow was standing right in front of him, he could see he was practically still a kid. He couldn't have been more than nineteen, twenty at the most. This wouldn't change anything, of course. He was just caught a bit off-guard, and the misjudgment felt all too much like an oversight, something ready to taint this experience. But the horse was already bucking. No matter how hard he tugged on the bit and yanked the reins, this beast was going where it wanted. The kid was already dead. He just didn't know it yet. There was no stopping this far in.

He'd meant what he'd said before about seeing a fool running around in the rain, only he didn't think the kid a fool for being caught out in the elements unprepared. He thought him a fool for the same reason he had thought his other three victims were fools. He thought them fools for not being able to see the obvious thing that was right in front of their faces: the fact that they were so close to death and didn't even know it.

Why can't they see what I truly am? he thought.

"S'pose it does," the killer said, "but I won't hold it against you. Whaddya need?"

"Thanks." The kid laughed uneasily. "Wouldn't happen to have a jack, would you? Whoever owned Old Reliable over there before me must have lost it. I have a tire and a wrench but no jack. I guess I should've checked at some point, before I needed one."

"Rookie mistake," the killer said, pausing and looking beyond the kid at the Pinto. "Yeah… yeah, I think I got one. Let me pull up, and I'll give you a hand."

"Man, you're a godsend, you know that?" the kid said.

The killer laughed. "Sure, sure, buddy, I'm a godsend all right. Give me a minute, I'll be right over."

Fool.

"Thanks, man."

"Don't mention it." The killer rolled up the window, put the truck back in gear, and rumbled forward into the space next to the kid's car. He shut off the ignition, killed the lights, and threw on his faded Red Sox cap. Reaching into his pocket, he felt the gun and adjusted the grip, making sure he wouldn't have a problem getting to it when the time came.

He opened the door and stepped out into the rain.

No mistakes.

CHAPTER 3

The sheriff, Calvin Lee Gaines, leaned back in his chair with his feet on the desk, reading a copy of *The Heartsridge Chronicle*. The fan on top of the filing cabinet was tilted down and blowing directly on the back of his neck. The mayor had been too cheap during budget reviews to allocate any funds to the department for air conditioning, so fans were the best they got.

"Says here those things'll start coming out any day now," Gaines said, keeping his eyes on his paper.

The deputy on the opposite side of the room punched away at a typewriter. He glanced up long enough to offer a bewildered look to Gaines but gave no response. He put his head back down and continued with his work.

"They really as loud as they say? I can't believe a little bug like that can make so much damn racket." Gaines tried again.

The deputy on the typewriter looked up once more. "Sorry, sir. I'm having trouble with this one. I can't for the life of me figure out what to put in this report. That lady's batshit crazy."

He was referring to Mrs. Garity. She'd called the station earlier that day to report a robbery at her house. When they went out to Lakeman Road to check it out, they'd found her pet Chihuahua, Marky, to be the only thing missing. He'd run away after she'd left the porch door open. The only thing stolen had been their time. "What was it she said again?" the deputy asked, grinning.

Gaines laid the newspaper down on his chest and removed his reading glasses. "Well, let's see. I believe her exact words were, 'The no-good colored boy from down the street stole my Marky for a sacrificial, devil, voodoo some-shit-or-other.'" He tried to mimic her thick Dixie accent (she'd moved up to Massachusetts from the south about ten years back), but what came out sounded more like deep-woods Maine.

The deputy laughed. "Can I quote you on that?"

"Have at it, Sam." Gaines stretched back, running his fingers through his short dark hair and interlacing them behind his head. After a moment, his attention shifted and he brought a hand to the window blind beside him. Forking two slats open with his fingers, he peered through. "Almost eight o'clock in the evening, and it's still eighty-five degrees out there. Christ sake, it's hardly even spring." He was eyeing the thermometer on the post outside the station. "Two days ago it's fifty and raining, today it's like Florida. Gotta tell you, if I'd known about the weather in New England I'd never have left Kansas."

Calvin Gaines was a big man who still looked very much like the corn-fed Midwestern boy who'd travelled north most summers to work the oil fields of the Nebraska panhandle—broad shouldered and fat fisted.

The deputy finished on the typewriter, pulled the page out, and laid it in a filing tray marked RECORDS. "This'll have to do. It's Saturday, it's getting late, and I need a beer." He walked to the coffee pot. "Now what's that you were saying?"

"Now or before?"

"Before. About the locusts."

"They're not locusts." Gaines lifted the paper again, replaced his glasses, and checked the article. "Cicadas. That's what they're called. You should know that better than me. *You* grew up here."

"Oh right. Those noisy little bastards," the deputy said, turning around with a fresh mug and leaning against the counter, his uniform sagging off him like wet laundry. They didn't make a size designed to fit someone with Sam Hodges's build. He was a young man, late twenties, with a tall, thin frame—thin being an understatement; there were pencils that had forty pounds on Sam Hodges—a pointy nose, and a tightly cropped military haircut. There was an air of clumsiness about him, the way his lanky legs seemed to call the shots and lead him as if they were pulling the rest of his body along. "You never had them out west?" Sam asked. "I thought they were out there, too."

"They are, I'm pretty sure, but never came around where I was," Gaines said.

Sam rubbed his chin. "To be honest, I was only eleven the last time they came around. I think they come every fifteen years or something like that. I remember my dad telling me that once."

"Seventeen," Gaines said.

"What?"

"They come every seventeen years. Not fifteen. Says it right here." Gaines smacked the back of his hand off the paper. "Feed for seventeen years underground, then emerge when the weather gets warm. And it's plenty warm."

"Right, right, seventeen," Sam said. "Anyway, I don't remember too well. But I suppose that's a good sign. If they were that bad, you'd think I would remember." He grabbed a napkin off the counter then dipped his hand into a white cardboard box and pulled out an éclair.

"Yeah, you'd think. Hey, those pastries are from this morning, probably pretty stale," Gaines said.

"I'll take my chances. Anyway, those things, the cicadas, they kind of just buzz a lot—" Sam seemed to reach for something in his mind to compare it to. "Like heavy power-lines. Lots and lots of 'em." He took a bite of the pastry, and his voice went soft and muffled. "You get used to it though. I don't remember losing any sleep."

"Well, either way, the mayor's up in arms. I think he's worried that they're gonna turn tourists off from the festival." Gaines brought his feet down and leaned forward. He caught the falling newspaper with one hand and tossed it on his desk.

Sam swallowed hard, his face darkening. "Never mind that buffoon. Harry Bennett just likes to cause a stir so he has something to rally around."

"No argument there," Gaines said.

"What does he want us to do, be on bug patrol?" Sam moved slowly toward Gaines's desk and took a seat in the chair beside it. "Son of a bitch probably bought us flyswatters to replace our service weapons."

Sam and Gaines both broke into laughter.

"Yeah, maybe," Gaines said, leaning forward on his elbows. "Big ones."

"That's nonsense. It's just some bugs," Sam said dismissively.

Gaines eased back on the sarcasm. "No, I get it. That festival is his baby. A lot of people in this town make a good bit of income off of next week's tourism. They prepare months in advance. Hell, I think I saw Mrs. Joslin buying her pie makings three months ago down at the grocery store. I know Bill Simms already did a dozen or so of them chainsaw carvings—you know, the ones he does of animals—and those things go for a few hundred dollars a pop.

This ain't just chump change to some of these folks. They take it serious. So does Harry."

"Hmph," Sam snorted in contempt, dismissing Gaines's words. "Spring Festival... never did like it. Too many tourists. I can't stand all those people. They think we're all just a bunch of rednecks here for their amusement. Norman Rockwell did us no favors."

Gaines placed his hands on his desk palms down. "Tell ya what, why don't you type up a complaint? I'll swing by Mayor Bennett's offices and drop it off on my way home tonight. Make sure you sign your name real clear, though. He'll want to know who to respond to." Gaines was smiling wide now, showing his teeth and dimpling his cheeks.

Sam waved him off. "He'd love that, I bet. Probably fire me."

"Oh, come on. He ain't all bad."

"Sure. I don't know. Just never really liked the guy."

"He bed your mother or something?" Gaines said.

Sam shot back a serious glance. "Really?" he said. "You want to speak like that about the woman who raised me?"

Gaines surrendered his hands. "Okay, sorry, I was only fooling with you, Sam. Didn't mean any disrespect... but I guess I have my answer." He sat back and laughed.

Sam smirked and picked up the newspaper on the desk beside him, tossing it at Gaines. "Jackass," he said.

"That's no way to talk to your superior—" Gaines was saying when the phone rang.

The receptionist, Carol Mathews, answered. Her voice filtered through to the back office. "Good evening. Heartsridge Sheriff's Department. How can I help you?" There was a pause of twenty seconds or so. Then: "Just a moment, Mr. Price." Carol leaned in through the window. A strand of her blonde hair fell over her eye as she bent forward, and she brushed it away with her hand. "Calvin, it's for you. It's David Price. He says it's urgent. Something about his daughter."

Gaines looked at Sam and shrugged. "Put him through in here, Carol. I'll take it."

Sam leaned back, smiling at Carol. She smiled back and then addressed Gaines. "You got it, Sheriff. Right away," she said, but lingered for a moment, shifting her gaze, making gooey eyes with Sam once more. The two had been dating for almost six months now.

"Carol?" Gaines said in a tone one might use with a child. She was only twenty-one, after all.

She broke her gape. "Yes, sir?"

"Now, please." His voice was stern but fair.

The young receptionist smiled once more at Sam, and her golden curls disappeared back through the window. "Sorry," she said softly.

Gaines looked at Sam, whose face was bright red and twisted into a half guilty, half love-struck grin. "Can't you two do that after work? Or do I need to get you fixed?"

Sam didn't answer, only looked down at the floor trying to hide his smile.

There was a click. Then a muffled voice once again: "I'm putting you through now, Mr. Price."

CHAPTER 4

David Price paced outside the bathroom door as his wife, Ellie, tended to their daughter on the other side. Ellie had told him to let her handle this, and so he had, albeit with great reluctance. He had no clear understanding of what had happened to Kara, but he knew she'd been hurt, and that was enough.

Coming from the bathroom, he heard the rising and falling pitches of conversation but nothing specific. He put his ear to the door and heard Ellie say, "Sweetie, this is going to sting a bit, but I need to clean that cut so it doesn't get infected."

Then there was silence, only a moment of it, but to David it felt like hours. His impatience—which was really only a father's concern for his daughter—got the better of him, and he knocked gently on the door. "Ellie? Ellie, what's going on in there? Is everything okay?"

The last question seemed foolish; he knew everything wasn't okay. If everything were okay, his daughter would not have come home with bruises on her face, crying hysterically. It had taken them an hour and two of Ellie's Valium just to get her to calm down and allow Ellie to take her into the bathroom and clean the cut on her lip. That was when his wife told him to wait outside. He had just stood there wide-eyed, feeling helpless, and for the first time, not a part of the family—*his* family. David didn't like the feeling of being asked to sit this out, but deep down he knew there was a reason. It was a reason he wasn't quite ready to allow to enter his mind. But he'd seen his daughter's face—the bruises, the cuts, and the ghostly look that haunted it. So he treated the notion like such an unfathomable scenario that it couldn't possibly be true. Denial was his poison, and he drank it greedily. No. No way. Not *his* daughter. *That* couldn't happen to her, not in *this* town. Heartsridge was home to only two thousand residents (population 2,038, according to the last census), and he couldn't for the life of him think of anyone capable of harming a teenage girl. It simply wasn't that kind of place.

Ellie didn't answer him. Instead, he heard the latch on the bathroom door click, and it opened. She slipped out, shutting the door behind her. Her face looked carved in stone. It was a look David had never seen before on her: unwavering strength. It was a face that could lead an army into battle. In a way, it comforted him. This was her show now; she was taking control of the situation.

"I think you need to go downstairs and call the sheriff's department. Tell Sheriff Gaines he needs to come out here. And make sure he brings Deputy Carlisle with him," she said, talking softly but concisely.

"Deputy Carlisle" was Deputy Catherine Carlisle, and of the fifteen members of law enforcement in Heartsridge County—which was made up of West Elm, Piermont, and Heartsridge—she was the only female.

"Why? What did..." he tried to say, but his words fell away.

Kara's face: the bruises, the cuts, the ghost. He knew exactly what had happened to his daughter, only he refused to vocalize or fully accept it. "Is she all right?"

"No, she's not all right. She was raped, David." Ellie closed her eyes and paused for a moment. She sighed. "I'm sorry, I didn't mean to—"

"It's okay. Don't apologize." David's tone was flat. He was off somewhere in his mind, processing what his wife had just thrown at him.

Raped. There it was. That word: *raped.* He tried to focus as his wife spoke, but his mind spun. He wanted to keel over and cry. Why hadn't he been there to protect her? She was his little girl, and he'd promised her he'd always be there. He couldn't understand how someone could do this to her. He felt as though he were drowning, trying to stay afloat while sifting through his mind for an explanation. But there were no explanations, and all he cared about right then was finding the man who'd done this to Kara and making him pay. David could picture himself beating some faceless perpetrator for what he'd done. He would beg for forgiveness but get none. He would cry that he was sick and couldn't help himself, but David would not listen. He would go on beating him until there was no more life to take. But... *Oh, God, I should've protected my daughter. What have I done?*

"Are you sure? How do you know?" he asked.

"That's what she told me." Ellie cast the hair from her forehead, folding her arms across her chest and cupping her elbows with her hands. "She needs to see a doctor tonight, so call Dr. Hornsby too, and tell him to make sure he has one of his nurses there. Can you do that?"

"Of course," David said, rubbing the side of his face and swallowing hard. "Jesus, how the hell did this happen?"

"I don't know. I can't even imagine. Who would do such a thing? I mean, she's only fifteen, for Christ sakes."

"Can you tell me what she said? Did she say who did it?" he said impatiently. The emotion was misplaced, and he knew it. He didn't know who or what to be mad at, so right now he was pissed at everything.

"No, she isn't saying. Not yet, at least, but she's still in shock, I think. When I ask her, she starts to get hysterical again and just shakes her head." Ellie brushed away a tear.

David leaned up against the wall, trying to calm himself. He placed a hand gently on his wife's shoulder. Ellie took his hand and squeezed it. "Did she say *where* she was attacked, at least?"

"No." Ellie shook her head. "She hasn't really said anything. But her feet and hands and knees are all covered in dirt. Honestly, I have no idea what happened…" Ellie trailed off. "David, raped? Really? Our little girl? How could this happen?" Ellie looked as if she might break into sobs, but she straightened, the strength returning, emotion swept beneath her face like crumbs under a rug.

"All right, go be with her. I'll call the sheriff." David took his hand off Ellie's shoulder.

"Okay." She hugged him. It was a long, lingering hug that was more like a pact to make it through this together. She turned around and slipped back inside the bathroom.

For the brief moment that the door was open, David could see his daughter sitting there on the side of the bathtub, staring straight ahead out the window, as if searching for something miles away on some distant horizon.

When the door was shut, he turned and made his way downstairs to call the sheriff's department.

"David, sorry Carol put you on hold, what can I do for you?" Sheriff Gaines's voice came through tinny and thin on the phone's receiver.

David paused for a moment, sitting on the stool in the phone nook by the kitchen. The alcove was recessed into the wall about a foot, a dim yellow lightbulb hanging overhead. The space was filled with old phonebooks sitting at odd angles in thoughtless stacks. There was a wicker basket overfull of mail, phone messages, and coupons, pens and pencils tossed lazily among paper clutter. Phone numbers were scrawled on wrinkled scraps. Some were his handwriting, and some were Ellie's. And then some were the sloppy and hasty writing that could only belong to a teenager—Kara's writing. He took a deep, slow breath.

He imagined his daughter where he sat now, talking, laughing into the phone. She would be leaned over, twirling the cord in her fingers as she talked about who said what to whom at school and what boys were *soooo cute!* There was an innocence there, an innocence that David feared might not return to his little girl. The idea tightened his stomach. He felt the back of his throat fatten as the urge to cry washed over him. It was all too real. How could this happen? He wanted to weep for her but beat back the feeling. He needed to be strong here. He shut his eyes hard, wiping his mind clear and reminding himself of what he was doing.

"Hello?" Gaines repeated through the receiver.

"Hi, Calvin," David said, opening his eyes and leaning forward to rest on his forearm.

"Was starting to think the line was dead," Gaines said.

"Sorry, I was just thinking how to say this, is all." In that moment, David had an immediate appreciation for how hard it must have been for his daughter to admit what had happened to her. He could barely bring the words to his own lips, and it hadn't even happened to him. Once he said it, it was final; it had happened. Truth absolute. This finality, this setting of the facts, brought sickness to his mind.

"I see. Well, if it's that type of thing, you might want to just come right out with it. Sooner you tell me, the sooner I can help. Carol said you'd mentioned something about your daughter? Is everything okay with her?"

David let out a long sigh. "Wish I could say everything was okay. I never thought in a million years I'd have to make a call like this."

There was a rustling on the other end of the line, and David could tell that Gaines had sat up in his seat. "What's happened?" Gaines asked with concern in his voice.

"My daughter was attacked, Calvin," David said, bowing his head as if dealt a hard blow. "Ellie and I don't know a lot yet. Kara just came home after work with her face pretty well banged up. She hasn't said much. Ellie's been trying to talk to her, but Kara's in shock I think."

"Attacked? Like somebody beat her up?" Gaines said.

"Well, yes... and no, not like that." David rubbed the side his face anxiously, holding back emotion. His leg shook, resting on the bottom rung of the stool. He didn't know what to say.

"Okay. Well..." A long breath came through the receiver from the sheriff's end. "How do you mean, then?"

"Ellie says Kara told her she'd been, well, you know, assaulted... sexually." He hung his head down all the way, his chin almost resting against his chest. "Raped," he said, almost whispered.

"Raped?"

"Yes," David confirmed.

"Jesus, what happened?"

"Well, like I said, she hasn't told us much. My wife's talking to her now, dressing a cut on her lip, but we had to give her a few of Ellie's prescription pills just to calm her down. She either doesn't know or won't say who did it to her."

There was a brief moment of silence. Then Gaines said, "Okay. Give me twenty minutes."

"Calvin," David added, "Ellie thinks it would be a good idea to call Catherine in on this one, maybe let her... I'm not telling you how to do—"

"Say no more. I understand. I'll call her now and be right over."

They both hung up.

David picked up the address book sitting next to the wicker basket, flipped through it, and found the number for Dr. Hornsby. He picked up the phone once more, and for the second time that evening made a phone call no father should ever have to make.

CHAPTER 5

The killer walked to the back of his truck and pulled an old rusty carjack from beneath a stained tarpaulin. A small collection of beer bottles rolled off into the bed of his truck as he lifted the canvas. The sound of it made him pause a moment. His father, when he was still alive, used to drink. *Remember those days, pal? Remember when the bin in the corner of the kitchen would start over-flowing with Pabst bottles, and you'd have to lug that bag down to Marcaurelle's bottle return and then buy the old man a pack of smokes with the money? The bag was so damn heavy, but the old bastard didn't care you were only twelve. And remember the time you dragged it on the sidewalk because you just couldn't hold it up any longer, and the weak plastic split open, and the bottles went spilling out into Mrs. Darby's front lawn? She came out to help, looking so sad to see you. Yeah, you remember that look; it's haunted you since. She pitied you. "Let me help you," Mrs. Darby had said, running inside to get another bag. Then she threw it in her station wagon and drove you down-town so you didn't have to lug it any farther. Remember that? Remember when she said she'd known your mother before she...*

"Oh man, I don't know what I would have done if you weren't here," the kid said.

The killer broke loose from his thoughts. He hadn't realized that he'd been staring down at the beer bottles in the back of his truck for almost a minute, lost in his reverie as the rain soaked the back of his neck. "What's that?" he said, looking up to see the kid standing beside him.

"I was just saying that I'm grateful someone was here." He nodded as if reaffirming his statement. Thin streams of water ran down his face, dripping from his nose and chin. He was a handsome kid with sharp features: thin nose, high cheekbones, a square jaw. Probably popular with the girls in school. Probably played sports and got good grades, too. "Isn't really the kind of place I'd want to spend the night waiting for a tow, you know?"

"No, no it isn't, pal." The killer lifted the jack out of his truck. "Here, let's see if this thing works," he said, pushing it into the kid's hands.

The kid smiled. "You mean you aren't gonna change it for me, too?" He laughed. "I'm only kidding," he said, turning and walking toward his car.

The killer didn't find anything funny about the kid's comment. *Arrogant little prick. Probably does want me to change his tire. Probably joked his whole damn way through life. People like him only grow up two ways: to be assholes or bastards.* This kid was surely both. He knew it. He could sense it. "No," he said flatly. "I don't think so. I bring the swine, you kill it."

"That's a new one, never heard that expression before," the kid said. He dropped to one knee at the flat tire, slid the jack underneath the edge of the car frame, and started to turn the jackscrew. "This shouldn't take long. You might just want to wait in your truck so you don't get soaked out here. You've already done more than enough to save my ass, no sense in getting pneumonia too."

"It's no bother, seems like it's letting up." The killer pulled his pack of smokes from his pocket, fingered one out, put it between his lips, and lit it. The brim of his hat spared it from the rain, so he let it hang in his mouth instead of pinching it between his fingers. "I got a long drive ahead of me—need to stretch my legs, anyhow."

"Where you headed?" the kid asked, keeping his eyes straight ahead and his back turned as he pried at the tire iron.

"West," the killer said. That might have been a lie, or it might not have. The truth was he didn't really know. He took a deep drag off his cigarette and exhaled slowly, watching the smoke twist in the low light and drift away into the night.

The kid removed the first nut, dropping it to the ground. "West, huh? All the way, or just a little way?" he asked, never turning around.

The killer tossed his cigarette to the ground and crushed it under the toe of his boot. Running his palm down the side of his jacket, he slipped his hand into his pocket. The gun was cool and hard. It was a mean piece of metal. He was staring hard at the kid, studying him, analyzing his every movement. He wondered if the kid could feel his eyes watching him. He wondered if the kid could feel what he felt: that closeness of death. Maybe the kid felt it, only he didn't know what it was. Like something hiding in the corner of a dark room, lurking, unidentified. "Haven't decided yet," he said, squeezing down on the gun and situating his grip.

The kid started on another bolt, twisted it around a dozen or so times, and it dropped to the ground. "That's cool. No plans. Just go where the road takes you kind of thing. I can dig it."

The killer placed his finger on the trigger, readying himself to pull it out. "Yeah, something like that." His adrenaline was surging now, bringing hyperawareness of everything around him. His stomach twisted and burned. He felt the urge to void his bowels. His heart beat like the drum of a war god. He loved and hated the feeling all at once. It was a sick brand of excitement.

A gust of wind howled, and the kid tucked his head down into his shoulder. "What a goddamn night for this," he yelled.

The killer lowered his shoulder into the gale, too. "Not your lucky night," he said, pulling the gun from his pocket and letting it hang by his side.

The kid dropped another bolt and moved on to the next one. "Tell me about it," he said.

"You mind if I ask you something?" The killer moved a few feet closer.

The kid leaned forward on the wrench, bobbing up and down with his weight to break the bolt loose. "Go for it," he said, his back still turned to the man now holding a pistol.

The killer took another step forward. He was only two feet behind the kid. "What were you doing up in Hanover? Girlfriend? School?"

The kid kept working the stuck bolt. "Yeah, got a girl, she's going to school up..." He trailed off, pausing for a moment. Then he continued, his voice devoid of all enthusiasm, replaced with a nervous hesitation. "...Up there." His movements slowed, like a wind-up toy run out of spring. "How'd you know where I was?" He craned his head around.

The killer had the gun raised, pointed at the kid's face. "Yeah, there you go. You see me now, don't you?"

"Jesus, man, what are you doing?"

"Get up."

The kid took his hand off the tire iron. The wrench stayed snugly on the last bolt. He rose to his feet, his hands up in front of his face. "I don't have any money, if that's what you're after."

The killer laughed. "You think that's what I want? Your money? You really don't know what this is, do you? None of you ever know until it's too late. I don't get it. How come you can't see?" He squeezed down hard on the gun, feeling the ridges of the metal dig into his palms—mean, powerful metal.

The kid kept his hands raised in front of his face, as if they would even slow a bullet. "What do you want?" he asked with a quiver in his voice.

"Turn around and start walking." The killer took a step forward. "Keep going 'til I tell you to stop."

The kid's face crumpled into fear and panic. He bowed his head down and away from the pistol. "Please, can't we just talk about—"

Before the kid could finish, the killer lunged forward and cracked him with the butt of the gun across the bridge of his nose, opening a deep gash. The kid stumbled backwards, grabbing his face. Blood poured out beneath his hands, between his fingers. The killer knew he'd broken his nose, had smashed it good. He'd felt it cave when he came down on it. The kid was leaning up against his car now, doubled over. Thin cords of red spittle stretched down from his face and were lost on the wet asphalt.

"Please, stop. What do you want? " he said, his voice muffled by his cupped hands.

"I want you to listen to me," the killer said. "Get up, turn around, and head that way." He pointed the gun to an opening in the woods behind the information booth.

The killer kept the pistol trained on the kid as he slowly straightened himself back up. Then, like a crack of thunder, a voice that sounded all too much like his father interrupted: *You're the only fool out here. You should have shot him when his back was turned. You're going to fuck this up. You're going to make another mistake.* The killer squeezed his eyes shut for a moment to shake the voice. "No," he whispered.

When the killer opened his eyes, the kid was still standing there, leaning up against the car, his hands at his sides, silently watching him with a confused, terrified look in his eyes. From his nose down, the kid's face was covered in bright, fresh blood. The killer regarded him for a moment, taking it all in. There was something very animalistic about the way the kid looked—something raw about the whole scene. There was an artistic element to it all, something that begged to be understood and appreciated. Captured and savored. He could feel it, some other level beneath the surface. If only he could capture moments like these, hold onto them; then he could revisit them with perfect clarity whenever he wanted to, without having to rely on a memory often clouded by anxiety and doubt. Then it hit him, and he almost laughed that it had been sitting right in front of him the whole time and he'd failed to see it. Why hadn't he thought of this sooner? He needed a camera. That was the answer to his problems. It would be the perfect way to document his outings and capture these perfect moments for later study.

And that was when he saw it; the kid was slowly lowering his left hand toward the wrench still stuck on the lug nut. The killer hadn't noticed at first, but the kid's fingers were dangling only inches from the tool. They were twitching, readying themselves for action. He looked down at the kid's hand and then up into his eyes. The killer stepped forward, opening his mouth to tell the kid to not move a fucking muscle, but it was too late. The kid bent down, grabbing the tire iron, and swung at the gun, cutting a wet gray streak through the air.

"Back off, you crazy fuck!" He missed, the wrench crashing into the back window of his Pinto. Glass popped and shattered.

The killer backed up and squeezed the trigger. The Luger barked once. Twice. A third time. The last bullet hit the kid square in the face, entering right above his upper lip. His head snapped back, and blood and bits of skull and brain matter covered the roof of the car like curdled blood-milk. He slumped sideways and slid down the side of the car. He caught for a moment on the side-view mirror, eventually dropping to the ground like a limp sack of bones.

"No, no, no, no, shit!" the killer yelled. He brought his hands to the top of his head, the gun still smoking and clutched in his forefinger and palm. "Why did you do that, you dumb fuck? You ruined it." He sprang forward and started kicking the kid's lifeless body. *Thwack thwack thwack.* "You asshole!" *Thwack.* "You goddamn maggot!" *Thwack thwack.* "This was going so well." *Thwack.*

When he'd exhausted himself, he stopped, caught his breath, and looked around. The rest stop was still empty, save for their two cars. He bent down, picking up two of the shell casings. The third he remembered hearing bounce behind him when he'd fired. He straightened, turning around. He didn't see it. Anxiety cut through his chest. He walked to his truck and dropped down on his stomach, looking underneath. There it was, shining dully from the fluorescent lights of the information booth. *Careless fool.* He slid his arm under and grabbed it. Standing, he shoved all three spent bullet shells in his pocket and stuffed the gun in his waistband.

He approached the kid. His eyes were open, staring blankly up at the sky. Rain water mixed with blood pooled in the corners of his eye sockets. His lips were parted, his top front teeth missing—

some were bloody, jagged shards. The killer knelt down and began rummaging through the kid's pockets. There was a wallet. He opened it, searching for anything of value. He found nothing, only a driver's license. He slid it out, putting the identification in his pocket without reading it. He wiped the wallet clean of fingerprints and tossed it into the Pinto through the broken window.

A car drove by on the freeway, sloshing over the wet road but continued without stopping. *But what if it* had *stopped?* Cold coils of panic tightened in his gut. He jumped up and went back to his truck, grabbing the canvas tarp. He spread it out on the ground next to the kid's body, rolled him into the center, and wrapped it up.

The kid was heavy, solid with young muscle, but he managed to get the body off the ground, slinging it up over his shoulder. He headed into the woods behind the information booth, carrying the kid almost two hundred yards down a lightly worn trail before spotting a small ravine and veering left into thick brush. He rolled the body down the embankment and into the gulch. Sticks snapped as it tumbled to the bottom, where it settled with a soft thump. He turned over in his mind whether or not he should walk down and cover the body but decided against it. It was better if he just got out of there. If someone pulled into that rest stop and saw his truck and that kid's car together, things would have to get a lot messier than they already were.

Before he turned and headed back to his truck, the killer set his eyes on the twisted, blood-soaked tarp sitting in the ditch. It was hard to make out in the dark, but his eyes were well adjusted by now. An arm protruded from a loose fold in the canvas. It'd probably come open on its trip down the hill. It wasn't so much the arm that caught his attention, though—it was the kid's hand.

All the fingers were balled into a fist, as though they were still curled around the tire iron, except his index and middle finger stuck out straight, flashing an unintentional peace sign. The image brought a smile to the killer's face. He wanted that camera now more than ever. This shot would have been his first masterpiece, a special little something to remember the kid by. He imagined he might call it *Peace Lover.*

After a minute, the killer peeled himself away and left.

When he returned to his truck, relief washed over him. Theirs were still the only two cars there. *But what if someone came and left while you were out in those woods? What if they saw your truck?* It was too late now. Nothing he could do about it. Next time he would be better.

In the truck, he removed his hat and jacket and then started the engine. Before he put it in gear, he reached into his pocket, fishing out the kid's driver's license. On the floor beside him was a metal ammunition can (another piece from his father's collection). He picked it up and opened the latch. Inside were packs of cigarettes. He removed them two at a time, putting them on the seat. Ten in total, a full carton. To an untrained eye, the ammo can was empty now, but in the bottom right corner, hardly visible, there was the smallest indentation. The killer pushed his fingernail into the space, prying up a piece of green sheet metal that served as a false bottom. He'd added that little touch himself, a neat little hiding spot to preserve his collection. Underneath, there was a folded piece of cloth to keep everything from sliding around. He lifted that out and put it on the dash, revealing the true bottom of the container. Placed neatly near one end were three licenses bound together with a rubber band, a gold chain with a cross hung on it, and six empty shell casings in a plastic baggie.

He held the new kid's license under a shaft of light: William Mathey, Bridgewater, Massachusetts, Born 2/19/58.

The killer rubbed his thumb over William's ID picture and smiled. Then he bound it with the other three in the ammo can, added the three newly spent shells to his collection, laid the cloth back over everything, reset the false bottom, and closed it.

The killer glanced down at his watch. It was almost three thirty. He had been at the rest stop almost an hour and a half. He needed to hit the road. He hadn't slept in almost twenty-four hours. On the seat beside him was a road map of Massachusetts. He picked it up and found where he was on Interstate 91. There was a motel about twenty-five miles to his west in Heartsridge.

He put the truck in gear and headed out of the rest stop.

CHAPTER 6

The edge of Kara's bed felt like a cliff off which she might leap and make this all go away. Her mother had just seen the sheriff's cruiser pulling into the driveway and had gone downstairs to meet him. Now she was alone again.

Kara sat staring down at her dirty feet. The thong strap of her flip-flops left a funny Y shape in the dirt on her feet. She knew it wasn't humorous, but somehow the grimy Y brought a faint smile to her face. It was something else to focus on. That was all. When her lip stretched into a smile, the cut cracked and began to throb again. Instinctively, she brought her fingers to her mouth. The cut was greasy, covered in ointment—her mother had been generous with the antibacterial. She got some on her fingers and wiped it off on her sheets, leaving two dark streaks on the linens. In a far-off way, it reminded her of the blood she'd tried to wipe off her legs at the creek, before she'd waded into those unforgiving, icy waters.

On the first floor, the front door opened. The spring on the screen door moaned as it stretched and then recoiled. The door banged shut, the thin wood bouncing against the jamb. Then up the stairs came the sound of people talking in concerned tones. Next was the intermittent shuffle of people walking through the downstairs hallway. After a few moments, the footfalls began to grow louder and sharpen as they traveled upstairs. It sent a flutter through Kara's stomach. She knew what they wanted. What they'd all want, eventually. They'd want to know who did this to her. But she didn't want to say. Once she said it, it was out there. She may have only been fifteen, but she was well aware of the situation that would arise when—*if*—she pointed a finger.

There was a soft knock on her bedroom door. "Kara?" a female voice said. It wasn't her mother's. "Kara, it's Deputy—it's Catherine Carlisle. Can I come in? I work at the sheriff's department."

Kara didn't respond. Speaking just felt like too much effort, like if she opened her mouth and tried, nothing would come out.

Catherine knocked again. "Kara... Kara, I'm going to come in, okay?" The handle turned with a squeak, and the door opened slowly.

Kara looked up and saw Catherine standing in the doorway. She didn't know the woman well, but she did know who she was—a side effect of living in a small town. Kara was surprised to see that the deputy was in plain clothes: white T-shirt, jeans, and a pair of tennis shoes. Kara studied Catherine. She was short and thin, small breasted, with dark hair she kept gathered in a ponytail. She was pretty but not beautiful. There was a power and a hardness to her. Kara could sense it like a granite aura, and somehow it put her at ease.

Catherine came in, leaving the door open behind her. Kara's parents stood in the hallway talking with Sheriff Gaines. Kara couldn't quite make out what they were saying, only that her mother kept repeating, "I don't know. I don't know. I don't know..."

"Kara, what happened, sweetie?" Catherine asked. The bed creaked when she took a seat next to Kara on the edge. "Your mother tells me you were attacked. Is that right?"

Kara stuffed her hands underneath her thighs, looking down at the ground and making small circles with her big toe on the floor. Why couldn't this all just go away? She could feel the deputy looking at her, inspecting her face the same way her parents had.

"Kara, I know this is tough, but if someone hurt you, we need to know," Catherine said, lowering her head, trying to make eye contact with Kara.

"I know," Kara said under her breath, and turned her head. Her eyes met Catherine's, and for a moment Kara thought she might let it all come spilling out.

There was a sense in her that doing so would relieve the pressure of whatever it was she was feeling—pain, anger, shame, guilt? She didn't know. But she did know that the truth was eating at her from the inside like a cancer. She wanted to tell someone. She *needed* to tell someone. But she couldn't because then everyone would know. How could she show her face anywhere after that? People talked in Heartsridge. Kara knew this firsthand because she was just as bad. She wasn't innocent when it came to gossip. When Sadie Matthews got her first menstrual visit in the middle of class a year back, bleeding right through her white jeans, Kara had been sitting next to her in homeroom. For the week after, she'd told anyone who would listen. Soon, girls giggled in corners, throwing tampons at Sadie as she walked down the halls. It got so bad that she stopped showing up for school altogether and just opted for summer school, as opposed to being teased relentlessly by the other girls.

"So tell me what happened. You told your mother you were raped. Is that what happened?" Catherine asked.

Kara closed her eyes, her bottom lip starting to quiver. She nodded vaguely and began to cry. "Yes," she whispered. Suddenly, she had a powerful urge to call Sadie Matthews and apologize, beg her forgiveness and ask to be friends. She couldn't understand why, but there it was.

Catherine picked up a thin blanket at the end of the bed and wrapped it around Kara's shoulders. "Okay. It's okay," she said, and placed her arm around Kara.

"I didn't even do anything." Kara continued to sob into the deputy's arm.

Catherine held her, shushing her gently, comforting her, but after about a minute or so, she pulled away, holding Kara at arm's length by the shoulders. She was still crying lightly, the rims of her eyes red and raw. Catherine was looking at her with a serious gaze. "Kara, I know this is tough, but we need to know who did this to you. Your mom says you won't tell her."

Kara broke down again, shaking her head and looking down at her feet. "No. No, I can't. You don't understand. If I tell you then it's going to be worse. I know it will. Please, just… just let me forget about this. It's not a big deal… really." Kara forced herself to stop crying, swallowing hard, attempting to gather her composure. "Honest, I'm okay. I'm just being stupid." She wiped her eyes on the blanket.

Catherine's lips parted. Then she tightened her face and shook her head, as if for a moment she couldn't believe what she'd just heard. "No… no, Kara, this is a big deal. What was done to you is serious. And we need to know who did this so that this person can't hurt anyone else."

Kara didn't answer, only stared straight ahead. Inside her a battle raged. Everything urged her to just say what had happened and have it be over with. But another part of her, the part that saw her being ridiculed and talked about, would not allow it. Yes, the edge of her bed was like a cliff, and yes, she may have wanted to jump off it, but she could not for the life of her find the will to leap. And it wasn't suicide if she jumped; it was peace of mind, closure, the last step before healing could begin.

Kara's parents and Sheriff Gaines stood in the room now, all looking on but saying nothing, their faces carved in stone.

"I'm sorry," Kara said. She fell over onto her bed, bringing her feet up and curling into the fetal position. "Can't this just go away?" She turned and stared blankly out the window beside her bed. "Just go away..." She trailed off to a whisper.

Catherine sighed heavily and leaned over to Kara. "It's okay, you did good. Don't worry about anything right now, sweetie. We need to get you to a doctor, though—"

In a lifeless voice, Kara interrupted and began speaking, not to Catherine or anyone in particular, just speaking. "He told me he would give me a ride home." Somewhere inside her a leak had sprung, small at first, but the immense pressure was causing it to widen in a hurry. "I said I could walk back, I didn't mind, but he insisted. He said it was getting late and that a young girl shouldn't be wandering the streets alone."

Suddenly, everyone she'd turned her back to had moved in front of her, but she hardly acknowledged them.

"Who, Kara?" her father blurted, and stepped forward. "Tell me who did this to you."

Ellie grabbed his arm and squeezed.

"Easy, David," Gaines said softly. "Catherine's got this."

David halted and looked back at his wife. She widened her eyes at him.

With that haunted lifelessness in her voice, Kara continued as if she were some sad doll whose string had been pulled, and this was her preordained recitation. "When I left Town Hall, I started walking home. He pulled up and offered me a ride. I said okay. He always seemed like a nice guy, so I got in. Then he said he needed to make a stop first, and he'd take me home after." Kara paused and took a deep breath.

"Where did he take you?" Catherine asked.

"We went to Baker's Pond. He said he needed to drop a check off at the water department. But no one was there when we pulled up. It was only us. He parked the car and told me to get in the backseat. At first I almost thought he was joking or something because he had a huge grin on his face. But when I started to ask him what he was talking about, he hit me. And then, well, he just… he wouldn't stop." Her face tensed, on the verge of twisting into tears, but she looked down at the floor and her face relaxed.

"Who, Kara?" Catherine leaned in, forcing eye contact.

Kara didn't answer, only breathed softly through her nose. She could see herself inching closer to the edge of that cliff in her mind. That ledge she could not force herself to jump off. Her toes were hanging over the side, and Kara leaned forward, holding on with only one hand to whatever it was behind her that anchored her. Slowly she felt her weight shifting as her fingers began to slip and then one by one let go. There was a moment where she felt as if she were falling out of control, but quickly, before she lost all purchase, Kara pushed off from her toes and leapt. This would be on her terms. "Mr. Bennett," she said. "It was Mr. Bennett." A strange ease washed over her with those words, a feeling of something restored. A piece of whatever she'd lost had just been returned to her.

A claustrophobic silence smothered the room, her last two words hanging electric in the air like the reverberating chime of an alarm bell after being struck.

Catherine looked back at Gaines, then to Ellie and David. They all looked as though they'd just been slapped across the face. Mouths agape. Eyes wide. Limbs frozen in rigid postures.

"Do you mean Harry Bennett? As in Mayor Bennett?" Gaines asked, breaking the silence.

Kara wiped a tear from her eye and sat up. "Yes," she said, and ran her tongue over the cut on her lip.

It still hurt, but the pain had lessened.

CHAPTER 7

Gaines paced back and forth in Dr. Hornsby's waiting room, stopping occasionally and pretending to analyze the cheap Van Gogh prints hanging on the wall. He was pretending because David Price and he were now alone together, and Gaines knew exactly what question lingered in the ether between them: Is your daughter lying? Harry Bennett was a bit rough around the edges, sure, and maybe he played a little less than fair when it came to town politics, but rape? Gaines couldn't believe it; the mayor was a happily married man. He didn't doubt that something had happened to Kara Price, but he could not in good conscience take the sole accusation of a fifteen-year-old as absolute truth right out of the gate.

Eventually he stopped in front of Kara's father, holding his hat in one hand and rubbing the back of his neck with the other. He exhaled slowly through his nose. He needed to get this out, needed to get it over and done with. And it wasn't because it needed to go into any file or onto any report. It was because he needed to hear it for his own peace of mind.

"David, I'm sorry," he said. "I know this is not the time or the place, but I need to ask you. And I'm not proud of it, and I don't like it, but it is my job to ask these questions and see the whole thing from all angles."

David looked up from his chair. His eyes were shallow and dark, his complexion wan and exhausted. He was a man at the end of his rope. Gaines saw sadness on his face, a sadness that he himself was afraid to even imagine feeling. *Put yourself in his shoes,* an internal voice threatened. But he didn't wish to wear those shoes. Gaines could not bring himself, even for the briefest of moments, to allocate his own daughter to such a terrible fantasy. The idea of it turned his stomach sour.

"Listen, I know what you're going to ask," David said. "My daughter just said Harry Bennett raped her. You need to be sure she isn't just some disturbed teenager making up a story for attention. I get it. It's a small town, and you're in the politics game. You don't want to ruffle any powerful feathers."

That was true; Calvin Gaines was a politician, although he hated to think of himself that way. Maybe a sheriff required election, but the job came first and foremost. Besides, politics had little to do with his concerns. He did, however, need to consider the fact that throwing around accusations like this could ruin a person.

He took a seat next to Kara's father and set his hat on the chair beside him. "Look, I'm no fool, David. I have no doubt your daughter has been through something terrible. I just need to be certain what that something is before I go haul Harry Bennett into the station and ask him if he raped a fifteen-year-old girl." His insides tightened like a twisted rope at his last sentence.

"She isn't lying," David said bluntly. "You probably think she is, but I know my little girl. I know when she's lying, and I know when she's telling the truth. Just the same way I'm sure you can tell when your Maddie isn't being straight with you. A parent—a father—can tell." He turned, looking at Gaines, his face ironed flat. "But I also understand this isn't just some ordinary open-and-shut case. I know you need to take care how you handle it. I just can't say I'm seeing it like you, right now."

It surprised Gaines how calm and level-headed David was being. He half-expected some sort of vigilante defiance from the man, like something from a movie, a father out for revenge, threatening to take matters into his own hands if he *didn't do something*! Instead what he was seeing was a man defeated. Help-less. He hardly knew David, their interactions limited mostly to the sidelines of their girls' soccer games in the fall or the occa-sional conversation down at Hawk's Pub when they bumped into each other. But Gaines knew David well enough to know he was a smart, reasonable man. Character aside, Gaines had expected some sort of fight or up-in-arms reaction from the father of a daughter who'd just shown up home beaten and bruised, claim-ing she'd been raped. He suspected it was possible that David Price was being plagued by his own good sensibility—a hard-wired voice of reason telling David to be rational when all he wanted to do was be irrational. Gaines may not have known the man well, but he had a hunch about this because somewhere deep down inside himself he felt a reflection of it.

"It isn't that I think your girl's lying, David. I just need to know more. We don't really have much yet." Gaines knew this was bullshit, because part of him thought—perhaps hoped—she *was* lying. It would definitely make his job a whole hell of a lot easier if she was. But that wasn't the real reason he questioned Kara Price's honesty. It was because a prideful piece of him did not want to believe that Harry Bennett, a man he'd spent so much time in the presence of, could do something so vile, and he, the sheriff, could be so blind to the monster that had been in front of him all along. What would that say about him?

And even if it turned out that Kara was lying, Gaines still couldn't ignore what was true—the evidence right in front of his face. He couldn't discount her bruises and the obvious signs of some kind of abuse. It was possible she hadn't been raped, sure. She could be faking it. Gaines had heard stories before of teenage girls crying wolf for some reason or another, complete with self-inflicted wounds, all in the name of attention. There was an obvious answer here, though, and he refused to accept it.

"I'm sure you're probably not in the mood for it now, but I need to ask you a few questions." Gaines plucked out the pencil that had been resting behind his ear and pulled a small notepad from his breast pocket.

David balled his fists and rested them on his knees. "Go ahead. But make it quick. When my girls are finished back there"—he pointed to the door beside the reception desk, the one with the plaque that read EXAM ROOMS, PATIENTS & MEDICAL STAFF ONLY—"I'm taking them home. And I'll warn you, Ellie is a hell of a lot smarter than me and far more perceptive, if she picks up on what I picked up on, if she sees that look on your face like I have, if she thinks you're calling our daughter a liar, you'll be lucky if she doesn't try and put you through that damn wall."

Suddenly Gaines felt vulnerable, exposed. He didn't think he had been so transparent. He'd planned to come right out and ask David if his daughter could be lying, but David had spotted the question and answered it before Gaines had even asked. For this reason, Gaines had denied his intention—or at the very least, tried to disguise it to soften its edge. He paused for a moment, letting out a long sigh. "Okay. I understand," he said. "You know I'm just doing my job, don't you? I really hope you can see that. And part of that is to be skeptical. If I took everything at face value, I'd have to believe every accusation. I'm not saying that your—"

David held up his hand. "Calvin, it's fine. What do you want to ask me? I don't know much more than you do, though. I think we've pretty much already said everything we can."

Gaines rose to his feet, standing in front of David. "Your wife—Ellie, I mean—said that Kara had recently started working at Harry Bennett's office. Is that right?"

"Yes," David said.

"And how long has she been doing that?"

"Not long. Today was actually her first day. She was supposed to do Saturdays for a few weeks, learn the ropes, you know, until school was out, then she'd be full-time for the summer." He rubbed the side of his face with his hand. "Ellie's friend, Gail Hatcher, she's a secretary down at the clerk's office, she offered to get Kara an internship a few weeks back. I guess there's some kind of co-op program at Town Hall."

Gaines wrote down the information and moved on. "Does your daughter have a boyfriend?"

David shook his head, looking down at his lap. "You mean has my daughter ever had sex? Is that what you're asking? Christ."

Gaines looked away for a moment, dropping his hands to his sides. "Like I said, I just need to get all the angles. Please just try and understand that."

"Not that I know of, but she never really talked about boys with me and Ellie."

"Okay," Gaines said.

"She hangs out with John Kinsey's kid sometimes. Ryan, I think's his name. Sometimes he gives her a ride home from school. I don't think they're anything more than friends. I've never noticed anything to suggest otherwise, anyway."

Gaines wrote down the name, underlining it in his pad: *Ryan Kinsey. Friend? BF?* "What about school? Everything been going okay for her there? I know she's a freshman, sometimes the seniors can be rough on the underclassmen. Has she complained about any bullying?"

David looked toward the door to the exam room. "As far as I know, everything's fine. But again, she's at the age now where she doesn't really tell us much unless we pry it out of her. For all I know, she could be valedictorian and I'd have to hear it from someone else."

Gaines could see tears welling in David's eyes. "Yeah, my girl's the same way." He smiled halfheartedly, trying to offer some levity in light of the shared paternal plight. David didn't react. Gaines moved on. "So, I know you said you don't know much about what happened tonight, but what *can* you tell me?"

"Not a lot. This is stuff we've already been over," David said, and shifted in his seat. He kept his eyes glued on the door to the exam rooms. "I was reading in the living room. Ellie was making dinner. It was around six-thirty, I think, and we were expecting Kara to be home from her first day soon. Ellie opened the front door to let some air in or check the mail or something, I forget, and that's when she found our daughter standing there." David broke his gaze and turned to Gaines. "That's it. After that we just tried to calm her down long enough to find out what had happened. Then we called you after she told Ellie she'd been raped."

"Do you know how she got home?" Gaines asked.

"No. Ellie said she was just standing there. I have no idea for how long. But I imagine she probably walked from somewhere."

"So you didn't see anybody drop her off? Didn't hear any car?"

"No. But I doubt Harry Bennett was going to deliver her to our front door after he raped her," David said sharply.

There it was again, that name: Harry Bennett. Every time Gaines heard it, his chest panged with anxiety. "So you never saw a car? Harry Bennett's or any other?" He could feel what he was doing, how he was posing his questions, trying to lead the whole thing away from the mayor. He knew it wasn't right, but he wasn't even sure he was doing it on purpose. It was more like instinct, self-preservation. It wasn't as though he had any plan in mind; he was only reacting.

"For fuck's sake, this is goddamn ridiculous," David said, slamming his fists down on the armrests of the chair. "My daughter just gave you a name: Harry Bennett. The mayor. I know it's not what you want to hear, but there it is. There is your lead. You need to be talking to him." David's calm resolve was gone. The rope he was at the end of had snapped.

Gaines cradled the pencil behind his ear, flipping his notebook closed and tucking it in his pocket. "Relax, David. I know you're upset." He took a step closer.

"Relax? You want me to relax?" David gripped the armrests and leaned forward as if he were going to launch himself to his feet, but he stopped, his voice shifting from anger to despair. "My daughter is back there right now having God knows what done to her, and you want me to relax after you act as though she's just some dumb kid looking for attention—"

"I never said anything like—"

"You didn't have to, it's obvious. It's all over your face," David said. "Look, I can appreciate that you're not confident in the word of a teenager, but she just told you what happened. You know how hard that was for her? At least act like that's significant and you're considering it."

"I am, and it is. I know this is hard—"

The door to the exam rooms opened and Kara walked out, her mother beside her with an arm around her shoulders. Behind them, farther down the corridor, Catherine was speaking with Dr. Hornsby and the nurse, Julie Bowen. When Catherine saw Gaines, she held up a finger to Julie and Dr. Hornsby, breaking away from the conversation. She headed down the hall toward the waiting room.

David looked up at Gaines. Their eyes met. Gaines looked down for a moment, then toward Kara and her mother. He looked back at David. "We're all done here for the night," he said. "David, you can take your family on home now. Catherine and I need to speak with Dr. Hornsby."

Ellie walked her daughter through the waiting room toward the exit. Kara never said a word, her gaze set firmly on the carpet, but her mother paused on the way by. "Thank you, Sheriff," she said, and touched his arm.

The guilt and shame was an unexpected punch. Seeing Kara's face again nearly floored him. He had done nothing deserving of any appreciation. So far all he'd managed to do was insinuate to the father of a raped child that his daughter might be making the whole thing up. *Thank you.* Those words were like flechettes fired from her mouth. "No need for thanks, ma'am. Just doing my job." He looked back at David but couldn't bring himself to make eye contact. "Get home safe and sound now. We'll be in touch."

"We will," Ellie said, and continued to the door. "Come on, sweetie, we're going home now." Then they were outside, walking back to the car, slow steps.

David rose to his feet. "I know you'll do your job, Calvin. You're a good man. Sorry I lost my temper before," he said flatly, patting Gaines on the shoulder. Then he followed his family.

The front door to the medical practice was glass, and through it, Gaines could see David catch up to his wife and daughter in the parking lot. He put his arm around Kara, but she pulled away toward her mother. The two parents glanced at each other, pausing briefly, then continued, David slouching, hands in his pockets. The rear of their car divided them. Ellie went right with her daughter under her arm, opening the back door for her, and David, alone, went left and got into the driver's seat. Gaines finally saw the true character David was playing in this tragedy: the outsider. And Gaines felt for him.

Catherine stood in the doorway, thumbs hooked in her pockets, watching with a suspicious look on her face. "What was that about?" she asked.

Gaines heard her but didn't respond. He continued watching as the Prices got into their car. There was the dull roar of an engine. Brake lights flickered. Then they were gone.

"Calvin? Sir? Hey." Catherine snapped her fingers. "You with us?"

"What? I heard you. What was what about?" Gaines said, turning back to Catherine.

She stepped forward out of the doorway. "I asked what was going on between you and the girl's father. There was some serious tension in here."

"Oh. Nothing. Don't worry about it," Gaines said dismissively. "What did you find out? Where's…"

Dr. Hornsby's tall frame filled the doorway behind Catherine. He brought a finger to the bridge of his nose and adjusted his glasses. Julie Bowen stood beside him, eyes down, writing in an open file. She was a short woman, with wide-set eyes, brown hair, and a chubby figure.

"So what can you tell us, Creed?" Gaines asked.

Dr. Hornsby stepped around Catherine, and then all four were standing in a circle in the doorway. "I'll let Julie fill you in. She did the exam."

Gaines's eyes widened, his fists on his hips. "What? Why didn't *you* do it? You're the doctor."

Everyone looked at Gaines, surprised.

"Calvin, the parents asked for it that way. Given the circumstances I'd say that was the right call. Besides, Julie's well qualified."

Gaines rubbed his forehead. "I know, I'm sorry, I shouldn't've said that." He looked at Julie then back to Dr. Hornsby. "No offense. It's just, well, you know who the girl's saying did this to her, don't you?"

"Yes. Catherine told me. I'm no detective, but—" Dr. Hornsby glanced briefly down at his feet, then back at Gaines. "But frankly, I have a hard time with the idea that... " He started to say something but trailed off. "Never mind." He shook his head and tugged nervously on his earlobe.

Gaines noticed a look on the doctor's face—in his eyes—and he recognized it immediately. It was the face of a man in disbelief, a man struggling with an idea that seemed completely unfathomable. It was what Gaines had been feeling since Kara Price had uttered the name "Harry Bennett" back in her bedroom. He picked up again. "So you can understand why I don't want to take any chances on this."

"Look, Calvin, I understand. But everything was done by the book," Dr. Hornsby said.

"Well, how can you be sure if you weren't in—"

"What? Do you want me to call Kara's parents and have them bring her back so I can reexamine her?" Dr. Hornsby snapped. "Put her through that again? Is that what you think I should do?"

"That wasn't what I meant, and you know it," Gaines said, raising his voice firmly. "I just need to be extra careful with this."

Dr. Hornsby stiffened his posture but said nothing.

"Cal," Catherine said softly, placing a hand on Gaines's arm. "Let's not forget what we're doing here. Can we just…" She didn't finish the thought. She didn't need to.

"You're right," Gaines said. "I apologize."

Julie clicked her pen, sticking it in the crease of the folder and closing it. She wasted no more time. "You two done?" she said, and took a step forward. She spoke clearly and concisely with authority. "There are definite signs that Kara was raped. The bruises on her inner thighs are consistent with a sexual assault. I also found some internal swelling and tearing. The problem is some of these are only signs of sexual activity, not necessarily assault. But taken in context, given the mental state she's in, the defensive wounds on her legs, the contusions on her face, I think it is clear what happened to her."

A sick, unpleasant feeling ripped through Gaines's body when he thought about the idea of human flesh tearing. "Jesus." He looked at Catherine.

She shook her head, the corners of her lips curling down. "Go on."

Julie continued: "I also swabbed her for fluids, but if this guy wore something, there might not be anything. The test might take a while for results, too. And once again, even if we do find semen, that doesn't mean anything more than she's had sex. It isn't proof of rape. There isn't much else we can do right now, either. That's the problem with these types of things, everything's pretty much circumstantial." She shut the file. "But if you ask me, whoever did this was a sick son of a bitch. Worked her over real good. Put her tooth right through her lip." Julie paused, looking around, then brought her gaze to Gaines. "You really think Harry Bennett did this?" she asked. "I've known him my whole life. I just can't imagine…" And just like Dr. Hornsby, she trailed off before she said something she might regret.

Gaines didn't say anything at first, only leaned down, picked up his hat off the waiting room chair and absently ran his fingers along the brim. Finally, he widened his stance, folding his arms across his chest. He glanced back at Julie and said, "I have no idea. But that's what the girl says. And that's all we have so far. As hard as it might be to hear, I have to consider it. But this stays here for now, okay? I need to figure out how to handle this." He replaced his hat on his head and turned to Dr. Hornsby. "And you agree with all this? With what Julie's said? Her assessment?"

"Yes. As I said before, Sheriff, Julie is quite capable of doing her job. I agree with her findings."

Dr. Hornsby had grown cold toward Gaines since their escalating exchange a few moments before. But Gaines understood it: if Creed Hornsby ever showed up at the sheriff's station and tried to tell him how to do his job, Gaines imagined he might be ticked off too.

"Can I get a copy of that report?" Gaines asked.

"Yes, of course. Might be a few days, though. It won't be complete until those tests results come back."

"Not a problem. I appreciate it. Give me a call if you think of anything I should know."

"Yours will be the first number I dial," Dr. Hornsby said. "Now, are we all done here? It's almost ten o'clock—I'd like to get home."

"I think so." Gaines looked at Catherine. She was leaning against the wall, looking exhausted. "Yes, that should do it for now. I'll call if I have any more questions."

"Okay," Dr. Hornsby said, putting his hands into the pockets of his lab coat. He turned to Catherine. "Deputy, it's always a pleasure."

Catherine came away from the wall and yawned. "Excuse me," she said, and held a hand to her mouth. "Likewise, Creed. Say hello to your wife for me." She looked at Gaines. "I'll be in the cruiser, Cal. Try to be quick, I need to get some sleep. I have to be at the station in five hours. Night, Julie."

"Take care," Julie said.

Catherine left the waiting room and walked out into the parking lot.

Julie excused herself, disappearing down the hall back toward the exam rooms. Sheriff Gaines and Dr. Hornsby were alone. Their eyes caught for a moment, but they both broke away. Gaines wanted to ask the doctor if he thought that perhaps Kara was lying about Harry Bennett being the perpetrator. He wanted to ask and find out that he wasn't alone in his thinking. It would provide some assurance that he wasn't completely terrible for entertaining such a notion if another respected member of the community also had doubt. But he could not bring the words to his lips, the same way he had not been able to flat-out ask Kara's father the same thing. He wondered whether it was out of fear or respect that he didn't ask. He wasn't really sure it mattered, though. "Goodnight, Creed. We'll be in touch," Gaines said, and turned to walk away. He stopped. "And sorry if I came across as an asshole. I didn't mean anything by it. I hope you understand."

Dr. Hornsby smiled politely—no eyes, flat lips. "Don't worry about it. You're in a tough spot, I can see that," he said, and walked Gaines to the door. "Listen, it's a damn shame what's happened to that girl, it really is. I know that, and you know that. But don't forget where you live, Calvin. Something like this can tear a small town like Heartsridge in half. Just keep that in mind. People protect their own. It's human nature. Take that any way you like."

Gaines didn't respond. He wasn't quite sure what the doctor was talking about. The whole thing sounded so obviously cryptic. *People protect their own.* What the hell did that even mean? Gaines tipped his hat, nodded politely, and walked out into the night.

In the car, Catherine was already asleep. Seeing her brought a familiar weight to Gaines's own eyes. He was exhausted. Thoughts of home filled his mind—his bed, his wife, holding her as he drifted off to sleep, making love. He thought of an ice-cold beer and a hot shower. He thought of Kara Price and Harry Bennett, and his chest tightened. He thought of his daughter. And suddenly, something inside him warned that this was only the beginning of something much larger, only the first of many tired nights to come. But he shook the feeling away, closing his eyes hard. The thoughts ceased.

When his mind was clear, Gaines started the car. He reached for the radio but stopped himself when he glanced over at Catherine sleeping beside him. No music tonight. He would wake her once he pulled up to her house. They could discuss the case later. For now, she could sleep. For now, he would drive in silence. And that was just fine with him.

People protect their own.

Chapter 8

It was almost quarter to eleven by the time Gaines walked in through his front door. The lights in the house were off. He sat down on the bench in the front hall, unlacing his boots and kicking them off one at a time. He removed his hat and hung it on a hook beside the door. "Home sweet home," he whispered, and walked into the kitchen. The hum of the refrigerator was a lonely sound in the darkness, especially after the day he'd had. He flicked on the light switch. There was a note on the table. He picked it up. It read: DINNER IN THE FRIDGE. PIZZA! TOO TIRED TO WAIT UP. XOXO.

Gaines smiled. He was finally where he wanted to be. The stress of his job rarely followed him home, and on the off chance that it did, he had ways of quelling it. He opened the fridge, bent down, and pulled out a beer. He saw the plate of cold pizza but passed it over. He had no appetite. He cracked the beer, draining half the can down his gullet. It was cold and made his throat sting, but it was a good feeling. He set the can down, unbuttoned his uniform, and hung it off the back of one of the kitchen chairs.

There were a few pieces of mail. He flipped through them. Nothing important. Then Gaines picked up the half-drunk beer, shut off the light, and walked upstairs, leaving his day, Harry Bennett, and Kara Price all behind him in the darkness of the empty kitchen. In the morning they would still be there, waiting for him. But for now, he needed them gone.

The door to his daughter's room was open when he got to the top of the stairs. He saw the bright pink sign—MADDIE'S ROOM, PARENTS BEWEAR—hanging on the door. It was the only colorful thing in the dull twilight of the hallway. He stopped and looked at it for a moment, staring at the crooked handwriting and the misspelled word: BEWEAR. He grinned at the sight of it. He remembered the day she'd made it, a rainy weekend about six years ago. His wife, Linn, had come down with the flu and he'd taken the day off to take care of her. Maddie, who was only about nine at the time, had spent the morning cleaning her room, not without ample protest, of course. After she was finished she appeared in the kitchen doorway clutching a pink sheet of construction paper. Gaines recalled the look of determination that'd been in her eyes. "I want to make a sign," Maddie had declared. "I want to make a sign so people know to stay out of *my* room." He had only been able to smile. The idea of explaining to a nine-year-old that he in fact owned all the rooms in the house seemed a little mean spirited. She seemed excited about the whole thing, anyway, and he hadn't wanted to take that from her. "Okay," he'd said, and got her the box of markers from above the fridge. "You make it and I'll hang it. Deal?" There was a cute smile, and she agreed to the terms.

He left her alone with the paper and the markers at the kitchen table while he went upstairs to check on Linn. By the time he'd returned, Maddie was nearly done. "Look," she'd said, and turned around in her chair, holding up her sign. "This means you, *Dad.*" That was when he noticed she'd misspelled beware. But he hadn't had the heart to tell her. He would someday, but not that day. Not then. Not when it was raining outside. Not when Linn was sick upstairs. Not when his daughter was so proud. Not that weekend.

Gaines reached out and touched the sign. It was curled around the edges now, most of the lettering had faded, but she'd never taken it down, and that meant something. He wondered if she remembered that day the way he did.

He pushed the door open a few inches and leaned in, sipping his beer and watching his daughter sleep. She was fifteen now. She'd grown up so fast, was in high school now. She was lying on her back and breathing softly, her leg hanging out from under the comforter. Gaines heard the squeak of his bedroom door opening behind him but did not turn around. He knew what came next. There were a few soft footsteps and then a warm body pressed against his back. A hand reached around his waist, rubbing his ribs. Then out of the corner of his eye he saw his wife's face lean forward and rest on his shoulder. "Hi, sweetie," she said.

"Did I wake you?" Gaines asked quietly. They were both watching Maddie sleep now. "I tried to be quiet."

"No, I was reading."

"Good." Gaines turned, bent down, and gave Linn a kiss on the top of her head. Her hair smelled of vanilla. "I thought Maddie was going to be at a friend's tonight."

"She didn't feel well. Came home early." Linn brushed a strand of hair away from her forehead, tucking it behind her ear.

"Everything okay?" Gaines turned in the doorway to face Linn. A blade of light from their bedroom illuminated the side of her face.

"Yeah. I think she was just tired," said Linn. "We made some pizzas and watched a movie. I left you some in the fridge."

"I know. I saw your note. Thanks, hon." Gaines smiled. "Anything I'd like?"

"Just cheese and veggie."

Gaines laughed gently. There were a few things he believed initially attracted him to Linn when they'd first met: one was her intense, steel-blue eyes; and the other was her penchant for easy humor—put simply, the woman loved any chance to make a lame joke. "I meant the movie," he said.

"I know," Linn said, smiling with a goofy look. "We watched my favorite: *Gone with the Wind*."

Gaines sniffed and grinned. "You actually got her to sit through that?"

Linn brought two fingers to her mouth, pretending to smoke a cigarette. "Every second, sweetheart," she said in her best Bogart impression.

"Great, now you can both quote it at the dinner table." He shook his head and laughed softly.

"That was the plan," she said. "Everything okay at work?"

Gaines nodded and rubbed the back of his neck. "Can we talk about it later? I've had just about enough for one day."

"Of course, sweetie." Linn pushed her face against his arm and gave it a kiss. "Let's see if we can't help you relax," she said, taking his hand, turning, and walking toward their room.

Linn drew her husband a bath. He slipped in and she massaged his shoulders. His chest. His stomach. Then she reached down into the water and gripped him in her hand. He groaned slightly and let out a sigh in the form of a laugh. Then she kissed his neck and he was hard.

"C'mon," Linn whispered into his ear.

Gaines pushed himself up and out of the water. She ran her hands down his muscled arms and then draped his bathrobe over his shoulders. Dripping wet, he held his wife's hand as she led him back to their bed. She lay down on her back and beckoned to him. He went to her. And when he finally tasted her lips and pushed himself into her slick flesh, he felt everything that wasn't right in his life, everything that wasn't right in the world, melt away. He was finally home, where he wanted to be. For now, Harry Bennett and Kara Price were nothing but a distant thought.

CHAPTER 9

The following day, Gaines took his family to church, as he did every Sunday. And while his wife and daughter listened to the sermon, he prayed silently for God to provide guidance on what he should do. No answer came.

Afterward, he called Catherine at the station and told her he would be taking the rest of the day off. He told her to leave the Kara Price case alone until Monday. She was reluctant, but agreed.

Gaines spent the rest of the day up at Baker's Pond, searching the area for anything to corroborate Kara's story.

He found nothing.

David and Ellie Price tried to go about their day as if everything were fine, but their eyes were always watching the phone, waiting for it to ring, waiting for some update on what was being done about their daughter's assault.

No call came.

————

Harry Bennett went fishing and washed his car.

————

Kara Price spent the day in her room, staring up at the ceiling, running her tongue over the cut on her lip, pretending to sleep whenever her parents came to check on her—especially her father.

————

And ten miles away in Greenfield, a man walking his dog in the state park off Interstate 91 found the body of a young man who'd been shot three times and wrapped in a tarp. The Monday papers would name it the fourth murder in a string of recent killings. The authorities finally decided the crimes were connected, attributing them to a serial killer they were referring to as The Highway Hunter.

CHAPTER 10

Something electric and new filled the air of Heartsridge, Massachusetts, on Monday. The cicadas, having already emerged from the ground the week before and molted, had taken to the trees and started to sing their springtime love song. It was an endless droning sound, a low hum with an underlying high-pitched chirping. Some found it to be a pleasant sound—perhaps because of what it represented: the continuation of life (simply put, sex)—but Harry Bennett was not one of those people. And as he stood on his front porch drinking the day's first cup of coffee, looking out over his front lawn, he imagined that if he listened closely enough he could hear each individual bug mocking him with its obstreperous mating call.

"I should cut every last one of these goddamn trees down," he muttered. "Then where would you go?" He smiled and took a sip of coffee.

"Been a while since I heard that sound," a tired voice said from behind him. "God, last time I did I was in my thirties." Harry turned and saw his wife, Allison, standing in the doorway nursing a mug of coffee and smoking a cigarette. She was obscured by the metal screen, which made her form look hazy, like an old newspaper print. But her white bathrobe stood out, offering a sharper outline of her body. She was a tall, full-figured woman with a soft, round face. Green eyes and a head of cascading deep red hair that flowed down to her shoulders like silk flames. She was also the daughter of Mark Warren, owner of Bentley Warren Gravel, where Harry had worked for twenty years before setting out on his own and starting Bennett Trucking and Hauling.

Allison took a long drag off her menthol Moore, the end glowing orange behind the screen. She exhaled a jet of smoke and it drifted outside, lost in the morning air.

Harry turned back, gazing out over the front lawn in silence. He hated that she smoked. He thought it looked trashy.

"And don't you dare think about touching those trees," Allison continued. "I heard what you said when you didn't know I was watching. My grandfather planted these before you were even born."

Harry turned his head toward her, snorting disdainfully. "Good for him, Ali. A real Johnny Appleseed."

"Johnny Appleseed planted apple trees... those are maples," she said snidely.

Harry's eyes narrowed, his jaw muscles rippling, but he offered no retort. He couldn't stand when his wife was disrespectful to him. Harry Bennett was a firm believer that women had their place in the world, and that place certainly didn't allow for backtalk. Sometimes he wondered if the only reason his wife had offered to use her trust fund to help him start his own company was so she could behave this way without consequence, like she was purchasing the rights to his dignity. The only woman in his life before Allison had been his mother, Ginny Bennett, and she'd never missed an opportunity to humiliate him as a child, so why should his wife be any different?

Once when Harry was eleven, one of his friends from school—Nate Brickwell (long dead from lung cancer now)—brought a backpack full of skin mags to school. He, Nate, Sammy Matheson, and Mookie Donner had looked at them under the bleachers of the Heartsridge Middle School gymnasium until their eyes nearly bled and their underwear just about split. The gym teacher, Ms. Birch—jokingly referred to by the students, and probably some of the staff, as Ms. Butch—had heard the four boys laughing under the bleachers. One second the boys were staring at the bare breasts and spread legs of some young harlot in the pages of a nudey magazine; the next, Ms. Butch was ripping the magazines from their hands and yanking the four boys, two collars in each fat fist, out from under the bleachers, through the gym, and into the principal's office.

That night when Harry had returned home, suspension slip in hand for his mother to sign, she had already gotten wind of what had happened. "Disgusting, sick, perverted little boy. Beg God for his forgiveness… Beg for his guidance!" she yelled, as she brought the belt down on her son's bare bottom over and over again. Harry had cried harder with each swing, but not as much as he cried at what she did to him next. For the next two hours, Harry sat in a chair facing the wall in the corner of the kitchen while his mother read the Bible to him. That wasn't so bad by itself, but the mouse trap she'd clamped down on his penis hurt like nothing he'd ever felt before. He sat there the entire evening, crying, and when his wails rose too high, his mother would stop reading, stand up, cross the room, smack him across the back of the neck and say, "You want another pincher? Might not be much to clamp onto, but *I'll* find space."

Whenever it came time for doling out punishment or pain, Harry noticed that his mother always accentuated her role in it: "*I'll* give you something to cry about." "*I'll* teach you to fart at the dinner table." "*I'll* make sure you never forget to comb your hair before church." *I'll* find some space on that little wee-wee of yours to inflict more torture. Other mothers might not be able to, but *I* can! As if she were the world's foremost expert on painful lessons, and she wanted to make sure this was known before she proved it.

This part of the punishment, the humiliation and hurt of the mouse trap, went on for most of that evening until Ginny was convinced her son's promises to never look at smut mags again were sincere. Then he was sent to bed without dinner.

These were the sorts of memories that remained of his mother. Not many sweet ones. Scars was far more accurate. He believed things might have been different had his father stuck around, had he not up and abandoned them before Harry was born, but his father had. And in a way, sometimes Harry actually understood and forgave the man he'd never met, because he knew his father must've known what type of woman he'd knocked up, and a child he didn't yet know just wasn't enough to keep him tied to a cretin like Ginny Bennett.

When she died five years ago and Harry gave the eulogy at the funeral, it took every ounce of strength to keep from laughing when he referred to her as a "loving mother and a wonderful person". He hadn't wanted to say those false kindnesses about her, but he was mayor by then, and it was what the people wanted and expected: the picture of a sweet boy and a loving mother. A boy with a normal childhood. No monsters in the closet. So that's what he showed them. Harry Bennett was a man of the people, after all.

"Have you seen Lilly around the house?" Allison asked, taking another long pull off her cigarette. "I can't find her anywhere. I don't think I've seen her since Saturday morning."

Harry smiled inside. He'd been waiting for this question. He knew it would come eventually. In fact, he'd looked forward to it. There was something about the thrill of lying that sated an emptiness inside him. He liked to see if he could be so good that even *he* would start to believe what he was saying. That, he knew, was how the best lies were told—when the liar convinced himself they were real. "I think I saw her yesterday out back. You check the basement and under the porch? Sometimes she goes in through the cellar window."

"I checked the basement. All the usual places, too. Nothing."

"Maybe she ran away. Cats do that sometimes."

"Not when they're pregnant."

"*Especially* when they're pregnant," Harry said. "They go off and give birth in some dark corner where nothing will bother them. I'm sure she'll turn up. Probably with the new litter in tow."

"Maybe," Allison said, unconvinced.

"You'll see." Harry turned around and looked at his wife. "She'll be back. I'm sure of it." He smiled, really trying to sell it. "Don't go asking the neighbors just yet."

There was a shared moment of silence, save for the buzzing of the cicadas, in which Allison seemed to be pondering her husband's words. Harry waited, pretending to focus on the front yard, but really waiting to see if his performance had been convincing enough.

It had been. "I'm sure you're right," Allison said. She opened the screen door and came out, placing her cup of coffee on the railing. She pushed a few strands of hair off her forehead, folding her arms loosely. "Will you drop the Fourth of July invitations off at the post office this morning?"

"What?" Harry said, looking over at his wife, who was now sharing the same mindless gaze out over the yard. She looked mesmerized.

"It's actually kind of nice if you let it be—the noise, I mean" she said softly, as if in that moment she was discovering the fact. She looked away slowly, toward Harry. "The invitations for the Fourth of July cookout, will you drop them off?"

"Can't you?"

"I have a hair appointment at High Wave in West Elm." Allison stubbed out her cigarette in the small glass ashtray beside her. She released the last of the smoke from her lungs through her nose. "It's in the opposite direction. Besides, you're going right by the post office. Just say yes—it feels so good to say yes, darling." She walked up and caressed Harry's cheek delicately, then patted it playfully. "That's what Dad always used to say, anyway."

Harry was only half paying attention. The moment Allison had mentioned High Wave, all he could think of were Eddie Corbett and Wynona Finn going at it in the back of the salon. He'd looked at those pictures a few times before he used them to blackmail Eddie. Besides the negatives he had in his safe, he'd kept a few of the good developed shots for himself. They were like a trophy, especially the ones with great shots of Nona's tits. "Fine. Go get them and be quick. I have a full schedule today."

"You're the mayor. You have a full schedule everyday." Allison rolled her eyes, turned, and headed for the door.

"I'm a busy man. What can I say?" he said with a proud grin.

"Say you'll drop off the invitations, Harry." The screen door shut behind Allison as she disappeared back into the house.

CHAPTER 11

Gaines walked into Deb's Diner and grabbed a seat on one of the worn-out red vinyl stools at the counter. Most of them were cracked and torn, scaly, like the ancient earth of a dry lakebed. The ones that saw the most traffic were patched with red duct tape, which was also polished down to its mesh backing. Hard years of blue-collar denim hides sliding up to the same counter for their same morning coffees had taken its toll. And every morning, Joanna Renault, the thirty-five-year-old daughter of the eponymous Debbie Renault of Deb's Diner, was the one there to greet these habitual creatures.

"How about a cinnamon donut and a cup of coffee, Jo?" Gaines said, and smiled.

Joanna looked up from the two cups of coffee she was already pouring. "Be right with you, Sheriff."

She'd worked there since she was a young girl, taking over when her mother's arthritis got bad. Now Deb only came in on the occasional Saturday or Sunday to run the register. And lately even those occasions had become fewer and fewer.

This morning, Joanna's hair was tied back in a tight bun, which accentuated her high cheekbones and her narrow, almost feline, eyes.

"Thanks, Jo. And how many times I got to tell you to call me Calvin?" Gaines laughed. "'Sheriff' makes me feel so old and official."

"Okay, well, coming up, then, *Calvin*," she said playfully, then picked up the two cups of coffee, taking them to a waitress standing at the end of the counter. She poured one more cup and made her way toward Gaines. She put the steaming mug down in front of him and smiled. "I swear, I don't think I've ever met a man who *hates* to be called by his title. Most men would love to be sheriff, I'd guess."

"I'm not most men." Gaines grinned, removing his hat and placing it on the stool next him. "And besides, I like my name. I'm afraid I'll forget it if I don't hear it every so often."

Joanna laughed. "Is that so? Well maybe we should get you one of these." She pointed to the nametag on her work shirt. It read JOANNA in sturdy black letters.

"Already got one," Gaines said, and tapped his finger on the shimmering brass pinned to the breast of his shirt.

Joanna leaned forward, pretending to squint at the tag below his badge. Then teasingly she said, "No, that won't do," and smiled, shaking her head. "It only has your first initial and last name. We need to get you one that just says 'Calvin', and nothing else. That way you won't forget it."

"You might be on to something, you know?" he said. "You got any extras back there?"

Joanna put a hand on her waist, the other on the counter, drumming her fingers absently as if in thought. She shook her head. "Sorry, fresh out. You'll have to check back tomorrow."

"You just want to see me again, don't you?" Gaines winked.

"You got me." She lifted her hands as if to surrender. "Guilty as charged, Sheriff... I mean Calvin."

Gaines smiled, rubbing the back of his head and feeling a little guilty. He knew it was natural to flirt, and maybe it was just his personality, but if he did it subconsciously, he reasoned it was only to recapture some seemingly lost part of his youth. He and Linn had been together since high school, and he loved her dearly. But she was the only woman he'd ever been with. Not that he saw this as a bad thing (his parents had done the same and they had lived a happy life), but sometimes he couldn't help being drawn to the idea of another woman.

But an idea was all it ever was. He would never take anything any further than a few shared laughs or some lingering glances. Sometimes he just needed a reminder he was alive. While he knew this was foolish, and on some level selfish, he did it anyhow. He believed the guilt resided in the fact that he and his wife had a great marriage and an active love life, yet somehow it wasn't quite enough. There was always the nagging question of what love might be like with someone else. He wondered if that curiosity was something that ever went away. How many women does a man have to be with before he isn't afraid he's missing out? One or a hundred? There probably wasn't any set number. Maybe it only depended on the man. Maybe one was all he'd ever needed.

"How 'bout that donut?" he said.

"You got it. Cinnamon, right?"

"That'd be great. Warmed a little if you could, too."

"Comin' up," she said, turning and heading toward the pastry case.

The moment she was gone, the distraction was lost. The guilty excitement Gaines had briefly felt was replaced with an intense feeling of dread. He suddenly remembered the uncomfortable conversation he was about to have that morning, the thing he'd been trying to forget about, the reason he'd been trying to lose himself in the flirtation with Joanna.

Harry Bennett. The name flashed in his mind, sending a flutter of panic through his gut like a surge of dirty electricity. He'd held off contacting the mayor the day before, hoping to find some reason to make it unnecessary, but he hadn't turned up anything. Not that he'd really believed he would. Harry Bennett was the only lead they had in Kara's case, and Gaines knew her parents would expect to hear something soon. In fact, he was surprised they hadn't called the station already.

Looking down, Gaines once again noticed the rotten condition of the stools, how worn and tattered they were. For a moment, he hated those seats. He remembered ten years back when Deb had reupholstered them all. They had looked so brilliantly new, then. It hadn't taken much to weather them in the years since—only the slow, everyday acts of life. Normal wear. And that, he supposed, was what was happening to him—the normal, consistent, wear and tear of getting along in years. He could feel it: the stiff joints, the sore back, the lack of energy, the slight paunch of his gut. He couldn't deny that he was getting older, and those seats were like some strange reminder of the fact. At least, today they were.

Behind him someone opened the door, the overhead bell jingling. Gaines turned to see who'd come in. He was expecting a familiar face. Seven-thirty in the morning at Deb's usually saw the same queue of people, day in and day out. But Gaines didn't recognize this man. The stranger had the face of a trespasser, someone who didn't belong. Gaines eyed him for a moment. The man wore an old army jacket with a peace sign taped to the back, and a faded Red Sox cap. He held a little black canvas bag. The man stood at the entrance for a moment, grabbing a paper off the stand and looking around. Then he made his way toward the back of the diner and sat in an empty corner booth.

"He's a photographer," Joanna said, and set Gaines's donut in front of him.

Gaines turned back. "What's that? Who is?"

Joanna smiled, flashing a don't-underestimate-me look. "I saw you looking at that guy. He's been coming in here for the last few days. Name's Bill, I think—a photographer from New Hampshire. He's staying at the motel." Joanna wiped her hands on a dishtowel and pushed it back into her apron.

Gaines dipped the donut in his coffee and took a bite. "How you know all that?" he asked, dabbing his mouth with a napkin.

"Give me some credit, would ya?" Joanna laughed. "Ninety percent of this job is asking people questions. The better you know someone, the better the tip. Not so different from your job," she said. "And I don't need to carry a gun or shoot no one."

"A photographer, huh?" Gaines said.

Joanna nodded, clearing a few dishes from the counter. "That's right, nature stuff, I think. He said he was here for the cicadas."

"I don't know who'd want a picture of those things, they're the ugliest bastards I've ever seen. A couple of 'em were sitting on my car this morning," Gaines said.

"Yeah, they're a little weird looking, but some people think they're neat. Me personally, I think they're peaceful in the evening. Maybe because the last time they showed up, I was a kid and it reminds me of that."

Gaines grumbled in disagreement. He thought: *How can anyone find peace in that racket?* To him it sounded like a giant machine in the sky. He turned, taking another quick glance at the man with the peace sign on his jacket. "Doesn't look like National Geographic material to me."

"Oh stop it, Calvin. He seems like a nice guy. And besides, if it wasn't for out-of-towners like him, people might never know this town even existed," Joanna said, and bent down to grab a stack of napkins from behind the counter. When she did, a necklace popped out of her blouse and rested on her lapel as she straightened back up. It was a small circle of silver wire with beautiful blue and green stained glass soldered together and framed inside the border. Joanna didn't seem to notice it had fallen out.

Gaines eyed it for a moment, watching the light dance on the colored glass. "That's a neat piece you got there." He pointed to it. "I've never noticed it before."

Joanna looked puzzled for a moment, but then she looked down, realizing what Gaines meant. "Oh, this is one of my favorites," she said, grabbing the glass medallion between her fingers. "I made it. Did you know that?"

"That's impressive," Gaines said. And really, it was, too. It was the type of thing he imagined his daughter would love. He'd never been the best gift-giver—Linn always beat him in that department—but this seemed like a real winner. "I had no idea you made your own jewelry. And here I thought the diner was your life."

"God no. This place just pays the bills. I'm not exactly competing with Tiffany's or anything. I only really sell to friends and family, but I do all right."

"I'd love to buy one for Maddie if I could. Her birthday's on Wednesday. For once I think I might get her something she'll like." Gaines laughed. "The sweater from last year never shed its tag. You got one you could sell me?"

"Not today," Joanna said, frowning in thought. "But I could make you one. It takes me a few days, depending on my free time. You could even pick the colors you'd like."

"That'd be great," Gaines said. "I like those colors." He pointed to Joanna's once more. "Make one like that."

"Well, I can make hers with the same colors, but each piece is unique, so it won't be *exactly* like this."

"Even better. A one-of-a-kind necklace. This is the year, I can feel it—the year I get her a better gift than Linn." Gaines laughed and Joanna shook her head, amused. "You ever consider a booth at the festival? I'm sure people would love this kind of thing."

"Yeah, I was hoping to do a whole bunch of stuff this winter so I could have enough to sell next year, but I said the same thing last year. Just isn't ever enough time."

"I've been looking for a career change. Maybe I could take over the diner and you can do your jewelry full-time. Split the profits."

Joanna smiled. "Eat your donut, wise guy." She walked away, continuing her patrol along the breakfast counter, wiping surfaces and clearing dirty dishes as she went.

On his way out, Gaines stopped to introduce himself to the man in the corner booth, Bill, the bug photographer from New Hampshire. He wanted to get his own read on the man. He probably was a nice guy, just like Joanna had said, but with what had happened with Kara Price, Gaines was on high alert and paying extra attention to everything. *Nothing wrong with being polite to a tourist*, he thought. And maybe that was all he was really doing—saying hello to a newcomer. But he couldn't shake the feeling that there was something off about the man, a gut instinct, perhaps. So he was worth a sniff.

When Gaines walked up, the man was screwing a lens onto what looked like a fairly expensive camera. Gaines felt a bit of relief at this validation of the man's story. His internal watchdog backed off a little.

The black bag the man had carried in sat propped open on the table, and inside were a few rolls of film and another, smaller lens. The man put the camera down, looking up and smiling feebly when he noticed Gaines standing beside him. The jacket he'd been wearing was bunched into a ball, stuffed in the corner of the booth. On top of it was the Red Sox cap. The black t-shirt he wore was tight across the shoulders and chest, revealing small ridges of thin, lean muscle. His face was narrow and rough with stubble. Hair past due for a trim hung down onto his forehead in thick red greasy strands. The man looked young but not too young. Gaines's estimate put him somewhere in his mid-thirties.

"Morning," Gaines said, clasping his wrist casually with one hand and holding his hat with the other. "Don't think I've seen you around here before."

"Morning, officer," the man said, and took a sip of his coffee. "I suppose that's because I'm not from around here. Just staying a few days over at the motel while I work."

"It's sheriff," Gaines said and tapped his badge, smiling . "Or just 'Calvin' is fine. We're not too formal around here."

The man stuck out his hand. His fingernails were badly bitten back. "Bill… Bill Sexton," he said. "From Woodstock."

Gaines met Bill's hand and shook. It was a firm grip. There was strength there. "New Hampshire?" he asked, already knowing the answer.

"That's right," Bill said, and smiled. "Born and raised."

The man's stained front teeth suggested he was a smoker. Gaines scanned the table quickly, spotting a pack of Marlboros beside the ashtray on the table. There were already two spent butts stamped out, filters bent and flattened.

Gaines looked back at him. "Well, Bill from Woodstock, New Hampshire, welcome to our humble town," he said. "And by 'work', I'm going to assume from the camera that you're a photographer."

"I am," Bill said. "More of a hobby, really. I'm here to do a piece on the cicadas for a local rag back home. Nothing fancy."

"I guess some folks find that stuff interesting," Gaines said.

"I guess so."

"Well, anyways, I just wanted to introduce myself and welcome you to Heartsridge. I'm sure I'll bump into you again if you're here for any length of time."

"Appreciate it," Bill said, and took another sip of his coffee.

Gaines put on his hat and adjusted his belt. "You should send a copy of whatever it is you're working on when it goes to print. Send it to the sheriff's department. I'd love to see it. I'm sure folks around here would get a kick out of it too."

The man paused for a moment, his lips parting as if his mind had stalled. Then he seemed to restart and said, "You got it." And his eyes shifted to something beyond Gaines.

Before Gaines could turn around, he heard Joanna's voice behind him. "Leave the man alone. We're short-handed today, and I need to take his order," she said, and smacked Gaines's arm with her dishtowel.

Gaines smiled. "I was only takin' a moment to be polite and introduce myself."

"I'm sure you were." She rolled her eyes and laughed. Then her attention shifted to the man, Bill, sitting in the booth. "Don't mind his interrogation, he just doesn't have any crime to solve."

Bill smiled politely.

"Okay, well I guess I'm done here. I should be going anyways," Gaines said. "Despite what Jo here thinks, I do actually have some work to do." And for a moment, Gaines's gut tightened at the thought of Harry Bennett. "Take care, Jo. Let me know about the necklace. And good to meet you, Bill. Maybe stick around if you have nothing better to do and check out the Spring Festival. It starts this week. It's a good time with a lot of nice people. Bound to be some good photos in it for you."

"Was already thinking about it," Bill said. "This place seems like it has a lot to offer."

"All depends what you're looking for," Gaines said. "Anyways, enjoy your stay.

Bill held up his cup of coffee, toasting their exchange.

Gaines nodded.

"Bye, Calvin," Joanna said.

Gaines tipped his hat and headed toward the door.

Outside, he headed left down Market Street, to the station to face the day. He could feel the sweat starting to prickle his back. The air was dense with the sound of the cicadas. Behind him a child called out: "Look, Mom, there's one."

Gaines turned around, spotting a young boy and a woman. He didn't recognize either of them.

"Don't touch it," the woman warned the boy. "I don't know if those things bite." They were looking at a large cicada sitting on top of a post office box.

The boy moved closer to it with his arm outstretched, his finger pointed. "I don't think they do," the boy said, continuing to inch his finger closer to the insect.

"I said don't," the mother said, swatting her son's arm.

The boy pulled his arm to his chest and rubbed it.

And suddenly, all of the unease that Gaines had felt toward

the man in the diner—the gut feeling he had originally had that something was off about Bill, the photographer from New Hampshire—evaporated into the sweltering morning heat.

The tourists were arriving. That was all. Same as every year. Soon the town would be swarming with them, just like the cicadas many would be coming to see.

Gaines walked on, Bill from Woodstock fading into a distant thought.

CHAPTER 12

"Is it all right if I stay home today?" Kara asked, standing in the kitchen doorway in her bathrobe. It was early morning on Monday. The sun had barely climbed above the trees. The cut on her lip was scabbed and healing, but it was doing so slowly. This was because Kara had developed a strange compulsion to repeatedly stretch her mouth and reopen the wound. She would split it, running her tongue over it, tasting the blood and fighting back tears, until the stinging faded and the whole thing became numb and clotted again. "I don't think I want to be around anyone, not until my face heals a little, and I don't think I—"

Ellie stopped her daughter mid-sentence. "Of course you can, sweetie. I was trying to let you sleep in, but I guess that didn't work."

"Guess not."

Ellie poured a cup of coffee. "We figured you could use a few days off. I already called the school and told them you were sick. You can go back when you're ready."

"Thanks, Mom," Kara said softly.

"Your father and I talked about it last night, and he wants to take a few vacation days from work so you don't have to be alone."

Both Ellie and David worked over in West Elm. She was an administrative assistant for a vice president at American Mutual Insurance, and he was a sales manager over at the dairy plant.

Kara looked down and away. Her stomach dropped. "He doesn't need to do that, Mom. Besides, I think I'd like some time to myself. I don't need someone to watch me. I'll be fine."

Ellie's brow wrinkled. "I don't know, Kara. I don't think your father's going to go for that."

"Why not?" Kara asked, and folded her arms. For the first time since she'd been raped, she felt some sort of will to stand up for herself. "I'm old enough to be on my own. I don't need him around all day asking me how I'm doing every ten minutes."

Ellie's mouth dropped open, and she angled her head. "Oh, I don't know... I just don't think he is comfortable leaving you alone right now. Not until—"

"Until what? They arrest Harry Bennett? 'Cause that's never going to happen," Kara said. "That's why I never wanted to say anything to begin with. No one's going to believe this ever happened." She hadn't wanted to discuss this, but it was too late. The words were flowing.

"Kara—"

"It's true, Mom, and you know it. So does Dad. I could see it on all your faces the second I told you who did it. I'm not stupid—there's no proof. I know that. It's my word against his."

There was a thud, and the sound of rattling water pipes reverberated through the ceiling. Kara knew it was the sound of the upstairs shower shutting off.

"That's just not true," Ellie said. "Just because he's the mayor and he's managed to hide the kind of monster he is from everyone else doesn't mean he's getting away with anything." Ellie's voice was stern now. Not in a scolding way, but in a way that suggested she might be trying to convince herself of her own words.

"Then why haven't they arrested him yet? Why hasn't the sheriff called and told us anything?"

"I don't know. But no one is getting away with anything. Do you hear me? I promise." Ellie was staring into her daughter's eyes with a hard look. "I need you to know that, okay? He will pay for this."

Kara *didn't* know that, but in this moment she knew it was what her mother needed to hear. "Okay, Mom," she said. "I believe you."

Ellie slowly calmed down, her face softening. "Look, I know this is hard and you're pissed off, and I don't blame you. We're upset, too. I can't imagine what you're going through. This type of thing just shouldn't happen, not in a town like this, not in *any* town to *anyone*, but you've got to work with us a little. I know you're old enough to stay home alone, but these aren't normal circumstances, and I know you know that. Dad's only trying to help."

Kara did understand that, and she did appreciate what her mother was saying. But that wasn't why she was feeling so defensive.

Kara found it was almost impossible to be in the same room as her father since being raped. She felt terribly guilty for feeling this way, but she couldn't help it. She had recently become aware of the recurring disquiet that flooded her when he was in her presence. She pretended she didn't know why, but she did. She hated to acknowledge it, hated that it was even there. But it was. Harry Bennett and her father were both men, and that was enough to close any sort of distance she ever managed to put between herself and what had happened. Being around her father, especially when he tried to console her, even if it was only with a gentle caress of her arm when he asked how she was doing, brought visions of what she'd been through, flashing in her mind like brilliant strobes of anguish. The hands that had once held her as a child now felt so rough and strong, so capable of hurting if they wanted. She knew it wasn't right, and she knew she loved her father and he her, but right now his love wasn't what she wanted or needed. Right now she just wanted to forget and move on, and the mere fact that David Price was a man made that difficult. It wasn't his fault, but it didn't matter. Kara hoped her mother would understand this without her having to spell it out. She was afraid that doing so would make real or permanent what she hoped was only a temporary affliction, as though the feeling would set like cement once it passed her lips. Eventually this feeling would fade and life would return to normal. Wouldn't it? It had to. She just needed time, that's all.

"Fine," Kara said grudgingly. "But I think I'd be more comfortable if it was you who stayed with me." She'd been staring at the floor. Now she looked up, meeting her mother's eyes, clouded with a new look—something like worry mixed with understanding.

"All right, that's okay," Ellie said, cupping her elbows with her hands and moving toward Kara. Her mother understood now. "Do you want to talk about it? What you're feeling is completely—"

"Not right now, Mom, okay? I just... I don't want to..." She trailed off.

There was another sound from upstairs. The bathroom door opening. Footsteps. Dresser drawers opening and shutting. Kara looked up nervously, then quickly back at her mother.

"It's all right, don't worry," Ellie said. "I'll talk to your father, tell him I'll stay home, instead. He can go to work."

"Okay," Kara said. "Mom, I'm sorry."

"Stop that. Stop that right now. You don't apologize. Not for anything. None of this is your fault."

Kara felt like falling into her mother's arms and crying but fought the urge. She liked the way her little reemergence of strength had made her feel; it was a glimpse of her old self. And she didn't want to wash it away with more tears. There had been enough tears already. *Toughen up, Kara.*

"Thank you," Kara said.

"Anything else, sweetie?"

Kara's demeanor livened as the anxiety that had coiled in her gut began to unwind. "Well, I am a little hungry. I don't think I've eaten for a couple days."

Ellie smiled, nodding. "You haven't," she said. "I was starting to worry I'd have to bribe you to eat."

Kara finally smiled, and when she did, she felt the corner of her lip start to crack. She stopped and slacked her lips. That pain was for when she was alone. It was her secret. She didn't want her mother to see it start to bleed, otherwise she knew there'd be another round of her mother's heavy-handed application of ointment.

"What would you like? Eggs? Toast? Oatmeal? All three?" Ellie said. "Whatever you'd like."

"Some toast would be fine. Maybe some tea, too?"

"You got it, just let me talk to your father real quick and call my office."

"Thanks, Mom. I'd like that."

Ellie kissed Kara's cheek and then walked past her, heading upstairs.

Kara pulled out a seat at the kitchen table, flipping through a stack of old catalogues, pressing her tongue against the back of her lip and stretching it outward.

Her eyes watered and the room around her blurred.

David was slipping into a pair of old jeans when Ellie walked in. He was still damp from the shower, which made them tough to pull on. He was hopping on one foot when Ellie entered the room. "What's up, hon?" he said. The pants finally gave and slid up.

Ellie sighed heavily as she came in, taking a seat on the edge of the bed. "We need to talk."

We need to talk. David cringed at those words. They were the four worst words he knew. Nothing good ever followed them. His body knew this, and his stomach began to sour almost immediately.

"What's the matter?" He ran his fingers through his wet hair and parted it to one side.

"Now before I say this, I want you to promise you won't overreact, okay?" Ellie looked up at him from the bed. There was vague look of guilt in her eyes.

David would make that promise to her because that's what it took to get the information flowing, but he knew that promises demanded were never as binding as promises offered. "I swear, I won't. Now what's going on?"

"Well, you can take your jeans off," Ellie said, smiling halfheartedly.

"Why?"

"Because you should go to work today."

"Stop doing that—stop being evasive. I hate that," David said. He wanted her to just say it. The sooner he knew, the sooner the anxiety he was feeling would disappear. At least, that was the plan. "Just tell me what's going on." He took a seat beside his wife.

She reached over and took his hand. Her fingers felt cold.

"Sorry, I'm not meaning to be," she said, pinching her lower lip between her thumb and index finger. Her nervous tic. She stopped. "I'm just trying to think of how to put this so it doesn't sting."

"Don't think so much. I'm a grown man, just tell me whatever it is and get it over with," David said.

Ellie took a deep breath through her nose. "All right… I don't think Kara is completely comfortable around you right now."

"What? What are you talking about?" David pulled away, turning and looking squarely at Ellie.

"Hold on, let me finish," Ellie said. "I think she is just having difficulty being around you because of what happened to her. It isn't anything you did. It's just what you represent."

"What I represent? That's ridiculous. I have done nothing but be loving to her." David was starting to feel like the outsider again, the third wheel. He was thankful that Ellie had this intuitive female connection with their daughter, but on the other hand, he hated it.

"I know you have, but that isn't what I mean. You've been great… but—"

"But, what?" David stood.

"But you're a man," Ellie said sternly, then closed her eyes and took another deep breath. "Sorry. What I mean is you're a man, and you're the last thing she wants around her right now."

On some level, David had known this, feared this, but he didn't want to admit it. He knew it was only a phase that would pass, but it wasn't happening fast enough. His daughter had been apprehensive since they'd left the doctor's Saturday night, but he'd glossed over it, chalking it up to the idea that maybe she just didn't want to be around *anybody*, not just him. "Did she tell you that?"

Ellie looked away as if thinking. "No, not exactly," she said. "But she didn't need to. It isn't anything you did—"

"Then how do you know for sure?" David's brain switched to overdrive, his thoughts beginning to race.

"David—"

"How do you know this is how she feels?" David said, fists on his hips, angry. He knew his wife was right, but he could not accept it easily. There was so much wrong in his world right now, and there was nothing he could do to fix any of it. Did Harry Bennett really think he could get away with this?

"And what do you mean, 'not exactly'? What did she say?" David looked toward the door. "Christ! I have no idea what's going on. She's said barely two words to me since…" David trailed off for a moment. "Is she awake? Maybe I should talk to her."

"Calm down. Yes, she's up. But I really don't think that's a good idea. She needs time and space. This isn't permanent, try to remember that. She needs to process everything on her own. If you try and force it, it's only going to get worse."

David paused, feeling the thickness in the back of his throat. "I fucking hate this," he said, and rubbed the side of his face with a flat palm. "How did I let this happen?" He sat down on the side of the bed, defeated. There was nothing he could do, and he knew it. In this moment, this was his life, and he knew he needed to accept it. Merge with it instead of fight it. That was the only way to stay afloat when drowning seemed inevitable: swim with the tide, not against it.

"Don't do that to yourself. This is the fault of no one in this family. You can't protect her every second of the day. There are things out there that you can't see coming. You couldn't have known something like this would happen."

"I know… it's just… I want to be there for her right now, and all she wants is for me to stay away from her. It goes against every instinct in my body."

"I know it does, and I don't blame you for feeling the way you do. But it's what she needs for the moment, so be strong for her that way. You're helping her, just the same. Trust me, she will come around, and we'll make it through this together. And I promise you that when we do, she'll be forever grateful to you. She's a confused kid right now, that's all."

David feigned a smile, briefly resting his head on Ellie's shoulder. Inside he was dying, but apart from that, his wife had spoken the truth: right now, he needed to be strong. And he would be.

"So you talked to her?" David said, straightening his posture and lifting his head. "What'd she say?"

"She came downstairs a few minutes ago while I was making coffee and asked to stay home. She seemed to be in better spirits than yesterday, though."

"That's good. So, what, are we going to let her stay home alone? I don't think that's a good idea. I know she doesn't want me around, but I can stay home and just keep my distance. I already called the office and told them I'd be out for a few days."

"No, that's all right, she won't be alone. I'm going to stay with her," Ellie said, the guilt resurfacing in her eyes.

David noticed. Perhaps this wasn't difficult for only him. Perhaps Ellie had her own difficult feelings about being the sole source of comfort for their daughter—guilt for a victory she never wanted.

"How?" David asked. "I thought we discussed this last night. You don't have any vacation time left at work. That's why I was going to stay to begin with."

"I don't, but it'll be fine. They'll dock me for the days I'm out, but we can afford it. It's either that or tell them what happened and hope for understanding."

"No, that's not an option. It's best we don't tell anyone about this right now… for Kara's sake. I can only imagine what it's going to be like once this gets out, if it hasn't already."

"It'll be hard, but we'll handle it. That's what families do." She kissed his cheek.

David smiled, leaned forward, and started taking off his jeans. "Guess I should get ready for work then."

"I'm sorry, sweetie."

"It's okay. Maybe it'll be good to take my mind off things." He didn't believe this, but saying it made him feel like it might be true. "I'll swing by the station and talk to the sheriff too, see what's going on. We should've heard something by now."

Ellie nodded softly. "Okay, let me know if you hear anything." She stood. "I'm going to make Kara some breakfast. Want anything?"

David considered the lead knot in his stomach. "No thanks. I'll grab something later."

Ellie brushed the side of her husband's face with the back of her hand and walked out of the room.

David listened as her footsteps faded down the hall, finally disappearing altogether. It was a lonely sound, he thought.

David got dressed in his normal work clothes: khaki dungarees, black socks, leather penny-loafers, a light-blue dress shirt rolled up to his elbows, and a red paisley tie. He looked at himself in the mirror, and for the first time ever, he was unhappy with the reflection that greeted him. What he saw was something pathetic. A fool. An outsider. His wife had said they would overcome this together as a family, but nothing about what was going on around him felt like togetherness.

He turned away from his reflection and headed downstairs, toward a job that for the first time in his career he did not respect. Everything he had once been proud of suddenly seemed so gray and insignificant.

From the base of the stairs, David could see into the kitchen. He could see his daughter's back as she sat at the table sipping from a steaming mug. Ellie stood at the counter, buttering some toast. He heard the scraping of the knife across the thin, crisp ridges of bread. Any other morning he would've walked in, kissed his girls goodbye, and left with a smile on his face and joy in his heart. But this morning would not be like that; this morning was a new kind of sorrow. So instead, David imagined doing all those things he could not do now.

In his mind, he kissed Kara's cheek. There were no cuts and no bruises. He would walk up behind his wife and hug her, kissing the back of her neck while Kara pretended to be grossed out by their affection. In his mind things were different. Better. Normal. In his mind his world was right.

He entertained these thoughts for a moment, let the feelings linger on the edge of his brain, and watched his family silently from afar. *The outsider,* he thought to himself. *That's what I am.*

Without saying anything at all, he left.

Outside, David started his car and sat for a moment, just thinking of how unfair it all was. Then he put the car in gear, and headed out of the driveway.

CHAPTER 13

Sheriff Gaines's cruiser was sitting empty in the shade at the far end of the Town Hall parking lot when Harry pulled in. He smiled faintly, continuing to his reserved spot. He parked, killing the engine.

His mind was on the young girl from the day before, the intern, the one he'd given a ride to. Glancing into the rearview mirror, he adjusted it so he could look into the backseat. He wondered if he'd cleaned it well enough. Harry studied his reflection for a moment, straightening his tie and brushing his hair from his forehead. Satisfied, he threw his arm over the seat and looked into the back of his car. One last check. Meticulous attention to detail was how he'd gotten ahead in life. Seeing the little things that others missed, finding angles to exploit, holes in the fabric of life. And because of this self-image, he couldn't bear the idea of getting caught because of some ignored, minor element he'd missed. He'd lost his temper and been foolish with the girl, but that didn't mean he had to go to jail for it. People like him didn't go to jail. What was coming his way was a minor blip on the radar. Next year it would be forgotten, and *he* would be the victim, not her. She would be a mixed-up teenager who'd tried to get attention by making slanderous accusations about a man in power. Why? Perhaps her parents had ignored her as a child. Who knows why kids do the things they do?

He was Harry Bennett, mayor of Heartsridge, a man of the people. That was what people wanted to believe, and people had a great tendency to believe what they wanted to. The facts, the accusations, the "he said-she said," the likelihood of things all went out the window when a person wanted to embrace a reality that they were more comfortable with, something easier on the palate. Plainly and simply, Harry counted on the public's own selfishness, their need to soothe themselves and put their own feelings before another's. And they would. They always would.

Selfishness was a human condition Harry had used to his advantage for most of his life. It was a universal quality that every person had ingrained at some primitive level. It was a form of survival. But the fact that people were ashamed to admit they ever dipped their toes in those self-serving waters made them vulnerable. People with something to hide, even when they're unaware they're hiding it, are the easiest to manipulate. Sometimes he only needed to show people had a secret to exploit it.

The leather of the backseat was glossy and pristine. Harry could still smell the scent of the cleaning solution he'd used. The space was immaculate. He'd made sure of that, scrubbed it clean of any evidence the day before.

As he looked into the backseat, Harry tried to imagine the face of the girl. *The little cunt with no respect.* Kara was her name, if he recalled correctly. But he couldn't remember exactly what she'd looked like. Instead of an image, there was only the clear memory of how his sense of her had changed in the moment she realized what was about to happen to her, the change in the atmosphere between them. It was not a recollection of sight; it was one of emotion, how he'd felt. It was power. He knew that feeling well. It was unmistakable. Dominance over another thing, another being. But her face was a blur. He didn't even think he could pick her out of a lineup if he had to. How he'd felt, though, that he'd never forget.

He'd heard her earlier in the day on her lunch break. She'd been on a personal phone call in the office—a boy named Ryan—saying how foolish Heartsridge and the mayor were for thinking that anyone still cared about the "stupid festival." The arrogance of it all had driven Harry's mind into darkness. A little teenage girl who thought she knew it all, thought she was better than he was, than everyone, giggling about how stupid Heartsridge and everything about it was, everything *he* cared about. She'd been trying to humiliate him and it drove him wild. He shouldn't have let his temper get the best of him. But he couldn't help it. There was no other option. The girl needed to be taught a lesson. She couldn't just go around doing and saying anything she wanted without consequence. His mother would've given him the mousetrap—or worse—if he'd acted that way as a kid. Still, he shouldn't have been so careless. Someone in his position could not afford to let his emotions call the shots. He'd only been that out of control once before in his life, and it was only luck he hadn't gotten caught then. It may have been a different sort of thing with that bully who'd stolen his shoes, but it was careless just the same. This time, he promised himself, was the last time he allowed himself to lose control. But something inside him had awoken.

Harry turned back and pulled on the latch, opening the door. He stepped out of his car, walking across the parking lot to the front entrance of Town Hall.

"You have a visitor," Brenda Fahey said as Harry walked in. "Sheriff Gaines. He's waiting in your office."

Brenda was Harry's secretary. She was short, fat, and unattractive, but she was good at her job. She reminded Harry of a pet guinea pig named Wesley he'd had when he was a boy. His mother had made him drown the animal in the bathtub after it bit her finger.

"Thanks, Brenda. He tell you what he wanted?" Harry placed his briefcase on the edge of her desk next to a half-eaten muffin. He took his suit coat, which he'd draped over his arm, gave it a soft shake, and slipped into it, smoothing out the light wrinkles with a flat hand.

"No, only asked if you were in." Brenda shook her head absently, her earrings jangling like Christmas ornaments. "I told him you'd be here any minute, and he asked to wait in your office. I said it was okay," she said with a look of hesitation. "It is okay, isn't it, sir? I didn't think you'd mind."

"Yes, that's fine. I think Heartsridge's finest can be trusted in my office." Harry smiled at Brenda and picked up his briefcase again. He eyed the half-eaten muffin once more, then his eyes shifted to Brenda's shirt. There were crumbs on her lapel. *Pathetic,* he thought. He would have a talk with her later about eating at her desk. It was unprofessional. But for now he'd let it slide; he had more important things on his mind.

Brenda smiled back, her cheeks bulging and creasing in all sorts of extra places. "I have a few messages too," she said. "All folks with last-minute questions about the festival. I told them they should contact the Parks Committee and not you, but I took their names just in case."

"Okay, good, thanks. I'll take those," he said, and took the pink message slips Brenda was holding in her hand. "You have my paper?"

"Right here." Brenda reached behind her and pulled a neatly folded newspaper off a bookshelf. "Full of sad news, as usual: a baby died in a house fire over in Agawam, a town destroyed by a tornado in Wichita, a serial killer who's shooting people on the side of the highway. Every day the world seems to get worse and worse. Honestly, I don't know how you even read this anymore. It would just depress me."

Harry took the paper out of her hand. "Yes, well, the world's a sad place, unfortunately. You should be happy you elected someone like me. The terrible state of the world is why I got into politics in the first place, to try and make things different for people here. The world may be a sad place, but the way I see it, our Heartsridge doesn't have to follow suit. I've worked hard to try and make this town better than the places you read about in here." Harry tapped the paper. He didn't know if he believed any of what he'd just said, but slinging bullshit like that had become second nature to him in the last decade of his life.

"You do a good job of that, sir. I hope you know that."

"And I'll continue to do so, so long as I have your vote next election." Harry smiled his politician's smile. "Do me a favor and hold all my calls until I'm done with the sheriff. Can you do that? I don't want to be interrupted."

"I'm on top of it, sir." Brenda clicked a button on her telephone and a red light lit up. "Anything else?"

"Yes, I almost forgot. Call the Parks Committee and let them know Eddie Corbett has agreed to let us use his parking lot for the festival. Tell them they need to set up signs off the highway and around town like we talked about and arrange someone to drive a shuttle bus. And tell them I don't want Paul Donniger behind the wheel—the man's a drunk. Get someone reliable."

Brenda whispered to herself as she scribbled down Harry's instructions. "Okay. Call committee, need signs and shuttle, no Paul Donniger. Got it." She looked up. "That all?"

"For the moment," Harry said. "I'll have more for you later. I should go see what the sheriff wants." He turned away from Brenda and headed down the hall to his office.

On his way, in an effort to distance his thoughts from the girl, he cracked open the newspaper and read the headline on the front page:

THE HIGHWAY HUNTER'S OUT THERE—
POLICE SUSPECT SERIAL KILLER IN STRING OF
GRISLY SHOOTING MURDERS.
FOURTH VICTIM IDENTIFIED OFF I-91.

When Harry turned the corner, he lifted his eyes from the paper. He could see Gaines through the open doorway to his office, leaning in close, inspecting pictures on the shelf beside his desk. Gaines seemed to be focusing on the one of Harry and his wife, taken last Fourth of July at his family cookout.

Harry centered himself, preparing for the conversation he imagined he was about to have. *You're Harry Bennett, a man of the people, a kind, nice, caring person. You've spent the last seven years helping the people of this town. They'll believe what they want, remember? And they won't want to believe this. They won't want to believe they elected someone capable of...*

Harry walked in.

Gaines composed himself and took his hands out of his pockets.

"Calvin, how are you?" Harry said, going to his desk. He laid his briefcase down on a stack of papers. "You hear about this?" He held up the front page of the paper. "They're saying there's a damned serial killer out there now. Just found another body off the highway. It sickens me." Harry walked around to his chair, took a seat, planted his elbows, and tented his fingers in an officious way.

"Yeah, I read about it this morning. It was over in Greenfield. They said four victims so far, all of 'em pretty much kids in their late teens and twenties. Twisted stuff," Gaines said, taking a seat in front of the mayor's desk. "Hopefully it won't scare people away from the Spring Festival."

Harry held up his hands and waved them humorously. "No blasphemy in this office," he said, and laughed. "These damn cicadas are already nuisance enough, never mind some psychopath on the loose. Regardless, I have a feeling this year's festival will be the best yet. We've been taking vendor applications since December, some from out of state. Sold fifty percent more than last year, actually. Seems like everyone has something to sell this year."

Gaines placed his hat on the chair beside him. "I don't know, Harry, I think the cicadas are actually a good thing for business. People seem interested in 'em. From what I gather, they're a kind of novelty. There's even some photographer here who's interested in doing an article."

Harry eyed Gaines for a moment, looking him over, trying to read his face without appearing to do so. What was his true business here? Had the girl kept her mouth shut like he'd told her too? He doubted it. But he bet for damn sure Calvin Gaines hadn't come to his office to talk about bugs.

"Is that so? Well maybe you're right, but all I know is I can't stand that racket outside," Harry said. "It drives me up the wall. Sounds like a dentist drilling in my ear."

"Oh, they're not so bad. I'm already starting to get used to them."

Harry leaned back, lacing his fingers over his stomach and laughing. "You sound like my wife. She says they're peaceful. I don't get it."

Gaines returned the smile. "Well, I wouldn't go that far. I wouldn't say peaceful."

"Fair enough," Harry said. "Anyway, what can I do for you, Calvin? Still after your air conditioners? 'Cause after this year's festival, I think we'll be able to help you out. The budget's looking flush right now."

Gaines's face slowly darkened, and he offered a polite but forced smile at the mayor's comment.

Harry noticed this, and his chest fluttered, a hot flash surging through his body. His palms began to sweat, his vision tunneled, his mouth dried. *Remember to breathe. They have nothing but* her *word against yours, so long as you covered all your tracks. These people are fools. Calvin Gaines is a fool. Just breathe.*

"No, actually I'm here about something else." Gaines looked down briefly, then his eyes lifted and met Harry's.

Harry maintained the smile on his face. The smile that said: *I'm your mayor, your elected official, I'm listening, now tell me what I can do to help you.* He'd held that fake look for seven years, so what was another few minutes using it to pretend he didn't know why the sheriff of Heartsridge had dropped by unannounced and was now wearing the look of a doctor about to deliver bad news?

"Any way I can be of assistance?" Harry asked.

"I don't know… maybe," Gaines said, shifting uneasily in his seat. His posture stiffened and he let out a long sigh.

Suddenly Gaines looked more official. The fluttering in the mayor's chest turned into full-on panic. But still, he maintained his outward composure, holding a natural expression. He had found over the years that, in times like these, his instincts took over, and the anxiety acted like fuel to push him through to the other side.

"Harry, do you know a girl by the name of Kara Price?"

There it was. The game had begun. *Breathe.*

Harry furrowed his brow, feigning uncertainty. "Kara Price? The name doesn't ring a bell. Should it?"

"Well, she works here at Town Hall... in your office, from what I understand." Gaines pulled his notepad from his breast pocket, flipped the cover open, and ran his finger down the page. "I believe Saturday was her first day, so maybe you don't."

Harry's eyebrows raised and he sat forward, resting on his elbows. "Oh, yes, the new intern, Kara, that's right. I only met her briefly. Haven't really had a chance to get to know her yet. But if she's working with Brenda, I'm sure I will soon enough. She seemed like a nice girl, though. Smart, from what I gathered. Why do you want to know? She get in some trouble?"

Gaines turned his head, looking toward the door. It was shut. He sighed again. Nervous. Fidgety.

Harry could see that Calvin Gaines, the law of Heartsridge, the only man who was in a position to actually harm him, was one of the first people to let his own selfish agenda cloud the truth on this. He could see the man struggling to believe something he did not want to. To do so would be to allow something sour to fester in his mind. Most people could not tolerate such disgust. Life was easier for folks when they believed monsters were only the children of imagination, not walking among them in the flesh. The truth might be a tough pill to swallow, but if there was no sickness, there needn't be a remedy.

"Here's the thing. I hope you know I'm only doing my job. I know you can respect that."

"Of course. Now what is it? The anticipation is killing me. Someone didn't die, did they?"

"No. No, not exactly," Gaines said. "But this girl, Kara Price—something happened to her on Saturday after she left here."

"What do you mean?" Harry asked. He was starting to feel comfortable now. He was slipping into the skin of the lie, wearing it, becoming it.

"Well, she showed up at home after work pretty roughed up," Gaines said, pausing. Then: "She said she was attacked... by you. Raped."

Harry looked down, smiling and shaking his head. He laughed nervously. "What? I mean, I'm sorry, I don't mean to laugh. But you're joking, right? This is a joke, Calvin. Tell me you're kidding."

Gaines didn't crack a smile, but Harry hadn't expected him to. "I'm afraid not. This girl is for real. She's claiming you did it. Her face is banged up real good, too. And Julie Bowen down at Dr. Hornsby's office examined her and confirmed that she's more than likely experienced, well, you know, some sort of sexual assault."

There was a pause between the two men.

Harry's face fell serious. "Jesus, Calvin, she's lying. Don't tell me you're even considering it. Don't be a sucker. You don't think I could do something like that, do you? For Christ's sake, I'm a happily married man, not a pervert."

Harry fought the urge to soften for Gaines, to pander to him; that wouldn't be typical behavior for him. The point here was to seem normal. Be himself, like nothing was off or different or amiss. Harry may have been a man of the people, but there was also a raw edginess to him that he wore on his sleeve, and anyone who knew him respected him for it. To hide that side of him now would seem suspicious.

Gaines held up a hand defensively. "I know, give me some credit here. I'm not jumping to any conclusions. I didn't say I believed anything. If I did, this conversation we're having would be down at the station. But you know how this works, I have to follow every lead, and since there's only the one—her accusation—I didn't have a choice. I had to come talk to you."

"Okay, so let's hear it then. What's her story?" Harry said. "What bullshit is she feeding you guys? I'd like to know what she's saying I did to her."

"She hasn't said much. She was real shaken up when I talked to her." Gaines looked at his notepad again. "But the gist of it is that you offered her a ride home from work and instead took her to Baker's Pond and had your way with her in the back of your car, after roughing her up some."

Harry threw up his hands. "I guess that's what happened then," he said snidely. "If she says so, then it must be true. So what now? Where do we go from here? Are you going to haul me in? Ruin the career I've spent almost a decade building, all because of some screwed-up girl's bullshit story?"

"Look, I'm not going to do that and you know it. We've known each other almost fifteen years, petty politics aside. I'm not going to arrest you, because there is no evidence other than her claims, but if there was, this would be going down differently. I know her father wants me to bring you in, but what's the point? You're not going anywhere, and like you said, I'm not going to destroy your career based on accusations alone, that would just be irresponsible and reckless. But you need to give me something, a reason she might have it out for you."

"Hell, I don't know. You have a teenage daughter, you know how irrational they can be. Maybe she just wants attention. Your guess is as good as mine."

"No argument there. But you didn't see this girl. This isn't just some act... not all of it, anyway. Someone worked her over good."

"I don't know what you want me to say. I don't know any-thing. Did you come down here looking for a confession?"

"No. I came down here looking for your side of the story."

"My side of the story? I have no side. Last time I saw that girl was when I left the office, and she seemed completely fine. There's my story, beginning to end."

"So you didn't offer her a ride?" Gaines asked.

"No, I didn't offer her a ride. They were still working when I left."

"What time did you leave?"

"I don't know exactly. Maybe around four or so."

Gaines scribbled something down in his notepad. "And what'd you do then?"

Harry rubbed his chin. "Went to Harrigan's, grabbed a six-pack, went home and sat on my porch for a bit, then did some yard work and took a trip to the dump."

"Anyone see you?" Gaines said.

Eddie Corbett came to mind, but Harry decided to leave him out of this. Eddie would keep his mouth shut about their meeting. He didn't need to involve him in this in any way. Not yet, at least. Only if his back were to the wall would he call on him.

Harry shrugged. "I don't know, maybe. People could've seen me. I'm sure if you ask Gary Trask down at Harrigan's, he'll tell you I was there." Harry paused a moment. "And I didn't see anyone else at the dump when I went, it was kind of late, but I know you'll find a bag of old campaign signs on the edge of the garbage pile. That's what I brought down there. You won't be able to miss it. I had to tie it shut with a blue rubber band because I ran out of plastic twist ties."

There was truth in these statements. Not in its entirety, but enough that if Gaines checked, he would find the answers Harry wanted him to. The best way to tell a lie, Harry knew, was to weave it with what was true. Anchor it to those shiny, authentic pieces. Sure, there were still gaps in his timeline, but Harry relied on the truths he *did* tell to smooth them over, like road tar patching the cracks in the asphalt of a weathered road. It was all cosmetic, only there to pass inspection from the state. Any real scrutiny would require further repair.

"But for the most part you were alone? No one to verify?" Gaines asked.

Harry scoffed. "Yes I was alone. That a crime?"

"No. I'm only asking questions. The more I know the better."

"Yeah, well they're questions I shouldn't have to answer in the first place." Harry leaned back, folding his arms.

Gaines continued writing in his pad, ignoring the mayor's remark. "What about your wife? Was she home?"

"No. As my good fortune would have it, she was up in Nashua at her sister's. Good timing, eh?" Harry said sarcastically. "If I'd known I was going to need an alibi, I would've told her not to go."

Once again, the sheriff ignored him and continued jotting down notes.

"Let me ask you something," Harry said. "What do *you* think? Do you think what this girl is saying is true? It seems to me there will be two camps to fall into on this matter, and I want to know where you'll be setting up shop."

Gaines stopped writing, but his eyes stayed down on his pad. After a moment, he flipped it closed and looked up. "I think you understand why I can't answer that."

Harry interlaced his fingers on the desk. "Yes, I know. You're the sheriff, you're in charge of this investigation, you can't go around town saying you feel one way or the other, need to be impartial. Look, I get it more than you know. Half the decisions I make in my job are the same thing. I have to let the people think they're the ones calling the shots, that their opinions and efforts are what bring around the change they want. But you and I both know that isn't the case. You and I both know there are a handful of people in this town who make the wind blow. It isn't anything against the rest, it's just that nothing would ever get done if we left it up to them to decide what they want. So yes, I understand what it is to seem unbiased on an issue. But right now, I'm asking you to step outside with me, take politics, take that badge and this office, this title of mayor, and forget about them. Man to man, what do you think? I need to hear it for my own peace of mind. Could you do that for me, Calvin? Could you do it as a friend?"

Harry laughed inside when he heard the word 'friend' slide through his lips. He knew he'd never been a friend to Calvin Gaines, but he wasn't sure the man sitting across from him knew that. Behind closed doors, Harry had done everything he could to discourage the out-of-towner-turned-sheriff without letting him know he was doing so. Things like the requests for new air conditioners, more deputies, new cruisers, and new service weapons when the old ones started jamming—they were all denied due to "budgetary constraints." It was never Harry's fault. It was the damn budget's. The money just wasn't there. Sorry, pal.

Only it really was there. Harry just never liked the idea of someone who hadn't grown up in Heartsridge taking on the role of head lawman in town. He wanted someone he could control, someone who would bend to his will, and that man was not Calvin Gaines.

Gaines looked toward the door again and then back to Harry. "I think the fact that you're not in handcuffs tells you where I stand. Let's leave it at that. And that's between you and I. If I hear that you've repeated that to anyone, we will be having a different sort of conversation. You understand me?"

"Of course," Harry said, flashing Gaines his palms. "You have my word. So what now?"

"Well, if I knew that, my job would be a lot easier," Gaines said.

"Can I offer my opinion?"

"Please do."

"Well, this Kara, she's, what, about fifteen or sixteen? Is that right?"

"Fifteen. A freshman in high school," Gaines said.

"A freshman, exactly," Harry said. "Girls at that age will do anything to impress older boys. Sometimes they flirt, and sometimes they tease, and sometimes boys get the wrong idea about what's going on. Their wires get tangled and what's being put out there is being received all wrong, in mixed messages. You get what I mean? You remember high school, don't you? How the younger girls acted toward you, especially if you played sports?"

"Yes, I recall."

"So didn't you ever have some I-wanna-impress-the-quarterback girl tease you to no end, lead you on, parked somewhere on a dark road, thinking you were about to score, only to have her turn cold and say take me home?" Harry smiled.

Gaines turned a thin shade of red. "Maybe a few times, but I always respected their wishes."

"Of course you did. I know the kind of guy you are, just the same way you know I'm not the kind of guy who could ever do what this girl's saying I did. But what I'm getting at is that there are plenty of boys who think they're invincible. I can think of more than a few in this town—in high school right now—who wouldn't be so morally bound, if faced with same situation. They might not take hearing *no* so kindly as someone like you or me. You get what I mean?"

Gaines shifted in his chair. "Yeah, I get what you're saying. It was the first thing I thought of when I found out what had happened. But still, why wouldn't she just say that if it's what happened?"

Harry laughed. "You sure you have a daughter? High school is one giant popularity contest, just like politics. If she made a claim like that against a popular boy, she'd be an outcast, not a victim. No one would ever want to talk to her again. And some girls would think that was worse than rape. Hate to say it, but it's true."

"I see what you're saying, but why you?" Gaines said. "Why point the finger at you?"

"Hell I don't know the answer to that any more than you do. Convenience, maybe. She had to blame somebody. If she's banged up like you say, she needed some kind of story. She spent all day in my office, maybe I was just the name at the tip of her tongue. But like I said, I don't know."

"I guess, but I'm not sure. That seems like a stretch."

"Really?" Harry said. "More far-fetched than me, the person who's spent his entire career making this town a better place, the person with a wife, the mayor of Heartsridge, the person with the biggest spotlight on him, raping a fifteen-year-old high school girl that works in my office? That's the believable scenario here? There's been a dozen other high school girls worked in my office on internships and not once was there a complaint of any kind. So just out of nowhere I'm going to start assaulting these women—let me correct that—these *kids*?"

Gaines put his hands up. "I know, I know. I'd be lying if I said hadn't thought the same. But do me a favor and tell me about Saturday. What type of interaction did you have with her?"

Harry rested his chin on his fist, tapping the side of his cheek with his index finger. "Let's see. I was in around nine. I spent most of the day in my office signing off on vendor licenses, calling a few local businesses to get sponsorships for the festival. I believe Kara came in at around ten. I met her briefly when I went to lunch. Introduced myself, like I do to all the interns. She was working with Brenda, filing old requisition forms and taking calls most of the time, from what I could tell. Like I said, she seemed like a nice girl. I left around four, and she and Brenda were still working, you can ask her on your way out. Then I went home, spread some bark mulch, took a trip to the dump. That's about it."

"Can anyone corroborate that?"

"Like I already told you, Allison was in Nashua. But I'm sure Gary down at Harrigan's will tell you I stopped in sometime after four to grab beer. And then there's the bag I dropped off at the dump. Other than that, I didn't see anyone that day, no. I'm not saying *they* didn't see *me*, but I didn't see them, you know?" Harry leaned forward across his desk, as if to tell Gaines a secret. "Between you and me, I don't get many days to myself, and I imagine you don't either, so I guess you could say I was enjoying the solitude of bachelorhood for the brief time I had it. That's not against the law, is it? Can't a man reminisce a bit about a time before wives and careers and just sip on some suds on his own, do some yard-work, nothing but him and his thoughts? 'Cause I tell you, if I have to come to grips with the idea that those days are completely behind me, I might just have to retire now." Harry fell back in his seat and smiled.

Gaines did too. "Believe me, you don't have to tell me. I can't remember the last time I got to do that."

"From what I gather, probably too long ago. It's important for a man to do that from time to time. Call it a tune up. It reminds him who he is and what's important. People like you and me,

Calvin, we're not made of stone and steel like most people think. We're something closer to wood—hard wood. Oak, like this desk." Harry knocked on the slab in front of him. "And after a while, life sands down our edges, rounds us, forms us to its will. It's our job to know when it's time to reform our boundaries, re-sharpen our edges. You catch my drift? That's what time alone does—it allows us to recapture our original design. And that's important."

Gaines nodded. "I can't say I've ever thought about it that way."

"Most don't," Harry said. "But just remember, these jobs we do, they can change us. It's an everyday battle to stay true to who we are. We measure ourselves by how sharp we keep our edges. And a man's ability to measure himself is important."

"That's real poetic, but that doesn't help me any right now."

"It isn't poetry, it's the truth. Don't forget that."

"I'll try not to," Gaines said.

Harry could sense the conversation reaching its natural dé-nouement. He was in the homestretch. "So look, I know you're going to have to poke around about this, that's your job, I under-stand, and I'm sure it won't be long until word of these accusations spread around town. If you fart at breakfast, everyone knows about it by lunch. I only ask that you try to be discrete about it, for now. I'm sure Allison is going to love this, and I'd like to be the one to tell her."

"I can respect that. What was said in here is between us," Gaines said.

"Okay, good. " Harry rested on his elbows, hands together, massaging his palm with his thumb. "Also, and I'm just getting your opinion, do you think maybe it would be good if I talked to Kara or her parents? Try and straighten this out on my own?

Maybe seeing me will remind this girl I'm a person who she's hurting, not just some grownup she barely knows."

"I don't think so. That PR smile of yours isn't fixing anything that easy this time. The girl's in a real bad way right now, and her parents aren't exactly on your side. I would just leave it alone and let me handle this. I'll sort everything out, but I don't think either one of us is making any new friends or earning any votes." Gaines looked down at his lap for a moment and picked at the knee of his pants.

Harry clutched the arms of his chair and sat up straight. "I'm afraid you might be right about that. I wish it didn't have to be that way."

"Me too," Gaines said, looking back at Harry.

"One more thing." Harry held up a finger. "When you figure out this girl is lying—and I know you will, you were elected sheriff for good reason—I want you to take it easy on her. By the sound of it, you're right, she's been through something terrible and might be a little mixed up. I think she's just making a mistake right now, and that is no reason she should have to pay for it the rest of her life."

"That's real kind of you, Harry. I can't say I'd be so forgiving."

"Of course, I understand," Harry said, and flashed a toothy grin. This one was for himself, congratulations for another victory. "Just feel free to ask me for anything you need to move this along."

Gaines picked up his hat, turning it in his fingers, and then placed it back atop his head. "I think that's all for now. I hope I didn't ruin your day."

"Just doing your job." Harry stuck out his hand. "Feel free to talk to Brenda on your way out if you have any questions for her. But I'm sure she'll tell you what I already did."

"I don't think that will be necessary right now," Gaines said. He stuck out his hand and the two shook.

"Okay, as you see fit," Harry released Gaines's hand and stood. He walked to his door and opened it. "If that's all, I have a lot to do to get ready for the festival. I hope you'll understand if I don't see you out."

"Not at all," Gaines said, rising to his feet and making his way to the door. "Call me if you should think of anything else."

"Will do, Calvin. But like I said, I've told you all I know. I have no doubt you'll find the son of a bitch who harmed that girl. I trust you, you're a smart man."

Gaines tipped his hat and walked out of the office. "Take care."

"Same to you."

Harry waited until Gaines turned the corner and was out of sight before shutting the door and pouring himself a drink. It was hardly past nine o'clock, but he deserved it. He'd earned it.

CHAPTER 14

The killer thought: *I am Bill, the photographer from Woodstock.*

Bill sat on the edge of the bed in the Heartsridge Motel. Beside him was his new camera—a Nikon. He'd purchased it three days before from a small shop outside of Heartsridge at a place called Joy's Camera & Photo. The woman behind the counter who'd sold it to him said it was the best they carried; it was what the professionals used. While he was there, Bill also bought everything he'd need to develop his own pictures, along with a beginner's instructional book: *The Art of the Lens,* by Deedee Stanhope.

It took him most of Friday afternoon and night, as well as a trashcan filled to the brim with ruined developing paper, but eventually Bill managed to get the solution ratios and developing times right. His first successful photo was of the peace sign on the back of his jacket. After this initial success, the rest came easily. He did four more right away: one of the TV on top of the dresser; one of his truck in the parking lot, which he'd taken from the window of his room; one of his bare feet on the tiled bathroom floor; and two of the kid who worked the front desk (these were also taken from his window, while the kid took out the trash).

Now all these primitive photographs hung proudly in his bathroom like trophies, secured with wooden laundry pins to a length of twine he'd purchased from the hardware store downtown. He'd replaced the bulb above the washroom sink with a safelight—a darkroom bulb. It painted the room a deep red when it was on. That might have been Bill's favorite part, the warm red tones surrounding him while he worked. It was womblike, a space of warmth, comfort, and creation. It was a feeling of serenity he'd never experienced before, and the closest, he imagined, to what a mother's love must feel like.

I am Bill, the photographer.

The next day, after figuring out how to use his new equipment properly, an urge to return to the rest stop visited him. It was an obsessive thought: What if he were to go back and snap a shot of the kid from Hanover? The kid was likely still in that ditch, wrapped in a tarp. His hand would still be sticking out, flashing that accidental peace sign. Still a chance for a photograph. It would be his first real piece of art, although he could not shake the feeling that going back there was somehow cheating. He needed to move forward, not backward. So he resisted the temptation. Returning to a crime scene was risky and careless, as well, and he needed to be smarter than that.

Bill grabbed his cigarettes off the nightstand and beat the pack softly against the heel of his palm until the tip of a filter edged out. He caught it between his front teeth, pulling it out, and lit it. He took a drag, sitting there a moment, recalling his morning at the diner. It was unfortunate he'd come face to face with the sheriff. He hadn't wanted to draw any attention to himself. But it wasn't the first time, and probably wouldn't be the last, that he'd conversed with locals in a town he was just passing through. It'd never bitten him in ass before, and he didn't think it would now. He'd be out of Heartsridge in a few days, and by then he'd just be another face fading into the background of these people's memories.

Bill tamped out the cigarette. Then he leaned down, pulling out the old ammo can he'd stashed beneath the bed. He opened it, unloading the packs of Marlboros and prying up the sheet-metal trap door at the bottom. He dumped the contents onto the hotel bed and unbound the collection of IDs, laying them out on the ugly yellow-and-brown bedspread. Next, he picked up the gold necklace and put it on. He removed the bullet shells from the bag and placed them around the IDs, arranging them like decorative flower petals. Rubbing the cross between his thumb and forefinger, he stared at the faces of the people he'd killed: William Mathey, Bridgewater, Massachusetts, born 2/19/ 58; Stephen Weagle, Burlington, Vermont, born 11/4/56; Sara Sexton, Portsmouth, New Hampshire, born 5/27/55; Kyle Giuffrida, Acton, Massachusetts, born 7/4/60. (*Good ol' Kyle, born on the Fourth of July. What a patriot. Thanks for the necklace, pal.*)

Bill reveled in the memories of each kill. William Mathey and his accidental finger pose. Sara Sexton—oh, how she'd smelled of lavender and cherry (she cried the most). Stephen Weagle, the man who'd tried to escape from the car when he saw the gun (it'd taken Bill an entire afternoon to clean the kid's blood off the upholstery). Then there was Kyle Giuffrida, the guinny who'd prayed to Jesus right up until the moment Bill pulled the trigger—only he wasn't going by Bill back then—and put a bullet through the bridge of his nose. They had all been fools. And they all got what they deserved.

Bill removed the necklace, re-bundled the IDs, scooped up

the shell casings, and placed everything back into the ammo can under the trick bottom. But before he sealed it back up and put it under the bed again, a thought struck him.

He went into the bathroom, his new darkroom, and stopped for a moment, looking at the row of photos hanging from the twine in front of him—his first six successfully captured and developed pictures. They were special photos, he decided. They were the beginning of something new, his first steps, the first words spoken by Bill the photographer. While he didn't see any real artistic value in them, there was something extraordinary about them. They were his earliest work, and so they had sentimental value. It was the same way a parent is proud of a child's preschool artwork: it isn't about content or how well crafted it is; it is about what it represents—a beginning with a promise. A promise of more to come. Soon the refrigerator would be covered in artwork, each better than the last. A trophy case of progress.

Bill unclipped the photographs, shuffling them in his hands. It was decided; he would place them in the box with the rest of his memorabilia. They belonged there. They would be at home there, mixed among the other relics reminiscent of an elemental time: Kyle, Sara, William, and Stephen. His first kills and his first pictures, comingling. They were the remnants of a childhood, a time of development, a time that was behind him now. He was full grown, had come into his own. He could feel it. He'd always thought he knew everything, thought he was so slick. But like any boy who is convinced he's a man, he was blinded by his own adolescent exuberance. He hadn't known shit when he'd first started. But now he did. Now he was ready.

I am Bill.

"I am," he whispered, and smiled.

Before Bill left the darkroom, his eyes shifted to a second

length of twine strung behind the first. Four pictures hung there. These pictures were different from the first six. These four pictures were more important. For two, he understood why: they were of his next kill, his perfect kill. He grinned wickedly at these two pictures, his heart starting to pound. Excitement. Nervousness. Palms prickling. Mouth drying. It was the nearest thing he'd felt to sexual arousal in a long time. The blood stirred in the associated regions and his spit thickened. *Joanna*, he thought. And then he whispered her name, his breath caressing his lips. "Joanna."

Yes, Joanna. Joanna and her perfect features. Joanna and those eyes that seemed to see into his very soul. Joanna and her sweet smile. Joanna, the waitress who knew his name—Bill. She'd talked to him, seen him in a way nobody had before. She was interested in him, had asked him questions. Who was he? What did he do? Why was he in town? His answers were lies, but they were true lies. In that moment, and from then on, he *was* Bill. He was Bill for her. He had to be, otherwise he was Nobody. He didn't exist. People couldn't see Nobody. People didn't care about Nobody.

I am...

Joanna was perfection. She was proof that flawlessness existed, and that was why he needed to have her and capture her perfection, immortalize her in death. Was this what love felt like—this need to absorb someone's essence? Was love this thing that burned inside him? It was impossible to tell. He had never experienced love before, so far as he knew. He might've loved his mother if she'd stuck around. But she hadn't, so fuck her. No, this feeling inside him was something out of focus, something closer to rage on the edge of desire.

He plucked the two pictures of Joanna from the second line and looked at them closely, running his fingers over the black and white prints. One was a shot of her locking the diner after her shift on Sunday night; the other was of her getting into her car. He'd sat in the shadows of the park across the street from Deb's Diner, waiting almost two hours to get those. He couldn't remember excitement like that since his first kill, Kyle. The waiting. The anticipation. He needed to feel her. Have her.

He examined the photos a few moments longer then shuffled them together with the others. They would all go in the ammo can, old and new together. One big happy family. In the end, in some future long away from this motel room, the box would tell the story of a life, start to finish.

At last his attention shifted from Joanna to the two pictures remaining on the twine. They were something special altogether, something he'd stumbled into on Saturday. Nothing he had ever intended, just the right place at the right time… depending upon how you looked at it.

That Saturday, his head burning with thoughts of returning to the rest stop to photograph William Mathey, Bill decided to go for a walk in the woods behind the Heartsridge Motel. He needed to clear his mind, thinking it would be a good place to practice using his new camera. Maybe get some shots of nature.

He'd just come upon a pond when he heard the girl screaming. Through the woods he could see a brick structure. There was a sign on the side of the building: HEARTSRIDGE WATER DE-PARTMENT. When Bill moved closer, he spotted a car parked alongside the building. In the backseat, a man was forcing himself on young girl. Bill waited, watching for a few minutes and snapping two shots with his camera. There was artistic value there, he was sure of it. Strong emotional content. And he'd liked the way it had felt to watch. Rape had never interested him; he had always preferred the idea of taking life rather than forcing unwanted love. But the voyeurism of witnessing it had excited him.

Now, two days later, looking at the pictures hanging on the clothes line in the red warmth of his darkroom in the Heartsridge Motel, they still excited him, and that meant something, so he took them down and stored them with the rest.

CHAPTER 15

David Price pulled into the parking lot, parking beside a red pickup truck and shutting off his engine. He looked up at the flickering neon sign above him. HEARTSRIDGE MOTEL: VACANCY. That was the best news he'd heard all day. Vacancy. It was exactly what he needed—someone to take him in, accept him. David breathed a sigh of relief, which felt oddly like gratitude. He glanced at the darkened NO beside VACANCY. Two harmless letters, but today they looked threatening. David half-expected them to light up the second his feet hit the pavement.

He had intended to go to work when he left the house thirty minutes before, but the closer he got to the West Elm Dairy Plant, the more the thought of work soured in his mind. The idea of going became exhausting. He wouldn't be able to get anything done at the office. His wife and daughter were home, dealing with this crisis together. He wanted to be there, too. He wanted to help, to console, to fix. But he couldn't. Not this time. His own daughter was uncomfortable around him because of what that son of a bitch Harry Bennett had done to her.

At first he'd driven past the motel, not even noticing it, but in his periphery his subconscious must've seen the flickering neon sign and planted a secret desire in the bedrock of his mind. Before he even knew it was there, a part of him acted. He hit the brakes, turning around and pulling into the parking lot. By the time he'd put his car in park, the murky thought which had been born in the bottom of his mind surfaced and came into focus. Even then, David did not understand where the desire came from—only that it was a real thing. What he did know was that the idea of escaping and being alone in that motel was the only thing making the knot in his gut unravel.

David stepped out of his car and walked to the front desk.

"What can I do for you, sir?" the kid behind the counter asked as David walked in.

David didn't recognize him, and that was good. He hadn't wanted to know anyone here, not today. Heartsridge was a small town, and most people either knew, or at least recognized, one another. But recently he'd noticed this wasn't so much the case anymore. Generations were growing up, replacing the familiar with the unfamiliar. Every day Heartsridge reminded him less and less of the town he'd grown up in. He didn't know if this was good or bad. His mother had always told him to embrace change, and he tried to remember this whenever possible. But here, in the place where his roots ran down to the nostalgic waters of the past, change seemed like sin.

"How much for a room?" David asked.

The kid ran his finger down a short list taped to the desk in front of him. "Eleven dollars a night during the week, sir. You here for the festival?"

"No," David said. "I just need a room."

"A room it is, then. Just one night?"

"Yes… no actually, I'll take it for the week. Monday through Friday. Can I do that?" David asked. A series of thoughts followed his words: *Why the hell can't I? I already told the office I'll be out for a few days, and if a few days should happen to come to a week, so be it! What do I care?*

"Not a problem. But so you know"—the kid scanned the list once more—"it's fifteen dollars a night on weekends, Friday and Saturday, during the festival. So it'll be a little more for Friday night. And it might get a little crowded around here starting Thursday, the rooms go pretty quick."

"That's fine, I'm not worried," David said. Then, for show, he patted his pockets. "You know, I lost my credit card, though. You take cash?" He couldn't have motel charges showing up on his credit card statement. Not that he was doing anything particularly wrong, but he didn't want to have to explain himself to Ellie. It was just easier this way.

The kid laughed. "This is still America, isn't it? Of course we take cash. You just need to fill this out." He slid a clipboard with a preloaded form secured in its metal grip. A pen dangled from the side, attached to a piece of frayed string.

David looked over the form briefly, filled it out, and signed it.

"How much do I owe you?" he asked, reaching into his pocket and resting his hand on his billfold.

The kid rubbed his head, glancing around. He picked up a calculator. "Just a sec," he said and started punching numbers into the keypad. "With tax, it comes to sixty-two dollars."

David removed his wallet, counted out seventy dollars, and handed it to the kid. "Keep the change," he said.

The kid's eyes widened. "Thanks, mister, that's mighty kind of you. Name's Pete. Don't hesitate to ring me if you need anything."

"Don't mention it, Pete. But I'm sure I won't call."

"Well, if you should it's no bother. I'll make sure you aren't disturbed." Pete turned around and removed a key from the rack behind him. "How about room seven? Lucky lucky seven?" He handed the key to David.

"That's fine," David said.

"Seven's down there on your left." Pete pointed behind David to a short covered sidewalk lined with numbered green doors. "Enjoy your stay."

"Thanks again," David said, turning around and heading out the door.

Outside, the whine of the cicadas split the air. David didn't notice them. His mind was too caught up in itself, tumbling and turning over, tangling his thoughts. There was so much to feel, so many emotions, internal conflicts, instincts he was forced to ignore, and everything seemed to be pushing and pulling with identical force in opposite directions, balancing out, creating an odd, numbing equilibrium. He had so much hatred, but only because he had so much love. He wanted justice, but revenge seemed sweeter. He found envy and jealousy in his wife's connection to their daughter, but he also had a great appreciation for her, for being able to soothe their child when he could not. In this moment, the task of sifting through all these internal divergences seemed too daunting, so he pushed them away, saving them for later consideration. He knew they would still be there when he was ready. Right now he just wanted peace and quiet. He wanted to forget, if only for a little while, the obsolescence and disquiet waiting for him back home.

David continued to Room 7, and as he fit the key into the lock and opened the door, it occurred to him that in all his years, he'd never once been in this motel. Motels were for tourists and people who cheated on their spouses. He was neither. Only that was no longer the truth now. He *was* a tourist, a stranger in his own land.

Inside, the accommodations were as he'd expected: ugly bedspread, small television, thick drapes, worn carpets, the stale smell of lives lived quickly and on the go. Existence measured in nights, not years or decades.

David sat on the edge of the bed, slowly removing his shoes. Then he turned on the TV and lay down, closing his eyes and listening to the sound of the local morning news.

"The body has since been identified as one William Mathey of Bridgewater," a reporter said on the TV.

David was asleep before the first commercial break. He dreamed of a better time, of a memory he hadn't even known he'd forgotten.

"Where do the butterflies go when the sun goes down, Daddy?" Kara asks as they walk through a field along the edge of night. Vast space lowers to dusk. Purple skies kiss the horizon in straight lines. "Do they sleep like us?"

David laughs. "I'm not sure, but I imagine they do sleep at some point, sweetie."

"Do they disappear?" she asks, stopping. There is a child's seriousness in her voice.

"No, they don't disappear. Do Mommy and I disappear when it gets dark? Do you disappear when the sun goes down and you go to bed?"

She balls her hands into clumsy fists, bringing them to her hips. "How am I supposed to know, Daaaaad?" she says, playfully annoyed. "I'd be asleep, silly."

"All right, wise guy," David says, and laughs again.

His daughter, barefoot and wearing her little purple sundress, hardly comes up to his waist. She is six. He reaches out and tousles her dirty-blonde hair. She giggles, turning her face up and exposing her tiny rows of tiny teeth. She runs ahead of him, turns, and lets her arms dangle in anticipation of a chase. Then she bows her head down, smiling mischievously. "Can't catch me," *she says, turning and running with clumsy six-year-old steps.*

He pursues as she tries to get away, scooping her up after only a few feet. His arms feel impossibly long and strong, like he could hold on no matter how far she ran.

"How can you run so fast?" she asks, between small rising and falling gasps. Her breath falls on his face. He can smell it. It's sweet like watermelon. Her lips are bright red. There was a lollipop.

"That's my job, sweetie. To be fast and always catch you when you stray."

"Stray?" she repeats, confused.

"Yes, stray. It means when you go away or wander from me."

"I won't go away from you, Daddy," she says, her face cramped into a look of concern.

"I know," he says, and brings his face in close and blows on her neck, tickling her. She laughs hard. The sound fills the empty park. To David it seems to brighten the world.

"Eeeew, Daddy-germs." She pulls her face away and wipes her neck.

He sets her down. "That's right, Daddy-germs." He makes a face at her. "Your mom's probably starting to get worried. We should get back soon." He glances toward the parking lot.

Kara's face darkens and she looks down at the empty glass jar her father is carrying. "But we didn't catch anything," she says nervously, like there may never be another chance like this one again. "You said we'd catch lightning bugs tonight."

"Okay, okay," he says, "We'll search on the way back to the car. Keep

your eyes peeled. If you look toward the darkest spots, it usually makes it easier to spot them."

They walk slowly, eyes scanning the horizon as they stroll back, but they don't see any of the glowing insects. David can feel the disappointment building in his daughter.

"Where are they? Where are the lightning bugs?" she keeps asking, more and more frequently, the closer they come to the parking lot.

They stop at the head of the little path that leads them through to the parking lot. Kara and her father turn to look one last time out at the darkening field. Still, there are no bugs. No little green flashes of summertime wonder.

Kara looks up at her father and then down at her bare, dirty feet, covered in tiny shards of splintered, dead grass clippings. Her lip trembles as she tugs on the edges of her dress, swaying side to side. There will be tears soon.

He sees this and bends to one knee, lifting his daughter's chin with a hooked finger. "Hey... hey, sweetie. Don't be upset. We can come back and try again tomorrow. Maybe they were just sleeping tonight."

She opens her mouth to speak. "What a fine fresh scent, Daddy. Look at the green and the white stripes. What a fine fresh scent," she says with an accent, her lips never moving. David doesn't recognize the inflection at first, but then he does. It's an Irish accent.

The world around him quickly begins fading to reality. The colors all around him run like a painting left out in the rain.

Kara opens her mouth again—a black hole without lips or a tongue. "What a fine fresh scent, Daddy. Gets a strong man fresh."

"What, honey? I don't understand," he says.

But the little girl vanishes, melting away with the rest of the world. He reaches toward the thought of her with his impossibly long arms, which now feel like a million tons each, but there is nothing to hold on to. She is gone. Kara is gone.

Colors run gray to brown to white to black. Darkness for a moment, followed by slow degrees of increasing awareness.

Awake.

David opened his eyes. A commercial for Irish Springs was playing on the television. He looked over at the clock on the nightstand. 12:12. Flashes of his dream flickered on and off in his mind, but for the most part, the recollection was foggy and far-off. He could feel that it was a pleasant dream, but the more he reached for details, the more he chased them away. Only the sensation lingered. Trace elements. But they were kind traces. Something had warmed his spirits. He was not consciously aware of what, but it didn't matter. The effects were real just the same.

He sat up, rubbing his face. *Four more hours,* he thought, looking at the clock. David turned and planted his feet on the floor. This grounded him, rooted him in the present. He was fully awake now, back in the motel room, sitting on the same ugly yellow bedspread, with the same tiny TV and the same stale scent.

David picked up the remote, shutting off the television. Silence blanketed the room. He stood up, walked to the window, and pulled the curtain aside. The red truck he'd parked beside was gone. His was the only car there, now. Not many people need a motel at noon on a Monday, he supposed.

The sun had gone away in his sleep. The sky was overcast and gray, and he could see beads of water collected on his windshield, puddles on the pavement—it had rained. He remembered the weather reports from that morning, the ones he listened to on the radio in the bathroom when he was getting ready at home, before his wife had come in and told him he needed to go to work, before she'd told him their daughter couldn't stand to be around him. He must've slept through the storms, although he still suspected there were a few more out there, dark clouds looming on the horizon and heading his way. He wondered if he would still be around when they arrived.

David turned back to the room, letting the curtain fall back against the window.

Again the clock on the nightstand caught his eye. The little black-and-white scoreboard numbers cartwheeling over and over again, keeping track of his time spent in the room, his time spent dishonestly when his family thought he was at work and his work thought he was at home. He was in limbo, holed up in a motel room, stuck some place between the two lies. But *some place* was the only place he'd been able to find relief from the racing thoughts, so right now it felt like home... or as close as he was going to find.

It was lunchtime. David wasn't very hungry, but the idea of a cold beer pleased him. He knew of a little tavern just outside of town in West Elm. He went there sometimes on his way home from work. At this hour the place would be empty, save for a few problem drinkers who wouldn't know him—or if they did, wouldn't remember him tomorrow. A pleasant relief came with this thought. The idea of being forgotten was somehow satisfying. At first he didn't know why, but then he did: it was freeing to have no identity, no one to be... or to not be. And then he understood something more: in this motel room, without his family, without a job to go to, without a purpose, he was not David Price at all. No. David Price did not exist in that place.

For the first time in a long while, he smiled.

CHAPTER 16

Sam and Catherine sat across from Gaines. He'd expected some sort of backlash for his decision not to arrest Harry, but he hadn't expected it to come from his own deputy. He wondered if perhaps Catherine being a woman made her especially sympathetic to the Kara Price case. It was dangerous for him to think so obtusely, but he couldn't deny the fact that she seemed to be taking a particularly strong—almost personal—position on the matter.

"His story checks out. What can I do? My hands are tied. Not to mention Creed Hornsby just called this morning and said all the tests they ran came back negative. And remember what Julie told us: nothing proves for certain that Kara was raped. It's all circumstantial," Gaines said. "Without any hard evidence, I'm not going to arrest him. That's just the way it is. He's a respected pillar of this community, and there is too much at stake."

And Harry Bennett's story did check out. After his morning meeting with the mayor, Gaines had gone down to Harrigan's Liquors and asked Gary Trask if he'd seen Harry come in around four o'clock to buy beer. He said he had. Then he drove out to

141

the dump and searched out that bag of campaign signs. It was there, tied with a rubber band just like Harry had said it would be.

But there were still holes in the mayor's story, gaps of time with no alibi. That was hard to ignore. Harry could have done those things just to lend some believability to his story. Sure. The man was smart enough to do that. Considering this, wasn't there a tiny piece of Gaines that was starting to think that maybe, just maybe, the girl was telling the truth, after all?

Catherine said: "I get that all the evidence is circumstantial. That's how it's always been with rape cases, barring a witness or other direct proof. But Harry's story doesn't prove anything. He was still alone with no one to corroborate where he was when he left his office. He could've easily come back and offered Kara a ride. Those aren't credible alibis he fed you. They're just insignificant noise. And if we can catch him in a lie, then that's gotta say something."

Gaines folded his hands on his desk. "You're right, his story doesn't prove his innocence. But just the same, that girl's story doesn't prove his guilt. Christ, all we have are stories. That's my point. I have to use my own judgment here, and right now that tells me Harry Bennett didn't..." He trailed off. "Listen. He may be a little rough around the edges, but he doesn't rape kids, is what I'm saying. People like that don't just walk around unnoticed."

Catherine slid forward in her seat. "Yes they do. It happens all the time. People like that exist everywhere. They spend their lives learning to blend in and go unnoticed. That's what psychopaths do," she said. "It's survival for them . . . it's an instinct."

"That's bull," Gaines said. "There's never been anything like this happened around here. No other victims. No other accusations, no incidents or reports of any behavior that would suggest that of him. A person doesn't just turn that way overnight. There are signs. A violent history. Something. *Anything.* You both have known him your whole lives. I've known him almost fifteen years. And what, we all missed an important detail like, oh, I don't know, he's a sexual predator? 'Cause if that's the case, maybe we should all turn in our badges. We may be a small town, but I like to think we're more capable than that."

The logic had run through Gaines's mind on repeat over the last few days. He'd internalized it, analyzing it, looking for holes. But now that he was stating his reasoning out loud, he had to wonder whether he was trying to convince himself or everyone else that it made sense.

"That isn't what I mean," Catherine said.

Gaines sat back, folding his arms defensively. "Really? Because that's what it sounds like to me. It sounds like you think Harry Bennett has been assaulting woman in his spare time as a hobby, and we've just been sitting here twiddling our damn thumbs, too stupid to notice."

"I'm just saying we shouldn't rule him out simply because you don't want to believe he would do it."

"That's a cheap shot, Catherine. Don't tell me what I believe or don't believe. I just think we can't be so irresponsible as to completely destroy a man's life without being sure of the facts. Is that so bad? You know what it would do to his career—his life— if we arrested him? He could lose everything... *we* could lose everything. Sam, back me up here, would ya?"

He wasn't sure if he believed it or not. Maybe it was only that the threat of ruining a person's life was the best excuse for inaction. But Kara's life had already been ruined. How was that fair? Gaines wasn't sure he really knew, anymore. When he chose to run for sheriff after Billy Surret died, he never expected to have to deal with any type of crime like this. Up until now, the worst things he ever arrested people for were drunk and disorderly or the occasional drug charge, and most of these were kids in their early twenties, with a chip on their shoulders. Kids who never left town for college, sticking around to become the next generation of townies who drank cheap beer, worked menial jobs, and were always content with the way things were, are, and ever would be. Life to them wasn't a series of growing experiences. It was a place to exist while the world went on without them, never knowing that if they'd just bothered to stick out their thumbs, they might have been able to hitch rides along to a better life. These were the type of people—the types of situations—Gaines knew how to deal with. He knew how to navigate a life like that. And that was fine and good and easy. But what he was at the center of now was a whirlwind of what-the-fuck-am-I-doing. He did not know the way here. He was a navigator at the wheel of a ship pointed toward storm clouds and a darkening horizon, and with each decision he made, he became increasingly aware of the clumsy footsteps he was taking toward some inevitable tragic end that was not even vaguely in sight.

Sam shifted uneasily in his chair, looking toward Catherine. "I gotta side with the sheriff on this one, Catherine. Without evidence or a witness, there isn't much we can do. We can arrest him, but no court will convict him solely on the word of this girl. The prosecution has to think there is enough evidence to win the case and unfortunately right now there just isn't. And you know me, I'm not exactly Harry Bennett's biggest fan." Sam turned, facing Catherine squarely. He spoke earnestly now. "But arresting him without proper proof is just reckless. I support the sheriff on that. If we're going to say to the public that we think he committed such a terrible crime, I think we should be damn sure. The rumors that'll surface about this will be bad enough, but people forget rumors. If we arrest him and it turns out he's innocent, no way, forget about it—that's permanent. That stays for life, whether he's guilty or not."

Catherine didn't respond to Sam. She turned back to Gaines, picking up where they'd left off a moment before. "I understand that. Don't think for a second that I haven't thought the same thing, but you seem to have already ruled him out."

Gaines rubbed his face. He was already exhausted with this. He just wanted it off his desk, out of his life, gone. "I haven't ruled anyone out. I've only said that without definitive evidence, I'm not arresting him. And besides, he isn't going anywhere. What are you worried about? If he did it, there's something out there to prove it. And I'll find it. But as of right now, Harry Bennett is off limits."

"So what then, if he's off limits? What other lead is there?" Catherine asked. "Where do we go from there? It's a dead end."

"There's a boy, Ryan Kinsey. David Price said his daughter and Ryan are friends. Drives her home sometimes. That type of thing. He's a couple years older than her, I think. Her father doesn't believe they're together in that way, but I don't buy that for a second. I'm going to look into him, to start."

"So… what? You think she was raped by *him*?" Catherine said in disbelief. "Why would she lie about that?" She paused for a moment, her lips parting as if she were suddenly receiving some secret message. Then her face tightened and she fell back in her chair, looking almost defeated.

Gaines noticed her peculiar look, but he continued. "I don't know. But what I do know is I have a daughter and I know how teenage girls can be. They aren't sweet and nice and honest all the time. They can be conniving and manipulative when they want to be, especially when they panic. Don't you remember? You were one once, weren't you?"

Catherine sniffed derisively.

"Listen, I'm not leaning any one direction on this," Gaines continued. "All I'm saying is we're still considering all possibilities. I'm just trying to let the dust settle a little and figure out where to go next. But I will say that it is not outside the realm of possibilities for a teenager to lie." He raised an eyebrow, pleased with his own insights.

Catherine scoffed, turning her head away. "You didn't see what I did, Calvin—"

"Don't you pull that crap," Gaines said sternly. "I was there. I saw the same thing you did. It wasn't easy for me either."

"No, not like me," Catherine snapped back. "I looked into her eyes. And what I saw wasn't a liar. What I saw was a terrified little girl."

Gaines sat upright in his chair and shrugged. "What are you after, here? What do you want from me? There is no hard evidence."

"I thought it was clear," Catherine said. "Bring Harry in here. Question him for real. None of this 'friendly neighbor' crap. Put the screws to him and he'll crack."

Gaines laughed and shook his head. "'Put the screws to him?' You watch too many movies. That isn't how it works, and I'm not bringing him down here. That's out of the question."

"You just don't want to harm his reputation... or maybe it's your own reputation you're worried about."

"Watch it. Don't forget which side of this desk you're sitting on." Gaines pointed at her. Then becoming self-aware of his rigid demeanor, he softened and lowered his hand. "And yes, that is exactly what I'm afraid of. I thought *that* was clear."

Catherine backed down. "I'm sorry. I didn't mean that. I just can't stand the thought of someone getting away with this. That's what's bothering me. If we don't do something soon, you know how it is, this will just go away and people will forget about it."

"Why are you so sure of this all of a sudden?" Gaines asked. "Saturday night you didn't say a peep. You fell asleep on the ride home. And now you seem positive beyond the shadow of a doubt. What bug crawled up your ass?"

Gaines saw her eyes shift to the floor, but they quickly darted back up. There was something more going on here, and he had a sickening idea of what it was. He didn't dare ask her, though.

"Call it a hunch. Women's intuition," she said. Her voice had taken on a less aggressive tone. It was more pleading, desperate.

Gaines sighed. "Deputy, I'm sorry, but that's not enough. I need more than intuition. I'm not arresting him without evidence and that's final. I don't want to hear another word about it." There was something about the way Catherine was acting, though. He was compelled to give her something, some piece to hang on to. "But if you want to talk to his secretary, Brenda, you can. And if you want to talk to Kara again, you can. That is completely fine. I'd actually prefer you be the one to do that. But be discreet and leave Harry alone. Sam, you go with her."

"Yessir," Sam said.

Catherine looked insulted. "I don't need a baby sitter. I'm fine on my own."

"This time I'm afraid you do," Gaines said. "This isn't up for debate. You got some sort of fire under your ass right now, and I don't want anyone getting burned by it."

Catherine bent forward, her elbows on her knees. "You saw that girl, you saw what she was like," she said, as if to appeal to Gaines's sensibility. "And it's just as hard for me to believe Harry

Bennett is capable of something like that, but we can't just turn a blind eye to what she's saying. Half the time when this happens to a girl, she'll just keep quiet. If she's decided to come forward and give a name... well... I'm telling you, she is telling the truth, and we should listen."

Gaines closed his eyes for a beat—a long blink, really—and opened them with a long contemplative breath through his nose. "I'm not ignoring what the girl's saying. You think I wanted to march into the mayor's office this morning and accuse him of raping a fifteen-year-old girl? You think that was fun? He can make my life—hell, all our lives—a lot harder if he wants to. If we find evidence that points us in his direction, then we'll follow it. Okay? That's the best you're going to get from me right now."

"Fine," Catherine said, looking away for a moment.

"But that doesn't mean you go tear the town open looking for it," Gaines said. "You can follow up with what I said: his secretary and Kara. But that's it for now. And I can't be any clearer about being discreet. You got me? Can you be okay with that? Because if I hear otherwise, I'll take you off this and you'll be tearing tickets at the festival."

"Yessir," Catherine said. "Is that all?"

"Yes. You can go."

Sam and Catherine stood, both replacing their hats.

"Sam, hold back a sec, would you?" Gaines said. "I need to talk to you about something."

Catherine looked at Sam. He shrugged. "I'll be out front," she said, turning and walking out.

"What's up?" Sam asked.

Gaines stood, walking around and leaning on the front of his desk, arms folded. "I need you to keep an eye on her for me. Will you do that? I want to keep this thing under wraps for now, especially with the festival coming up. I know it will get out sooner or later, but I'd rather it be later. Just make sure she doesn't go making a mess of this, okay?"

"No problem. That all?"

"Yes. You can go. I'll see you tomorrow. I'm going to get out of here early tonight. Have a few things to do."

"All right, sir." Sam turned and headed for the door. When he reached it, he stopped and turned around. Then, cautiously, he said, "Just so you know, sir, I'm on your side," and walked out.

My side? Gaines hadn't known there were sides. But deep down he knew what the deputy meant, and even more importantly, it felt good not to be alone.

"Jesus, give me a break, would you?" Gaines said to himself.

David Price was pulling into the parking lot of the sheriff's department as Gaines walked to his cruiser.

Gaines looked down at his watch. It was almost six o'clock. He wanted to get home. It was his own fault, though—he should've contacted the Prices by now with some kind of update. But there was no new news to give. And he imagined that what he *did* have to tell them would not go over well. His disagreement with Catherine was just a taste of what he expected he was about to hear from Kara's father.

David killed the engine and stepped out, leaning against his car with his hands in his pockets. He appeared to be in his work clothes, but they looked slightly disheveled. Wrinkled. Un-tucked.

Gaines could immediately tell there was something off about David. The way he held himself was more aggressive. He didn't look like the defeated man he'd spoken with in the waiting room of Dr. Hornsby's. He looked like a man with an agenda, and Gaines knew exactly what that agenda was.

"Evening, David," Gaines said, and stuck his thumbs in his pockets. "I'm sorry we haven't contacted you yet. I've been meaning to, but wanted to wait until we had something solid."

"Something solid?" David scoffed under his breath. "I'm sure you did, Sheriff," he said louder, and turned his head and looked toward the fading sky in the west. He scratched the side of his face, swallowing hard.

"Everything okay? You don't look so good," Gaines said.

David laughed unenthusiastically, turning back and looking Gaines in the eyes. Gaines could see how bloodshot, glassy, and distant they were. The man was drunk.

"What do you think, Sheriff? My little girl's been raped, she doesn't want me around her because I make her uncomfortable, and it's Monday and I doubt you have Harry Bennett locked up back there." David pointed at the station behind Gaines. "So what do you think? Does that sound *okay* to you?"

Gaines could feel clouds of guilt and sympathy stacking inside him, darkening his mind. He remembered the way Kara had pulled away from her father in the parking lot of Dr. Hornsby's. He remembered how the car had divided the family— David walking alone to the driver's side as his wife and daughter, embracing, walked together to the other side. Now, with David standing in front of him, Gaines could see that the distance between the man and his family had been far greater than the width of a car. He truly did feel for him.

"You have a few drinks tonight, David?" Gaines asked reluctantly. He could smell it from where he stood. Gaines didn't have any intention of giving him any trouble for it. He just wanted to know what type of conversation he was about to have.

"I had a couple beers with lunch. Don't worry about me. I'm fine," David said. His speech was a little slurred, but not so slurred as to suggest he was a person who would forget this conversation tomorrow.

"Okay," Gaines said. "If you say you're fine, let's leave it at that."

David didn't respond directly. He only looked toward the station again and said, "So be straight with me. Can you do that?"

"Of course."

"Have you arrested Harry Bennett?"

Gaines's stomach wrenched. He looked down for a second, but then back up, quickly meeting David's eye. He owed the man that much. He owed him the respect of looking him in the eye. "No," he said. "We haven't arrested him." Then, just like that, Gaines felt some floodgate opening and he began to pour out explanations. He wanted—needed—David to know why. "I'm sorry, but we just don't have enough evidence right now. I know this is hard, but your daughter's testimony simply isn't sufficient to prove his guilt. We're still looking into everything, and we're still in the beginning stages, but we can't arrest him and risk destroying his life without—"

"Just stop, okay? Stop. I'm not stupid. I know that if you haven't arrested him yet, you probably never will," David said, holding up his hands. "And that's what I came down here to find out. I needed to rule out hope. My family has already been through enough. Waiting on hope where there is none would be the last nail in the coffin. I needed to know, and now I do. The son of a bitch will get away with it."

"That just isn't true. We're still gathering evidence, talking to people—"

"I have no doubt you are. But I've heard all I needed to."

And like that, David seemed to revert back to the calm and level-headed man Gaines was familiar with, the man he'd seen in the waiting room two days before.

"I promise you. Whoever is responsible will be held accountable. We only need some more time," Gaines said.

David laughed, shaking his head. It was an angry gesture. "Do you even hear yourself? You're one of the smartest people in this town, but you're too stupid to see you already made up your mind two days ago."

Gaines felt as if David had just socked him in the gut. He didn't want to believe the words he'd just heard. Or maybe he did. He didn't even know, anymore. On some subconscious level, he and David had just had a different, more-truthful exchange, and somehow all of Gaines's cards had been exposed. He was vulnerable, just like in the waiting room when they'd first spoken. In a way, he felt some kind of anger towards David for revealing this secret. A secret that Gaines, up until this moment, hadn't been fully aware of. He'd sensed it, especially during his debate with Catherine, but he had not seen it in its entirety, in all its ugly glory. It was like some monster that was hiding in the shadows. Gaines had known it was there, had heard it rustling, breathing, chewing on the bones, but he'd never gotten a clear glimpse of it. Now David had just shone his light into the shadows, revealing what lurked there. It was an ugly thing, a confused thing, with blood on its teeth and fear—not hate—in its eyes.

"I'm sorry you feel that way, David," Gaines said, and no longer had any desire to explain himself to the man standing in front of him. The guilt and sympathy that had started to brew in him quickly faded. What right did this man have to throw accusations like that against him—*unfounded* accusations? *I can see where his daughter gets it,* he thought, almost said. He caught himself, immediately feeling sick for thinking it. "Listen, you okay to get home? Because if not, I can drive you. Otherwise, I have to get going myself."

David smiled a halfhearted smile. "I'm fine, Calvin. Sorry if I came off as rude. Was never my intention."

"Look, I know this is hard, but I promise you, in the end, justice will be served."

"I have no doubt of that," David said, turning and opening the door of his car. He slunk in, rolling down the window. "Take care, Calvin."

"I'll be in touch. Take care of your family. They need you now more than ever," Gaines said.

David forced a smile, started the car, and pulled out of the parking lot.

Gaines watched his taillights grow smaller until they reached the end of Market Street and disappeared around a corner. The sound of his car faded in with the sound of the cicadas, vanishing like smoke in the air. Then out of nowhere, Gaines remembered what Dr. Hornsby had said back at his office on Saturday as he was leaving. At last he thought he understood what the man's comment had meant.

He brought his hands to his face and rubbed his temples despairingly. His thoughts raced and his head pounded. A million unresolved questions wanted to shroud him in darkness, where one threatening phrase repeated in deep red letters, flashing like an alarm:

People protect their own. People protect their own. People protect...

CHAPTER 17

Catherine found herself thinking about her time in high school as she and Deputy Hodges sat in the cruiser outside Brenda Fahey's apartment, waiting for her to arrive home from work. More specifically, though, Catherine was thinking about Dickie Hume.

Dickie had been her first in so many ways. He was her first real crush. Her first real kiss. Her first real love. There were boys before Dickie, sure, but they were just that—boys. Boys her own age. Boys she'd known since kindergarten and gone to preschool with. Mostly they were the friends she was destined to share youth's awkward romantic moments with. Innocent summer crushes. Kisses stolen under the stars at the park during a game of spin the bottle. Hearts pounding while holding hands. Tongues tied. The thrill of uncovering an entirely new and fun and exciting world of possibilities.

But none of these clumsy, adolescent forays into sexuality compared to what she experienced with Dickie. With him the experiences were beyond novelty. With him, the things she felt left lasting impressions on her soul that forever shaped how she saw the world and her future in it. In her mind, that was how she defined real.

Catherine and Dickie had met in high school when she was a freshman and he a senior. Dickie was tall and handsome, lean, with sharp-angled muscle. His blue eyes sat hard and dark against the chiseled features of his face. His dirty blond hair was usually swept behind his ears, some missed strands always spilling lazily across his forehead. Dickie wore his good looks humbly, as though it was more a burden than a blessing to be handsome and well-liked. It was almost as if he didn't want to be seen. He was soft-spoken, but when he did speak it was with a deep, confident, steady voice, as if he were choosing each word so carefully.

It was no wonder Catherine was shocked when Dickie offered her a ride home from school one afternoon. She was only a fifteen-year-old freshman, after all. She didn't think he even knew who she was.

"Need a lift?" He'd stopped to ask as she walked home that afternoon, the engine of his Plymouth rumbling low and powerful beside her, the heat of the car's undercarriage breathing on her legs. He had one hand on the wheel as he leaned out the window, grinning, wearing his black and orange varsity jacket. It took Catherine a moment to open her mouth and reply, but somehow she managed a smile and a nod.

He gave her a ride to her house, and they sat talking for twenty minutes in her driveway. The whole time she was so nervous, wondering whether or not her mother was watching from the living room window, about to come outside at any moment to ask to be introduced to Catherine's new friend. It would have been so embarrassing. But she had a feeling Dickie would have enjoyed it. She had a feeling he would charm her mother the same way he charmed everyone else. It was his nature, his instinct, to be liked. Her mother had never intruded, though. And the two sat and talked uninterrupted, their eyes never breaking contact, the only two people in the world.

Dickie did most of the talking, and mostly he talked about how he'd just broken up with his longtime girlfriend, Cadence Marlow. Catherine didn't care that he was going on about another woman. He could've talked about pretty much anything and she would've donned the same awestruck smile and listened with the same level of delight.

Dickie ran through all of the reasons he thought he and Cadence's relationship had come to an end. But what Catherine recalled understanding most clearly, when she accessed these long-forgotten memories, was that Cadence had wanted Dickie to apply to the same colleges as she did so they could stay together after high school. Dickie had refused to agree to that. He said he'd always known that part of growing up was going out into the unfamiliar world alone, living life without a tether, and he didn't think that he could do that with something as familiar as her by his side.

Catherine listened and nodded, listened and nodded, too nervous to chime in with her own thoughts. It went on like this for a little while, but eventually Dickie accused himself of being a bore and a fool for offering her a ride home only to pine over an ex-girlfriend, so he stopped. He apologized, saying a few more things that Catherine once again just nodded her head to, smiling, and before she knew it, she had plans to go see a movie with Dickie the following Friday. It was a date, the first of many.

It went like this for two months: Friday night dates. Rides home from school while other girls looked on in jealousy. Long nights parked up at The Point, the low rumble of his car idling away while they made out with the heat blowing on her legs. Him sliding his hands up her skirt. Under her shirt. Her moaning. Her face flushing red. Her toes curling. The Rolling Stones on the radio. Why did he taste so good?

Never sex, though. Even when he begged for it, she would refuse. She knew what their relationship really was. It was great and fun and wild and exciting, but she knew it wouldn't last; he was off to college soon, and she remembered how he felt about being tethered to something familiar. That conversation never left her mind for the duration of their relationship, always reminding her to be ready to lose him.

At the time, she was still a virgin, and as much as she loved Dickie she did not wish to give herself fully to someone who would more than likely forget about her within months, if not weeks, of leaving. Catherine was young, but never stupid or naive. She knew how the world worked... even Dickie's world. What she felt and experienced with him may have been real by her definition, but she understood that that did not make the relationship everlasting or meant-to-be. Their time together had been great and fun and had changed her in ways she would never be able to put into words. She would forever cherish their moments together. Or at least, that's what she'd thought at the time, before these cherished memories soured.

Everything changed the night of the dance. The night *he* changed. The night she changed, too. It was Dickie's senior prom. He invited her to go and she happily accepted. She even bought a new dress with the money she'd saved working shifts down at Woolworth's.

The dance was fine and good. They had a blast. They'd even kissed in the middle of the gymnasium during the last slow dance. It had been so romantic. But afterward was a different sort of time.

Dickie and some of his friends rented a few rooms at the Heartsridge Motel for a place to hang out after the dance. But it was more than just a place to hang out. It was a place to party, a place to drink alcohol purchased illegally, a place for some of the looser girls to sleep with their dates. She had been to parties with Dickie before, parties with drinking and drugs and where there were rooms dedicated to fooling around. She wasn't a square. But this was different. This place made her skin crawl. There was a raw energy in the air. She remembered feeling it on her skin. And the fact that it was a motel made the whole scene seem depraved. It just felt off, and she wanted to beg him to go somewhere else. But instead she held her tongue and went along with Dickie. He was leaving soon, after all. Why not appease him? He seemed excited about going.

A few of them—all friends of Dickie's—ended up together in one room, drinking Schnapps, smoking cigarettes, having some laughs. But slowly, couples broke off, disappearing to more private quarters to have some fun, and before long she and Dickie were alone. They started doing their usual stuff: necking, kissing, hands on each other. This time it wasn't enough, though. Eventually Dickie whispered in her ear that he wanted to sleep with her. He had asked many times before and had always laughed it off when she spurned his attempted advance to home-plate, but this time was different. This time he had a dark, glassy, mean look in his eyes when she pulled away.

Exactly when and what happened after that was a blur. She was pretty well buzzed by this point. She remembered him standing up, getting mad, but then suddenly becoming calm and insisting they drink more. The subject changed and she drank, not wanting to be a stick in the mud. She drank more than she ever had, and that was where her recollection of the night went out of focus. The memories she had were all snippets of him on top of her, her trying to get up and feeling helpless, feeling sick, feeling pain. Then him laughing. Then she must've passed out because everything went black.

The next morning she woke up naked and alone in the motel. The room smelled of cigarettes and booze. The sheets were cold, and there was a spot of blood beside her. Her head pounded viciously. She couldn't recall much of what had happened, but inside she knew. She went into the bathroom, sat down in the tub, and ran the shower. She cried for close to an hour, maybe two. But once she left that room, she left it all behind. She never cried again, and she never told anyone. The only person punished for what happened that night was her. Grounded for two weeks for not coming home.

The following Monday, she saw Dickie in the hall at school. He walked right past her, not so much as a smile. The two never spoke again. Three months later he left for college in California. She never saw him after that. He died in a drunk driving accident his freshman year. There was a girl in the car. She died on impact. Catherine always wondered if Dickie was on his way to do to that girl what he'd done to her back at that motel the night of the dance. If he was, maybe he'd done the girl a favor by killing her before he had a chance to do worse.

"What time is it?" Sam asked, pulling Catherine's mind back to the present.

"What?" Catherine said, slowly turning to him.

"I asked what time it was." Sam flipped his hat around in his hands. He was bored. "What if she doesn't come home right after work?"

Catherine looked at her wristwatch. "It's almost quarter of six," she said. "She'll be here. I've known Brenda since we were young. Never met a more boring woman in my life."

"What's your point?"

Catherine knocked the hat out of Sam's hands. "Knock it off. That's obnoxious."

Sam picked it up, placing it in his lap. "What crawled up your ass?"

Catherine ignored it. "My point is that Town Hall closes at five everyday. By five oh five the place is a ghost town. She probably stops for a bottle of wine, some groceries, and then it's home to feed her cat and watch TV. You can practically set your watch to it, you'll see."

Sam laughed, shaking his head, then turned and gazed out the window toward the front stairs of Brenda's apartment building.

Catherine continued. "Calvin could've spared us a stakeout if he'd just let us go down to her work and catch her there. Who cares if people see us talking to her?"

Sam turned back. "You know he's just doing his job, right? You can't envy him right now. He's trying to be discreet about this until we come up with something more. Suppose that girl comes forward tomorrow and points the finger at someone else? What if that boyfriend of hers—her friend or whatever, the one Calvin's looking into—*did* have something to do with this?"

"I just don't find it believable that she would lie about that. If this kid did it, she would just say it was him." The second she said this, she cringed inside. She knew this wasn't true. She knew girls lied about this type of thing all the time. In Catherine's case, her lie had always been to herself. She'd chosen never to ever tell anyone she was raped, to deal with it in her own way. But she was sure—pretty sure, anyway—that Kara wasn't lying. She'd seen the truth on her face the night she went to her house. Catherine's heart listened to Kara. She was telling the truth.

Sam smirked. "That's not true and you know it. People lie all the time. And until you see the motivation, the lie never seems possible. But once you do see it, well, you never know how you missed it."

"I'm sorry, but I just don't think she's lying. Though I can see *you're* already toeing the line."

"I'm just saying that we could all lose our jobs if this goes down wrong. He's lookin' out for us more than you think. He's a good man who was dealt an impossible hand… he's just trying to play it as best he can."

"Spare me the poker metaphors, would you?" Catherine said, rolling her eyes. She knew Sam was speaking the truth though; Gaines *was* a good man. He'd always been a great boss to her, had always put the town, the people, before himself. And maybe that's what he was doing now: trying to spare the town from this grotesquery. But Heartsridge didn't need to be spared; they needed to know that the man they all trusted, the man they voted for to run their town, was a monster. She just needed to prove to Gaines that Harry Bennett was lying. But she couldn't deny the one very real obstacle she'd heard over and over again: there just wasn't enough evidence to arrest Harry for this crime. She didn't know what she would find talking to Brenda and Kara, but she had to try.

"Well, looks like you were right," Sam said.

A yellow Volkswagen pulled into a parking space in front of Brenda's apartment. A portly woman carrying a bag of groceries stepped out and walked toward the building.

"That's her," Catherine said. "Wait here."

Sam looked like he might argue about going with her, but he didn't.

Catherine opened the door, walking briskly across the street. She caught Brenda at her door while she was fidgeting with her keys.

"Brenda?" Catherine said, stopping at the base of the stairs.

Brenda started, spinning around quickly. "Oh, you scared me. What're you doing here, Catherine?"

Catherine put her foot on the first step, leaning on the hand-rail. "Like to ask you a few questions about something, if I could."

Brenda's forehead wrinkled. "Okay... sure," she said in a puzzled tone. "Come inside. I need to put this bag down. I'm not the young lady I used to be."

Catherine said nothing. She and Brenda were roughly the same age, mid-thirties, but Catherine didn't feel old in the same way the woman standing in front of her, struggling with a bag of groceries, seemed to. For this, she felt a peculiar air of self-righteousness, knowing she'd made it through the last fifteen years of life in far better condition than her counterpart.

"No problem," Catherine said. "This'll only take a few minutes."

Brenda smiled, turning and slipping the key into the deadbolt. She unlocked the door and disappeared inside.

Catherine followed.

The interior of Brenda's apartment was almost exactly how Catherine had imagined it: worn-out rugs; the sharp, ammoniat-ed smell of cat urine; thick drapes pulled snug over the windows; a couch piled with layers of quilts and hand-knit afghan blankets.

In the pile of blankets, Catherine saw a white and black cat raise its head and then yawn into a long stretch.

"There's my widdle pwincess," It was a slur of embarrassing baby-talk. "We hungwee my widdle darling?" She shut the door behind Catherine, plopping her bag of groceries on the counter and going to the couch. She made a series of high-pitched smacking and kissing noises directed at her cat, until she scooped it up in one arm and brought it over to Catherine. "This here is Joan, as in Joan of Arc." Brenda laughed, pressing the cat against her face, covering its head in kisses. The cat writhed and then jumped from her arms. She chased it with her eyes until it disappeared into a back room. Then she brought her attention to Catherine. "Sorry. Haven't seen my girl since this morning. I promise I'm not a crazy cat-lady. Well not completely, at least," Brenda said, and laughed.

Catherine was hit by a sudden thought: *This could have been me—one false move and I could be living this gem of a life.*

But was she really so different? They were both single (she presumed this of Brenda). They both lived alone. They were both the same age. Neither made much money...

Catherine smiled politely. "No need for apologies." She looked vaguely around the apartment. "Cozy place you have here."

Brenda waved her off. "Who you kidding? This place is a sty right now. I've been meaning to clean it, but with the festival coming up, Harry has me too busy with paperwork. I'll get to it eventually." She hesitated a moment. Then: "So what did you need to talk to me about?"

"Kara Price," Catherine said bluntly.

"Kara Price?" Brenda's face scrunched. "The new intern? What about her?"

"She worked with you on Saturday, from what I understand. Is that right?"

"Yes. It was her first day," Brenda said. "I was training her on some basic stuff, like how to take calls, how the filing system works—mostly busywork she'll be doing during the summer. Why? She in some kind of trouble?"

"We're just looking into something. Nothing I can discuss, unfortunately. Hope you don't take offense."

Brenda's eyes lit up. "Oh, how exciting. A scandal," she said, smiling.

"Not exactly. But I'd love your cooperation. It could be a great help."

"Anything," Brenda said.

"I really just need to know about the end of the day on Saturday."

"Like what?"

"To start, what time did you leave?"

Brenda tilted her head, bringing a finger to her chin. "I think we finished up around a quarter to five. I remember because I heard the bells chiming down at St. Christopher's as I drove through town on my way home."

"And what about Kara? Did she leave when you did?"

Brenda nodded enthusiastically. "Yes. I showed her how to lock up Harry's office and how to close up for the day. Then she left and headed toward the grocery store." She looked down at the floor for a moment, then quickly back up. "I probably should have offered her a ride, I know, but I just wanted to get home. I hadn't felt well all day. She said she lived close by, anyway."

Catherine felt something against her leg. She looked down and saw Brenda's cat brushing against her. "And what about Harry? When did he leave?" Catherine asked, back to Brenda, watching her face and her eyes closely as she accessed the memory and answered. Catherine had started to entertain an idea: What if after years and years of working for the most powerful man in Heartsridge, Brenda, the secretary with nothing to love but her cat, had developed a crush on the man she worked for? And if that were the case, would she lie for him? Would he even have to ask her to? Or would she just do it out of instinct to protect him, to protect herself from losing something she cared about?

Brenda's face offered nothing, only that dumbstruck look that seemed to live there.

"Harry? Well... let's see. He left before we did, maybe an hour or so earlier. Told me he wanted to get some stuff done around his house."

"Did you see him after that?" Catherine sighed thinly, folding her arms. She could feel this going nowhere.

"No. The next time I saw him was this morning," Brenda said. "This have something to do with Sheriff Gaines coming to see him?"

Catherine inhaled, her lips parting.

Brenda noticed and threw up her hands. "Right, right. I forgot, you can't tell me anything. Forget I asked."

"Thank you."

She was starting to feel a frightening hopelessness growing in her. She was realizing that Calvin was right; there was no evidence. Brenda was telling her exactly what they already knew, and without revealing what had happened, there was little else Catherine could do. She was starting to wonder if maybe her best bet would be to wait for the rumor to get around town—and she knew it would. Once it was out there, they wouldn't need to be so discreet. Once it was out there, someone might come forward as a witness. And while she had plenty of doubt the latter would happen, there was at least some hope there.

There was a moment's pause between the two women. Then Brenda said, "Is there anything else? I don't know if I'm being at all helpful."

"You are. I really appreciate your cooperation," Catherine said. "One last thing—did you notice Harry acting strange or angry or different in any way?" Catherine could hear desperation in her own voice. She was reaching for something—anything—that could point her in the right direction. There were no answers here, though, and she knew it.

Brenda narrowed her eyes, thinking. "I don't think so. He was a little stressed, but that's normal this time of year, with the festival a few days away," she said.

"Okay," said Catherine. "I think that's all."

Brenda laughed softly. "Well, I don't know if I helped, but I hope you got what you came for."

"Thanks, Brenda," Catherine said. "I'll be in touch if I think of anything else I need to ask you. I can see myself out."

"Sounds good. We'll be here," Brenda said, apparently referring to her and the cat. "Take care, Catherine."

When she returned to the cruiser, Sam was just finishing up a conversation on the dispatch radio. "All right, I'll tell her," he said, and then hung up the radio.

"Tell me what?" Catherine said as she shut the door and started the engine.

"Promise not to shoot the messenger?"

"Yes. What is it?"

"Well, Calvin wants you to hold off on going to the Prices'. Said her father came by the station a few minutes ago and was pretty bombed. He doesn't think it's a good idea to go poking around right now."

Catherine put the car in drive and pulled out into the street. "That's fine. I'll do it tomorrow."

"Everything go okay in there?"

Catherine came to the stop sign at the end of the road. "This is just pointless," she said. "Everyone's going to know about this soon enough. I don't see why we have to be so quiet about it. Having to tip-toe around makes it damn near impossible to figure anything out."

"You think Calvin doesn't know that?" Sam said. "He just doesn't want to be responsible for letting the cat out of the bag. Give it a week. Wait until word spreads, and then I'm sure he'll give you some more leeway. Harry isn't going anywhere. What's the rush?"

"I know, I was already considering that... but I have my concerns."

"Like what?"

"Like in a week, after this *really* gets around, Harry Bennett will be the victim, not Kara. Christ, that's already how it is, but it'll be on a larger scale once it gets out to the masses. Without evidence, Kara's accusations will just be lies. That's how people will see it—that's how they *are* seeing it. Every single person who has found out so far has refused to believe that the magnificent Harry Bennett could be capable of such a thing, and I think that is exactly what he was counting on. That's why Calvin won't do anything—he doesn't want to be on the losing side when this comes to a head. It's going to be a witch-hunt. You'll see."

"Can you blame him?" Sam said coldly. "What would you do in his shoes?"

And for the first time, Catherine wasn't wholly certain she knew. It was true: arresting Harry now would be career suicide, and she couldn't ignore that, but it felt so wrong to do nothing.

She glanced in the rearview mirror and saw the sun lowering below the trees. As the day waned behind her, she drove, her thoughts shifting back to Dickie Hume.

CHAPTER 18

"I'll tell you why," Harry Bennett said resentfully, "because she wants attention. That's all women ever want—attention." He downed the rest of his bourbon. "Drama is the last drug of the desperate whore."

"Calm down," Allison said. "You sound ignorant when you talk that way."

"Well, it's *true!*" Harry yelled, slamming his palm against the wall. "Why else would this girl make up something so terrible? Attention. That's all."

Harry had spent the last ten minutes breaking the news to his wife about Kara Price's accusations against him. He was prepared, though. He had practiced the conversation in his head more times than he could remember. It was just one more lie to sell, and he was good at that.

"Lower your voice, the neighbors will hear you." Allison shushed him. She tried to put her hands on him, but he pulled away.

"Oh, who cares, Ali?" He shrugged exuberantly. "Who fucking cares? Who cares if they hear us fighting? It's life. People fight."

"Put the drink down. You've had enough. You're drunk, Harry. I know you're upset but—"

"Yeah, well, you'd be drunk too, if you had the day I did. Anyone come to your office and accuse you of raping a fifteen-year-old girl today?"

Allison pursed her lips but said nothing.

"I didn't think so," Harry said, walking past her to the living-room bar and topping off his glass. With his back to her he grinned proudly, quickly stifling the smile before he spoke. "Talk to me about being drunk when *that* happens to you. You know what this could do to my career?" He turned and took a seat on the arm of the couch, staring absently at the floor, really trying to put on a show.

"Yes, Harry, I do. That's why I'm trying to figure out how we should handle this. You need a clear head right now," Allison said, and came into the living room.

"*We?*" Harry scoffed and ran a hand through his hair.

"Yes, *we*. Don't for a minute think that you'd be where you are today without my help. It isn't you alone out there. It isn't Harry Bennett versus the world, whether you think it is or not. Where'd you get the money for your campaign? Where'd you get the money to start the trucking company? You'd still be shoveling gravel if I hadn't helped you."

"Don't speak to me like that." He pointed a rigid finger at her but caught himself, lowering his hand and his temper. For a moment, he felt the darkness tunneling in, but he beat it back. *This isn't the time to lose it, Harry.*

Harry cringed at what she'd just said. *The money! The goddamned money!* She was throwing that in his face. He'd always suspected that she held that debt over him, but she'd never said it… not until now. There was truth in it, though. He *had* needed her money in the beginning, but now he was making plenty of his own. Financially, he didn't have use for her any longer, but she still had value to him, especially now. Her social influence was undeniable. Her life seemed to be one giant game of telephone, and when she whispered into the ear of Heartsridge, the message was always received clearly and quickly. Allison would be the one to keep Harry in the town's good graces. She would be the one ensuring the right facts were heard and the right opinions were held. Defending himself would not look nearly as good as being defended by a strong woman like Allison Bennett. Surely a woman of her caliber would not stay with—and defend—a guilty man. Her resolve and her dedication to him would be his absolution.

"Why are you so concerned?" he asked in a calmer voice. "This isn't your problem. I don't need a lecture. I only told you so you'd hear it from me."

"Not my problem?" Allison laughed in disbelief. "Do you really think this won't affect me, too? Yours isn't the only name that is being dragged through the mud." She paused, head shaking. "Who is she anyway? You still haven't told me her name. Is it someone I know?"

"I don't know. I'd never heard her name before. She's some new intern I only met once. Her name's Kara, I think… Kara Price."

"Price? I know the name, but I don't really know the family."

Allison made it her business to know everyone, especially being the wife of the mayor. Aside from raising a child and making a home for her family, it was the closest thing she had to a job. She seemed to take it almost as a failure when she didn't know someone.

Harry absently stirred the ice in his cup with his finger. "Why would you? They're clearly bad people. Anyone who'd raise a daughter like that isn't proper company. They're trash. Have to be. How else would you get a screwed-up kid like that? The little bitch is trying to ruin me."

Allison began rubbing the gold pendant on her necklace. "You said Calvin Gaines talked to you. What's *his* take?"

"They have nothing. There's not a single shred of evidence that I did what this girl is saying. Calvin thinks she's lying too, in fact. All she has is her story and a few cuts and bruises. Anything could have happened to her. She could have marked herself up... or some high school boy... I don't know..." Harry trailed off into his glass of bourbon.

"Did he tell you he thinks she's lying?"

"No, not in so many words. But he didn't have to. Calvin's a smart man. He wouldn't let some kid string him along. The county made the right choice when they elected him. I was wrong about him. I'm glad he got the job."

Harry rose from the couch and crossed the room toward his wife.

He bent, set his glass on the coffee table, and then gently put his hands on Allison's shoulders, never breaking eye contact with her. "This is all such a mess. I don't know what I did to deserve this. But it will be okay. I don't care what happens. I don't care what people think or what rumors go around. All I care about is that *you* know I would never do anything like this." He paused for dramatic effect. Then: "Honey, you don't believe her, do—"

"Don't even ask me that," Allison snapped. "If I believed it I wouldn't be standing here. And have faith in your people—they won't believe this either. They've trusted you for almost a decade, they won't stop now. We just need to get ahead of this."

Harry released one hand and turned away, shaking his head, pinching the bridge of his nose between his thumb and finger.

"God, this couldn't have come at a worse time. I already have more on my plate than I can handle with the festival a few days away."

"I just don't understand why this girl would accuse you of this," Allison said. She didn't appear to be listening to her husband. She was stuck in her own train of thought.

"I don't know. Your guess is as good as mine." Harry paused, pretending to be hit with a recollection. Then after a moment, he said, "You know, Calvin was saying that maybe it was a boy from school who did it, a boyfriend or something along those lines. He thought maybe this girl's boyfriend—or whoever—did this to her, and she didn't want to get him in trouble or be ostracized, so she pointed the finger at me. I guess to a high-school kid I'm as much a nobody as anyone. I just happened to work with her that day, so I was it." Harry paused again and watched his wife's face turn slightly. He had her attention so he continued. "I don't really know how much I agree with that theory, but hell, what do I know? I'm not a cop. But Calvin seemed pretty keen on the idea." Another lie. It had been Harry who had really put that idea in Gaines's head.

Allison paused for a moment, her eyes darting around the room. "Or like you said, she only wants attention. Or maybe it's money she's after. Doesn't really matter what her motive is, at this point. All that matters is that we aren't the last to the party. Action is better than reaction with this, and we don't have long before everyone knows about it."

It was as though a switch had been flipped inside her. Allison was getting revved up. Harry could see the cogs and gears in her brain starting to churn. If only she knew he was the one who'd set them in motion. If only she knew the whole conversation had been about leading her to this point. Lighting a fire under her ass. Making her feel unappreciated so she felt as though she had something to prove. Getting her to prove they were a "we." But she didn't know all that, and she never would, because Harry was always two steps ahead. More importantly, his talent for believing his own lies was too thoroughly practiced to contend with, which made it nearly impossible for someone with even the smallest morsel of doubt to hold their ground against him. That doubt was like stress cracks in a person's foundation, and he could spot those weaknesses in an instant and chip away in all the right places to bring down what was built atop the faults.

"What do you have in mind?" Harry asked.

"You said her name is Kara Price?"

"Yes."

"Well, if she wants attention, I'll make sure she gets it," Allison said.

Harry smiled inside, but his face kept the look of concern. "What do you mean?" He knew exactly what she meant. It was what he'd been after all along. Allison would be his personal PR team behind the scenes. She had access to the mainline of the town's rumor mill. "What're you going to do?"

"I'm going to tell the right people the truth before they hear the lie. That's how you beat something like this. Who wants pie after they've already had cake?" Her face steeled as she lit a cigarette and inhaled deeply.

"Maybe I underestimated you." Harry flashed his smile.

"That's your biggest weakness, Harry. It always has been. You only see people as you want to see them, not how they truly are."

CHAPTER 19

The shopping bags sat on the end of her bed. They were a small mountain of glossy boutique totes full of new clothes, shoes, and expensive makeup. Kara held out her fingers, inspecting her freshly painted fingernails. Rose Red was the color. That's what the woman in Newburyport had told her and her mother, anyway.

Their girl's day had helped. For the first time in two days, Kara felt happiness creeping back in. It wasn't a superficial happiness, either. It wasn't happiness bought by the almighty dollar. She would be lying if she said she hadn't enjoyed being spoiled a little, but her delight did not reside in the bags at the end of her bed, nor was it lacquered onto her nails. The happiness was that of subsiding pain. Like the pleasure felt after banging your knee. The pleasure of the hurt fading. The kind of happiness that can only come after something has been endured. Happiness that wasn't really happiness at all, only the slow ascension back to normality. And that was what had been so great: the day had felt like a normal day. Just two girls out for an afternoon, doing a little shopping. That's all. They had even stopped for lunch at Captain Jack's and gotten Kara's favorite—lobster rolls.

Kara glanced over at the clock on her nightstand. It was 9:25 on Monday night. Her parents were already asleep. She and her mother had returned home at around five o'clock from their day in Newburyport, and Kara's father had arrived home drunk shortly afterward. Her parents had argued briefly in whispers in their bedroom, but it had ended more quickly than it started. Kara had never seen her father drunk before. It left an uneasy feeling in her stomach. She knew she probably had something to do with it, and a part of her felt bad for him. A part of her wanted to reach out and hug him, apologize for everything, apologize for what had happened to her, apologize for the new uneasiness she felt around him, tell him she would be better soon, tell him that she only needed some time. But she couldn't. Something about it just seemed so awkward. Perhaps it was because for her entire life, the tides of consolation had flowed toward her, and now the idea of reaching out to her father in a gesture of reparation, swimming upstream against that tide, seemed so cumbersome in her mind. Things would right themselves on their own. They had to.

It had been two days since Kara was raped, and she was starting to see glimpses of a life where every single thought did not land her in a fit of anxiety. Sometimes she found that ten or fifteen whole minutes had gone by, and that scene from the back of Harry Bennett's car hadn't replayed once. It was something, Kara imagined, she might never get over completely, but it seemed that if she worked at it, she could block it out bit by bit. And if that was the case, then she would devote all her will to forgetting the past. Find a secure closet in her mind, stuff everything toward the back, and shut the door. Lock it and throw away the key. Maybe put up a sign—DO NOT OPEN!—as a reminder, in case she ever found herself standing at the threshold in a moment of weakness. What other choice did she have? It had happened, and now she needed to move on and put it behind her. Besides, was it even *that* bad? It was just sex, after all. She was planning on losing her virginity this year, anyway. Sure, the way it had happened was wrong. But was it really as bad as everyone was making it seem? If *she* could get over it, perhaps everyone else could, too. It just wasn't a big deal, okay?

Kara ran her tongue over the cut on her lip and bit down on the scab. Pain flared, and her lower eyelids immediately gathered tears. But they weren't tears of sadness. They weren't tears of any emotion. Just a physical reaction. She would have had the same results if she'd stared at the sun. She had spent so much of the last forty-eight hours trying to flee from the thoughts and the memories, the emotional hurt of being raped, that in this turmoil she had learned a new skill: to harness the physical pain for good.

The little cut on her lip was like a safety switch, and pressing it pulled her into the present and out of whatever dark hole the thoughts had led her down. There were no reflections of the past here, no meditations on the future, only the present moment. It was just her and the pain throbbing on her lip. It even had its own little heartbeat, as if it were alive. That was calming, in a way. In these little eddies of peace, these brief moments of serenity, Kara found the strength to move forward. Inches and millimeters at a time, she was putting distance between herself and the back seat of Harry Bennett's Cadillac. Her methods weren't ideal, but they worked, and they were her own. That was important.

Kara was even beginning to entertain the idea of returning to school later in the week. She didn't know how much longer she could stand being cooped up in the house. Sometimes she would go hours without speaking a single word. In the instances when she became aware of it, she would say whatever word happened to be on her mind, simply so she could remind herself what her voice sounded like... or that it still worked. A return to society seemed like a welcome idea. And the week leading up to Spring Festival was always the most exciting time of the year to be in school. Teachers didn't give out work, and students got together and decorated the hallways and the gymnasium with vernal themes. She had done this in middle school the year before, but this would be her first time participating in the high school version. Kara thought maybe she didn't want to miss that.

What if she saw *him*, though? A twinge of panic rippled through her. Kara knew Harry Bennett hadn't been arrested, and from what she'd heard of her parent's argument a few hours before, she didn't get the impression he ever would be. That was what her father had been yelling about. It was the only part of the fight that had made it through their bedroom door with any clarity. It wasn't a surprise, though. She had never expected that Harry would be arrested. A part of her had always understood that he'd probably done what he'd done because he'd known he would get away with it. And right now, Kara would take a return to normality—which she was slowly beginning to recognize, even if it was happening by small degrees—over revenge or justice. She shuddered at the idea of it all being drawn out for weeks or months in a courtroom and in the paper. Gone and forgotten was just fine with her.

She had no doubt her parents would continue to demand justice. But as far as she was concerned, moving on was the best remedy. It was the only solution that didn't send a shiver of panic through her, and she was sick to death of feeling that way. Always on edge, always on the verge of tears, stomach raw with acid, muscles sore and tired from no sleep.

Kara laced her hands behind her head, lay back on her bed, and closed her eyes. The edge of sleep danced on the insides of her eyelids, flashing shades of white and black and red and blue, electric images that didn't quite align with her conscious mind.

Then a voice shook her out of it: "Where you been, stranger?"

Kara opened her eyes and sat up.

At first she didn't see anyone, but then the voice spoke again and she recognized it. "Over here."

She looked toward the window and saw Ryan Kinsey's face pressed against the screen, smiling mischievously. "Ryan? How the—"

He drummed softly with his fingers on the windowsill. "I found a ladder around back. Don't worry, I was quiet. I didn't wake your folks."

Kara swung her legs off the bed and crossed to the window. "What're you doing here? You can't come in."

"Good to see you too," he said sarcastically. "You forget you have a boyfriend?"

"I'm sorry. I've been real sick. A stomach bug," Kara said, holding her abdomen, turning her face away. The light in her room was dim, so she thought he probably couldn't see her bruises. "I was meaning to call you."

"Yeah, yeah. I'm sure. That's what they all say. There's someone else, isn't there?" Ryan joked and then tapped lightly on the screen. "Now c'mon, let me in, just for a sec. I haven't seen you or heard from you since Saturday. I won't stay long. I parked up the street."

Kara cupped her elbows and crossed her legs awkwardly, almost losing her balance but steadying herself. "I don't know, Ryan. Now's not a great time." Kara looked him in the eyes for a moment, turning away quickly when she remembered her face.

"I'm not leaving until you let me in," Ryan said slyly. "How can you deny your Prince Charming? I climbed all the way up this here tower to see my fair maiden."

Kara felt the beginnings of a smile. A part of her had anticipated feeling the same unease around Ryan that she felt around her father, but so far she sensed none of it. She was actually kind of glad to see him. It felt like another step in the direction of normal.

There was something innocent and less threatening about Ryan. It was, perhaps, because he was still very much a boy and not a man. He did not carry that threatening look of hard age in his eyes—the look all men, at some point or another, possessed once life smacked them around a bit. Bitterness, the little twinkle of anger and frustration that flashed when tempers ran high. She had seen it in Harry Bennett's eyes moments before he'd hit her. She'd seen something like it three years before in her father's eyes when he had caught her trying a cigarette behind the garage. Her father had never laid a hand on her, though, only yelled and screamed until she was sure his head was going to explode. She couldn't deny that maybe what she'd seen in her father then had been something different, though, something more good-natured. For a brief moment she felt guilty for comparing Harry Bennett to her father. They were nothing alike. She needed to remember that, repeat it like a mantra if need be.

"Fine," she said. "But only for a few minutes. If my dad catches you, he'll kill you. He still thinks we're just friends." Kara pinched the clasps at the bottom of the screen, lifting it a few inches. Ryan took it from there and opened it quietly the rest of the way.

"Why are you afraid to tell him?" he asked as he swung a leg over the sill into her room. "I don't see what the big deal is."

"Because you're older than me, and I don't think he'd like it."

Kara walked away from the window. When she turned around, Ryan was standing right in front of her. She kept her head down.

"We haven't even really done anything, yet. We basically *are* just friends," he said, and laughed.

But she didn't. She didn't laugh because she *had* done something. Not that it was on her terms—if she wanted to get technical, it had been done *to* her. But any way she looked at it, one thing remained true: she was no longer pure. What she had been saving for Ryan had been taken from her, and now she didn't know if she had anything left to give. Or if she wanted to. Whatever desires she had felt were extinguished, and she doubted they would ever return.

"So, what's wrong with you? You don't look sick. And if you are I'll take my chances." He leaned down to kiss her, hooking a finger under her chin, and lifting her face to meet his.

Something automatic responded inside Kara, a new reflex. Her stomach tightened and she pulled away. "Don't," she said.

"What's wrong?" Ryan said. But before she could say anything, his attention shifted. "What happened to your face?" He leaned in, inspecting.

Kara pulled away completely, bringing her hand to the side of her face.

"It's nothing," she said. "I was sleepwalking when I had a fever and fell. I don't remember it, but my mom said it could've been worse. I was a little delirious." Where had this lie come from? She hadn't thought about it once; it just came to her.

Ryan's eyes thinned as he looked her over. For a moment, Kara was certain she was about to have a talk she wasn't ready to have. Eventually she would have to tell Ryan about what had happened to her, but it would be when she was ready. And she was not ready. But then he said: "Oh well. Looks like it hurt, klutz. Maybe they should strap you in like at the loony bin." He turned away from her, looking vaguely around the room.

"It did—it does," Kara said, keeping her fingers over the wound. "My mom gave me some stuff to put on it, and it's helping."

"Is that why you won't let me kiss those beautiful lips?" Ryan turned back to her with his charming smile.

Kara volleyed one back and nodded. Her lip cracked, and she flinched. "Yes," she said. "Only until it heals. Then it'll be okay. Are you mad?"

"Of course not. I can wait. We got all summer, baby."

"Thank you. Did I miss anything at school today?"

Ryan began wandering around her room, picking things up, inspecting them and putting them back down.

"Nah, nothing really. Alex Holt and Philip Lang almost got into a scrap in the parking lot after school. Got broken up before anything real interesting happened, though."

"What were they arguing over?" Kara asked. It felt good to get back in the loop of gossip.

"Who knows? Probably a girl... it's always a girl." Ryan scanned through the clutter on top of her bureau.

"They're idiots, if you ask me... the both of 'em. What girl could possibly be involved with them?"

Ryan laughed, thumbing through a yearbook he'd found sitting on her bureau. "No idea. I didn't care enough to ask. This you?" He held the yearbook toward her, the spine propped open with his index and middle finger.

Kara saw the picture he meant. It was her class photo from the year before, when she was still in middle school. Her dark hair was in pigtails. Although it was only twelve short months in the past, it seemed like a lifetime ago. "Put that down," she said, and grabbed it out of Ryan's hand.

"Jesus. Okay. I didn't mean to get you all worked up."

Kara's face went cold, and she shushed him. "Quiet. I think someone's awake." She turned and looked nervously at her closed bedroom door. Someone was stirring.

"What? I don't hear—" Ryan was saying when the sound of footsteps started coming down the hall. His eyes widened.

"Hide. Lay down underneath my bed."

Ryan got on his back and slipped under her bed, drawing his feet up.

Kara got under the covers and shut off the light.

The footsteps stopped outside her room, and for a moment, Kara was sure her door was going to swing open. But after a few seconds the footfalls picked up again and passed. Distantly, she heard her father clear his throat and go into the bathroom, his slippers shuffling across the floor.

She flicked the lights back on. "C'mon, Ryan. You gotta go. Trust me. It just isn't a good time for this."

"Okay, okay, fine," he said, and slid out from under the bed.

"Hurry, before he comes back. He'll probably come check on me." She knew her father wouldn't, not after what she had told her mother that morning. He hadn't even said goodbye to her in the morning when he left for work, and for as long as she could remember, he had never failed to do that. He was keeping his distance, and Kara could feel it like a cold and hollow cloud between them.

Ryan went to the window, lifting a leg over, riding the sill between his legs. He searched for footing on the top rung of the ladder below. "Will you be in school tomorrow?" he asked urgently as Kara shooed him out.

"I don't know. Maybe. If not tomorrow, Wednesday or Thursday. I'm starting to feel better so I'm sure it will be soon. And put the ladder back."

"Okay. Geez. Relax. You want me to fall and break my neck? You know you really don't seem sick."

Kara ignored him. "Just hurry," she said. Her father might not come in and check on her, but her mother certainly would. Hearing the footsteps outside her door had spooked her.

"Fine, fine, all right." And like that, Ryan was back on the ladder, looking into her room as if he had never entered in the first place. He pinched the screen clasps and carefully slid the window back into place. His face became a haze behind the gray mesh of the screen, floating like an apparition in the night. "I hope you feel better," he said.

"Thank you," she said, bringing her hand once more to her lip. "I'll be back soon."

Then he smiled that charming smile and descended. "Later, alligator," he whispered.

She stayed at the window and watched him until he faded into the darkness. A moment later the ladder pulled away from the house without a noise, and he was gone.

A few minutes went by, then very faintly she heard a car door shut, and an engine rumbled to life in the distance.

She listened with a faint smile on her face as the car drove away. Maybe there was hope for her, after all. Maybe life could just pick up where it had left off. What had happened to her did not need to define her. It didn't have to be who she was. And it didn't have to determine who she would become, either. It was time to move on.

Gone and forgotten.

The sound of the car faded into the night. When her room was still again, Kara shut off the light and closed her eyes. Sleep didn't come easily for her, but eventually it found her and held her in a dark, dreamless embrace.

CHAPTER 20

David awoke at four o'clock on Tuesday morning with a dull headache and a sour, rough tongue. His mind was a grim slog. It felt as if his brain had been switched out for a wet, cardboard replica that threatened to disintegrate into a pile of mush if not handled gently. Fragmented recollections of the previous evening wandered through his head. A conversation with Calvin Gaines in a parking lot. An argument with Ellie. Kara didn't want to be around him. The motel. Lucky Lucky Room 7. *What a fine fresh scent, Daddy.* He hadn't even had that much to drink: six or seven beers, tops… maybe a few whiskey backs. He owed the hangover to lost tolerance; it had been a while since he'd put that many down. He was no longer the sort of practiced drinker he'd been as a bachelor. A good thing, he thought.

But among these hazy, formless memories and post-booze morning thoughts, one stuck out the most. It was a thought with crisp, clean edges, one that didn't pass on through but instead lingered ominously without any promise of fading. It was something he'd concocted in drunken anger the night before, bits and pieces of rationality and irrationality stitched seamlessly together by the threads of alcohol into something illusively coherent. David had fallen asleep turning it over in his mind, but he'd expected his enthusiasm for it to be gone when the sun rose on the new day. That was the way things like that usually worked, he'd thought—like running into an old friend drunk at a bar and making plans that both parties know in their hearts will never be carried out. In the morning the plans were forgotten, and everyone moved on with their lives. No harm, no foul.

This wasn't like that, though. The idea had followed him through sleep, anchoring itself to his mind in an almost obsessive way. It had followed him—stalked him—into sobriety, enthusiasm and all. In the early-morning twilight, it retained its appeal, making more sense now than it had when it was merely the mad whiskey dream of a desperate man.

Beside him, Ellie slept, snoring gently with her leg kicked out above the covers. He would not wake her.

Swinging his lower half off the bed, he sat up and rubbed his face, working the sleep out of his eyes. After a moment, he rose to his feet quietly.

By 5:05 David Price had done six things: taken a shower; brushed his teeth; gotten dressed in his work clothes; downed three glasses of lukewarm water (for the hangover, of course); popped two aspirin (also for the hangover); and grabbed the pistol from the safe in the basement.

A half-hour later, he was pulling into the motel parking lot, parking in the same spot as the day before. The red truck was there again, and for some reason this pleased him. He didn't know who it belonged to, but he found comfort in knowing that at least he wasn't alone. Somewhere, in some secret vein of his consciousness, he thought: *You and me, pal. We're in this together.*

David killed the ignition and his car grumbled to a stop, revealing the still silence of the early morning. It was 5:33, and the sun remained just below the horizon. The cicadas had yet to awake and resume their noise. David found their absence deafening, as if a pair of invisible hands were cupped around his ears. He was one of the few who enjoyed the sound of the bugs, but not because he thought it was beautiful or sappy or nostalgic or anything like that. No, he liked them because their sound was a distraction. It was something arbitrary to focus on, such as how even in the winter he needed the sound of a fan in his bedroom to fall asleep, white noise to cut through dark thoughts. Without something to occupy his mind, he felt as if he might just disappear from the world, fade into some still, silent void of nothingness—oblivion.

The pistol, a Smith & Wesson .38 Special, sat on the seat beside him wrapped in an old red bandana. David picked it up, slid it into his pocket, and then stepped out of the car.

The DO NOT DISTURB sign hung askew on the door handle just as he'd left it. *Lucky Lucky Room 7.* There was the faint sound of music coming from beyond the door. For a moment he was confused, but then he remembered he'd forgotten to shut off the alarm he'd set for himself the day before. David removed the key from his jacket pocket, pushed it in the lock and turned it. The music sharpened as he walked into the room. It was Carly Simon singing "You're So Vain." Kara loved Carly Simon. He grimaced. David shut the door behind him and moved to the clock radio. He pressed the off button. Carly's voice vanished abruptly. Silence again. David looked around the room, the stale cigarette smell like a dirty sweat sock under his nose. After a moment, he pressed the button again. He let the music play as he lay down on the bed and closed his eyes. Kara loved Carly Simon.

With a hand on top of the Smith & Wesson, David fell back to sleep, his heart on fire.

CHAPTER 21

Bill was watching her.

Joanna, her body long and arched, reached for the plastic flatware sorter high on the shelf behind the counter.

"Be right with you, hon," she said, her head turned slightly so Bill could see only a suggestion of her face. It was a nice suggestion, he thought.

"Take your time."

Joanna's calves were so smooth and well shaped, like two teardrops. He stared as she raised up on her toes, then on to one foot, the frill of her server's uniform brushing delicately against her legs.

She got a finger on the sorter, tipped it toward her and brought it down into her hands. She placed it on the counter beside Bill and offered a smile. "Life would be a whole lot easier if I were six inches taller," she said. "I should fire whoever put that up there." She laughed.

"Suppose you should," Bill said, perching a cigarette between his lips and lighting it. He took a drag and smiled behind the smoke.

Joanna slid an ashtray in front of him. "Truth be told, I'm probably the one who put it up there. Coffee?"

"Black."

"Menu?"

"Not today."

"All right, well, that was easy. One black coffee it is, Bill."

He warmed inside. "You remembered," he said.

"Of course I did. You've been coming in here the last few days. I never forget a face or a name. How's the big bug shoot? Glamorous? Everything you'd hoped? Is our little town going to be in *National Geographic*?"

"It's coming along just fine. I've got some great pictures back at the motel," Bill said, leaning forward onto the counter and grinning. "But I don't think you'll be seeing anything in *National Geographic*."

Joanna laughed. "That's a shame," she said. "I hope you're enjoying it here."

"I am. I'm thinking I may stick around 'til Thursday. Maybe do another piece on your festival. That seems to be the real story here."

"Well, look at you. We might make a local of you yet."

A man in a faded black-and-red Texaco hat interrupted. "Thanks, Jo," he said, and dropped a dollar and some change on the counter.

Joanna lent her attention to the older man. "Thanks, Paul. Take care, now."

Bill looked up at the man. *I should fucking kill you! We were talking. Get lost before I put this goddamned cigarette out in your fucking eye, you old faggot!* Bill moved a hand to his lap where he could feel the shape of the switchblade (*click-click... click...*) in his pocket. It would be so easy to just stand up and drive the blade into the side of the man's head, right in the temple. But he stopped himself, biting down hard on the inside of his cheek until he tasted blood. He couldn't lose focus. He was here for Joanna, to study her, not to kill some old hick who could never understand their connection. He was too smart to ever act on an urge brought about by anger, though. That was how people got caught. Their emotions got the best of them, and consequence took a backseat to satisfying a rabid craving for blood.

The man turned and walked away.

Bill shifted in his seat, watching as he exited the diner. How easy it would be to follow him out to the street and bash his brains in with a chunk of asphalt. Maybe another time. He was here for something far more important. He was here to work on his craft. He would capture Joanna's essence. He would soon immortalize her, and someday people would be able to see what *he* saw and understand why he'd had to kill her. But like any great artist, he needed to be able to understand his subject—his muse—before he attempted to define her to the world.

"That was Paul Donniger," Joanna said, recapturing Bill's attention. "Old fool's been drinking himself stupid for as long as I can remember. Last week he rear-ended a school bus. No one was hurt, but I think they're finally going to take his license for good."

"Every town has one," Bill said, immediately thinking of his father.

"That's the truth," Joanna said, sighing. "Okay, one coffee, coming up." She turned and headed to the waitress station.

She walked so gracefully, each step so purposeful and clean. Pure. Perfect. And she'd remembered his name. Oh God, how good that had felt. He couldn't believe she remembered.

"I remembered too," Bill said softly, so completely lost in the idea of her.

Joanna stopped and turned back. "You say something, hon?"

His words were never meant to be spoken aloud. He'd got caught up in his own thoughts. But instead of retreating from the situation, he repeated himself awkwardly. He couldn't control himself; he needed her to know. "I remembered too," he said, almost yelled, leaning forward on the counter.

"Remembered what?" she said, puzzled.

"Your name... I remembered your name. It's Joanna."

Joanna looked at the waitress standing at the end of the counter, and the two exchanged a funny look. She turned back to Bill. "Oh. Okay. Glad to hear it." She continued to the coffee machine.

Too eager. She doesn't care that you know her name. She knew yours because it's her job. It's all a job to her. That's it. Can't you see that?

It was his father's voice again.

Bill tamped out his cigarette in the ashtray, reached into his pack, and fingered out another. He lit it while Joanna poured his coffee and talked with the waitress down at the other end. The two women giggled a few times, looking his way.

They're laughing at you. They think you're a fool. A stupid, pathetic little fool who couldn't even get a hard-on if he tried.

Bill squeezed his temples and closed his eyes, tipping his head down.

"So you remembered my name, huh?" Joanna set the mug in front of him. "That's more than I can say for most of the folks just passing through. I'm usually '*Hey You*' or '*Miss*' or my favorite, '*Hey, Toots.*'"

Bill didn't answer. His head was pounding.

"You okay?" Joanna asked.

After a few seconds, he removed his fingers from his temples and looked up. "Headache," he said. "Migraine. I get 'em bad sometimes."

"Oh, geez, I get those every so often. They're godawful. I might have some Excedrin in the back, if you need it."

"I'll be okay. The caffeine in this coffee should do the trick." Then without missing a beat he glanced at the nametag on Joanna's blouse and changed the subject. "I know it says it on your shirt, but I remembered your name, too. I just wanted you to know."

Joanna cocked her head half-sideways and wrinkled her nose. "Okay, I believe you. You sure you don't want any Excedrin or something to eat? You look a little pale. Got some fresh pies from Peggy Joslin. She makes the best in town."

"No. Not hungry. The coffee'll be just fine."

"Okay, then. Give me a holler if you need anything."

"What do I owe you?" Bill reached for his wallet.

"For the coffee? It's on the house, hon. But let me know if you change your mind about the pie or the pills."

Joanna turned and walked away.

For the next few minutes, Bill sat and drank his coffee, sipping it slowly while the headache passed. They never lasted too long and only seemed to come when his father's voice presented itself, screaming behind his ear. This one had been particularly bad, though.

He watched Joanna discreetly from the corner of his eye as she worked. Occasionally, his mind wandered to areas he didn't expect: Glimpses of his hands on her soft flesh. Her warm breath on his neck. The smell of her. The taste of her. She was perfection, and he had to have her. But in what way? For a moment, he wasn't sure. For a moment, he wondered what it would be like to be inside of her hot, slick flesh.

"Bill, the photographer. I told you I'd see you again," someone said, breaking his concentration.

Bill turned and saw the sheriff leaning against the counter a few seats away.

"Hello," Bill said. "Had a feeling I'd see you, too." This was true, and the feeling was not a good one. The feeling was dread. It was one thing for Joanna to recognize him and remember his name. (*Soon she won't be alive to recall me to anyone.*) But it was another for him to be recognized around town by law enforcement. How many tourists did Heartsridge see this time of year? A few thousand? More? And how many of them would the sheriff remember when they were all gone? At least one, Bill now knew for certain, and that was no good.

"Yeah, you'll see me here just about every morning," Gaines said. "Best coffee in town."

Bill forced a pleasant look onto his face but kept his head angled away so as to not give a full look at his face this time.

Joanna spotted Gaines and made her way down the counter. "Morning, Calvin."

"Hey, Jo. Can I just grab a large black to go? I'm in a bit of a hurry this morning."

"Sure thing," she said, and smiled. "Oh and I finished that necklace you wanted."

"Already? That was quick," Gaines said.

"Well, you seemed excited about it so I wanted to make sure I got it done sooner rather than later. Turns out I'm a bit quicker than I gave myself credit for."

"I guess so," Gaines said. "Want me to pay you now?" He reached for his back pocket.

"Can't this second. It's in my car at the moment. Think you can stop by this afternoon? I can run out and grab it when I'm not so busy." Joanna looked down the counter and gestured to the full restaurant.

With Gaines and Joanna caught up in conversation, Bill decided to make his exit undetected, stepping back off the stool and drifting away like smoke in the breeze. He walked out the door as an elderly couple entered. He didn't look back until he was across the street.

Outside, he watched from his truck, looking in through the diner's front window, the window he'd watched Joanna through the previous two nights and where he would watch her later. Gaines peered around, looking for Bill, the photographer from New Hampshire, but seemed to give up rather quickly.

"Nice knowing you, Sheriff," Bill said, and smiled. "See you never." Then his eyes settled on Joanna, who was walking back toward Gaines with a to-go cup of coffee in her hand. "I'll see *you* later, darling."

CHAPTER 22

"Hey, Ali," said Elsie Francis, the heavyset, gum-chewing red-head who ran the Ciao Bella Nail Salon in Heartsridge. "Wasn't expecting you today."

"I know, Else. I was hoping you could squeeze me in. I'm in a bit of a rush. Think you can help me?"

Elsie smiled and looked around the room. Two other women—employees—were sitting in the back at manicure tables, reading magazines, empty chairs across from them. "It's nine o'clock on a Tuesday morning, not exactly our busiest hour," Elsie said. "I think we can fit you in."

Allison may have been the mayor's wife, but she was never one to abuse her influence over people. Knowing she could if she ever needed to was just as good. Showing it was classless, she had always thought. What good was power if she needed to prove to people she had it?

Allison reached over and touched Elsie's arm. "Oh, you're a lifesaver. Thank you, thank you, my dear."

"Don't mention it. C'mon over, I'll do you myself. We haven't

195

seen you in a while."

"In too long," Allison said. "I've been so busy these days." She followed Elsie to the back of the salon, taking a seat in front of a nail table.

Elsie dropped down across from her. "Let's see those hands."

Allison put her hands on the table.

"Oh wow. It *has* been too long," Elsie joked. She took Allison's hands in her own and inspected them. There was power in Elsie's hands—a soft, precise power that suggested long years of doing the same delicate task with hard conviction. "Geez, have you been biting them or running them through a wood chipper?" She flipped them over and back again a few times.

Allison laughed. "Old habits, I'm afraid. Been a little anxious lately."

"We got quite a job ahead of us." Elsie picked up a cotton ball and pressed it against the mouth of an acetone bottle, tipping it upside down quickly and then righting it. "Gimme those," she said, and in rapid succession she swabbed each one of Allison's nails. The liquid sat wet on Allison's skin for only a moment and then evaporated with a cold breath. Elsie fished through a drawer in front of her, found a nail-file, and went to work. "How's that handsome husband of yours?"

Allison snorted. "Hah, what handsome husband? Harry, you mean? Maybe fifteen years and thirty pounds ago. You try sleeping next to that snoring machine every night, or watching him pick his teeth with the corner of a matchbook, sitting in his underwear watching *Jeopardy*, screaming the wrong answers at the TV. After fifteen years of that, I forget what handsome is."

Elsie laughed and shook her head. "Oh, you're terrible. At this point, I'd take any man who can keep me warm at night."

Allison smiled, but sidestepped the subject of Elsie's failing love life. She was here for a very specific reason. "Are you doing the festival again this year?" she asked. "You did well the last few years, didn't you?"

"'Did well?' That's an understatement." Elsie huffed, her thick chest heaving with excitement. "We did *great* is more like it! Saw more money in those four days than I do in three months here. And this year me and the girls are stepping it up a notch. We're doing nails, face painting for kids, a whole bunch of stuff. We even have some homemade creams and lotions to sell."

Allison brightened, feigning excitement for Elsie. Not that she wasn't happy for her, but she had an agenda that required all of her focus. "I guess you weren't kidding. It sounds like you've really got a good thing figured out."

"You got that right," Elsie said, sobering. "So what's got you so tense that you almost chewed your fingers down to the knuckle?"

Allison conjured a serious face for a moment and then shook it away. "Don't worry. I'm fine. It's nothing really." Dramatic pause. "Well, actually it's not nothing, but I'm not supposed to talk about it. It's pretty serious. The sheriff's department is involved."

Sheriff's department. She used those two words deliberately. Heartsridge didn't see a lot of excitement, so anytime law enforcement was mentioned, people listened. They needed that little bit of exhilaration in their lives. And once they got a taste, they were like sharks that had smelled blood.

"C'mon, Ali. You know the deal here. This place is just like the doctor's office. What you say here stays here. It never leaves these four walls."

The corners of Allison's lips twitched, threatening to curl up into a sardonic grin, but she fought it, never breaking from her act. She knew that what Elsie had just said was very untrue. That was the point, though, wasn't it—to get the story out there? To start the smear campaign against Kara Price, the girl spreading lies about her husband. What was said inside Ciao Bella most certainly did—barring some sort of divine intervention—leave those four walls. It left those four walls and spilled out into the street like the angry, charging bulls of Pamplona, eager to find something—anything and anyone—to trample and gore. Ciao Bella was the ocean that fed the rivers of gossip, and the rivers all flowed to the dining room tables of Heartsridge's residents, where rumor-fueled conversations took place over cold glasses of milk and pork roasts and mashed potatoes.

Allison cocked her head slightly off-center. "Well, I suppose it really doesn't matter. You're probably going to hear it sooner or later, anyway," she said. "You might as well hear it from a reliable source before the story gets all turned around and inside out."

Beads of sweat started to tickle the back of Allison's neck as her skin flushed from nerves. Suddenly, the manicurist's light she sat under seemed all too much like an interrogation lamp. But why should she feel that she was doing something wrong? She was only getting the truth out there before the lies, right?

"That's the spirit, doll. Let it out." Elsie smirked like a kid who'd coaxed a parent into buying them a new toy. All she cared about was the gossip, not about how getting it might affect the person spilling it. It was selfish business.

In Allison's case, the effect of sharing the information was entirely the point. In fact, prior to going to bed the night before, her fingernails were freshly done from her visit to High Wave Salon over in West Elm. She had been going there for the last three months. That was the real reason Elsie hadn't seen her in a while. The truth was that they did a much better job. Regardless, Allison had removed the fresh coat from High Wave and chewed her nails so she would seem in dire need of Elsie's services when she arrived (deep down, part of her knew that the nail-biting had not been voluntary). Ciao Bella and Elsie Francis were merely tools she would use to get a job done. Nothing more. The illusion of friendship may have seemed present when the two women sat across from one another at that manicure table, but no true allegiances existed. And that was what she was counting on: the moment she walked out that front door, Elsie would spill the gossip to anyone who would listen. Allison would never be foolish enough to think otherwise.

"I don't know if you know this or not, but when Harry became mayor, he started an internship program for high school students," Allison said. "The kind of thing for kids who are interested in a summer job or want to get a look at what goes into running a town. A lot of them just want to have something to put on their resumes when they enter the job force. It's been pretty successful, too. Had a lot of good feedback over the years."

Elsie nodded as she filed. "Yeah, I remember Ruth Wheeler mentioning it when her daughter worked down at town hall last summer. That's a good thing your husband's done."

"Yes, I think so. Or at least, I thought so. It only takes one person to ruin a good thing like that. And I'm afraid that's what may've happened."

Elsie's face lit up with curiosity. "Whadya mean?"

Time to sell it, Allison. Lay it on thick.

But she didn't need to sell anything. The words she was about to speak were very real. And in the midst of this thought she recalled the theater classes she had taken while attending Emerson College. She'd always wanted to be an actress. But she'd never had the opportunity—or the guts (were the two really so different?)—to pursue her passion. On her first day of class, her teacher had offered what he regarded as the most valuable piece of advice he'd been given about acting. Pacing back and forth across the stage, he'd said: "My future thespians, if you wish to give a convincing performance, you must find a real emotion deep within yourself, and then you must nurture it until it becomes you. Then, and only then, will an audience give themselves to you." That was what she was doing now.

"God, I don't even want to say it," Allison said, shaking her head and looking pained. "It makes it seem so real when the words come out of my mouth. And I know it's not, but still, it doesn't make it any easier."

She did know it wasn't true. She did! That girl was lying. Her husband—her Harry—would never do something like that.

Honey, you don't believe her, do you? Harry had asked her.

And she was sure she didn't. Wasn't she?

"Oh, geez, I guess it *is* serious," Elsie said. She put a bowl of warm, soapy water on the table and guided Allison's free hand into it. "All right, continue, I'm listening."

Allison leaned her head down, rubbed an itch on her nose with the back of her wrist, and then straightened. "Apparently one of the students working down at his office—a girl—decided to start a nasty rumor about Harry. It's just so obvious she's doing it for attention."

"Really?" Elsie said. "What's she saying?"

Allison bit her lip, looked down, and then up into Elsie's eyes. "The worst things, Elsie… the worst kind of things you can imagine. The girl is sick, I'm sure of it. Mentally ill. The stuff she is accusing him of is just so terrible." Allison closed her eyes dramatically—a slow, thoughtful blink. *Do you see how hard this is for me?* the look said. "She's saying he assaulted her… put his hands on her."

The nail-filing stopped. Allison took that as her cue. She met Elsie's eyes again, checking her audience. The beautician was roped. "What?" Elsie said, almost yelling it.

Allison looked nervously at the two women on the other side of the room then back to Elsie. "Quiet, quiet."

But of course she wanted Elsie to be too loud. It was all for show. The more tightly someone asked that a secret be contained, the faster it seemed to spread. It was as if the information were a hot coal fresh from the fire, glowing white hot, and whoever touched it had no choice but to hold it for only the briefest time before tossing it to another, who would in turn do the same. The hotter the ember, the longer it burned, and the more people it reached. And this baby was one hot mother.

Appearing to rein herself in, Elsie said, "I'm sorry, but… *what?* That's insane. I don't believe it." She was whispering now, but it was somehow louder than her natural voice. "Harry? Are you joking?" She trailed off into a headshake.

The women in the back continued to read their magazines. They were more than likely pretending now, turning the pages at regular intervals, staring blankly at blurred words and pictures as they focused all their efforts on eavesdropping.

"It gets worse," Allison said, "there's more."

"You bet your ass there's more. There better be. You can't leave me hanging like that. I need details, hon."

"She's saying he raped her. Can you believe that? My Harry, raping a fifteen-year-old girl? Not to mention the fact that at the time she claims this to have happened, Harry was home. I know it for a fact. I called him from my sister's when I was away on Saturday. I'm sure the sheriff will be able to check the phone records soon enough. That will put an end to this nonsense. But dammit, Elsie, this is just so unfair. This could really damage

Harry's career, and he's worked so hard. You know how people are when they hear a rumor—they believe what they want, whether it's true or not."

Why had she just lied? She'd never called him.

She knew Harry could never do these things he was accused of. His character was strong enough to stand up to an unfounded accusation like this alone without her adding false alibis to the story. There was no evidence he had done anything at all. It was only a mixed-up high school girl crying wolf. Maybe she had a few bumps and bruises, but that didn't prove anything.

So why had she just lied?

"Jesus, Ali, are you serious?" Elsie said, completely captivated. "I thought you might have something big on your mind, but nothing like this. This is full-blown. Like right out of a movie." Elsie was high with excitement, her face glowing with questions. It was obvious she was trying to hide it, but she was doing a pitiful job.

"I'm afraid I am serious," Allison said. "And the worst part is that there really isn't much we can do other than wait for the sheriff to do his job. I just feel so vulnerable. Someone can say whatever they want about you, and the next thing you know your life is upside down. I'm sure once they prove that this girl is lying everything will be okay. But what if the damage is already done? That's what really scares me. I think it scares Harry, too, but he'd never admit that outright."

"I'm so sorry. I can't believe it." Elsie's gears slowly started to turn, her jaw reengaging as she began to chew her gum again. Then the nail file started up, and she carried on: "Who is she, anyway?"

"The girl?"

"No... Mother Teresa. *Yes,* the girl. Who else would I mean?" Elsie bobbed with laughter again.

"Her name is Kara Price. I don't know her or the family. I don't think they go to our church—or any church, from the sound of it—otherwise I don't think this'd be happening. Probably godless people."

Elsie's face twisted into a painful look of concentration, as though she were searching her brain for a face to match the name. Then—*Eureka!*—she found something. "Price? Get out! I know a Price... Ellie Price. I'm surprised *you* don't. She's a nice woman. Comes in here about once a month. You'd think it wasn't possible to stay off your radar, Ali, especially in a town this size. Can't say I know her too well, though."

"She must be Kara's mother," Allison said. "And something tells me they aren't the kind of people I'd want on my radar. I can only imagine what type of person it takes to raise a girl capable of such awful deceitfulness. It's deranged, is what it is."

"Fair enough," Elsie said. "But like I was saying, she always seemed like a kind woman. But again, I don't really know her. She isn't a huge talker, if I recall. She's a relaxing type. Closes her eyes and doesn't speak when I work on her. Some people do that. They find the whole thing calming. And I guess I understand that. Some people like to chat, others don't."

"I guess you know what type I am. I wasn't supposed to say a word about this. Harry would kill me if he knew." Allison said, shaking her head. "Did that woman ever mention her daughter? Say she had emotional problems or anything?"

"Hah. Honey, all teenage girls have emotional problems. Don't you remember being young? The hormones of puberty? But I don't recall her ever saying anything like that, no. I mean I knew she had a daughter, but that's about the extent of it. Like I said, she doesn't really talk too much when she comes in."

"I know. I'm just looking for anything to..." Allison trailed off into tears. Her acting teacher would be so proud. "I'm sorry. Oh, just look at me. I'm the mayor's wife. I'm supposed to be composed. I guess I'm still in shock about this whole thing. I only found out yesterday, and with the festival coming up... this just couldn't have come at a worse time."

"Oh, please, honey, don't apologize. Here, take this." Elsie handed Allison a paper towel.

Allison wiped her eyes. "I just don't get it. What would make a girl say such terrible things?"

"Well, hon, I think you probably hit the nail on the head earlier."

"What do you mean?" Allison folded the paper towel and dropped it on her lap.

"Attention. The girl probably just wants attention. What kid doesn't?" Elsie dabbed Allison's fingers with another cold swab of acetone. "Harry's a teddy bear, I can tell. Not a mean bone in his body. In my line of work, being in the service industry, you learn how to read people. And he's one of the good ones. You lucked out, Ali, really. Don't let some high school girl with something to prove make you doubt that."

Oh, how wrong Elsie was. There *were* mean bones in Harry's body—and more than a few. Allison had seen them. There were times when Harry lost his temper, never in public, but behind closed doors. Usually it was when he was drunk, but not always. He'd frightened her on more than a few occasions, to the point where she'd left and gone to her sister's for the night. It was in these times, and only these times, that she was thankful they had no children; she could only imagine the toll her husband's erratic behavior would have taken on them. These occurrences of unwarranted rage were always followed by an apology the next day, and gradually things always seemed to return to normal. But it sent a chill down her spine. When it happened, it was like Harry was a different person. And there was that scar on his hand, too, of course.

That scar, the thick white one on his knuckle. Harry had told her the story behind it the day after they got engaged. It almost made her reconsider marrying him altogether. But he'd convinced her otherwise, said it was just a stupid mistake from childhood. It was hardly the innocent adolescent mistake he'd made it out to be, though. He had waited after school with a lead pipe for that bully and shattered his kneecaps. Then he beat the kid's face to a pulp with his bare hands and sent him to the hospital in a coma. It was all over a pair of sneakers the boy had taken from him. Allison always suspected that she and her husband shared two vastly different definitions of the word "mistake." Mistakes could be forgiven and repaired with time—reconciled. The only reason Harry never got in trouble was because by the time the kid came out of his coma, he didn't remember anything. And by then the family had moved out of town to live closer to the hospital where the kid was slumbering away in a dreamless sleep, living a counterfeit childhood, breathing and being fed through tubes.

Only two people knew that secret about Harry: Harry's mother was one, and Allison was the other. Allison had unknowingly accepted membership to an exclusive club when Harry had told her that secret, and it was a membership she'd never wanted. Up until the day of her wedding, it had been in the back of her mind, but after she said "I do" there was no returning the keys to the clubhouse. Allison felt she would have been better off never knowing. Sometimes she wished he'd lied to her about it when she asked him how he'd gotten the scar, said something—anything—but the brutal truth. Lying isn't always bad, after all, not when you're protecting someone from the truth. Not when your intentions are…

(*You don't believe her, do you?... I was home doing yard work...
The sheriff has nothing... The little bitch is trying to ruin me... She's
lying.*)

Allison's mind stalled for a moment. She physically shook her
head to clear the thoughts.

"You okay?" Elsie asked.

"Yes. Sorry," Allison said, and then continued. "I guess attention is just the only motive I can think of. Why else would she do
this? Harry can't come up with any reason she would have it out
for him. She'd only worked for him a day. Not exactly enough
time to hate your boss. I just don't get it. Why Harry?"

"Who knows? Kids these days are all screwed up. That's why
I never had any."

Allison had a hard time believing this was the real reason Elsie Francis was sans children at the ripe age of forty-one.
Obnoxious, overweight, and single were the first three things
that came to mind. It made much more sense than something as
broad as "kids these days are all screwed up."

With those last snide thoughts, Allison suddenly became
aware of the anger inside her. It was a hidden anger, teetering on
the knife's edge of stress and grief, being misdirected at Elsie
Francis. And she wasn't even sure what she was angry about. Kara Price and her lies, or was it Harry? A notion struck her at once
and tightened her stomach: Maybe she was mad at her husband
because somewhere inside her she was starting to realize that
maybe... maybe he was capable of much more than she gave him
credit for.

*Enough of those thoughts, Allison. You've been married to him for
twenty years. You know this man.*

Allison altogether avoided Elsie's comment about having
children. It was not the avenue this conversation needed to go

down. "I wish there was something I could do to make this all just go away," she said.

"Oh I wouldn't worry about it too much. From what you tell me it sounds like this girl's just throwing stones. Anyone who knows Harry won't think twice. This too shall pass," Elsie said. "Let the cops do their jobs. Sheriff Gaines is a smart enough fella. I'm sure it won't be too difficult to prove a fifteen-year-old kid is just out for kicks. I've known Harry as long as I can remember, and he has never been anything but a nice, good man."

"None of it makes sense." Allison said. "We'll probably never know why she's doing this. But I guess you're right—the teenage brain isn't exactly rational. Worst thing is that after this is all over and settled, she'll probably get a slap on the wrist. But Harry... Harry's name will be forever tied to that awful word: rape."

"Nonsense. I think you're wrong. I for one don't believe a word of it, and I promise you I'm not just saying that because, well, let's face it, you're the mayor's wife, and I feel obligated. That forward enough for ya?" Elsie laughed again.

In this moment, Allison saw that she'd succeeded in her intents. She didn't understand this from Elsie's words; it was her demeanor—the lightness with which Elsie had been receiving this information. There had never been any revulsion in her eyes, no placation in her voice, nothing that would suggest a woman masking her true feelings. Elsie's sense of humor was a good indicator, too. The show of jokes in the wake of such heavy news could only mean that Elsie was on board with the story. *The truth! It's not a story,* a voice screamed in her head.

"Thanks, Elsie. That means a lot."

"What'd the sheriff say? Has he offered any insights? Tell you what *he* thinks happened?"

Allison cleared her throat. The rest of this was a breeze. She was home free. "Harry talked with Calvin Gaines yesterday. He came to his office in the morning. I don't know exactly what was said, but from what Harry told me, it sounded like the sheriff thinks the girl is making it up, too."

"Well then, there you go. Don't sweat it."

"Easier said than done. But maybe you're right."

Yes. Maybe she was right. She shouldn't sweat it. Perhaps this too would pass, and perhaps the doubt she felt, the burgeoning suspicion of her husband's honesty, was all just a normal reaction.

But something still lingered. There was a question, one she'd been trying to ignore, and it flashed bright and insistently in her mind, refusing to go away until she acknowledged it: *If* Harry had (and she stressed *if*) done these things, would she still lie to protect him... to protect *them*? To protect herself?

And the scariest thing about that question was that she didn't know the answer.

"Have you gone and talked to the girl yourself?" Elsie asked. "Try to appeal to her decency?"

"No. Harry wouldn't allow that," Allison said, her tone becoming almost impatient but not rude. "You know, I think I'd like to change the subject. Is that okay?"

Her job was done now. She'd planted the seed. It wouldn't be long until it germinated and broke through the soil.

Elsie held up her hand and nodded. "Not a problem, doll. I can tell this ain't something you want to talk about. Sorry if I pried a little too much."

"No. Not at all," Allison said, and for the next twenty-five minutes, the two women talked about anything else. They talked about the lotions and creams. They talked about which vitamins made their skin glow and which made their hair thick and shiny. They talked about the cicadas. Allison learned a trick to use to remove wine stains from clothes. They spoke of actors on whom each had crushes—childhood and currently. They spoke of many things, but they did not speak of Harry Bennett and Kara Price again. Allison knew that talk would be saved for when she was gone from the salon, when the chatterboxes could gossip amongst themselves unabated.

That was fine with Allison. She'd served her purpose. She'd protected herself and her husband, made sure the truth got out there before the lies. Yes, that was what she'd done. She'd protected them. And Harry thought they weren't a team? This would show him otherwise.

When Allison finally did leave, it was with great relief. She stepped out into the warm morning air. Closing her eyes briefly, she took in the sweet smell of spring. She breathed deep, happy to be free of the sharp scents of acetone and nail polish and the constant smacking of Elsie Francis's gum. The cicadas were going full at it, and the sound was, as she'd always felt it to be, peaceful and calming.

She headed down the sidewalk, along to the next stop on her campaign, Peggy Joslin's bakery. She felt like Johnny Appleseed, her bag of seed a bag of gossip. And she would be careful how she sowed.

But dear God, what if Harry actually had…

No. Never mind. He never would. That was just foolish.

CHAPTER 23

Catherine was late.

She'd called ahead that morning and spoken with Ellie Price about coming to see Kara, but that was before Sheriff Gaines had called a meeting to go over the security and traffic plans for the festival. It had lasted nearly all afternoon, and after the meeting, Gaines had finally said what she'd been anticipating. He made it clear that he wasn't going to be dedicating all his resources to the Kara Price case at the moment. It simply wasn't the time, and there were no new leads to go on. Of course he would stick to his word and still allow Catherine to go talk to Kara, but that was with an understanding that if she didn't find any "actionable evidence," then she was to leave it alone until after the festival. They weren't closing the case by any means. Definitely not. They were only tabling it until they had the resources to pursue it properly, *after* the festival. And did she understand that?

She had understood, albeit grudgingly.

But she was still late.

Catherine should've been at the Prices' at three o'clock. That was what she'd told Ellie when they'd spoken on the phone. Now it was almost a quarter of five. She stepped out of her cruiser and walked up the driveway.

Looking up, Catherine recognized Kara's bedroom window. It had only been a few nights before that she had been glancing out of it nervously as she tried to comfort Kara. At the time, she had seen the view from the window but never really acknowledged the things she was seeing or where they were in relation to the rest of the world. Now to her left was the weathered picnic table sitting beneath the three pine trees, and beyond that was the mulched garden bed with the granite birdbath—all things that she'd seen previously from the window, but things that hadn't made sense to her at the time. Suddenly she felt as if something in her head had come into focus—a new understanding—and the space around became uncomfortably familiar.

Catherine knocked on the door.

Ellie opened it after a few moments.

"Hello, Mrs. Price. Sorry I'm late. Hope I didn't keep you waiting. Got hung up down—"

"Hi, Deputy. Nice of you to show up," Ellie interrupted coldly.

Okay, so there it was. There would be no more superficial kindness from the Prices. They were fed up. Their daughter had been raped, and she'd identified her attacker, but still, nothing had been done. Their faith in the law was lost. The public service they'd paid for, bit by bit from their paychecks through taxes over the years, had proved unreliable and useless.

"You're right. There's no excuse. I can only imagine how frustrated you must be at this point," Catherine said, ashamed.

Ellie laughed derisively. "Ha! Yeah. I guess you could say we're frustrated. Sure. That's one way to put it."

Catherine couldn't help but notice that Ellie had made no

gestures to suggest she was ever going to invite her in. "I know this has been tough. And I wouldn't be any less upset if I were in your shoes. In fact, I'd probably be handling it worse. It may seem like nothing is being done, but I assure you I am not letting this go. I want to talk to Kara again and see if I can find something useful. The other night when we were here, emotions were running high, and it's easy for important details to be skipped over or forgotten when that's the case."

"Useful? How much more useful could she be? She told you who did it. Isn't that enough? The sheriff's department has done squat with that information. Why would anything be different with this?"

"Well, I'm sure it seems that way, but we need to find a way to implicate—"

"Yes, I know, there isn't enough evidence. That's all I've been hearing."

Catherine felt her temper starting to slip. Didn't this woman know Catherine was the only person fighting for her daughter? "No. There isn't. But that's why I'm here. I need every detail, otherwise that bastard is going to go free—" Catherine caught herself. "Listen. I'm only trying to help, Mrs. Price. If you'd like me to leave, then just say so and I will."

Ellie's face darkened briefly and then went flat. "She's around back, if you want to speak with her." She opened the screen door and stepped aside. "Straight through to the back porch."

"Thank you, ma'am." Catherine took a step forward.

"And listen to me"—Ellie gated the doorway with her arm, forcing Catherine to stop—"she seems to be doing okay today, so don't push her. I want that monster in jail, but not at the cost of my daughter's sanity."

"Of course not," Catherine said. "We all want the same thing, here."

"I'm sure we do," Ellie said with a hint of hostility. Then she lifted her arm.

———————

Kara sat on the porch steps, rubbing the dog's ears, scratching under his collar and behind his head, crooning those nonsensical, almost infantile words that only a pet-owner can conjure. She was in good spirits today. After a moment, she stopped and picked up the tennis ball between her feet. Without hesitation she pitched it to the back of the yard. Geronimo, their chocolate Labrador, broke away from the affection and darted after the ball, snatching it mid-bounce before it disappeared into the tiger lilies.

"Good boy," she said heartily.

He returned to her, proud as ever, tennis ball clenched in his jaw, as if he hadn't just done the same thing twenty-five times in a row and received the exact same praise each time. Kara wondered whether he remembered those previous fetches, or if his mind reset each time she threw the ball. Or perhaps the dog just had an innate ability to release the past and simply enjoy the moment no matter what had come before. Maybe to the dog, the game of fetch was very much like Kara's lip was for her: a sort of talisman that summoned her mind to the present. She smirked at that thought, not because it was really that funny, but because: was she really trying to relate to a dog?

"God, Kara, you've been away from society too long," she said, amused.

From behind her came the sound of voices, her mother and another woman. They were speaking in the front of the house.

Geronimo forced his snout into Kara's lap, trying to drop the slimy tennis ball again. "Hold on, Mo," Kara said, absently rubbing his head while she listened. She figured it out after a moment: the second voice belonged to Deputy Carlisle. Kara recognized the underlying toughness of it. Almost immediately she remembered that her mother had mentioned to her that someone from the sheriff's department might be coming by that afternoon to speak with her again. Her stomach tightened. Another round of *Can You Tell Me What Happened?* She hated that game. There were no winners. It was a fool's game. If she'd known more than what she had already said, she would've said it.

"Great. You want to take my place, Mo?" She looked down at the dog. His head was cocked at an angle, his eyes honest with curiosity and anticipation. All he cared about was another round of fetch. She envied him. "I didn't think so," Kara said, and pried the tennis ball from his mouth. She threw it to the end of the yard and Geronimo gave chase.

The screen door yawned open behind her and then shut solidly, the spring clattering against the wooden frame. Then came the sound of footsteps behind her. There was a timid quality to them. It was something she had grown to recognize in the last few days. It was the sound of people walking on eggshells. *Don't frighten the wounded pup.*

"Kara?" Catherine said. "It's Deputy Carlisle, we met the other night. You have a few minutes to talk?"

Kara turned around, looking over her shoulder. "Okay, I guess."

Catherine took a few steps closer. "You mind if I sit?"

"Sure."

Geronimo returned, tail wagging, ball in mouth.

Kara once again pried the ball free, but this time she didn't throw it. Instead, she put it on the ground behind her back and let it roll away on the porch, leaving a thin, dark trail of slobber.

Geronimo sat, head cocked to the side, confused, and let out a small whimper.

"Go away, Mo," Kara said, scratching his head dismissively and pushing him gently aside.

Catherine took a seat next to Kara on the step. "Cute dog. What's his name?"

"Geronimo... We call him Mo." Kara wiped her hands on her jeans.

"Did your mom tell you I was coming?" Catherine asked.

Kara turned and regarded the woman. The Catherine Carlisle sitting beside her now, the one wearing a uniform, was a far cry from the woman who had consoled her in her bedroom wearing a T-shirt and jeans three days before. That woman had been Catherine Carlisle. *This* woman was *Deputy* Carlisle, the professional.

"She did," Kara said. "To be honest, I'd forgotten. I just remembered when I heard you talking out front."

"That's okay. I understand. I'm sure this is probably the last thing you want to talk about right now. I would've forgotten, too."

Kara forced a smile. She knew Catherine was trying to be amusing, but what Kara wanted right now wasn't for this woman to try to be on her level. All Kara was hearing was: *Hey, I can relate. I understand. I'm hip. I'm funny. Trust me. We're the same, you and I. Not so different after all. Now tell me about the rape and spare no details.*

"So what did you want to know? I already told you everything," Kara said.

Catherine removed her hat and tossed it beside her. Then she leaned back and rested on her hands, taking in the view of the back yard. Long sigh. "So how've you been holding up?"

"I'm doing all right," Kara said. "I think I'm ready to get back to my life soon. I can't stay home anymore. I'm going crazy."

"I think that's a good idea. It'll be good to surround yourself with your friends," Catherine said, followed by a short pause before she continued. "Listen, I want to get this right out there before this goes any further. If you don't want to talk, or if you want to tell me to take a hike, that's fine. I would completely understand. Especially after how little we've done to bring you and your family the justice you deserve. I also don't want to come down here and treat you like a child. If you want to answer some questions, that's great. It would make my job a lot easier. But if you don't, then that's fine too. I promise I won't keep anything from you, Kara. But you need to promise me the same. The lines of communication need to be fully open for this to be worthwhile. You understand?"

Kara said nothing at first but found she was nodding in subconscious agreement without meaning to.

"I need you to answer me, Kara. I need to hear it. I need to know you follow me, otherwise this is a waste of time for both of us."

Kara swallowed hard. "Yes. I understand."

"Okay. Good," Catherine said. She leaned forward, wiping the dust off her hands. "Now like I was saying, I don't want to keep anything from you, and I don't want to treat you like some little kid who can't handle the truth. So here it is. There is no evidence of the rape other than your bruises and your accusations, and that isn't enough. That's why Harry hasn't been picked up yet. Maybe you already know this, maybe you don't. I'm not sure what your parents have told you. But there it is. Without more, Harry won't get brought in... *ever*. I know it doesn't speak highly of the justice system. It's just the way it is, unfortunately. But you might not even really care about what happens to him anymore. Am I right? You just want this over with so you can get on with your life? I wouldn't blame you."

Again, Kara nodded unintentionally. She was captivated by the sudden, blunt honesty of Catherine. She'd expected more consoling dialogue, where the ultimate goal was to coerce information out of her with a gentle hand, but what she was getting instead was raw and real. And for the first time since being attacked, she felt she was being treated with respect and not pity. There were no fragile touches here. Just two equals having a conversation. "Yeah, I guess so," Kara said. "I am sick of the whole thing, to be honest. It just seems like it would be a lot easier to forget about the entire thing."

"I'm sure it does seem that way right now," Catherine said with slight hesitation. "But I hope you know how brave you were, Kara. Coming forward with this was not easy. I know that first hand."

"What do you mean?" Kara said. But what she was thinking was: *How on earth could you possibly know? You don't know how hard this was. Not unless...*

Catherine glanced down briefly, as if too ashamed to make eye contact with the world. "You're going to make me spell it out, aren't you? I thought I was being clear enough. But okay, fair is fair. I said I wouldn't keep anything from you." She laughed nervously, pausing for a moment. Then: "I was raped when I was just about your age, Kara. So when I tell you I know what you're going through, I'm not just saying it... I really do know."

Kara looked at her oddly but genuinely. She didn't know how to respond at first. Was this woman for real? Or was she just trying to gain trust? Kara didn't think so. After what she'd been through, she couldn't imagine a person lying about a thing like this. In fact, she would be willing to bet everything she cared about that Catherine was telling the truth. She could see it in her eyes and on her face. Perhaps a week ago she might not have recognized the look, but now she did. She did because it was staring her in the face every time she looked in the mirror.

"What happened?" Kara asked timidly. It was strange being on the other side of this line of questioning. But it was a good strange. Not that she was happy to hear of another's misfortune, but it put her at ease to be out of the spotlight, even if it was only for the moment.

"I trusted the wrong person, I guess you could say. A boyfriend from high school, a real slick kind of guy who always seemed to say the right thing at the right time." Catherine leaned closer to Kara as if she were about to impart some kind of secret knowledge. "Be careful of those types… trust me," she said earnestly. "Someone who seems too perfect is usually hiding something." She leaned back and continued. "Anyway, I dated him for a little while and things seemed great at first. The only bit of tension between us ever was that I refused to sleep with him because he was going off to college and I was one of those unlucky—or lucky, I still haven't figured that out—saps who actually wanted to save myself for the man I would marry. And he just wasn't it. For a little while a part of me thought he might be, but that was just young lust. I'm sure you're familiar with what I mean."

Kara's face flushed, and she flashed an embarrassed smile. "I'm sure I don't know what you're talking about—"

"Yeah, yeah. 'Course you do. I was your age once. I remember what it was like. It's just us girls here. You don't need to be shy. It's all normal teenage behavior, sweetie."

Kara gave a faint smirk and shook her head. Then she focused on her feet. She had never really considered anything she had ever done before as being lustful. That word just seemed so adult. Could she really think of herself that way? Doing adult things? Having adult feelings? It made her feel funny to think about it, and she didn't know why.

Catherine continued: "Anyway, he invited me to his prom, got me drunk—well to be fair, I got myself drunk, but he helped for sure—and then he took advantage of me. I don't remember a lot, but I remember enough." Catherine's face went cold and distant. "Enough to know that what happened was not consensual. He never talked to me again after that night, only smiled at me in the halls whenever I'd see him at school. God, I can still see the smarmy smile. Sometimes I just wanted to walk up to him and rip his damn lips off."

It was clear to Kara that Catherine was trying hard to speak easily about something that was quite difficult for her. And for a moment, the woman sitting beside her did not look like a grown woman at all. For a moment, what Kara saw was a scared little girl, something similar to herself but also very different.

"So what happened after?"

"What happened? Well… nothing. I never told a soul. Not until now, anyway." Catherine's face brightened, and the chilled look evaporated. "For a while, it was only me and him that knew what had happened that night. And then a little while after, he died in a car crash. That just left me. I was the only one who knew. And I'll tell you, it's a terrible thing to have to harbor a secret like that alone. Eats you up. It was like that for a long time, too… until now, I suppose. You're the first person I've actually ever told about this." She turned to Kara and smiled sincerely, nodding. There was a look of relief—or something like it—in her eyes. Perhaps it was the look of a burden lifted.

"Did you have something to do with his car accident?" Kara

asked, her eyes wide. She felt stupid immediately after that question passed through her lips.

Catherine let out a whooping laugh. "Ha! No, darling, I didn't. I'm no murderer. I mean I can't say I didn't think about getting revenge on him ever, but I never acted on anything. No, that accident was just the world's way of righting a wrong. That happens more than you'd think. Karma, I guess, if you believe in that sort of thing. I didn't always, but now I'm thinking maybe I do. I won't lie and say I wasn't happy when I found out he'd died. It sure didn't make dealing with what he'd done to me any easier, though. That part still, well, hurt like hell inside. It isn't easy to have something like that taken from you. It's losing a part of yourself, and you mourn it just like you'd mourn losing anything that was important to you: with time and strength."

"Does it ever change? Does it get easier?" Kara asked with a hint of desperation in her voice.

"I wish I could tell you it does. Unfortunately, it never gets easier, you only get used to it. And I know that's a tough truth to hear. But it will do you good to know that you can't forget a thing like that. It's a part of you now. A scar. It doesn't have to be who you are, but it is a part of you. You need to accept that you'll have to live with it. Don't run from it, just beat it back whenever it tries to consume you. That's how you win. It sure as hell isn't fair, I know, but it's the reality of the situation. And you have to be honest. Not with everything, if you know what I mean, but at least with yourself—that's most important. Don't live a lie. I know it may sound a little strange, or that I'm being a little harsh, but I think you understand what I'm trying to say. You do, don't you?"

"I guess so, yeah," Kara said. And she did. She'd always understood. Even when she'd convinced herself that forgetting about the rape and moving on was the best medicine, she'd understood.

"Sometimes I wish I'd spoken up and told someone," Catherine went on. "I don't know if anything would've come of it, but I should've tried, at least. I think it might have given me a better sense of justice. Death was too easy on him. I would've liked it better if the whole world knew what type of monster he was. Wounds heal a lot faster when you don't keep them covered, you know?"

"Yeah, well, sometimes I wish I'd done what you did and not told anyone. It would've been easier, if you ask me," Kara said.

Catherine leaned forward, rubbing her hands slowly on her shins. "I know you think that now. But believe me, it isn't. I always told myself that the reason I kept quiet was because I didn't want to give that bastard the satisfaction of taking anything else from me—like my pride, for instance—or I thought people would look at me different if they found out. Label me a tease who'd deserved it or something. But the truth is, I was just scared. That's all it ever boiled down to. I was afraid of what would happen. That's why I never spoke up. I just wanted to salvage my life. And back then I thought stuffing it under the rug was the only way to do that. It wasn't the best choice, now that I look back on it. Probably it's the reason I haven't ever had a decent romantic relationship. I never dealt with it like I should've."

"Why are you telling me all this?"

"Honestly, I don't know. I think at first I was trying to get you to trust me so you'd talk to me candidly. But now I don't know. It kind of just burst out of me. Maybe I just saw an opportunity to finally tell someone who could relate." Catherine shook her head. "Look at me. I'm supposed to be the grown-up here, and it turns out I might've been looking for support in you."

Kara straightened her posture and tried to elongate her body, as if for some reason she needed to show this woman that she could be strong. "I'm really sorry that happened to you, Miss Carlisle." She was stuck somewhere between Deputy and Catherine, so she settled on Miss. "But I still don't really understand what it is you want from me. I've already told you what happened. I'll admit maybe I've been a little afraid, and I've been trying to ignore what happened. But I promise I haven't kept anything from you."

Catherine sat up straight again. More professional. "I know. But did you ever think that maybe when you were in a rush to forget the attack, maybe you missed a few details about what occurred that evening? Things you might not even know you know? I'm not accusing you of doing this on purpose, but sometimes it happens. You were really upset at the time."

"I don't know. I guess so, maybe."

"Do you think I could ask you some questions? Would that be okay?" Catherine asked.

Kara folded her arms, cradling her elbows, and said, "I don't mind. Go ahead."

Catherine twisted at the waist to face Kara. "Okay. Now you feel free to stop at any time if you'd like."

"I'll be fine," Kara said.

"Can you start by telling me about Saturday again? Maybe tell me about work."

"Sure. Saturday was my first day. It was kind of dull, to be honest. I spent most of the time working with a woman—I think her name was Brenda—just filing papers and answering phones. I can't say I was looking forward to an entire summer of doing that, but I knew it would look good for college, so I guess it's worth it."

"Brenda Fahey," Catherine said. "I know her."

Kara nodded. "That's right, yeah."

"And when did you first meet Harry Bennett?" Catherine asked.

"He stopped in to introduce himself later in the day. And a few times when I was on the phone he walked by and stuck his head in but never said anything. I didn't really talk to him. Mostly he just worked with his door closed."

"Do you remember seeing him leave for the day?"

"Yes. He came in and told Brenda he was leaving. He said he had errands to run and work to do at his house. I didn't think twice about it at the time, but I remember Brenda making a comment after he walked out. She thought it was funny he told her he was leaving because she said he never told her when he was coming and going. Said he always came and left as he pleased. And she wasn't sure why he told her this time. It seemed like a joke, is all."

"Do you remember what time that was?"

"No. Not exactly," Kara said, lowering her arms over her stomach. "Maybe around three or four o'clock. I know we locked up at five, and he left an hour or two before that, so yeah, I'd say around three or four. Definitely."

"And what happened after he left?" Catherine asked, her questions coming faster now.

"Nothing," Kara said. "We just continued working until it was time to go home."

"And when you did leave, what then? When did you see Harry next?"

Kara narrowed her eyes, thinking. "Brenda showed me how to lock up the offices. That took a few minutes. Then she got in her car and left. I could have asked her for a ride, but I didn't want to be a bother, and it was nice out so I didn't mind walking. I left the parking lot and decided to take Union Street, you know, the road that goes by the grocery store, so that I could take the cut-through path that connects to Durham Street. I was about halfway there when I heard a car pull up beside me. It was a big red car. I'm not sure what kind. It drove alongside me for a second and I kept walking, ignoring it. Eventually I looked, I mean like really looked, and I recognized the driver. He smiled at me and said hello. It was Harry Bennett. He stopped me and asked what I thought of my first day working in the Mayor's Office. Then he asked where I lived, and when I told him, he said that it would be dark before I got home and that I shouldn't be walking the back roads all by myself. That's when he offered me a ride. I said no at first and said I liked to walk, but he kept insisting. And to be honest, I felt like I kind of had to say yes, you know? I mean, he was my boss and I didn't want to come off as rude. It just felt wrong to turn down a favor from the mayor. You know what I mean?"

"I do," Catherine said. "And I'm sure he knew it too."

Kara continued: "Okay. Well, after I got in, he turned around and started driving in the other direction. I didn't think anything about it at first because Union Street wasn't the best way to get to my house by car anyway. So I thought he was just going to take me back through town and drop me off that way. But he didn't. He turned before we even got back by Town Hall and drove toward Baker's Pond. He told me we were taking a detour. I didn't think anything of it at the time, but now that I think about it, he was acting kind of strange. He kept looking all around as if he was trying to find something. Like turning his head and taking extra long at each intersection, looking down every street. He seemed nervous, I guess. Fidgety. And he kept talking about how these bugs might ruin the Spring Festival and how important the festival was to the town. And he asked me how I felt about it. If I knew how important it was to the town."

"And what'd you say?"

"I said I did. I mean, I don't really go to it anymore. Not like I did when I was younger. It's not as fun when you aren't a ten-year-old. But I said I was aware of how important it was."

"Then what happened?"

"He got real quiet after that. He didn't speak again until we showed up at the water department. When we got there he pulled into a spot at the far end of the lot. I remember thinking that was weird too because the place was empty, he could've parked anywhere, and he chose a spot nowhere near the building. By then I sort of had an idea something was up. I mean, I had no idea what was actually about to happen, but I could sense something was wrong. He shut off the car and turned to me. Then he smiled at me all weird. His eyes were all watery and dark. It was almost like he was a completely different person from the man I'd met earlier. God, I can still see that face when I go to sleep at night. It was like he was possessed or something." Kara stalled for a moment and felt herself biting down on her lip. She caught herself and stopped, continuing with what she was saying. "He said he was going to teach me some respect. He called me a spoiled little brat or something along those lines... and that's when he hit me."

"Respect?" Catherine cut in. "Why would he say that? Had you done something that day that he'd gotten mad about? Been disrespectful?"

"I don't know. I don't think so," Kara said. "If I did, I don't know what it was. Like I said, I barely said twenty words to him."

"Okay. Go on."

"After he hit me, he got out of the car and started walking around to my door. I pushed down the lock but the window was down and I couldn't roll it up in time. He got the door open and he dragged me out and pushed me into the backseat. He was talking to himself the whole time. I remember that. It was really strange. He kept saying something about me being a liar. I couldn't really understand everything he was saying, but I kept hearing the word 'liar' over and over again… that and 'little bitch'. He kept calling me a little bitch with no respect. At first I tried to fight back, but he was too strong. He pinned my arms down, and eventually I just gave up and let him do what he wanted. I thought he might kill me if I didn't."

Kara brought her hand to her face and wiped her eyes. There were tears, but she couldn't remember crying.

"Are you okay?" Catherine asked, and put her hand on Kara's shoulder. "We can stop. We don't have to go any further with this if you—"

"No. I'm fine," Kara said, and stiffened her body. "Really. I am."

"You sure?"

"Yes. I wanna finish. I'm almost through."

"Go on, then."

"When he was done he told me to get out of his car. He told me that if I'd bled on anything that he'd come back and teach me another lesson. Then it was over and it all became kind of a blur. Almost like a bad dream. The next thing I know I was sitting there in the parking lot watching as his car drove away. I couldn't tell you if the whole thing had lasted two minutes or two hours."

"How did you get home?"

"I walked. Took the back roads so nobody would see me. My face was bleeding pretty badly, and I didn't want to have to explain to anyone what had happened to me. At that point I thought I would never tell anyone what had happened. I was sure of it. Anyway, I walked to the Saver Mart and took the path. Then I stopped and cleaned myself off at the creek before I went home."

Catherine sighed. This next question seemed as though it pained her to ask. "Do you remember anything funny about his body? Any distinguishable marks?"

"What do you mean?" Kara asked, confused.

"Like a birthmark or anything? Something that only certain people could know about? Certain people like his wife... or his doctor."

"Oh. No, I didn't notice anything. I had my eyes closed while he was... you know—"

"Okay. That's okay." Catherine put up a hand and waved it dismissively.

"I'm sorry. I can't think of anything more," Kara said. "Did I at least help a little?"

"You did, sweetie. You helped a lot. And you don't need to apologize. I'm the one who's sorry. I'm sorry I had to put you through that again."

There was a doubtful look shadowing Catherine's face. It was a look that told the truth behind her words. The expression was akin to the look on Geronimo's face when Kara ended their game of fetch. The look was disappointment.

"That's all right. It's not so hard to think about anymore," Kara said, a faint, reassuring smile surfacing. She wanted to show Catherine that everything was okay. That she would be okay. That everything would be okay. That whether or not Harry Bennett ever saw the inside of a jail cell would not change the fact that she, Kara, would find herself again.

But was that really true? Would everything really be okay? She couldn't know for sure. But what she did know was that the familiar taste of blood was on her tongue again. The familiar taste that came when she brought her mind to the present by way of her secret trick.

Kara wiped the back of her hand over her lips. When she pulled it away there was a thin streak of blood.

"You all right?" Catherine asked. "You're bleeding."

"Yeah, I'm fine. This stupid cut just won't heal," Kara said. "I don't know why. I've tried everything, but it won't heal. Every time I think it's getting better, it opens back up." She felt guilty for lying; she knew exactly why the cut wouldn't heal, but this time she didn't even remember toying with it.

"Here." Catherine handed Kara a tissue. "Take this and put pressure on it."

Kara took the tissue and did as she was instructed. "Thank you," she said.

And for the next few minutes, while the bleeding stopped, the two of them sat and looked out over the backyard, neither saying a word. There was nothing left to say. No questions left to ask. No answers left to give.

This moment was a peaceful pardon from their lives, a brief glimpse into the heart of something beautiful. The electric hum of the cicadas drowned out any unpleasant thoughts and swept away the rubble of both of their recently excavated minds. There, in those few minutes, there was only nature. There was only there. There was only then. And after a while, when the moment had run its course and the space between the two women filled with tired sighs, shifting postures, and the anticipation of parting words, Kara reached over and took Catherine's hand and held it tight. She thought Catherine might need that.

And she needed it, too.

Catherine waited until the Prices' house was out of view until she pulled the car over and began to cry. She cried for herself. For the joy of release from her secret. She cried because it still hurt. Because it felt good. But mostly she cried for Kara because there was nothing she could do for her.

Harry Bennett was going to get away with what he'd done.

Chapter 24

"Is it true, Dad? Is Kara Price really telling people she was attacked by that mayor guy? Whatsis name?" Maddie Gaines asked casually between sips of milk.

Gaines, leaning over his plate of meatloaf and mashed potatoes, sat bolt upright and coughed. His eyes began to water. "What'd you just say?" he said with a choked voice, trying to clear the food out of his windpipe. "Where did you hear that?" He looked at his wife, who looked equally perplexed. "Did you—"

Linn leaned back, insulted. "Oh don't even *think* about it. I haven't said a word," she said, waving her hand at her husband. She shifted her attention to her daughter. "Honey, who told you that?"

"Why? What's the big deal?"

"Who, Maddie?" Linn repeated.

"Samantha's mom," Maddie said. "She was talking about it on the phone when I was over there after school. Is it true, dad?"

Gaines paused, his fork and knife poised in his hands. "Maddie, we're not discussing this. Just drop it. You shouldn't talk about things you don't know anything about."

Maddie didn't seem interested in letting it go. "Samantha's mom says she made the whole thing up for attention. She even cut her own face just to make it look like it happened. Can you believe that?"

"Then Samantha's mother doesn't know *anything*," Gaines said sternly, praying his daughter would let it go. But he knew her too well and had little hope that she would move on until she got the answer—or reaction—she was fishing for.

"Mad, stop," Linn said. "Your father asked you to stop talking about this."

"Why? It isn't like it's a secret," Maddie said, her face wrinkling with disapproval. "If Mrs. Daviosa knows about it then half the town already does. She told everyone when Jenny Graham got pregnant. So you can guess… She's probably already called the *National Inquirer*. So why can't I ask if it's true? I have a right to know, don't I?"

"Rights? You're a teenager. You don't have rights. Not until you're living on your own and paying your own bills," Linn said, picking up her wine glass, folding her free arm across her chest, and tucking it under the other. It was a mother's drinking pose.

"*Seriously?* That's so stupid!" Maddie wailed. "Wouldn't you rather I hear the truth from Dad? I mean, he knows better than anyone what's going on."

"We're handling it," Gaines said, steadily losing patience. "That's what's going on. It's a law enforcement matter. So stop talking about it and just drink your milk. Got it? I would like to enjoy my dinner… Can I do that?… Please?"

"Fine. Geez. You don't need to lose your head over it. I was only curious."

There was a long beat of silence, and slowly the sound of utensils on plates resumed with awkward hesitation.

Then: "All I'm saying is I go to school with Kara. She sits near me in social studies. I just want to know if I'm sitting next to a psycho or not. You know, only a loon would make up something like—"

"Enough!" Gaines yelled, and brought his fist down on the table. Plates jumped with a clatter. "I don't want to hear another word! You understand?"

"Okay, sorry, you don't have to get so upset," Maddie said calmly, moving the food around her plate but never eating.

Gaines's face had tightened into an angry glower, and he was pointing a stiff finger at his daughter. He lowered his hand slowly. "You don't know a damn thing about this. And Samantha's mom should keep her mouth shut. She shouldn't be spreading those kinds of stories. Kara Price is just a kid. It's irresponsible. Martha Daviosa is the only psycho you should be worried about." He pushed back from the table, went to the fridge, and grabbed a beer. "I lost my appetite," he said, and stormed out of the room.

Fading behind him, Gaines heard Linn scolding their daughter: "Why do you have to provoke your father like that? He's been under a lot of stress lately."

He opened the back door and stepped out onto the deck before he heard Maddie's response. But it didn't matter; he knew the true answer: his daughter wasn't what had provoked him at all. Maybe she hadn't let up with the inquisition when he'd asked, but so what? Most times, he adored that about her. He adored her persistence. It was something that he always imagined would take her places in life. She didn't deserve to be yelled at that way. No, what had set him off was something else.

Since Saturday, Gaines had been trying to assure himself that Harry Bennett was innocent. For his own comfort, he had needed to believe that a man he thought he knew so well wasn't capable of such a terrible crime. But if it had been so easy to suggest that Kara was lying about being raped, when there was nothing but conjecture to support such a thing, then how could he really say he was qualified to judge a man's character? Because now he understood that he hardly knew himself. Never in a million years did he think his own actions could ever be so cowardly. Here he was, though, sitting on his deck, drinking a beer, cozy and safe, while Kara Price was being dragged through the mud by the likes of Martha Daviosa, and Harry Bennett was still sitting, giant fucking PR smile on his face, behind that fat desk of his, running Heartsridge. It was so wrong. He was just as bad as they were. Worse.

It was all because of that little kernel of truth Gaines had seen shimmering in the black heart of the matter, the oily thing he'd latched onto and founded his campaign against the truth upon: there wasn't enough evidence. Those four words—*There isn't enough evidence*—had become like some sick slogan for the Kara Price case. Sure, there wasn't enough for a solid conviction. That was true. But he couldn't deny it had almost felt like a relief when he had discovered that. At the time, it had seemed like some kind of lucky loophole, something that served to make his job—his life—easier. But now he saw it for what it really was: a way to avoid dealing with a truth he was too afraid to confront. He supposed he had known that all along, but he could no longer hide from it. It was eating him up from the inside like a cancer.

People protect their own.

The thought stirred the bile in his stomach and made him want to lose what little dinner he'd put down. But he had only been thinking about his family. It wasn't just that he was afraid for himself; he had been scared for Linn and Maddie, too. His decisions affected them just as much, if not more. He needed his job, and if he arrested Harry and nothing came of it he'd be done. What then? What about bills? The mortgage? Maddie's college fund? And it was true, dammit! There wasn't enough evidence. Harry would simply go free. It would be career suicide for him. A useless hop into the flames, all in the name of honor. Gaines could admit he'd been afraid and been a coward, but he couldn't bring himself to agree he had made the wrong choice. He wanted to see justice for Kara Price. But he wanted to do so without sacrificing himself and his family.

Samantha's mom says she made the whole thing up for attention, his daughter's voice repeated in his head.

The words made him cringe. They sounded so vindictive, as though Kara were some kind of deranged villain. It took him a moment to realize why hearing that had soured him so much, and then it became clear: the words were his own. Maybe not verbatim, but he'd uttered a similar phrase more times than he cared to recall. And now he could only hope he wasn't the cause of Martha Daviosa being armed with the same logic. How had she even heard, anyway? Only a few people knew about this. He knew it would get out sooner or later, but he didn't expect it so soon. He hoped he wasn't responsible for that, some way or another.

"You okay, hon?" Linn's voice came from behind him. "You know she's just being a teenager. She's curious, is all. You knew this wouldn't be a secret for long."

Gaines turned. Linn was standing in the doorway. "Yeah, I know. I'm sorry. I just have a lot on my mind. I shouldn't've gone off like that."

"I know. But she knows she was pushing your buttons, too. She's always liked to get a rise out of you."

Gaines laughed and shook his head. "Well, the kid's got a talent for it. That's for sure. But this wasn't her fault. Hope she isn't upset."

"Maddie? Please. She was smiling when you left the room." Linn stepped out onto the porch. "She's a tough one. She gets that from you."

Gaines took a long sip of beer then said, "I don't know... maybe."

"You remembered it's her birthday tomorrow, didn't you?" Linn asked, changing the subject. "She wants me to take her to the DMV after work so she can get her driving permit. God, she's growing up too quick."

Gaines brought a hand to his head. "Shit. No I didn't forget that," he said. "But I did forget to pick up her present. I had Joanna down at the diner make her a necklace. Did you know she did that? Made jewelry?"

"No, but that sounds like a wonderful gift," Linn said. "I'm sure she'll love it. You trying to dethrone me or something?"

Gaines laughed. "I hope so. It's this neat little pendant thing. I thought she'd like it. I told Joanna this morning that I'd be down to get it later. I wanted to give it to Maddie tomorrow morning before school so she could wear it."

Linn leaned against the porch column. "So go get it. The diner's still open."

"Yeah, I guess I'll have to." Gaines took another sip of beer and smiled. "Or maybe I can have Sam pick it up and drop it off. He drives right by on his way home." He checked the time on his watch. "Should be done with his shift in an hour."

"You're really that lazy?"

"What good is having deputies if they can't run a few errands for you from time to time? Besides, it's been a long few days," Gaines said, "and I've had a few of these already." He held up the beer can. "Probably shouldn't drive."

"Probably not. No." Linn smiled.

"Go on inside, I'll be in soon." Gaines leaned down and kissed Linn on her forehead. "I need a few minutes to clear my head."

Linn placed her hand on his chest and rubbed gently. "Okay, hon. Take your time."

She turned and walked back inside. When she was gone, and he was once again alone with his thoughts, Gaines's mind wandered back to that dark place—the place where the truth waited for him. The place where he could no longer pretend he wasn't aware of what he'd done to protect his own.

CHAPTER 25

His heart thumped in his throat.

"So you know what I think?" Sam said, a love-struck smile spread wide across his face. He was leaning on one arm through the small slider-window that connected the dispatcher's booth to the back office of the sheriff's station, talking to Carol Matthews. The hand he kept in his pocket fondled the diamond engagement ring his mother had given him. There was no grand plan, no extravagant ploys, just a movie, some popcorn and a quick *hey you wanna get married, babe, because I love you and want to spend my life with you.*

Carol spun around in her chair, her golden curls sweeping across her shoulders as she turned her head. That night and always, she was beauty's finest hour, and Sam Hodges couldn't for the life of him figure out what it was he had done to land a girl like her. It was, perhaps, one of those instances where one didn't question good fortune, only accepted it. All he really knew for certain was that he wanted her to be his forever. In sickness and in health.

"No, what do you think?" she asked, returning the smile.

They were young love, still wet behind the ears and all wrapped up in the honeymoon phase of their relationship. There was still so much to discover. There was so much excitement. There was magic.

"Well, I'm glad you asked," Sam said. "What I think, my dear, is that I should take us to the drive-in in Agawam and catch a late show tonight. We're both outta here in an hour, so whadya say, beautiful?"

"I wish I could. But remember I told you my Nana's been staying with me while my parents are in Florida." Carol pouted playfully. "I'm sorry, Sam. It's only for a few more days."

"The more the merrier," Sam joked, smiling mischievously. Nervous humor. "All three of us can hop in my backseat. It's pretty spacious. I'm sure we'd all fit."

"Gross." Carol shook her head and laughed. "You know, I wouldn't put that past you, horndog."

"I don't know if I'd put it past your Nana. I saw the way she looked at me when I met her."

"Fresh." Carol reached up and pretended to slap Sam's face.

"Okay, okay, sorry." Sam surrendered. "Why don't you come over to my place, then? Just for a little bit? I'll drive you home later."

"I can't. Her nurse only stays until ten, and I can't leave her alone. She needs help with things."

Sam hung his head in an exaggerated way—a man accepting defeat. "Fiiine. I give up. Next week, though. Next week you're all mine." He released the ring in his pocket and pulled his hand out. It would have to wait. And in a way, it was a relief. Not because he was unsure but because the anxious knot in his gut disappeared. It would return, he knew, but for now it was gone, and he could breathe normally again.

"I promise," Carol said.

"I guess I need to find something else to do, then. A date with my television, a six-pack, and my couch, I suppose." Sam laughed.

"Hey, that doesn't sound all that bad," Carol said.

"Well it depends on what I'm comparing—"

The phone rang and Carol held up a finger. "One sec." She picked up the receiver. "Heartsridge Sheriff's Department, how can I help you?"

Sam pushed back out of the window, turned his back, and pulled the ring out of his pocket. He looked at it and sighed, undoing the button of his breast pocket. He dropped it in and patted the pocket thoughtfully. Weren't the best things worth waiting for? And while he did believe that old adage to be true, he still felt the sting of disappointment.

There was a tap on his shoulder, and he turned around. Carol was holding the receiver to her chest.

"It's Calvin," she said. "Wants to talk to you. Something about a necklace."

Sam wrinkled his face in confusion. "A necklace?"

"Yeah, that's what he said. I don't know."

"Oh, ah, okay, put him through to my desk. I'll grab it there."

"Okay," she said. Then Carol reached out, grabbed his uniform, pulled him toward her, and kissed him. "I swear next week I'm all yours, handsome," she whispered, then winked at him. She put the phone back to her ear. "I'm putting you through now, Calvin," she said, and smiled devilishly at Sam.

He stumbled backwards, reeling from the kiss, grinning stupidly, and banged his shin on a chair. "Next week," he said. "Okay."

The phone on his desk started to ring.

CHAPTER 26

Joanna was in the kitchen locking the back door of the diner when the flash startled her.

Her immediate thought was born out of instinct from years of working in an old building with bad wiring: One of the overhead bulbs in the kitchen must've blown again. It happened all the time. But that on-hand idea crumbled when she turned around.

Bill stood there with his camera clutched chest-high in his hands. Joanna recognized him immediately. The dark beard scruff. The strands of copper hair tucked beneath that tired old Red Sox cap. The ratty, olive-green army jacket. In the past she had thought him to be a rugged but handsome enough man, attributing his unkempt appearance to his being a photographer. Because, well, artists were like that—so caught up in their craft that sometimes they forgot to take care of themselves. It was a novel idea, and one she could relate to quite well when she thought of the rare occasions when she had a day off to work on her jewelry. How sometimes she could wake up before the sun, throw on a pot of coffee, and spend all day soldering stained-glass pendants on her

living room floor, never changing out of her pajamas and sometimes never even brushing her teeth. But there was something very
different about Bill now. No artist, just a stranger with a camera.
She saw it right away. He was there, but he was a different person.
There was a dark, shallow look in his eyes. If what her mother had
always said—*Eyes are the windows to the soul*—was true, then the
windows she peered into now sat nestled in a vacant structure.

"Oh… hey, Bill. You startled me," Joanna said with hesitation,
sliding the keys to the diner into her apron pocket. "I didn't hear
you come in. Hope you didn't come for a late dinner 'cause I'm
closing up for the night."

What she aimed to say was: *Did you just take a picture of me?
And what are you doing in my kitchen?* Those were more important questions, the questions she really wanted to ask.
However, a part of her already knew the answers. Maybe not fully, or clearly, but she saw their shape, the same way you could
make out a hand in front of your face in a dark room. And maybe
that was why she already felt a cold sweat prickling at her palms
and heard a tremor in her voice as she spoke.

"Hi, Joanna… Jo. Can I call you Jo? I think I really do like
that better," Bill said, then immediately brought the camera up,
wielding it almost like a weapon. He took another picture before
she could respond.

The bulb flashed and Joanna was blinded by the blue-white
light. "*Ah!* What the heck? Knock it off. What are you doing?"
She bent her neck down and rubbed her eyes with her fists. Her
back pressed against the cool steel of the back door. When she
lifted her head again, all she could see were two silver spots floating where her vision should've been. She looked toward where
she'd last seen Bill, blinking hard and narrowing her eyes. She
could hardly make out his silhouette, but in the bottom of her

periphery, she could see his old, scuffed, leather boots starting to walk closer.

"You're perfect, you know that?" Bill said. His voice was low and flat, completely different from the voice he had spoken with in the past.

Attempting to restore her sight, Joanna continued to blink desperately as she reached out her hands, feeling for the wall, and then trying to move along it. "What's the matter with you, you fucking psycho?" she cried out. Her shoulder banged into a shelf, and a rain of pots and pans clattered to the floor. For a brief time, the noise blinded her completely, two senses temporarily erased by overexposure. She was completely vulnerable, swinging her arms around wildly. "Stay away from me. Just leave me alone."

Then another flash.

But this time, her head was turned away. She continued around the perimeter of the kitchen, trying to listen for the shuffling of his footsteps. After a few feet, she kicked something, and it slid with a thin scrape across the floor—a long butcher's knife. She traced the sound and saw it come to rest underneath the sink, spinning lazily on its hasp. The shimmering spots temporarily etched into her corneas from the flash still floated like metal ghosts in the center of her vision... but her vision was restoring.

"Please hold still, Jo. When you keep moving like that, it's hard to get you in focus," Bill said calmly. There was an eerie playfulness in his voice, like a cat toying with a cornered mouse.

How quickly her world had changed. A minute ago she was locking up the restaurant, preparing to head home and curl up on her couch with a glass of wine and her new limited-edition copy of *To Kill a Mockingbird* (her favorite book). Now she was trapped in the back of the diner with some guy she barely knew—if she knew him at all (in this moment it occurred to her that Bill the photographer from New Hampshire could just as easily have been Bill the rapist from Florida or Steve the murderer from Des Moines)—who was stalking her with a camera.

Another flash.

Joanna kept her head pointed away, down at the floor. "Stay away from me. This isn't funny, asshole. You want me to call the sheriff?" But her threat was so obviously empty. The phone was in the front of the restaurant, through Bill... or Steve... whoever he was. The man with the camera.

On the heels of this thought, as Joanna continued slowly along the perimeter of the kitchen, trying to make her way to the swinging doors that led to the counter, she acted in desperation, falling to the ground on purpose, and landing with her hand near the butcher's knife. For a moment she was out of view from Bill, kneeling behind a prep table on the greasy kitchen floor. Seizing the opportunity, she slid the knife into the front of her apron.

"Jo, where'd you go? I don't want to hurt you. I only want some pictures."

Joanna held a beat longer, staying out of sight behind the table. Her vision was almost completely restored now.

"Jo... Jo, are you there? Come out, come out, wherever you are," Bill said. He started to move toward her, no more than fifteen feet away.

Still she stayed, not ready to face what might be next.

What if he really was just a weirdo and didn't mean any harm? What if he just wanted some pictures? Maybe if she obliged, he would leave on his own. Maybe he was just a pervert and wanted something to jerk-off to later. Whackos like that existed, didn't they? Not as bad as murderers but worse than thieves, somewhere right in the middle, in a place without violence. If she were in better spirits, she might've laughed out loud at the naïveté of her thoughts. This guy didn't want anything short of blood.

A loud crash startled Joanna, and a stack of plates scattered across the floor. She flinched, holding a hand over her mouth to stifle a scream.

"*Jo!* Get the fuck out here! I mean it! Or I'll gut you right in your own kitchen like a goddamn pig!" Bill shrieked, and then there was another loud crash as he threw a tray of flatware toward her. A few loose spoons and forks came to a rest around her. She rose to a crouch, resting on her toes. Then she slid a hand into her apron and felt the knife.

"Okay," Joanna said, and rose to her feet, her hands up at her sides. "What do you want? Just tell me and maybe I can help you."

Bill was standing no more than ten feet from her now. "There you are," he said. "Now hold still." He brought the camera to his eye, winking the other closed.

Joanna clamped her eyes shut in anticipation of the flash. She wouldn't be blinded again. There would be no hope if she couldn't see. A warm red flash blinked behind her lids. When she opened them, Bill had the camera hanging idly around his neck on a strap, resting against his diaphragm. One hand was dropped to his side, the other tucked in the pocket of his jacket.

Bill removed his hand.

It took Joanna a moment to process what she was seeing. Her first thought was that Bill was holding some tool or attachment for his camera. Whatever it was looked metal and hard-angled. Something old but with a purpose. But it didn't take long—fractions of a second that played like thick, slow minutes—for her to realize, especially when he pointed it at her, that what she was seeing was a gun.

And its cold dark eye was staring her straight in the face.

Sam may have been sans a fiancée—for now, anyway—but at least he was finally off work for the night, and that was still something. Better than nothing, he reasoned.

His shift had ended at nine thirty. By ten thirty, Sam Hodges planned to be halfway through a six-pack of Miller, his feet up on his coffee table and, with any luck, drinking away the dull disappointment he felt over having to delay his marriage proposal. It wasn't like he'd planned any grand spectacular surprise for Carol that had fallen through. But it also wasn't just a spur of the moment thing, either. He'd planned, on some level. He'd taken important steps beforehand: obtained a ring, asked her father's permission (he'd said yes), picked a place to ask her. Sure, the drive-in wasn't the most romantic place, but it was where they had their first date, and Sam couldn't help but think that that meant more than nothing. He knew she'd see that, too. So while it may not have been him down on bended knee atop the Empire State building with balloons falling and champagne flowing, it had still stung a bit when it hadn't happened. But the drive-in wasn't going anywhere. It would be there the following week. So would he, and so would she. He only hoped his courage would be, too.

It was safe to say that the first beer couldn't come fast enough for Sam. The only reason he was making a pit-stop now at the diner and not beelining it to his apartment was because Gaines had called and asked him to stop at the diner to pick up a necklace for his daughter and drop it off at his house on the way by.

Eric Clapton was well into the second chorus of "Lay Down Sally" when Sam pulled into the diner parking lot and put the Ford into park. He let the radio blare, leaving the ignition on and drumming his fingers against the steering wheel. He didn't exit the car right away. Sam had a pet peeve when it came to turning off a song midway through. It was a crime on some level; he was sure of it. So he let it play and looked at the stillness of Deb's Diner.

The front of the diner was empty. No customers. No waitresses. All the lights were still on. Joanna was probably in the back. Sam imagined he would see her any minute, emerging from the kitchen through the two swinging doors, her arms full of plastic dish bins or some such. She was probably closing up. The sign was turned around in the front door. SORRY WE'RE CLOSED.

Clapton crooned, and Sam tapped his foot along with the beat.

Before long, the song faded out and the DJ returned, reminding listeners that Mr. Clapton would be playing a show in Boston in the coming month and tickets were going fast. Sam turned the dial, and the radio clicked off. As if *he* could afford Clapton tickets. The silence fell over the scene like thick smoke. Sam turned off the car and stepped out.

The diner remained empty. No sign of Joanna. No sign of anyone. Maybe she'd locked up and forgotten to shut off the front lights. Sure, she'd only been doing the same job her entire adult life and had never forgotten something like that, but maybe tonight was the night she had. Sam pulled on the door handle, expecting it to be locked, but it opened. The doorbells jingled in familiar fashion above his head.

"Hello? Jo? You here? It's Sam," he announced. "Calvin told me he was supposed to stop by earlier for a necklace or something. As you can see, he forgot." As Sam spoke, he moseyed around the diner, looking at things he had seen in there a hundred times before but had never really looked at: cracks in the floor tiles, stubborn coffee rings on the table, loose grains of sugar on the counter, a water stain on the ceiling.

But still, there was no answer from Joanna.

"You here, Jo? Or you getting senile? You forget to lock the front door and kill the lights?" Sam asked, focusing his voice toward the swinging doors behind the counter, the doors that led to the kitchen.

No answer, but there was a sound—a faint, dull thud and a light clattering. The sound of keys.

Sam smiled, lifted the counter section, and walked behind to the waitress area. "You hiding back here?" He cautiously pushed one of the swinging doors open. "Can I come back here? I know it says employees only but—"

She wasn't there. More silence. The fluorescent bulbs flickered overhead. A slow and lonely sound of water dripping in the sink. The fresh scent of Bleach.

"Hell are you?" Sam said to himself, scanning the room. Then his eyes fell on the back door. There was a set of keys hanging out of the deadbolt lock. He walked over to them and went to grasp them, stopping when he noticed specks of blood on a few of the keys. To his left he spotted broken plates and scattered silverware.

Call for backup, an internal voice urged him. That was standard operating procedure: sign of trouble, call for support.

But was it really a sign of trouble? A few specks of blood on a set of keys? Some broken plates? She probably dropped a dishbin and cut herself. It was a restaurant, for Christ's sake. People hurt themselves all the time in kitchens. Joanna was probably just out back taking the trash to the dumpster.

Sam hadn't even realized it, but he'd moved his hand to his pistol, and his body had tensed.

Realizing this, he unclenched. "Too many movies, Sam," he said, shaking his head. He took his hand away from his gun and grabbed the doorknob. He twisted and pulled. The door opened into black.

The back parking lot was a wall of darkness, especially from where Sam stood in the bright light of the kitchen doorway. "Jo, you out here?" he said, narrowing his eyes and using his hand to shield the light.

There was another sound. Something muffled. Then a grunt and the sound of whispering.

"Who's out there?" Sam rested his hand back on his pistol, his heart starting to pound in his chest.

"Jo, you out here? Is that you?" He took a step forward into the night. His eyes adjusted, but only slightly. The light from the diner poured from the back door, casting his long shadow, framed in the cockeyed canvas of light painted on the asphalt.

Another muffled grunt, then a hollow thud. The sound of someone being struck.

"This is Deputy Sam Hodges, come out where I can see you," he said, lowering his voice. It made him feel a little foolish when he did this, like he was trying to be something he wasn't.

Sam's sight continued to adjust as he inched his way out into the parking lot, black slowly turning to navy-blue. He unclipped the strap over his holster, readying his weapon.

Something cautioned in his head: *It's probably just Jo messing around. She'll walk out from the dark any minute with an empty trashcan, a silly grin across her face. Don't go drawing that pistol yet. You'll look like a scared, rookie fool.*

Sam stepped aside, out of the glow from the restaurant so he could see more clearly. When he did, the light travelled beyond him, revealing a red pickup truck at the far end of the lot, fifty feet away.

At first it was nothing, only a vehicle he didn't recognize. Then there was a Red Sox cap hovering in the night, two eyes, then four eyes, tucked back in a corner beside the truck, between the dumpster and the fence. From there the scene filled itself in. All the pieces connected and clicked into a clear, coherent understanding.

The man had his hand over the woman's mouth, her eyes wide with terror. "Joanna," Sam whispered to himself in disbelief. Then he yelled it: "Joanna!" His adrenaline pump kicked in, and the world became fast and electric. Vivid. "Joanna? What the hell is going on—" Sam began to say, as his slow, cautious movements quickened and he moved toward her.

Joanna managed to pull the man's hand away from her mouth "Sam, no, stop," she yelled.

But Sam was already charging in her direction, pulling his pistol from its holster. Then he saw why she was screaming. Sam caught sight of the man's gun, and his world, his life, immediately slowed. Everything stopped, and for a moment his eyes locked with the man's, shadowed beneath the brim of his hat. Sam's only thought was a quick and simple one: *Okay, fine.* It didn't make a lot of sense, but Sam understood it. The darkness around the man flashed yellow, and his gun clapped twice.

Sam felt it before he heard it.

The first shot caught him in the gut. The second caught him in the chest and spun him sideways—a one-two punch that sent him reeling to the ground. For a moment he thought his ears were ringing, but it was only the sound of screaming.

"Sam!" Joanna yelled, her shriek cutting the night.

Sam rolled onto his side and coughed. Blood sprayed from his mouth and ran warm down his chin. Reaching for his dispatch radio, there was another sharp clap and another searing punch of pain. This time the bullet struck his back. Immediately his legs went numb. But he still continued pulling the radio from his chest and bringing it to his mouth.

He pressed the call button. "This is Deputy... This is Deputy Sam Hodges. Dispatch... I..." He coughed again and tasted the hot iron in his blood. His vision began to tunnel and fade to gray. His tongue felt fat and clumsy, as if from too much Novocain. "Dispatch... This is... This is..." He couldn't get the words out. Everything was happening so fast, and he was suddenly so tired. But as his mind muddled, a thought stuck with him: *Thank God Carol went home and somebody else is working dispatch.*

A boot-clad foot landed against Sam's shoulder and rolled him over. There was a scrape as the man slid Sam's gun along the pavement, out of arm's reach. Sam could see the man clearly. He didn't recognize him. Joanna stood behind him, her face bloodied, her wrists bound together with what looked like tape. She was crying.

"You couldn't just leave us alone, could you?" the man said. His eyes were wild and frantic. "You had to be a goddamn hero. Now look at her. Look what I had to do to this perfect woman. The sign said closed. Couldn't you read?"

"Go for dispatch. Sam, is that you?" a man's voice crackled on Sam's radio.

Bill bent down and clicked off the receiver. Standing, he raised the gun, the barrel opening wide and black to Sam, who was panting in shallow, quick breaths. Then Sam set his eyes on Joanna, and his face slowly lifted into a bloody smile. His lips limned with blood and his face paling, he resembled a clown dressed in cop's clothing. With a last effort, he brought a hand to his breast pocket and rested his palm over the engagement ring meant for Carol. He looked Joanna hard in the eyes, hoping she understood that something there was important.

The gun barked a last time, and Sam's world went black. And that was okay. He wasn't scared, only sad for those who would hurt for him.

Like that, Sam Hodges was dead.

Joanna felt the blood drain out of her face. Something inside her had snapped.

"C'mon," Bill said, turning back to her and grabbing her neck. "Get in the truck. It's time to go."

But when he faced her squarely, Joanna pulled her hands out from the front pocket of her apron, wrists unbound. She had managed to cut the tape. The blade flashed dully in the moonlight as she threw her weight forward and drove the butcher's knife into Bill's gut up to the hilt. She didn't think she'd be able to, but something—survival or seeing her friend shot—provided more than enough strength. She felt a hard scrape as the blade sank in and slid against his spine. Bill let out a guttural groan, stumbling backwards and dropping the Luger to the ground. Joanna stood back from him as he looked down at the knife sticking out of his torso, his hands palm-up at his sides. There was an honest look of confusion on his face.

Bill fell to one knee, holding his gut and doubling over. His camera, still hanging around his neck, seemed to pull him down in slow motion. Finally it slammed off the ground as he collapsed, and the lens shattered.

Joanna stepped forward and kicked his gun as far away as she could into the dark and ran to Sam, kneeling beside him. "Sam, Sam, Sam," she said—pleaded—but he was gone. His eyes stared blankly out into the night sky, searching the stars for something beautiful.

After a moment, the sirens started. Very faint at first—the station was a few miles away—but they were coming. Someone must've heard the gunshots, or whoever had been on dispatch when Sam had radioed had known something was wrong. Joanna placed her hands over Sam's eyes and shut them. Then she lifted the hand he had placed over his chest in his final moments and felt his breast pocket. She'd seen him gesture to it right before Bill had fired the final shot. There was something there. She opened the flap, reached her fingers in, and felt something cool to the touch, something hard but delicate. She slid it out. The diamond ring shimmered in the ambient light of the parking lot.

Her heart sank. "Jesus," she said, and sighed heavily.

The still moment was broken by a wet gurgle. Bill rolled onto his back, gasping and trying to pull the knife from his stomach with no luck. He lifted his head off the asphalt and touched his chin to his chest, trying to analyze his wound. "What did you do to me?" he said deliriously, letting his head fall back against the ground with a hard thud, like a dropped melon.

The sound of sirens was steadily growing louder. It wouldn't be long before they squealed to a stop in front of the diner.

Joanna pocketed the ring. It didn't belong in an evidence locker down at the station; it belonged with its intended recipient. She'd known Sam Hodges and Carol Matthews were a couple, and she could only imagine why he was carrying around that ring. Young love that never got to grow. What a terrible, sad thing to understand.

Another cough and a long gurgle spurted from Bill. Joanna reached over and picked up Sam's gun, scooted backward, and held the revolver clumsily in both hands. She had fired one once before, with her father when she was just a little girl, and so she knew the basics. Cocking the hammer back and pointing it at

Bill, Joanna decided if that bastard moved again or made another noise, she'd fire a shot of lead right into his ear.

"Don't move, you hear me?" she said, and waited a few beats.

She received no answer or acknowledgement.

Then after another thirty seconds or so, she noticed Bill wasn't moving at all. He had stopped breathing. His eyes stared coldly off-angled back at her, black and deep-set. A bead of blood ran from the corner of his mouth and pooled on the ground. In the darkness, it looked like motor oil.

Joanna dropped the gun and stood. There was too much death back there in that parking lot, and she wanted to feel the safety of bright lights and open space now. Slowly, she made her way to the street.

Red and blue flashers were flickering up the street as she took a seat on the curb. But it was too late; there was nothing left to save.

While she waited under the orange glow of the street lights out front, a cicada landed next to her on the hood of a car. She looked at it. It lazed about for a moment, jerky and chaotic, fluttering its wings occasionally but making no sound. It stopped, and for a moment Joanna was sure it was staring at her, its head turning from side to side, analyzing her. She gazed back at it, her mind numb, her nerves seared and raw. Then in some strange association to what had just happened, a sour thought emerged: There really are some hideous creatures in the world, creatures humanity could get along without. And she didn't feel like tolerating that at the moment, whether she was right or wrong about it. Suddenly she had no patience for seemingly useless, ugly things.

Joanna flicked her hand in the direction of the bug and it took to the air, vanishing beyond the light, one of God's own mistaken creations darting off into an unknown future, in pursuit of some hardcoded purpose that would never be fully understood by it or anything else.

CHAPTER 27

According to the ID Gaines pulled from the man's wallet at the scene, Bill Sexton, the photographer from Woodstock, was actually Leslie Charles Millis from Belchertown, Massachusetts, a small town about forty miles east of Heartsridge. Gaines put in a call to the police department in Belchertown at a little past midnight but only got some rookie from the nightshift who didn't seem to know much of anything. Gaines said he would call back in the morning.

Also found in Millis's pocket was a room key belonging to the Heartsridge Motel. Attached to the key was a little brass key fob with the motel's emblem—the silhouette of an eagle perched prominently atop a roof—stamped on the side. Below the emblem, a large 6 was engraved. On the reverse it read: PLEASE RETURN KEY UPON CHECK-OUT.

Now laid out before Gaines on the two folding banquet tables they'd set up in the basement evidence locker of the Heartsridge sheriff's station was everything they had found in Room 6 of the Heartsridge Motel.

"You okay?" Catherine asked as Gaines unpacked another box of evidence. "I know Sam and you were friends. He was a good guy, always liked him. Me and his sister were real close when we were younger. I just can't believe this. It doesn't seem real. It hasn't sunk in yet, you know?"

She was opposite him, talking as she worked, labeling evidence bags. Mostly photography equipment they'd found set up in the bathroom of Room 6.

"I'm fine," Gaines said. He wanted desperately to talk about something—anything—other than how he felt. "Let's just get all this stuff checked in so we can get outta here. It's been a long night."

"Okay… was just trying—"

"I know, and I appreciate it. But now just isn't the time."

The door opened behind Gaines, and one of the younger rookies—Deputy Gerund—walked in with another box. "This is the last one," he said. "Where you want it?"

Gaines let out a long breath and squeezed his temples. His head pounded and stomach acid nipped at the back of his throat, either from the beers he'd had earlier or from the guilt he felt for having sent Sam to the diner in the first place. Probably both. He knew it should be him laying on a cold steel slab across town in the coroner's office, not his deputy… his friend.

"Wherever. Find a spot," Gaines said sharply, and pointed to the end of the table. "There's fine."

Deputy Gerund set the box down and lingered for a moment.

"You need something?" Gaines said.

The rookie looked down. "Sir, just want to say I'm sorry. I didn't know Deputy Hodges all that well, he was a few years older'n me, but from what I gather he was a good guy and good at his job. It's a shame to lose someone like that."

Gaines softened. "Yes… Yes it is. Thank you, Deputy." He paused. Then sincerely, "How many hours you been on, Sean?"

Gerund looked up. "Since yesterday morning… so going on eighteen now, sir. But it don't matter, I could do twenty more if you need."

"No sense in killing yourself. Catherine and I can handle this stuff. You should go home and get some rest," Gaines said. "The festival's starting Thursday, it'll be another long few days, and I can't have my guys falling asleep on duty."

Gerund smiled politely. "Yessir. I'll see you tomorrow then." He turned and walked out.

Gaines flipped the lid off the box Deputy Gerund had brought in. He recognized the items from when they were back at the motel. There were a few bags of photographs, mostly improperly developed pictures they had pulled out of the rubbish bin in the room. There were a few nature shots: some trees and rocks and clouds—amateur stuff. There were some pictures of feet (presumably Millis's own), and some of random things in the room: the TV, the bureau, an ashtray, the bed. There didn't appear to be any rhyme or reason behind the shots. They all seemed so elementary and random. In fact, the only universal truth that all the photographs shared was that none of them revealed anything about Leslie Charles Millis other than if he actually was a photographer (and Gaines doubted that now), he was a piss-poor one. So why was he in Heartsridge, then? He imagined the guy was probably just passing through. But Gaines wasn't so sure the answer really even mattered anymore. Millis was dead, and so was Sam. Nothing would change that. Sometimes these things happened for no good reason whatsoever. There had been both crime and punishment. Wasn't that enough to start the healing process? Gaines's mind was a blizzard of unrelenting thoughts that screamed like high gales: *Hodgesisdeadhodgesisdead... the festival... the festival... fuck... leave me alone... this is too much... don't forget about Kara Price... don't forget Harry Bennett is probably a rapist who will get away with it and you're just as bad for letting him skate... people protect their own, they kill for their own, remember that... and oh yeah, almost forgot, Hodges is dead and his blood is on your clean hands.*

He didn't know how to even begin to process it all, so instead he did his best to shut it all out. Just focus on the moment. One thing at a time.

HODGES IS DEAD PEOPLE PROTECT THEIR OWN YOU DIDN'T WANT TO DRIVE BECAUSE YOU'RE A COWARD THAT'S WHY HE IS DEAD THAT'S WHY KARA WILL NEVER SEE JUSTICE.

He shook his head in an attempt to cleanse his mind and continued logging the evidence.

The last item in the box was the metal ammo can they had found hidden under the bed, the one full of cigarettes. It was an old ammunition can that read .50CAL in faded yellow stencil letters along the side. Gaines took it out and set it on the table next to the bags of photographs. He opened it, removed the five packs of Marlboros, and slid the ammo can to the end of the table, giving it no further inspection.

"You calling the Staties in on this?" Catherine asked.

"I don't think so. What's the point? Maybe if the man responsible for shooting Sam wasn't sitting stiff across town I would. But as it stands, there isn't really anything to investigate."

Gaines expected a contrarian view from Catherine on the subject, but instead she said, "That's probably for the best. They'd only bring a media circus, and that's the last thing any of us need this week."

"No, you're right, we don't need that," Gaines agreed. "Best thing to do is wait until we hear something from the Chief of

Police over in Belchertown. Maybe he knows something more about this Millis guy that'll shed some light on the whole thing. Either way, we'll run his name and the plates on that truck. For now, he can stay on ice until we figure out what to do with him." Gaines paused in thought for a second. "And I'm positive I've heard that name before."

"What? Millis?"

"No. The fake he gave me when I first met him: Bill Sexton. I know I know that name. It's been buggin' me since I pulled his real ID back at the diner. I thought so when he first said it, and I'm even more sure of it now. But I can't for the life of me remember where I heard it."

"Can't say it sounds familiar to me," Catherine said, picking up the evidence bag with Millis's driver's license in it. She looked it over for a second, her eyes thinning. "Bill Sexton, huh?" she said softly to herself. "We even sure this is our guy's? I mean, I know whoever is over at the morgue is our shooter, but are you sure this is his license?" She gestured to the ID photo. "I guess it looks like him enough, the red hair and all. But this is expired, and the DOB on this is faded and illegible."

"I noticed that. Here, let me see it again," Gaines said, extending a hand. Catherine tossed him the bag. He caught it and studied it for a moment.

The man in the license picture had a full beard and short, copper-colored hair. Take away the facial hair and it was a dead ringer. Same nose, same deep-set eyes, same thin face.

"Try and picture him without the beard. It's him. I had a conversation with the guy a couple days ago and looked him right in the eyes. This is him, I'm sure of it."

But he wasn't sure of it. He was *nearly* certain. He was *pretty* confident. He was a lot of things, but "sure" wasn't one of them.

Thinking about it, Gaines couldn't actually remember the last time he'd really been sure of anything. He'd spent the better part of the week, ever since Kara Price, living in some strange gray area where every decision he made felt like suicide. Maybe he just wasn't cut out for this job anymore. Maybe he never had been. The last decade had been nothing more than speeding tickets, drunk drivers, and the occasional fist-fight or property dispute. It had softened him... or at the very least, he'd allowed himself to get comfortable. And that was dangerous with a job like this, where he never knew what the next day might have in store. Just because rape and murder wasn't something that happened in Heartsridge didn't mean he should be so unprepared to deal with such atrocities when they did.

"If you say so," Catherine said.

There was disbelief in her voice, and it furthered Gaines's own self-doubt. Why couldn't she ever just agree with him? Why did she have to be so...

He tossed the license back on the table with the rest of the evidence. Then Gaines's eyes settled on the green, metal ammunition can one last time. Something about it had seemed strange. It was a bit odd for someone to use such a bulky thing to carry around cigarettes. But then again, the man had shot one of his deputies and tried to kidnap—most likely murder—a woman too. So who was Gaines to think that he could understand the motivations of someone like that? Who was Gaines at all? That was starting to seem like a recurring question as of late.

Suddenly, Gaines made a faint connection to the conversation he'd had with Harry Bennett a couple of days before. Not that he actually valued anything the man had to say, but it had seemed to ring true in the moment: *People like you and me, we're not made of stone and steel like most people think. We're something closer to wood, and after a while, life sands down our edges, rounds us, forms us to its will. It's our job to know when it's time to reform our boundaries, re-sharpen our edges. It reminds us who we are.*

Gaines couldn't help but wonder if that was what was happening to him. Had he lost his edge? The thought that it might be the case made Gaines feel an overwhelming wave of exhaustion.

Outside the birds had just begun to chirp. A few early-to-rise cicadas had started their lonesome soliloquies, and sleep was becoming necessary. It had been a long night. That was the only thing Calvin Gaines was certain of.

It was 3:45 in the morning on Wednesday.

CHAPTER 28

Around noon, after Gaines managed to steal a few hours of sleep in an empty holding cell, he picked up the phone and tried the Belchertown police a second time.

It rang twice, then a man picked up. "Belchertown Police Department."

Gaines cleared his throat. "This is Sheriff Calvin Gaines calling from over in Heartsridge. Could I speak with the officer in charge please?"

"Just a moment." There was a beat of silence, followed by rustling on the other end of the line. Then: "What is this regarding?"

"I think it'd be best if I went over that with whoever's in charge," Gaines said.

Another pause. This time Gaines heard muffled voices on the other end.

The man returned and said, "Just a moment, please."

Thirty seconds or so went by, then an older voice picked up. "This is Chief Tim Walsh. What can I do for you, Sheriff?"

"Hi. Hello. Sorry for the theatrics," Gaines said, "but we have a bit of a serious matter on our hands over here."

"Not a problem. Hope it's nothing *too* serious," Walsh said. "What can I do for you?"

"Well, unfortunately, we had a shooting last night," Gaines said, and sighed. "The worst of it is we lost one of our deputies. A good man. It's been a really trying twenty-four hours, to say the least."

"I'm sorry to hear that. That's never easy. It's the worst part of the job," said Walsh, his voice tightening up—a serious tone.

Gaines could hear the sincerity. "Yeah, it's a real shame. Young kid, too," he said.

"Well, you have my condolences. Anything we can do to help?" Walsh asked.

Gaines sat upright and shuffled the selected copies of evidence sitting in front of him: motel statements, pictures from the scene, and a copy of the ID they had found in the man's wallet. "The person responsible, he'd been staying locally for a few days. Said he was a photographer from up north. But that was a lie, of course."

"You have him in custody?"

"Not exactly in custody, no, but we got him." Gaines stalled briefly. "He's dead."

"Oh," Walsh said, sounding relieved, if not happy. "Well, maybe there's justice after all."

"I suppose. Anyway, we found an ID on the guy. It says he's from Belchertown." Gaines scanned the copy of the license just to make sure, even though he'd seen it a dozen times. "I was hoping maybe you'd heard of him. We ran the plates on his truck and they came back stolen, so no luck there. We're running his name, too, but that always takes time. I was hoping maybe you could help us shut this case a little quicker. We got our hands full as is."

"Glad to, but heck, I hate to think someone like that came outta our town. Though I'm not foolish enough to think it isn't possible," Walsh said regretfully. "What's the name? I'll see what I can do."

"Leslie Charles Millis." Gaines verified with the copy once more. "That's what his driver's license says, anyway."

There was a pause on the other end of the line, followed by a few reluctant laughs. "Are you screwing with me? Pulling my leg? Who put you up to this? Frank?"

"I'm afraid I don't follow."

"Charlie Millis is dead," Walsh said.

"Dead? Are you sure?" Gaines felt waves of frustration starting to crash against the front of his mind. A fear that he would have to start from scratch started to enter his mind. He didn't have time. He just couldn't catch a damn break this week. Suddenly, his head started to ache.

Walsh cut the laughter and said, "As a goddamn doornail. No doubt about it. Hanged himself after he had a stroke. I don't know who you have sitting in your morgue, but it sure as hell isn't Charlie Millis."

"Then why is his ID sitting in an evidence bag in the basement of my station?"

"I don't know, but sounds like whoever it is..." Walsh trailed off as if an old thought had struck him. There was a moment of silence on the other end of the phone. Then, curiously sincere, he asked, "What does this guy look like?"

"About six foot, skinny, red hair, a crooked nose that looks like it might've been broken a few times," Gaines said. "Maybe forty years old. It's tough to tell, his license is old and the DOB is faded. Looks to be expired, too."

"Christ almighty... I wonder..." Walsh muttered.

"What?" Gaines said impatiently.

"It's a long shot, but Charlie Millis had a son, Gordon... Gordon Millis." There was a slight hesitation in his voice. "But no one's seen him in years. He was the spitting image of his old man. God, I can't remember the last time I heard that name."

"You think that's who it is?" Gaines asked.

"Maybe. Don't know. But I can't think of anyone else who'd have Charlie Millis's driver's license and who you'd mistake for the real Charlie Millis, provided the ID hasn't been altered. I can't know for sure without having a look myself. I could take a drive there if you'd like. Tell you for certain."

"Don't trouble yourself," Gaines said. "I'll have one of my guys head over there now with a copy of the license and some pictures of the body for a positive ID."

"That'll work too," Walsh said, almost sounding disappointed.

"Okay, good. That helps a lot," Gaines said. Finally, something was going his way. "So this guy, Gordon Millis, what's his story? Got any info, if it is him?"

"Hell, where to begin? What a sad thing that was. I don't think I've thought about that kid for ten years."

"Well, enlighten me if you could. I'm still trying to understand why this happened in the first place," Gaines said.

"It's been a while, but you don't forget a thing like this, unfortunately."

"Whatever you can tell me, I'd appreciate it," Gaines said. "All we got over here are questions... I could use some answers for once."

Walsh breathed a long, pensive breath. "Okay. Well to start, Charlie Millis was a terrible drunk. I mean, this guy—what a real piece of work. I picked him up more times than I can remember on drunk and disorderly charges. But that was the least of his problems. He was a real grade-A scumbag. For a while, he was married to a real sweet woman, Elizabeth, I think was her name, and he developed a bad habit of slapping her around after he'd hit the bottle. About once a month we'd get a call from a neighbor who'd heard yelling and screaming coming from the Millis house and who was sure Charlie was about to kill his wife. We'd show up, she'd have a shiner or a rosy cheek or a bloody nose, but she'd refuse to press charges—that's usually the case with these things, you know—so we'd just make Charlie sleep it off in the tank and release him in the morning. Nothing else we could really do. It was awful. Made me sick sometimes."

"If you ask me, people like that deserve the chair," Gaines said. He felt compelled to state his position, to prove he felt the same disapproval for that kind of abuse. For a second, he wondered if he felt that need only because of how poorly he'd presented his true position recently regarding the accusations against Harry Bennett. It was, perhaps, a poor, desperate attempt at redemption.

"Couldn't agree more," Walsh said. "Anyway, all the while this was happening, they had this kid, Gordon. At this point he couldn't have been more than a few years old, and he witnessed this type of thing probably daily. I remember every time we'd show up he was sitting in some corner of the house, knees curled up to his chest, just watching his father smack his mother around. The thing was—and this always struck me as odd—the kid never cried, not once. He always just sat there calmly, even when we walked in to break it up. It was probably shock, but it sure did give me the creeps. What kind of kid wouldn't be upset over seeing that?"

"I can't imagine," Gaines said, finding it hard to find any real sympathy for the person who had possibly just shot and killed his friend.

"You don't want to, that's the truth. Trust me. But listen, it gets worse," Walsh said. "So eventually Charlie's wife leaves him. Can you blame her? That's not a life if you ask me. I didn't understand it for a while, you know, how a mother could abandon a child like that, but I guess everyone's got a tipping point. I'm not saying she was a bad mother, she was just trying to survive. I think I get it now—it's instinct. Truthfully, Charlie probably *would've* killed her eventually had she stuck around. But without a woman to beat up on, Gordon became the next best thing. Poor kid never stood a chance." Walsh paused a moment. "I know you probably don't want to hear me offering pity for this kid, not if he actually is the one who shot one of your guys. It's just how I remember it, that's all."

"It's okay, I understand. Go on."

Walsh continued. "After his wife left, things changed a little. Not for the better, though. Charlie was a little more discreet about how he handled his boy. What he did, he did behind closed doors, and we stopped getting the calls from his neighbors. But every so often we'd get a call from a concerned teacher or someone who'd seen Gordon around town with a black eye or looking roughed up. Really everyone knew what was going on, but how can you stop family stuff like that? It's always more complicated than it seems. Anyway, I tried talking to Gordon more than a few times, but he always clammed up and denied anything I was suggesting."

"What type of kid was he?" Gaines asked.

"He was smart, you could tell, but always a few degrees off dead-center, if you know what I mean. When I'd speak to him, his eyes were there, you know, but there wasn't much behind 'em. Tough to tell if he was born that way or just turned like that."

"When's the last time you saw him?"

"Well, eventually he left for college, which was probably for the best. He wasn't really cut out for war. Kind of a loner, you know? I heard it had pissed his father off something awful, which was why his old man offered to pay for his schooling—told him to go and never come back. A parting gift, I guess you could say. So Gordon left and stayed gone a long time, almost ten years. Then his father had a stroke, a real bad one that paralyzed him and put him in a wheelchair. Shortly after that happened, I bumped into Gordon in town. He said hello with no mention of what he'd been up to for so long and then went on his way, like he hadn't been gone all that time. I don't know how he'd found out about his father—I don't think he had any other family—or why he cared, but for some reason he came home to take care of the old man. And if you believe the popular opinion, he did just that."

"What do you mean?"

"About a month after I ran into Gordon, he showed up at the station and said his father had hanged himself, and he said it with those same cold eyes." Walsh paused for a moment, then said, "That was the last time I ever saw Gordon Millis. I think it's the last anybody ever saw of him. I don't think he made the funeral, if you catch me."

"So he murdered his own father? Is that what you're telling me?"

"No, I didn't say that. We never found any evidence to suggest Gordon killed him... never any to the contrary, either, though. But sure, there were more than a few people who were curious as to how a paralyzed man climbed a set of stairs and strung himself from the banister. And I'd be lying if I said I wasn't one of 'em."

"Did you ever open an investigation? At least try and track him down? I mean, if you really thought he killed someone, didn't you…" Gaines didn't follow the thought through to its obvious conclusion; they both knew where it led. And what was the point, anyway?

There was a beat of silence between the two men.

"As far as I was concerned, there wasn't a need to," Walsh said earnestly. "Charlie was dead. The ME declared it suicide. And I just figured Gordon went back to whatever life he'd been living before he came back. Everyone was better off, it seemed." He cleared his throat, his tone livening. "You still want to send those photos along? See if we can't ID your DB?"

"Yes. I'll send someone within the hour. Soon as you know something, give me a call. And thanks for your help."

"Of course, Sheriff," Walsh said, followed by a sigh. "And I truly am sorry you lost a man, even more so if Gordon Millis did it."

"Me too."

Gaines hung up the phone.

Two hours later he had his positive ID on Gordon Millis.

CHAPTER 29

On Thursday, with renewed hopes of getting on with her life, Kara returned to school. She had prepared for what she might be met with, knowing that her secret was no longer a secret, knowing that some version of it was out there floating around. Her mother had warned her that she'd received a call on Wednesday from her friend Meredith Drinkwater, asking if this terrible thing she had just heard about Kara was true. It was the inevitable nature of such a small town. No secrets here. And Kara had known there would be some kind of reaction to it. But this? It'd be a lie to say she thought it would be this harsh or directly mean—this cold. The sudden impact of the mean gesture she was looking at on her locker admittedly rocked her; she wouldn't deny that. It pushed her close to that familiar ledge she'd spent the last few days backing away from, the ledge that fell away into that familiar dark chasm of despair she'd clawed herself out of, one helpless thought at a time. Hard days giving way to hard hours, giving way to hard minutes, giving way to impossible seconds, each a seemingly impassable hurdle. But she held strong. This would not drop her. She'd come too far.

This is a part of you now. It is a part of your life.

Kara said nothing standing in front of her locker. She closed her eyes and clenched her jaw, fighting back the urge to cry and scream and pound her fists. There could be no reaction.

Kara opened her eyes.

It was a quarter after eight. Fifteen minutes before first period. That's all. Just another day at school.

She looked left down the hall and saw a group of girls standing in a small circle giggling and looking her way. Some she even recognized to be girls she thought were her friends. To her right she heard similar low-hung laughter but didn't look; she wouldn't give them the satisfaction.

Breathing deep, Kara fixed her eyes again on the graffiti scrawled across her locker. The word SLUT was staring back at her, written in thick black permanent marker. *Be tough,* she thought. *Don't give them the response they want.*

(Slut? Is that really what they think of me?)

She squeezed the latch on her locker and swung the door open.

At first she was startled by what happened. Jumping back, she clutched her chest and almost fell. Her backpack slid sideways, hanging unevenly off one shoulder. Immediately her face flushed and went hot. Then she heard the gales of laughter rising in a raucous crescendo. And this was all before she really knew what was going on.

Papers were sliding out of her locker. An avalanche. They flowed down and spread out like some sort of kaleidoscope eruption. Different colors poured out into a confused pile of reds, yellows, whites, and blues all juxtaposed against one another. It took a moment for her to comprehend what she was seeing, but eventually she understood what all the papers were. They were old flyers from Harry Bennett's various elections and campaigns. Hundreds of them. Some she immediately remembered seeing hung on telephone poles around town, one year, two year, maybe three years ago. Kara continued backing away. One fluttered to her feet, spinning in its own, small, lateral vortex and landing right side up. And then there he was: a black and white headshot of Harry Bennett smiled upward at Kara. Below the picture was a slogan: ELECT HARRY BENNETT, HE'S NOT AFRAID TO GET HIS HANDS DIRTY.

Kara's adrenaline kicked in, and she slammed the locker shut. There couldn't have been more than twenty kids in the corridor, but the laughter roared like a stadium. She felt as if she had shrunk to an impossibly small size. She re-shouldered the fallen strap of her bag, and before she knew it, she was running towards the ladies' room down the hall.

While she ran, the world around her slurred into a million shades of gray, except for one thing that remained in focus: her friend, Haley Richmond. They had been friends for years, and as Kara began to break left to push open the door to the bathroom, she saw Haley and caught her eyes. She was laughing in a small group of girls, girls Haley and Kara never palled around with. New friendships, already? When the two made eye contact, Haley was quick to slacken her face and cut the laughter, her eyes immediately darting to the floor.

"What's going on out here?" a teacher yelled as Kara pushed open the heavy oak door to the bathroom and went in. It was the last thing she heard before the acoustics of the tiled floors and concrete walls of the lavatory enveloped her in cool silence.

Kara entered the first stall she saw, shut the door, removed her bag, and sat down hard.

Suddenly, everything that she had worked toward, all the inner peace she had managed to find in the wake of a shattered life, vanished like it had never existed. What a fragile thing it truly had been after all. It seemed her progress was only cosmetic, like a broken bone that had just started to set: on the surface it felt hard to the touch, but the depth of her wound ran profoundly into the composition of her sense of self, akin to a sprained soul. And that was where the injury was far too fresh to accept the applied weight of everyday life because, so far as she could tell, life was cruel and unfair. She had been a fool to think otherwise. She had been a fool to think she could handle this—that she could live with it.

A dime-sized drop of blood spattered onto her knee as she stared down, trying to slow her breathing and fight her tears. Kara wiped the back of her hand across her mouth. Pulling it away, she saw the familiar streaks of blood. Without meaning to this time, she had reopened the cut. She gathered a small length of toilet paper, bunched it, and pressed it against her lip to stop the bleeding, just as Catherine had showed her back at her house. But this time the pain seemed different. She tried to harness it as she'd done before, to use it to center herself, to pull her mind into the present, away from the dark thoughts, but couldn't. Now it was just plain, dumb, useless pain, and it was overwhelmingly relentless.

Kara heard the flat murmur of people talking outside the bathroom door. They seemed to stall for a moment, then slowly fade. Just some students passing by. Maybe they'd already forgotten all about her and moved on to the next thing. When it came to matters of adolescent bullying, that was how it often went. Kids had short attention spans when it came to teasing. Out of sight, out of mind. If she stayed away, maybe they would move on and forget about her.

But Kara doubted it would be that way this time. This time, people were under pressure to choose a side, and whatever corner they decided on would have consequences that reached far beyond the halls of Heartsridge High School. It was her or the Golden Boy, Harry Bennett. Who they picked spoke volumes about who they were and what they stood for, so people were choosing the safe bet: Golden Boy. Kara was smart enough to understand that, but not strong enough to accept it. She wanted to be, but couldn't force it if she tried. And she *had* tried. She just wasn't built that way, and for the first time since Harry Bennett laid his hands on her—*the ones he's not afraid to get dirty,* she thought (true to a sickening degree)—Kara Price longed for her father, for someone to protect her the way only a father could. But she had pushed him away, and now she had no one to save her.

The first-period bell sounded. Outside the bathroom, students flowed into their classes. Teachers shut their doors, locking out latecomers unless they had a pass from the front office. Right on cue, the school fell into its silent state of production. For those wishing to escape and cut class, this was the best time to make a break for it—no one knew whether you were coming or going. Kara planned to be going. She was sure of that. There was nothing here for her.

She stood and walked out of the stall, tossing the small wad of bloody tissue into the trash. She pulled a piece of paper towel from the dispenser and blotted beneath her eyes. No way in hell would anyone see her cry. Then she opened the bathroom door and stepped out into the hall.

"Hey," Ryan said, catching her off guard. He was standing a few feet away, his backpack hung in a too-cool-for-school way off his shoulder. "What's up?" His tone was sullen, none too thrilled to see her.

Kara froze in her tracks. "Hi," she managed. But even that one word seemed to struggle to find its way out. Her throat had slammed closed. It felt as though she'd swallowed a fat marshmallow.

"Can we talk?" Ryan asked, tucking a few strands of hair behind his ear. "I haven't seen you in almost a week."

"Ryan, I'm sorry but now… now just isn't a good time," Kara said, and looked nervously down the hall beyond her boyfriend. The papers were still there, spilled out around her locker as if it had just vomited them out and hadn't even had the decency to wipe its chin.

Ryan's face fell, becoming dark and serious. "No. It can't." He adjusted his backpack with one arm.

"Ryan, please. I'll tell you everything later." Kara just wanted to get out of there before some teacher tried to stop her and she was stuck there the entire day, reliving the embarrassment from fifteen minutes ago. People laughing, talking, whispering.

"I can't believe you lied to me… You lied to everyone. My dad's friends with Harry Bennett. I've known him my whole life. Why would you say something like this about him? For fuck's sake, you won't even screw me and now you're going around saying Harry screwed you? *Raped* you? What is that? You know how embarrassing that is? How embarrassing it is for someone like me?"

Kara's jaw fell slack. What he was saying didn't even make sense. It just seemed belligerent. Who was this boy? It wasn't the person she'd known. "What? How could you?" The words barely escaped her disbelief. "You're just like the rest. Ryan… I… I can't believe this…"

Ryan stiffened. "We're done, Kar—" But before he could finish the words, Kara reached up and caught Ryan across the face with the hardest slap she could muster. Her palm flashed hot with the satisfying, thick connection of flesh on flesh. The crack echoed down the hall.

Disbelief quickly broke to anger. "You don't know *anything!* You... you *fuck!*" she yelled, and then felt the onslaught of emotions threatening to burst out, starting to press harder on her weakened defenses, promising escape. She charged past him, trying to hold in her tears. Her shoulder connected with his and sent him awkwardly against the wall. His eyes peeled wide with surprise as he held his cheek.

Kara continued running past her homeroom, past her locker, past all the cruel flyers strewn on the floor as a sick reminder of what she was running from. And then, finally, she was at the front entrance, her hands shoving with all their might to free her from this place. She would get out of that hellhole before anyone saw her shed another damned tear. In fact, she would never set foot in that school again. Isn't that what they wanted, anyway? To close their eyes in the face of this monster and have it be gone when they opened them again? Children afraid of their own imaginations, unable to discern reality from dream... or in this case, nightmare.

It's a part of you now, Kara... it's a part of you.

But she didn't want it to be a part of her. She didn't want this to be her life. It wasn't how her story was supposed to play out. Who would want to live a life like this?

Somebody save me. I'm drowning.

Before Kara knew it, she was home. She'd walked the whole way, never lifting her gaze off the ground, lost in thought, completely oblivious to the world around her. A half-hour had gone by like a second. Now looking up, the driveway was empty. Geronimo was sleeping beneath the picnic table, a half-empty water bowl beside him. The closed house was a lonely sight. Her mother had gone back to work to make up for the personal time she had taken off to be with her daughter and wouldn't be home until almost ten tonight, and her father had pretty much been MIA since Monday. Kara had wanted space, not for him to disappear. He was supposed to know his little girl needed him.

That's your fault! a voice screamed in her head. *You said you couldn't be around him. What did you expect when you practically said he was as bad as the man who raped you?*

Recently her father had been leaving early for work and coming home late, avoiding her, not saying much to anyone. The shuffle of his slippers down the hallway in the little hours of the night was the most she had heard from him. It wasn't much, but that little noise had become a comfort to her. It was as if he was speaking to her through some weird code, a secret father-daughter talk that existed on some indestructible plane in a dimension beyond the fallout, a place life couldn't touch. This wasn't true; she knew that. He wasn't really communicating to her with his footsteps, but if he was then she imagined *shuffle-step... shuffle-step... shuffle-step* meant "I love you, sweetheart. It'll all be better soon. Don't give up." That was what her father would tell her. Yes. Those would be his words.

That inner voice spoke up again: *You've really made a mess of things, haven't you, Kara? Wouldn't it be better if the monster just disappeared so everyone could finally sleep?*

Sleep. Yes. Sleep was a good idea.

Kara unlocked her front door and went inside. She wanted to sleep now. Let the monster close its eyes. Let it dream about a time when it was a little girl with hopes of being a princess. That was an easier time. *That* was a life worth living.

CHAPTER 30

It was just after four o'clock in the afternoon on Thursday when Harry Bennett took the stage.

"Ladies and gentlemen. Thank you... thank you. Is it that time of year again already?" He waved slowly and appreciatively, flashing his thick smile, oscillating from left to right like a cheap desktop fan, acknowledging the applause. "Thank you. It's a pleasure to be here. Thank you. My goodness. You're too kind. Thank you." The crowd continued clapping for their Golden Boy, drowning him out—and he loved every second of it.

It was the opening act of the Spring Festival: the Mayor's Speech. Mostly it was a local crowd today, but the street was still swollen with the energy of excitement.

Harry looked out over the sea of native attendees and admired the scene, scanning row after row of upturned, smiling faces; hopeful eyes that stared out at him from the patchwork of bright, summer clothes donned by the crowd during this premature, springtime heat wave. It was a collage of whites, reds, blues, beiges, and yellows. Short-shorts and tank tops. T-shirts and low-cut sneakers. Khakis, not denim, because blue jeans were simply too hot for the occasion. Along the side of the street were the pastel boundaries of the crowd, where the elder Heartsridge women were camped in their beach chairs along the sidewalks, talking heads turned to one another, sunglasses dark against their paper-white skin. Too-clean, never-worn hats sat atop gray, permed curls. Behind these veteran women stood their husbands, wearing the flat, tired look of men who had come to terms with the fact that their lives were in their final stretch—sad-happy grins set hard into deep wrinkles, concerned less about what lay ahead and more about the way things used to be. The cicadas buzzed on, droning their seventeen-year song, reinforcing the notion that summer was here early. Their sound seemed to thicken the humidity, teasing the air with their electric noise. But no one seemed to mind. It was high times for Heartsridge. And at the head of it all, in the center of Pride's Square, where the main stage had been erected, Harry Bennett stood at his podium, dressed in his white linen suit, looking out, smiling, prince of all he surveyed.

But even as Harry enjoyed his applause and his admiration, his eyes were busy examining the crowd, searching, gauging, evaluating his people. Occasionally he would meet the eye of someone he knew well. He would nod and smile but then quickly move on. Because it wasn't the people—the ones he might call friends—who he was concerned about; they would always stick by his side and believe what he told them. No, he wanted to see the faces of those who only knew him from a distance, knew him through talk and rumor, indirectly. Those whose opinions of him swayed with whatever way the wind blew. They were the people who mattered. They were his customers, the ones who bought or rejected the Harry Bennett product.

He'd already been stopped in the street half a dozen times by someone who wanted to tell him they'd heard an awful rumor about some troubled girl who was trying to get rich by spreading lies about him, but that wasn't enough. It was reassuring to hear, however Harry still wanted to see the loyalty on a grand scale. He wanted to see it in the face of the crowd. He wanted to see that he was still their Golden Boy. And as far as he could tell, he was. His wife had been right all along. They were a team, and she had managed to score, perhaps, the game-winning point. He couldn't have done it without her. He had never held Allison Warren Bennett in higher regard than he did in that moment.

"Okay... all right... thank you," he said, trying to add an inflection of seriousness to silence the crowd. He placed both hands on the corners of the podium and leaned forward into his words. The applause slowly died to a murmur. "I'd like to thank you all for coming, although I have to admit, I think you'd all be here regardless of whether my ugly mug was up here or not." He smiled and the crowd laughed. Then he took a sincere tone. "But that is what is so great about tradition, ladies and gentlemen. That is what I find so special about this town—that we care about the things that have made Heartsridge what it is today. We embrace our roots, and that is important. It speaks highly to what we stand for. It speaks to our strength as a community. In the face of tragedy, we still persevere. We still show up to ensure that the things that matter most to us won't waver."

"That's right, Harry. You tell 'em," someone in the crowd shouted. There were a few laughs, which faded quickly.

Harry offered a good-natured smile, glanced down briefly, and then straightened his posture. "Now, I know all of you've heard by now the terrible thing that happened to one of our own. Many of you knew Sam Hodges. He was a good man who died protecting a tradition of this town, one that is most important above all, one that many of us, I'm sure—me included—take for granted: the right to feel safe on the streets of your town. He was doing his job, and unfortunately the good Lord decided it was his time. It's a sad, awful thing, and it is with a heavy heart that I ask you all—whether you're religious or not—could we please take a moment to pray for Sam Hodges? I ask you to offer a moment to pay your respects to a man who sacrificed himself so that others could walk the streets at night without having to look over their shoulders. Please take a moment."

The crowd went silent and Harry closed his eyes, dropping his head. They were still his, and he knew it for sure now. To follow a man into prayer is an undeniable show of faith, respect, and allegiance—three things not offered lightly and certainly not to someone who is guilty of rape. Yes, he still had them. He was still their leader. The crowd remained heads-down and would for as long as he asked them to.

David Price stood silently at the back of the crowd as the town offered their prayers, his eyes remaining fixed on Harry Bennett. The mayor was barely an inch tall from where he stood, but David could imagine that smug, two-dollar smile just the same.

He was so sick of it, seeing the way the mayor manipulated people with his blue-collar charm, like some discount southern gentleman, the way he shoveled shit and sold it as gold behind that fake exterior. He didn't understand how anyone could fall for it. Couldn't they see what he really was? It didn't take a genius to notice it, to see what lay beneath. David had spent the last couple of days following Harry to and from his office, following him to bars and restaurants, on errands, meetings, learning his routines, learning when he was most vulnerable.

David wasn't so naïve as to think he would get away with what he aimed to do, but he could live with that. What he couldn't live with was doing nothing and allowing Harry Bennett to get away with what he'd done to Kara. A part of him wanted to shoot Harry then and there, right up on stage—it was maddening to see how much praise and respect he still garnered from so many—but he couldn't do that. There were too many people who didn't deserve to witness something like that, especially the children in the crowd. It would scar them forever, and David didn't feel he had the right to inflict that kind of damage on the innocent. Instead he would wait, and he would be ready when the time was right, like a hunter. He'd come this far, built the nerve, and made his peace with God. It was justified.

As David watched, shifting his weight from his heels to his toes, he thought two things: how much he missed his daughter's smile; and how even in the heat, the revolver's steel felt cool against his skin, tucked into his belt. And in that moment, he had a sudden feeling that some kind of end was near, some kind of resolution. It felt right. He would protect his family. He only hoped they would understand why he had to.

"Thank you once again, ladies and gentlemen," Harry said, his voice crackling through the speakers. "That was a mighty fine way to kick off the thirtieth anniversary of the wonderful tradition of Spring Festival. Such a marvelous, heartfelt show of respect, admiration, and gratitude for one of our own fallen friends. I truly have never felt more proud to be from the humble town of Heartsridge than I do right now, standing before so many friends and family."

The crowd began clapping again, and Harry let the sound drown out his words.

David kept his stare hard on the mayor, wondering if Harry could feel just how close to his own end he was.

CHAPTER 31

Something wasn't sitting right with Gaines as he walked through the crowd in Pride's Square, listening to the final words of Harry Bennett's speech. The name Bill Sexton still floated on the edge of his mind. A chord had been struck that would not stop resonating. It seemed like a waste of energy to continue chasing the alias after the case was closed—it had probably just been a spur-of-the-moment choice by Millis. It could just as easily have been Paul or Dan or John, but he would have bet his life on the fact he'd heard that name before, recently too. He didn't see the point, though. They had a positive ID on the shooter. Sam was gone, and the gun had been sent to the FBI for ballistics, which could take weeks to return any information on where the gun came from. There just didn't seem to be any reason to pursue the case any further at the moment. Yet Gaines could not shake the feeling he had missed something. It all felt too clean and tidy.

His thoughts were interrupted.

"Now, folks, I hope you enjoy the next few days. I know I will. And be sure to eat a slice of pie for me. Heck, make it two. My wife is making me watch my figure," Harry Bennett said, and patted his stomach in a show of humor.

The crowd laughed and then roared with applause.

Gaines watched from the sidewalk as the town ate it up.

The mayor stepped back from the podium and started to wave with his body slightly bowed, a sign he was finished. A drum roll began, followed by a thunderous bang that made Gaines flinch. It always made him flinch, every year, even though he was ready for it. But this time it was especially startling.

The ceremonial cannon blast echoed off buildings and up and down Main Street. A small billow of white smoke drifted lazily around the firing crew in the commons. The crowd roared louder. Band music began to play. And Gaines still couldn't shake the name Bill Sexton.

"Thank you again, ladies and gentlemen. Please have fun and be safe." Harry walked off the stage and started shaking hands.

Gaines turned away, back into his thoughts.

"Calvin, oh Calvin, yoo-hoo." Someone gripped his arm gently. Before he turned, he already knew who it was. He recognized the way the voice seemed to harmonize with itself. It was a sentence spoken by two people simultaneously.

"Hello, girls," Gaines said. "Always a pleasure to see you two."

It was Gertrude and Dolly Thayer, smiling overenthusiastically in their matching white summer dresses. They were twin sisters well into their eighties who had both lost their husbands within a year of each other, a story they were always more than happy to tell to anyone who would lend an ear.

"Hi, Calvin," Gertrude said, fanning herself with a paper fan. "Can you believe how hot it is today?"

"Not even June, and already I feel faint," Dolly added in almost an identical voice. She was also armed with a fan. It was like speaking to one person, the way they finished each other's thoughts and movements.

"Sure is. Picked a heck of a weekend for the festival," Gaines said. "Hope you two are keeping—" But before he could finish the thought...

"Say, did you hear about that girl? The one who's claiming she had an affair with the mayor?" Dolly asked abruptly.

"Yes, Calvin, did you hear?" Gertrude repeated.

Both their faces had tightened into serious scowls. It was all they'd ever wanted to discuss. They waited in anticipation to hear what the sheriff of the town had to say on the matter.

Gaines sighed. "I'm sorry to disappoint you, ladies, but that isn't something that I'm going to discuss. And I don't think you should be, either."

The Thayer sisters looked at each other and smiled. "So it is true," they said in unison.

"Oh, what terrible, terrible lies. Why would a girl say such things about a good man like Harry?" Gertrude said.

"Yes, why indeed?" Dolly touched Gaines's arm with an air of dramatics.

"I'm sorry, ladies. You'll have to excuse me." Gaines turned and walked away.

"I knew it. I knew it." He heard them saying to one another as he removed himself. They had gleaned what they wanted from that brief exchange, and Gaines could only imagine everyone else was doing the same.

An affair? Is that how the story had broken, or had it morphed into that the way rumors do? Now there were two names at the fore of Gaines's mind: Bill Sexton and Kara Price. The witch-hunt had begun. It wouldn't be long before torches were lit and sickles were sharpened—if they weren't already.

Gaines saw Catherine standing opposite him on the street. She nodded, and he walked over.

"Hey, Catherine. Had enough, yet?" Gaines smiled kindly, trying to offer some lightheartedness to cut through the tension that had materialized between them recently. He wondered if in some way Sam's death would restore their relationship, a common grief they could bond over. But even if it did, he doubted it would last. Eventually, Kara Price would be brought up again, eventually tempers would clash. He had told Catherine they would revisit the case after the festival, and part of him hoped she would let it go, but a larger part knew she wouldn't. Maybe that was a good thing, though.

"Hey, Calvin." She returned a soft smile. "How's it going?"

"Not bad. Could use a beer, though." He had an urge to relay the conversation he'd just had with the Thayer twins, but that would only ignite a fire.

"That makes two of us," Catherine said.

Gaines laughed. "Hey, let's say you and I grab a drink later down at Hawk's after we're done here. It's been a while."

Catherine seemed surprised, but then her face fell into a look of accord. "Sure, I could do that."

Gaines smiled, but then his attention shifted. Beyond Catherine, in the commons, was a group of teenagers smoking cigarettes in a gazebo. "Excuse me a sec," Gaines said.

Catherine turned and followed the sheriff's sightline. "Give 'em hell, Calvin," she said.

"I will," he said, already moving toward them.

Before he arrived, the cigarettes were stamped out and butts flicked aside. The kids blew out their smoke in a hurry, trying to look nonchalant. They all appeared to be underage, but that didn't matter—Gaines wasn't about to give anyone a hard time for smoking under the legal limit; he already had enough on his mind. If they wanted to kill themselves, that was their prerogative. He was the sheriff, not their fathers. He just didn't want them doing it in a public place that was full of families.

"All right, you guys, go find an alley or some other place to burn your smokes."

"Sir, we weren't—" one of the kids, the leader of their little gang, started to say.

Gaines cut him off. "Save it. The festival's only four days, guys. Take it someplace else for now."

"Yessir, sorry," said the kid, looking down and away, his acne-covered cheeks flushing with embarrassment. "Not a problem." He started coming down out of the gazebo, and his four friends followed. Before long they disappeared into the crowd.

Gaines stayed back a minute, surveying the scene.

Looking down, he noticed one of the kids' crumpled cigarette butts. He crouched and picked it up. "Why the hell am I cleaning this up?" he said softly under his breath. "Punks."

He stood and made his way to the trashcan beside the gazebo, shaking the crushed filter in the palm of his hand like a lone die. As he did so, his mind went back to Bill Sexton—*Gordon, not Bill*, he had to remind himself—specifically to all the packs of Marlboros he had discovered inside that metal ammo can tucked under the bed.

That had been strange. He couldn't understand why Millis would carry around something like that and hide it under the bed in the motel room if it was only filled with cigarettes. It seemed needlessly cumbersome. The logic didn't line up. Sure, Gordon Millis was a lunatic who had gunned down one of his deputies, so perhaps reason and logic didn't apply here. But Gaines believed there were just some things that were universal truths across the human condition, one of which was that people, in general, seek convenience. And there was nothing convenient about carrying your smokes around in a ten-pound steel box. Maybe he'd overlooked something.

"How'd it go?" a voice startled him, and he turned on his boot heel.

Catherine was standing there. "You picking up trash now? Quite a demotion from sheriff," she said.

"Funny. It was just some kids. They got the idea," Gaines said. He tossed the butt into the trash beside him. "You think you'd be okay without me for an hour or so?"

Catherine looked around. "Shouldn't be a problem. We have six other deputies here. Why? Something wrong?"

Gaines rubbed the back of his neck. "No, just wanted to check on something back at the station."

"You leave the iron on?" Catherine laughed.

Gaines smirked. "Just something that's been bugging me, that's all. It won't take long."

CHAPTER 32

Kara awoke to a boom. It thumped in her chest and echoed in her heart. It was the ceremonial cannon. She recognized it. The faint sound of cheering came quickly after that, barely audible over the cicadas' late-afternoon chatter. Over the last few days she'd come to notice that the sound the cicadas made seemed to thicken as the day went on, becoming deeper and deeper as the day faded, until it seemed the sound set with the sun and merged with the night. There was another eruption of far-off applause and cheering, and suddenly Kara understood who everyone was cheering for—Harry Bennett. The name struck like lightning in her head. Then as her mind continued its ascent from sleep, her thoughts slowly went back to that dark place that scared her.

Kara could only imagine how her name was being tossed around in that crowd. People who didn't even know her would be regurgitating some version of the story they'd heard. None of them knew the truth. But even if they had, she doubted they would have cared. Everyone from her school was surely there, recounting the great prank they had played on that Price girl, the liar who deserved it. A week ago they would've been looked down on for an act like that, punished, but today they were probably heroes: the boys—and girls (she suspected many were involved)—who had shown that nasty girl what happened to liars.

She looked over at the clock on her bedside table. It was 4:12 in the afternoon, and now the tinny sound of brass band music was replacing the applauding citizens of Heartsridge. She knew these sounds so well. Spring Festival was officially underway.

The house was still empty, as far as Kara could tell. She went to the window to check. The smell of fresh-cut grass twirled around her, riding a warm breeze that caressed her face and batted her hair. It was a comforting, nostalgic aroma, one she always associated with the start of summer vacation, only now it felt more like an ending than a beginning. She put her hands on the windowsill and leaned forward, her forehead pressing against the screen as she peered down into the front yard. The driveway was vacant, just as she'd expected. Just as she'd feared. A part of her had wanted to see her father's car parked there, come home to rescue her. As if maybe he could sense what she was thinking about now. Maybe he would arrive just in time to save her from herself.

That was all she wanted: someone to save her. She sure as hell couldn't do it herself. She'd tried and she'd failed. Enough now.

Turning away from her window, away from hope, she looked through her open bedroom door and could see into the bathroom diagonally across the hall. It was so white and clean. So pure. She'd never noticed that before. Something inside Kara pushed her toward that room, almost as if being led there at knifepoint by her despair. Deep down, she knew she didn't want to go. But she didn't have a choice anymore. It was out of her hands. Something far more powerful was at work now.

The phone began to ring as Kara walked into the hallway. She looked toward the stairs at the end of the hall and paused, listening to the ringer clatter away. She did not go answer it. After a few more rings, the caller gave up, and the house was once again silent.

Kara turned away and walked into the bathroom, shutting the door and locking it.

CHAPTER 33

"Hey, Sheriff. Whadya doing back here? The festival's that way," Deputy Briggs said, pointing to the door.

Briggs was a part-time deputy filling in for Carol Matthews, who was currently on a leave of absence. She'd asked to take some time off because of Sam, but Gaines doubted very much she would ever return—and he didn't blame her.

"Forgot I had something to do," Gaines said, continuing past the deputy, down the stairs, and into the evidence room. "Can you buzz me through?"

Deputy Briggs pressed a button, and a loud rattle buzzed from the door.

"Thanks, Arlo," Gaines yelled up from the basement landing. Then he went into the evidence room and shut the door behind him.

The fluorescent lights flickered overhead and painted the room in medical tones. Against the back wall were the folding tables, end to end, three in a row, with all the evidence from the Gordon Millis shooting. At the far end, on the sparsest table, was a bag Gaines did not recognize. As he walked toward it, something inside the bag caught his eye: HEARTSRIDGE COUNTY SHERIFF'S DEPARTMENT. It was the embroidery on the sleeve of Sam's uniform, the one he had been wearing when he was shot. There were brown splotches of dried blood on the inside of the evidence bag. It must've been dropped off by the Medical Examiner that morning.

This is all your fault! a voice screamed from somewhere in his mind.

Gaines averted his gaze. The sight of it was making his stomach squirm like a bucket of eels, and reminiscing on regret wasn't why he was here now anyway. He was here for a purpose. He had come with a certain question in mind: Why the cigarettes in the ammo can? Something about that was odd and had elicited a peculiar curiosity in him. He was missing something. He could feel it, like a misalignment in his brain.

On the opposite end of the tables was the green ammo can, a small yellow evidence tag hanging from the lid handle. Beside it in a bag were the five packs of Marlboros.

Gaines walked to the table and opened the bag. He pulled out each pack and inspected it. They were all unopened and fresh-looking. To be sure, he peeled one pack open and dumped out the contents. Cigarettes and loose flakes of tobacco landed on the table. Gaines plucked a pencil from his pocket and sifted through them, looking for something—anything. The first pack turned up nothing. Then Gaines held up the empty pack, closed one eye, and peered inside. Nothing. He shook it to make sure there wasn't something stuck. Still nothing. Then he did the same thing to the remaining four packs until a small pile of cigarettes and tobacco sat before him on the table.

Gaines dropped the pencil among the cigarettes, pulled a seat over, and sat down. "Waste of time," he said, resting his face against his open palm. He wasn't even sure what he had really expected to find. Maybe an answer that justified or made sense of his friend's death? Or something that made the whole thing seem less pointless?

He leaned forward and hooked a finger under the lid of the ammo can, sliding it to the edge of the table. Gaines peered in, making sure it was empty. It was. He removed his finger.

He grabbed the bag that all the cigarettes had been in, pinched it open, and then with a careful hand he wiped all the Marlboros back into it. The loose-leaf stuff he blew off the table and allowed to scatter to the floor.

Some thorough cop you are, he thought.

For the next fifteen minutes he sat there in silence, staring at the scene, racking his brain, trying to find and overturn some unseen rock in his head. So far all he had been able to do was make a mess of the evidence and get tobacco all over the place. He supposed it really didn't matter. It wasn't as though there was going to be a trial. The evidence would be stored for a little while, then eventually destroyed.

Gaines checked his watch. It was nearly five o'clock. He should probably be getting back to the festival. As sheriff, glad-handing was important at town events. People expected to see him, to talk with him, to air petty grievances they wanted addressed, and today especially, to ask about Kara Price and Harry Bennett. Suddenly Gaines wondered if, perhaps, the only reason he had come down to the evidence room at all was to escape the very people who had elected him in the first place. Maybe he had concocted, and convinced himself of, this thin idea about the cigarettes and the ammunition box being strange, just so he could remove himself for an hour or so.

On the heels of that thought, Gaines spun around in the chair to leave and head back to the festival. As he swiveled, the chairback struck the table and the front edge of the ammo can. There was a loud rattle as the chair jarred the container, and that was followed by an even louder crash as the green metal box fell to the floor.

Gaines stood abruptly. "Shit, God, Christ, fuck it all," he muttered through clenched jaws.

The ammo can bounced awkwardly a few times on its edges and then came to rest on its side, spilling something out onto the floor. Small pieces of metal clinked and clanged in high-pitched symphony, like a fistful of change, only more hollow-sounding. One landed at Gaines's feet. He bent and picked it up. It was a bullet shell.

He held it up to the light for a second, then placed it on the table. He picked up the metal box and looked inside again. This time something was different. The bottom of the container was lifted up a few inches. It was a false bottom, akin to a magician's prop or a drug smuggler's suitcase. He set it down and pried the metal bottom up all the way. His heart pounded in his chest. This was something important. It was the something that didn't make sense. There were a few more bullet casings in an unwrapped plastic baggy, but he brushed them aside. In one corner there was a small collection of driver's licenses bound with a rubber band. Gaines removed them and scanned through the bunch. There were four: William Mathey, Kyle Giuffrida, Stephen Weagle, and Sarah Sexton.

Sarah Sexton and William Mathey... Bill Sexton!

The name finally made sense. It was an amalgamation of Sarah Sexton and William Mathey. But who were they?

And like that, it hit him. How could he have missed it? Why

hadn't his mind gone there before, especially after all the press and newspaper coverage? He had just read those names in an article a few days before.

"Jesus," Gaines whispered.

Laying down the licenses, Gaines reached back into the ammo can and fished out a gold necklace with a cross attached to it. He placed that on the table, too. There was one last thing at the bottom. It looked like photographs, face down. Gaines lifted the edge of one with his fingernail and got a grip on them. He shuffled through them slowly. At first Gaines thought he was looking at more of the same pointless pictures they had found in Millis's motel room, but he quickly realized they were more than that. The first photos that caught his attention and suggested he had discovered something more were pictures of Joanna Renault, presumably taken from somewhere outside the diner at night.

The next two pictures made Gaines reach for the chair.

"No," he said. He could taste his lunch in the back of his throat as he stared down at the pictures. The girl had been telling the truth all along. But deep down he'd always known that. He wanted to believe that up until this moment he'd only been doing his job "responsibly", waiting for proof before he arrested someone on such a character-damning charge as rape. But he knew there was more to it than that.

Dr. Hornsby's voice played on repeat in his head: *People protect their own. People protect their own. People... Protect...*

Gaines held the two pictures, one in each hand, his eyes shifting frantically between them. They both showed the same thing: Harry Bennett on top of Kara Price in the backseat of his Cadillac. Gaines dropped the photos on the table. He didn't need to look any longer to understand what he was seeing. Gordon Millis may not have been a skilled photographer, but he had captured two clear shots of what was going on. He didn't quite know *why* Millis'd had pictures of this, only that for some reason he *had*. And more importantly, he doubted Harry Bennett had any idea they existed.

Then, like a play-by-play being projected onto the silver screen of his brain, Gaines recalled everything about the night Kara broke down and revealed her attacker. How he had doubted everything she said. How at first, he couldn't believe Harry would do such a thing. How even as he began to accept that perhaps Harry wasn't as innocent as he claimed, he had still focused so intently on that small shadow of a doubt, the idea that Kara could be lying, forcing himself to believe what he wanted to believe. But that wasn't even the worst part. The worst was that the doubt he held onto felt all too much like hope. But hope for what? That she was lying? Or that it would all just go away on its own somehow and he wouldn't have to deal with it? *Coward*, he thought.

The answers to those questions were powerful, revealing truths that hollowed his gut. His first instinct was to push them away in his mind, ignore them. Self-preservation and all that. But instead of shying away from the ugliness, he met it head-on, eyes open, dukes up, and for the first time since Saturday, Gaines knew exactly what he needed to do and was prepared to do it. No more hiding.

He dropped his ear toward his shoulder and pressed his radio call button. "Catherine, you there?"

There was a short delay, then Catherine said, "Yeah, Calvin, what's up?"

Gaines looked hard at the pictures in front of him. Finally, he asked, "Where's Harry Bennett?"

CHAPTER 34

Harry made three rounds through the crowd with his wife on his arm, shaking hands, talking to vendors, making small talk, welcoming those from out of town, and pausing for photo-ops. But his focus remained on gauging his people, seeing how the recent rumors were taking to the streets. Was the kindness he was receiving feigned or genuine? Did he have loyalty or distrust? That was what he wanted—needed—to know. He watched the body language of everyone he walked near, met the eyes of every person he spoke with, reading faces, looking for tells like a poker player who'd just bluffed and wanted to know if he was going to be called. But it was quickly becoming clear that he was home free, and it was all thanks to his wife's well-placed seeds of gossip.

He took Allison's hand and squeezed it gently, a demonstration of his appreciation for what she'd done. "Thank you," he said.

She smiled back at him, but something haunted her face.

Allison discreetly pulled her hand from Harry's and said, "They love you, Harry. They always will. You never needed to worry." There was a disquieting tone to her voice, something like regret.

Harry put his hands on his hips and looked around, smiling proudly. "Yes. Yes, I suppose you're right. You were right all along. I should never have been so worried about all that nonsense. Thank you." He leaned in to kiss her, but she offered her cheek.

"Not here," she said. "I don't want to end up on the front page, kissing. They did that last year. It was cheesy."

"I never knew you to be so shy," Harry said, studying his wife's face.

"Well, I guess I am today. This heat's getting to me, I think," she said, and pulled away from Harry. "I'd like to go find a cold drink. You don't need me anymore, do you?"

"No, go find some shade," Harry said, rubbing his fingers across his forehead and massaging his temples. They were starting to pound. "I don't need you anymore."

She turned and began walking toward the food vendors.

Harry laughed to himself, almost in an impressed way, as he watched her go. All that time he had spent worrying about how others felt about him, and he had missed the thing right in front of him. She'd been so convincing. He actually thought Allison had believed him, that she stood by his innocence. But the only reason she had helped him at all was to protect her own interests. Because no one—especially a spouse—could spend over two decades with someone and not have any idea what kind of person they were. No one could be so stupid and naïve. *That* is what people—the papers, the news, all media—would say if the real truth had been first to the street. Her name would've been dragged through the mud along with his, and *that* would have been a scandal. Instead, now it was only a mish-mash of rumors, all suggesting the same thing: a troubled girl trying to tarnish a good man.

Harry didn't know when or how his wife had drawn her conclusion about him. Perhaps she had known all along. He didn't hate her or love her any differently in light of this. He only understood it and accepted it. She would be cold to him from now on, as long as they were together. That was the game. Maybe someday she might come around. Probably not. He wasn't entirely sure. The one thing he was certain of, though, was that she would never voice her true feelings to the world, and that was all he cared about. The cost to herself would be far too great. It would be a suicide worse than death, especially for a woman of her disposition.

"Harry, can we talk?" a voice spun him around. It was Eddie Corbett.

"Eddie, my friend, how the hell are you? Been meaning to call you." Harry slapped Eddie hard on the shoulder, spreading a smile on thick.

"I'm sure you have," Eddie said, squinting into the sun, face pulled into a scowl. "Can we—"

"Talk? Of course." Harry draped his heavy arm around Eddie. "Walk with me," he said, and he began leading Eddie away from the crowd, toward the commons. "I'm in a good mood today, Eddie. What do you want to bend my ear about?"

"I think you know, Harry."

They reached the gazebo in the commons. It was vacant. Harry cocked his elbow and rested it on the railing, folding his hands in front of him, leaning casually off-center. "What? The pictures? Is that what you're worried about? I told you they're safe."

"Yes, the pictures… *and* the negatives. I want them gone. I held up my end of the bargain. I gave you use of my parking lot. Two of my tenants already complained. They could break their leases because of this."

"Okay, okay, relax. I know you held up your end. And no one's breaking any leases, I'll see to that. But it's only Thursday, and I'm going to keep those pictures as an insurance policy until Sunday—then they're yours. I promise. I just need to be sure you won't renege on your word the second I give you what you're asking for. Then I'd really have a mess on my hands."

"How do I know you won't hold onto them and pull the same shit next year?"

Harry laughed. "You don't. That's the beauty of me being here and you being there. You'll just have to trust me."

Eddie stepped back and balled his hands into clumsy fists, his face clouding over. He looked around cautiously for a moment and then said, "I've heard what that girl is saying about you... the gist, anyway. Jeannie hasn't shut up about it. Keeps talking about how tragic it all is that someone would make up something so terrible about such a wonderful guy like Harry Bennett."

"Well, that's real nice of Jeannie to support me. I always respected her opin—"

"Cut the bullshit, Harry. You may have the wool pulled over all these people's eyes, but I know the real you. You're as fake as they come. Now, I don't know what happened between you and that girl—and honestly I don't care, the sheriff can sort that out—but I do know that you're certainly not the saint they think you are."

Harry's eyes shot open in surprise. In all the years he'd known Eddie, the man had never shown even a hint of the confidence he was showing now, and it scared him. "You really think I could do what that girl is claiming?"

"I don't know, and I don't care. That isn't my problem. That's *your* problem," Eddie said, seeming to further his courage. "But I do think you're arrogant enough to think you could get away with something like that, so you tell me."

Harry straightened his posture, trying to intimidate Eddie. He'd gotten his attention. "What are you getting at?"

Eddie didn't back down. "I'm saying that it didn't take me all that long to see you for who you really are. And I'm sure if I showed people where to look, they'd see it too."

"Suppose I *do* hold onto these pictures, what'll you do then? What if I tell you that you'll never see them, and you can spend the rest of your days wondering if Jeannie is going to wake up one morning and find a nice surprise pinned under her windshield wiper, or at work, or at your kid's school, or hung on telephone poles for all I fucking care?"

"I'll take my chances, if that's the way you want to go. I brought this on myself, I can accept that, but I sure as hell won't let you ruin my life without me doing the same to you. Jeannie finds out, she'll divorce me for sure, and then you'll just have a pissed-off, middle-aged man out there with nothing to lose, with no goal other than to take you down. And I'll do just that. I'll make sure people know the real Harry Bennett. I'll show them the guy who drowns house pets, you sick asshole. That really something you want to deal with?"

Harry and Eddie locked eyes. It was a standoff. The two held fast on each other, neither man breaking, like a game of chicken. Then out of nowhere, Harry smiled and laughed. "Well, hell, Eddie, it looks like I was wrong about you after all. Got a little fight in you yet."

Eddie said nothing, only continued his stare.

Harry grabbed Eddie's shoulder again and gave him a gentle shake. "All right, okay, here's what I'll do—like I said, I'm in a good mood today, feeling trustworthy, you know?—I'll head over to my office and grab what you're after and bring 'em back to you, and you can do with 'em what you'd like. How's that sound?"

"When?" Eddie asked flatly.

"All business with you now, huh?"

"When, Harry?" Eddie repeated.

Harry could see he had pushed the man to his breaking point, given him no avenue of escape, and that was a dangerous thing to do. It made a person fight to the death if they thought it was the only way to survive. And besides, he really didn't need those pictures anymore, anyway. He'd just wanted to toy with the man a little. He'd done that, and now it was time to let him out from underneath his thumb. "Shoot, right now if you'd like. I can be there and back in twenty. Can you live with that? You're welcome to come with me if you'd like."

"No, don't bring them here. Meet me at the dump in an hour. I want to watch you burn it all, just so I know for sure," Eddie said. "I want this over and done with."

"You have my word," Harry said.

Eddie scoffed. "Not sure that really means anything to me, but I know you'll do it. In the end, you always do what's best for you. Well, when your temper doesn't get the best of you." He smiled derisively at Harry, as if to say *I've got your number*.

And he did.

Harry almost lost it at that but caught himself before he hauled off and hammered the guy in front of fifteen hundred people, which would only serve to prove Eddie was right. Instead, through a clenched jaw, he said, "You know, I really was wrong about you." But Eddie didn't offer any sign of acknowledgment or that he cared. He only turned and walked away.

Harry waited until Eddie was out of range before breaking down in a fit of muttered expletives. He had waited because he didn't want Eddie to know how effectively he had riled him.

After he composed himself, Harry walked out of the commons,

away from the crowds of people, and toward the Woolworth's parking lot where he had parked earlier. Harry slunk into his car. He could take care of this before anyone even noticed he was gone All he had to do was go to his office, meet Eddie at the dump, burn the photos, and come back. Easy as pie. And it would get Eddie off his back. Of course, he would save one or two negatives just in case the little shit decided to turn on him. What choice did he have? Eddie had proven to be a bit more spirited than Harry had ever thought him to be. Allison had been right: sometimes he did underestimate people. For now, he would let Eddie think he had won this battle; it was safer that way.

He pulled out onto North Main Street and headed to his office, taking the back roads to avoid being seen. His mind still reeling from his exchange with Eddie, Harry never noticed the Oldsmobile station wagon tailing him.

He continued, and David Price followed.

CHAPTER 35

Ellie Price picked up the phone in her office and, for the third time in an hour, called home to check on Kara. Once again there was no answer. It was 5:02.

CHAPTER 36

It was like a valve inside him had opened, and finally Gaines could hate Harry Bennett freely, without hesitation and without needing to think rationally or responsibly. No more obstacles. No more worrying about ruining careers or a lack of evidence, because there it was, sitting beside him on the front seat of his cruiser. But this came at a price to his conscience. There was a sour realization underlying it all: he hadn't earned this sudden, well-defined thirst for vengeance. The pictures he'd found were an undeserved license to feel the way he did. It's easy to call a bluff when you can see all the cards.

"You find him yet?" Gaines spoke into his radio as he pulled out of the station.

Catherine's voice came through on the receiver. "No, I just did a lap through Pride's Square but didn't see him. He was here about fifteen minutes ago, though. Not sure where he is now. If I see him, you want me to tell him you're looking for him?"

"No. I don't want to spook him."

"Spook him? What's this about?"

"Just keep looking," Gaines said. "I'll tell you when I get there. And if you find him, don't let him out of your sight."

"Does this have to do with Kara? Did you find something? Is that why you left?" Catherine asked eagerly.

Gaines held the radio silent for a beat and then said, "Yes... but it's more than that. Just hold tight and I'll fill you in when I get there."

"I knew it," she said. "What is it, a witness? Is that it?"

"Catherine, just hold tight, I'll be there in a minute. I'm heading by Town Hall now. And if you do see Harry, don't—"

Something caught Gaines's eye as he crested the small hill before Town Hall. Harry's red Cadillac was parked in its reserved spot in the parking lot.

"Yeah, yeah, I know. I won't do anything without you," Catherine said.

"No, hold on, wait a second. I think I just found him," Gaines said, applying the brakes and slowly pulling in beside Harry's car.

"What? Where?"

Hesitating, Gaines said, "I'm looking at his car here at his office."

"Must've snuck out," Catherine said. "I didn't see him leave. You sure it's him?"

"I doubt Harry would lend out his car, so I'd say so, yeah." Gaines killed his engine. "Listen, you should make your way over here."

"Can you at least tell me what I'm walking into?"

Gaines hesitated no more. The cat was out of the bag. "He did it," he said bluntly.

"How do you know?"

"I found proof. I'm going to arrest him. I just thought you might want to... well... I thought you might want to be there when the cuffs go on. You were the one who..." He trailed off but knew Catherine understood.

"You thought right. I'm heading there now."

The radio fell silent.

Gaines grabbed the two pictures off the passenger seat and stepped out of the car.

CHAPTER 37

Harry Bennett's silhouette moved behind the frosted pane of glass in his door as David Price moved up the hallway, toward the office. Halfway there, he removed the pistol from his waistband and cocked the hammer. His heart was pounding so hard it felt like it might leap out of his chest. His fingers itched with nervous sweat as he tightened them around the gun's grip. It was now or never. Once he opened that door there was no turning back, and he was at peace with that. This had to be done. It was the only way anyone could move on. His family needed justice. So he would give it to them.

David stopped when he reached the door. Closing his eyes, he took a long, deep breath and thought of his daughter. He pictured Kara's smile and how long it had been since he had seen it.

Remember what he did, a voice played over and over again in his head. *Remember, remember, remember, remember...*

But of course he would remember. How could he forget?

The door swung open in one quick motion, and David scanned the room. Harry was now sitting at his desk, a small lockbox in his lap. Behind him, a large safe was cracked open.

"Can I help you?" Harry said, sitting up straight.

David entered the room and raised the gun, pointing it at the center of Harry's chest.

Harry leaned back in his chair. "Whoa, whoa, whoa. Now hold on a minute." At the sight of a gun he instinctively raised his hands. "I don't know what you want, pal—"

But everything after the word "pal" fell on deaf ears. Right then, the look on Harry's face spoke loudest to David. Harry hadn't the slightest clue who he was. "You don't even know, do you, you son of a bitch?"

"Know what?" Harry said tentatively. "All I know is you have a gun pointed at me. I'd really appreciate it if you lowered it so you could tell me what's wrong."

"Me! You don't know *me!*" David yelled. Then, sobering, "You take my daughter away from me, and you don't even know who I am." He took a step closer. Under the harsh office lights, David's defeated appearance was undeniable: bloodshot eyes, unshaven face, sunken cheekbones, greasy hair. Desperation's last stand.

"I don't know who you're talking about. But I didn't take anyone from you. And you're right, I don't know who you are. I know you're a local, I've seen you before, but I can't say I know you. Maybe if you told me your name—"

"Oh, go fuck yourself with all that country-charm bullshit. You raped my daughter, and now you want to try and pretend you care about getting to know me?" David tightened his grip on the gun.

"So you're David Price... the girl's father," Harry said, as if it all made sense now. "And that's what this is about? Your daughter?" He allowed his hands to drift downward. "Mr. Price—David—I don't know what you've been told, but I swear by my life that what your daughter is accusing me of never happened. I could never do such awful—"

"Shut up! Just *shut* your goddamn *mouth!*" David snapped. "Everyone else may buy into your bullshit, but I don't. I know my girl. I know when she's lying. And she isn't. You really think I'd be standing here if I wasn't sure? Do you?" He ran his free hand frantically through his hair, sweeping it to the side. "Now stand up. Stand up and look me level in the eyes. I want to hear you admit it." He didn't *want* to hear the words; he *needed* to hear them. They were his validation, his final assurance that what he was doing was right and just.

David raised the gun higher and stiffened his arm, fixing his aim on Harry's face and taking another half-step forward.

Harry flinched back. "Listen, just calm down. You don't know what you're doing. Your daughter isn't telling the truth."

"I said stand!" David swept the gun a few inches to the right of Harry's head and fired at the wall. The pistol cracked, and a picture fell to the floor in a chorus of broken glass. He reset his aim on Harry, whose head was now ducked down and away from where the bullet had struck.

"All right. Jesus. Okay. You win," Harry said. He lifted the lock box off his lap, setting it on the desk. "But just listen to me. If I did what she said—"

"Kara. Her name is Kara," David interrupted. "You can't even say her name, can you?"

"Okay, sorry… Kara. If what Kara said is true, where is the evidence? Besides what she claims, where is the proof I did what she said? You're just going to execute me based on what your teenage daughter said about me? She's lying." Harry's words were calm and calculated. "I don't know why she is, but she is. Maybe she needs help."

"I know you did it. I know my girl. I know—" A figure registered in David's periphery, and he turned to look.

"Christ, David, what are you doing?" Gaines stood in the doorway, his pistol drawn but aimed at the floor. "I heard a gunshot. What's going—"

"Stay out of this, Calvin. I didn't want to involve you in this," David said.

"Little late for that." Gaines took a small step forward.

"Sheriff, get this nut out of my office," Harry said.

David turned back to Harry, reinforcing his aim. He began to apply pressure to the trigger. Just one bullet and Harry Bennett was gone. That simple. Justice served.

"Don't say a word, Harry," Gaines said. "David, stop, please. Don't do this. He isn't worth it."

"I know he isn't, but my daughter is."

"I know she is, David. I know she is. But if you kill him, what good'll that do her?"

"Listen to him," Harry said. "Take that pistol off me. We can talk this out."

"Harry, I swear to God I'll shoot you myself if you don't shut your damn mouth." Gaines took another slow step into the room.

Harry's face darkened, but he kept silent.

Gaines lowered his arms more, his gun down by his side, still in both hands. "David, please, just listen to me. It's over."

"No, it's over when he's dead. He took my daughter from me. He took my Kara. You know she won't even talk to me? Did you know that? Every time she sees me, all she can think of is him. He can't get away with this." Two fat tears streaked down David's cheeks.

"You don't understand," Gaines said earnestly. "He's not getting away with anything. Not anymore. You need to listen to me."

Harry's eyes widened. Why wasn't he going to get away with it? He sure as hell was!

"'Listen to you?' Is that what you want me to do?" David said, his voice cracking. "So far you've done nothing. Not a damn thing. If you'd done your job, I wouldn't be here right now. So why should I listen?"

Gaines took another step. "I know. You're right. I screwed up. I should've done more. But my hands were tied, and it wasn't that simple." He was making excuses for his cowardice. His stomach tightened with guilt, but he would need to worry about that later.

David looked pleadingly at Gaines. "Please, just turn around and leave. Do that one thing for me. Wait for me downstairs if you'd like. I won't put up any kind of fight. I'll go with you after this is over. Just leave for now. Please."

"I can't do that, and you know it. I can't allow you to just murder someone… and I don't think you really want to either. But look, I'm going to put my gun away so we can talk." Gaines slid it carefully back into his holster and showed his hands. "You need to know something before you pull that trigger."

"How'd you know I'd even be here?" David asked, his tone breaking in confusion as though something new had connected in his brain.

"I didn't. I'm not here for you, David. That's what I'm trying to tell you. I'm here for Harry."

"What do you mean? I don't understand," David said, his eyes still set hard on Harry.

"I came to arrest him. That's why I'm here. Not to stop you. That was just good timing, I suppose. But I can't arrest him if you pull that trigger," Gaines said, slowly easing toward David, hands up.

"Hold on. What?" Harry said, taking a step forward and ignoring the gun pointed at him, as if it had never fazed him to begin with. "Arrest me for what?"

"Get back!" David yelled, nearly driving the barrel of the gun into Harry's eye socket.

Harry backed up but continued: "Arrest me for what? Are you out of your damn mind, Calvin? I thought we already talked about this. That girl is spitting lies like snake venom. She has it in for me, and I don't know why. You can't believe—"

"Just stop, Harry. You're done. I know you did it," Gaines said, looking Harry dead in the eyes. He wanted him to know he was for real. "Hell, I think I always knew you did it, but now there's proof."

"Proof? What proof?" Harry wrinkled his face.

"Let's talk about that in a second," Gaines said, gesturing to David. "In case you didn't notice, Mr. Price here has you fitted for a toe-tag."

David looked over at Gaines. "What are you talking about? What did you find?"

"You don't want to know that right now. You need to trust me on this. I know you got no reason to, but please, I'm begging you, give me the gun. He's going to jail, and I promise you that'll be a whole lot worse." He knew if he showed David those pictures, rage would take the place of any reason he had left inside him. There would be no stopping him after that.

"But you don't get it… my daughter… she…" David was losing focus, and the gun was beginning to tremble.

"Yes, I know. And I don't blame you. I can't say I would be doing the same thing if I was you," Gaines said. "But you're a better man than me, so just give me the gun and go home. Go tell your family that it's over. Go tell Kara."

Again, Harry stiffened nervously. Why was he going to jail? Why was Gaines so certain?

David started lowering the gun. "How're you just going to let me walk out of here? You can't do that. Not after this."

"Yes I can, and that's exactly what I'm gonna do. I owe you at least that much."

David grappled with the decision, tightening and then re-tightening his fingers on the pistol grip, lowering his arm a few inches and then raising it again. He'd come so far. There was no turning back... or maybe there was.

Harry remained calm as the gun trembled in front of his face.

"You deserve every damn bullet in this chamber," David said coldly to Harry. "I should put you down like the sick dog you are. People like you shouldn't be allowed to live." He reset his aim one last time, stiffening his arm to steel, grinding his teeth, clenching until it felt like his molars might pop. His finger danced softly against the cold curve of the trigger. So easy. One pull and he's gone. But was that the best justice for Kara? A father kept behind bars might only serve as an awful reminder, make it impossible for her to live a normal life. Finally, David dropped his arm, the gun hanging listlessly in his hand. "You aren't worth it," he said.

Gaines moved the rest of the distance to David and placed his hand on the pistol. David didn't fight it but kept his hate-rich stare on the mayor.

Harry angled his head back and narrowed his eyes. "I'm sorry you feel that way. But I promise you you're mistaken. Whatever the sheriff thinks he has or knows I'm sure will prove to be another lie. This is all just a big misunderstanding."

David glanced over at Gaines, who shook his head, as if to assure him that Harry was wrong: there were no misunderstandings. "I don't think so." David turned away from Harry and walked to the door, stopping next to Gaines. "I really hope you know what you're doing."

"I do. You did the right thing," Gaines said, and patted David's arm. "Now go home. I'll be by when I'm done here." He leaned forward and tucked David's pistol behind his back. "I'm going to hold onto this for now."

David offered something close to a smile but said nothing. Then he walked out of the room, down the hall, and was gone.

When David was out of sight, Gaines shifted his attention back to Harry. The room had grown thick with the tension of unresolved conflict. "Calvin, you've got to be fucking kidding me." Harry threw his hands in the air. "What's the matter with you? Have you lost it? I'm telling you, as mayor, it's an order, go arrest him. You can't just let him walk. He pulled a gun on me, for Christ's sake. I'm the mayor. That wasn't just some empty threat. He was going to kill me if you hadn't shown up. You and I can talk about this Kara Price stuff later. I assure you, whatever you've heard, it's just more rumors—"

"I don't think so, Harry. You're done talking. Sit down," Gaines said, pointing to the chair. "I don't take my orders from you. I take them from the people who elected me. I work for them, and it's about time I actually started to."

Harry scowled. "You really want to go this route? Once you head down this path, there's no turning back."

Gaines took a firm step toward the mayor. "I said sit."

A hateful look washed over Harry, but he obeyed, lowering himself slowly back into his chair. "You have no idea the shitstorm that's in for you. You're going to be finished, all because some high school girl has some fucked-up grudge against—"

"Finished? Really? Because I was thinking the same thing about you." Gaines slid two fingers into his pocket and produced the photographs, throwing them on the desk in front of Harry.

"Whadya make of these? Because *I* think they are pretty clear. Don't you?"

Harry leaned forward and inspected the pictures. His face slowly fell into a frown, and his lips parted. "Where did you get these? This isn't me," Harry said dismissively. There was a desperate, nervous quality to his voice. "I don't know where you got these, but someone's pulling your leg."

"Oh really?" Gaines said, leaning on the desk and looking down at the pictures. "So that isn't you?" He pointed to the clear shot of Harry. It was unmistakably him. "And that isn't Kara Price? And that isn't your car with your matching license plate? 'Cause it sure looks like it to me—and I'm sure it will look like it to a judge and jury, too."

Harry placed both hands on his desk and shook his head, his eyes darting between the pictures and Gaines anxiously. "This isn't what you think—"

"I know what I think. I think you're a smug son of a bitch who thought he'd never get caught. You fooled a lot of people—hell, you fooled me—but it's over. People will know who you are." Gaines hadn't really been fooled, though. Worse. Harry had forced him to see a character flaw in himself he had never known existed: cowardice. And that was far worse than being fooled. From now on, that would be what Gaines saw when he looked into a mirror: a man too selfish, too afraid, to do what needed to be done. For that, a large part of Gaines wished he hadn't stopped David from pulling that trigger.

"You're dumber than I thought if you think people want to hear the truth. You really think they don't already know? They'll hate you more than me for rubbing their faces in it. People believe what's easiest for them, just like you did." Harry interlaced his fingers over his head, leaned back, and started laughing.

"Without these pictures, you'd be right back on the other side of the fence, same place you were two days ago."

"Maybe. You're probably right. But it doesn't change the fact that you're going to jail." Gaines slid his handcuffs off his belt.

Harry eyed them. "Okay, fine, you got me. You caught the bad guy. Big deal. The little cunt deserved it. Nothing changes that. You should've heard the way she was talking about this town—about our traditions—like it… like we were all just some big joke to her."

"She was fifteen, Harry. *Fifteen!* Same age as my daughter. Now stand up and put your hands behind your back. Let's get this over w—"

"I don't give a shit!" Harry screamed, snapping forward and slamming his hand down on the photos. "She was old enough. She was old enough to learn her lesson and take her damn medicine."

Gaines backed up a step, his hand instinctively moving to his gun. "Relax, Harry. I'm not going to tell you twice. I'm not here to debate with you. I'm here to take you in. You can talk all you want at the station."

Harry's eyes curled up at their corners and he cackled again. It was a loud, mad, insane laugh. "Or what? You're going to shoot me? Is that it? You'll put one right between my fuckin' eyes?" He took his finger and pressed it hard against his own forehead. "Blow my brains out? That what you wanna do, Cal? Wanna be the hero, Sheriff? Do it. Do me a favor."

The moment was escalating. Gaines would've waited for Catherine had he not heard a gunshot and come to investigate. Control was slipping away from him. The hairs on his neck were on end. His face thumped to the beat of his heart.

Harry stood and leaned forward on his desk, smiling wickedly. "Let me ask you something, Sheriff—is this all the evidence you have? Do you have anymore photos, or are these all of 'em?"

Gaines straightened his shoulders and stuck out his chest. Harry was a big man, but so was he. The veiled threat hung in the air. "I'm not going to ask you again. Turn around." His right hand hovering near his gun and his left clutching the handcuffs, he began moving around the desk toward Harry.

"No problem," Harry said, with an I-know-something-you-don't smile. He turned around and faced his open safe. His hands remained at his sides, his fingers itching like a gunslinger's directly before a duel. The moment Gaines noticed this...

"Calvin, you up here?" a voice called from down the hall. It was Catherine. "I thought you were going to wait for me." She rounded the corner.

Gaines turned and looked in her direction. "I got this."

Catherine's eyes widened, and her face set to stone. She reached for her revolver. "Gun!" she yelled, and began to draw.

Gaines looked back to Harry. He was turning away from his safe. The nickel-plated pistol glimmered as it cut a swath through the air and set its sights on Catherine.

Gaines sidestepped into the line of fire, his pistol half out of its holster.

Harry fired.

The bullet struck Gaines in the chest and spun him sideways. The handcuffs flew out of his hand. There was another bright flash and a loud crack as Harry pulled the trigger again. This time it caught Gaines in the arm, and he fell against the wall, sliding to the floor. His gun tumbled beneath the desk. It felt as if he had taken two blows with a sledgehammer. His breath was immediately out of reach, his throat hot with trespassing blood. He coughed, and blood sprayed out onto his hands and down his chin. The room sounded muffled, as though he had his fingers in his ears. Everything around him was moving slowly. The walls and the ceiling started to turn and spin, his mind detaching from his body. His thoughts became thick and clumsy. His face tingled, and his hands went numb. He tried to look up, but he couldn't find the strength. His chin against his chest, blackness enveloped him, and he was unconscious.

"Cal!" Catherine yelled, and took two steps toward him, but Harry fired on her, striking the wall. Small cloud-bursts of drywall exploded with each shot, crumbling to the floor with the sound of dense sand. It was happening so fast. She had imagined this type of thing a million times—what it would be like, how she would react. But this was the real thing. Actions were quick. Life and death hanging milliseconds apart.

Harry fired again, the bullet striking inches above her head. He stepped out from behind his desk and stood beside Gaines, who was breathing shallowly on the floor, head down. Harry ignored him and moved into the doorway. A fearless man with everything to lose.

"You want a fucking lesson, too?" he screamed. "'Cause I got seven more with your name on them, Deputy."

Catherine ducked into a recessed doorway. Quietly, she radioed in for backup and an ambulance.

CRACK! CRACK! Harry rattled off two more shots. The wooden molding of the doorjamb splintered, fragments landing in Catherine's hair.

How many shots was that? Catherine tried to calculate: *seven... no, eight... maybe it was six?* It was the kind of thing she had always envisioned being able to keep track of in a situation like this—that little piece of knowledge that would save her life. But in the end, it all boiled down to dumb luck and guts, it seemed.

"Where the hell did those pictures come from?" Harry called down the hall. "I gotta tell you, I'm really curious."

Pictures? Catherine didn't yet know about the photos. "Put it down, Harry. I don't know what you're talking about. I don't know anything about any pictures. Let's you and me just talk." But who was she kidding? That never worked. This was well past negotiation. Only one of them would be walking away from this.

There was a beat of silence. Slowly the void filled with the approach of sirens.

"You called your friends? You bitch. You shouldn't've done that." There was a sarcastic malevolence in his voice that sent chills up Catherine's spine.

CRACK! CRACK!

The bullets shook the framing beneath the wall and vibrated against her shoulder. She peered around the corner. Harry was in the doorway to his office twenty feet away, gun fixed on her position. Beside him on the ground, Gaines was unconscious, blood soaking the front of his shirt. There was no sign of life, but she only caught a glimpse before Harry fired on her again and she was forced back into cover. She managed to squeeze off one blind round. It struck the window beside the door, shattering it into a rain of broken shards. She needed to conserve her ammunition. She was outmatched. Harry's pistol was a semi-automatic that seemed to hold an endless supply of bullets. She only had six—now five—rounds, plus a spare six on her belt. But her revolver was a bear to reload quickly.

"I was wondering if you were ever gonna use that thing. That's good, I'd like a little fight," Harry said. "Most girls never fight back. Kara didn't. She just cried like a little baby. Are you gonna cry, Deputy?"

Pressed flat into the doorway, she gripped her gun tightly,

breathed deep, and closed her eyes for a moment. "You got this, Catherine," she whispered to herself. There would be no waiting for backup. She was on her own.

Then something occurred to her: every shot Harry had taken at her had been high, presumably aimed at her head and torso. *Shoot for the center of mass,* she recalled from her training. That's what he was doing. He was shooting where he *thought* she was, and where he thought would inflict the most damage. If Catherine went low Harry might be caught off guard just long enough to buy her a clean shot.

She peered out again to set the bait.

Harry bit and fired, this time the round cutting through the hollow corner of the wall and striking behind her. Debris burst against the side of her face.

Harry was slowly making his way up the hall, opening up his angle on her. A few more feet and her cover would be gone. It would turn into an all-out mess of gunfire on each other. No reason or tactics, just empty the pistol and pray your bullets land first.

Catherine crouched as low as she could and waited, making sure no part of her could be seen.

Harry couldn't have been more than fifteen feet away now. "Calvin's not looking so good, Deputy," he said. "You going to let him bleed out? I'll let you tend to him if you'd like. Just come out here. I promise I won't—"

Catherine leaned out, low on one knee. Harry had his gun aimed high over her head. His face fell flat.

And before he could relock Catherine in his sights, she squeezed the trigger.

CHAPTER 38

Kara slipped into the tub, the frigid water stealing her breath as she submerged. This wasn't what she'd planned on—if anything, she'd heard hot water worked best to open capillaries—but in building up her conviction, she'd filled and drained the bath four times in the last hour. Each time she'd fill it, she'd sit on the edge of the tub, staring into the water, then lose her nerve and yank the plug. She'd stay and watch it completely empty out, listening to the slurping sounds the drain made as it drank up the last bits of water. Then she'd find her resolve, fill it up again, and do it all over. So now the water-heater was empty, and cold water was all that remained for her. Tough luck, but compromises could be made for the occasion. Cold water would suffice. And wasn't going out with a chill just perfectly ironic, anyway? A little secret joke between her and God. It was just like the creek where she had washed herself clean after Harry had raped her, even if the two were only comparable in a symbolic way. What she was after now was a different kind of cleansing, but a purifying act just the same. Blood could be washed off. Cuts could be cleaned out, patched, healed. Sweat, tears, and dirt could be wiped away. That kind of stuff was surface grime, cosmetic damage. But how do you clean a soul? How do you deal with internal filth? How do you purge pain so deep-rooted that it's become your identity? Simple. This was how. A deep breath. Two cuts. Slowly fade to darkness while all the poison drains out. Clean.

Kara's shirt sucked against her stomach as she slid deeper into the water, her breath returning in slow, steady drags.

When she was a kid, she used to spend hours in that very same tub, pretending she was a frog, a fish, some aquatic thing, blowing bubbles, seeing how long she could hold her breath, rubbing her eyes raw with soapy water, until her mother or father would come in and make her get out. But there was no one to make her get out now. The house was empty, save for the ghosts of childhood memories. And those nostalgic glimpses into a better time only served to edge her toward release.

Beginning to shiver, she slid her hand farther down the porcelain ledge of the tub and picked up the razor resting on the soap tray. It was a straight blade with a pearl handle. Her father had bought it for himself a few years back and had been so proud of it, proclaiming on the day that he walked through the front door with it that from then on he would shave like a "real man." That lasted exactly one day. A failed attempt, which led to him looking as if he had wrestled a barbed-wire fence using nothing more than his face, decommissioned the razor. He kept it in the bathroom, though, refusing to throw it away, as if doing so would be admitting defeat. So there it sat on the soap tray for years, growing rust but holding its edge just fine. Sharp as ever. Kara smiled at the thought of her father's bleeding, toilet-paper-dressed face. How he had insisted that the razor was defective and his unsteady hand was certainly not to blame. The man had pride; she couldn't deny that. The way she had treated him the last few days was, perhaps, her only regret in this moment. But regrets, like secrets, were acceptable things to carry to the grave. They're honest weight, the burden of which is the holder's right to bear.

She opened the razor and ran the blade over the back of her hand, testing the edge. A thin, dark thread began to sweat blood. A drop traced her wrist and dripped into the tub, diluting into the water. Defined then gone, just like her.

The phone rang again, but Kara ignored it. She slipped deeper into the water until her ears submerged and all she could hear were her own steady breaths.

CHAPTER 39

A jet of blood sprayed from Harry's neck as he staggered backwards, backpedalling slowly until he was back in his office and sitting on the edge of his desk. He slapped his hand over the gunshot wound, but it did nothing. Dark crimson oozed out in thick pulses. "You bitch," he gurgled, still clutching his pistol.

Catherine held her position in the hall, her revolver held tight on Harry. "Drop the gun."

He said nothing, only panted stiff breaths with an angry grimace. The lower right side of his face was painted in fresh blood, where a large flap of flesh hung down from between his fingers.

"C'mon, Harry, put it down." Catherine rose off her knee and got to her feet.

Harry stared down, wheezing, the gun hanging by his side. Either he couldn't talk, or he wouldn't. Small breaths hissed from his nose as blood started to darken his shirt in a hurry.

Catherine cautiously walked toward him, her gun held fast on his center of mass. "Harry, I won't tell you again."

Both understood what came next. The mayor of Heartsridge

looked up at Catherine, and their eyes locked. She could see it—a clear view of the immediate future. A predestined fate hanging in the space between them. It was going to happen whether she wanted it to or not. Harry smiled at her balefully, bearing his bloody teeth, then the pistol twitched in his hand and his arm rose toward her.

Catherine fired twice, the revolver bucking in her hand. The bullets struck Harry's chest and he jerked back, sprawling over his desk, his gun dropping to the floor. There was a long, wet gasp, and finally, his mouth fell open and he lay motionless. Silence blanketed the room, and time stopped. Her ears rang. It had all happened so fast. It didn't seem possible that taking a life was only a matter of moving your finger an inch. So easy. So quick. Pull a trigger, and it's here one second, gone the next.

Catherine held her gun on Harry for a moment longer, frozen in her firing stance, waiting for him to get up. "Harry?" she said doubtfully, but there was no answer.

The sound of sirens and screeching tires were no longer far-off, pouring into the parking lot right outside Town Hall. Finally, Catherine lowered her gun and rushed to Gaines, surprised to find that he was still breathing. She pressed two fingers against his carotid. There was a pulse—faint but there. He moved his head to the side, and his eyes fluttered open. He reached up and placed his hand on hers.

"Hold still, Cal. I called an ambulance. You're gonna be fine." Catherine applied pressure to his wounds.

Gaines grimaced. "I can't hear them anymore," he whispered.

"Hear what, Cal?"

"The cicadas—I can't hear them." His words were disconnected and slow.

"Just focus on the sound of my voice and hang on."

There was a loud crash as first-responders came in through the front door.

"Up here," Catherine raised her head and yelled. When she looked back Gaines's eyes were closed.

"Cal... Cal, c'mon, stay with me." She tapped the side of his face. Nothing.

Deputy Gerund and another rookie appeared at the end of the hallway and rushed over, guns drawn, followed by two emergency personnel with medical kits and a gurney.

"What happened?" One of the paramedics knelt beside Gaines and began assessing him.

Catherine stumbled for a second, her mind reeling. It was a good question. But she fought through the shock. "Gunshot... two of them. One in the chest, the other I think in the arm."

"All right, we'll take it from here," someone said. She couldn't be sure who; the scene was so surreal. She was in the midst of some cruel dream, and before she knew it, the sheriff was being carried down the stairs with an oxygen mask over his face.

Catherine stood and interlaced her fingers over her head. They were sticky with her colleague's blood. It took a moment, but finally she breathed, reality setting in.

"Jesus, what went down here?" Gerund asked, holstering his revolver.

The second deputy emerged from Harry's office visibly shaken. "I can't find a pulse. I think he's dead." There was a brief pause, then he said, "I ain't never seen a dead body up close before." He shook his head. "I can't believe you shot Harry Bennett. Shit. What the hell happened?"

Catherine looked around. "I don't know—not exactly. I walked into it. It all happened so fast..." She trailed off when her eyes fell on the bloodstain Gaines had left behind on the floor.

Silence filled the hallway, and Catherine looked up. The two deputies, baby-faced and doe-eyed, were just standing there, staring at her.

Why aren't they saying anything? she thought.

And suddenly a startling realization hit her: with Sam gone, and Sheriff Gaines in God knows what condition, she was the senior officer. This was her show now, and they were waiting to be told what to do.

"All right, this is a crime scene now," she said, a new, powerful clarity taking over. "Deputy Gerund, you go downstairs and make sure only badges get up here. The media is going to be all over this. We got plenty of part-timers on this week for the festival, so call 'em in if you need to."

"Yes, ma'am," Gerund said. He headed downstairs.

"You—" Catherine stalled. She didn't even know the name of the deputy standing in front of her. She glanced down at his tag. "Conroy, is it?"

"Yes, ma'am," he said.

"Conroy, find a phone and call the coroner. Tell him we have a body, don't mention who yet. Let's see if we can't keep a lid on this as long as possible. To be safe, don't talk to anyone who isn't with the sheriff's department. Got it?"

"Yes, ma'am," Conroy repeated.

"And after you do that, get to the hospital. I want an update on Calvin every half-hour. Can you do that?"

"I'm on it."

"Good. Okay. Try the offices down at the end of the hall for a phone." She gestured behind him.

"Sure thing, ma'am." Conroy headed toward a stretch of offices at the opposite end of the hall. Catherine didn't know if anyone was obligated to take orders from her, but she was giving them, and they were listening.

Behind her, Harry Bennett lay sprawled out over his desk, waiting to be officially pronounced and taken to the morgue. Catherine walked over to him. A few feet away on the ground was his pistol, the handle smeared with blood. She left it for now. His eyes were still open, staring up at the ceiling. A pool of dark blood slowly oozed across the desktop like lava, seeping from his neck, dripping over the side and onto the floor. The scent of death hung thick in the air—a mixture of iron, gunpowder, and human waste. There was a good possibility Harry had voided his bowels in his final moment.

Catherine took the whole picture in, allowed herself to understand all of its true colors. She had just killed a man—that color was the brightest—and the scariest thing about that was the realization that it didn't bother her. A lot of what had just happened twisted her up inside: getting shot at, almost dying, Gaines's uncertain future, being thrown in charge. But killing Harry was not on that list. Perhaps it was because she was justly defending herself. Or perhaps it was because she knew what kind of man Harry Bennett was, and the world was a little better without someone like that.

Her mind was on fire. How the hell was she going to explain this? People would demand to know exactly what had happened, why this young deputy killed their beloved mayor. Forget that the sheriff had been shot. Forget that Harry had fired first. Because what had Harry *really* ever done to deserve this? Not him. He was a saint. It must've had something to do with that liar, that girl who was saying those awful things. This was *her* fault, not Harry's. Catherine could see exactly how this would play out. Anything to preserve their idea of the man they had elected to lead them.

She slowly circled the desk, playing the scenario on repeat over and over again in her head. What proof had Gaines been talking about? He had told her he had found something, some kind of evidence, and Harry had yelled something about pictures during their standoff. She had no idea what he had been referring to. Then something caught her eye as she came around the back of the desk, something pinned under Harry's shoulder. It was the corner of a photograph. Black and white. Catherine reached down and carefully pinched the edge the pictures between her fingers, dragging them out from underneath Harry. They slid slow but firmly, greased by blood, and then released. The images were partially obscured by dark red streaks, but what they depicted was still clear.

Looking at the photographs, she took a seat in front of Harry's body and waited for the coroner.

Later, when they arrived to take his body, Catherine would still be sitting there. And when Harry was finally zipped up and carried away, she would allow Dickie Hume to go right along with him.

CHAPTER 40

His hands would not stop shaking. Even when he pulled into the driveway and shut off his car, David could not hold steady. He had almost killed a man. He would've gone through with it, too, if the sheriff hadn't shown up. That was the truth, and it was enough to shake him—shake any man, he reasoned. Knowing how close to the edge he had come. How close to making a decision that would have drastically altered his life forever.

Until ten minutes ago, David wasn't sure he would ever see his home again. But here it was, right in front of him now: the red front door; the black shutters; the weathered, gray shingles; the crooked chimney. It was a beautiful sight, and looking at it, he couldn't help but picture Kara and Ellie both inside, waiting for Daddy to come home. In a different time, that was the case, but not today. Although that wasn't to say that it was outside the realm of possibility. Maybe things between him and his daughter weren't the way they once were, but for the first time in days, he had a restored hope that they could get there again. It would just take time. And time he had.

He glanced at his watch: 5:39. Kara should be home. In the haze that had been the past few days of his life, he remembered a conversation from the night before. Kara had gone to school today. It was her first day back. He hoped it had gone well. She deserved a return to something normal. And Ellie was working late. That was why her car wasn't there. Then he remembered a discussion about Kara staying home alone. Both he and Ellie had reluctantly agreed to allow her to. But if Kara was home, why did the house look so empty? Even though it was still light out, Kara always at least turned the kitchen light on when she was home. They'd fought about the electric bill more times than he could remember. Looking through the bay window in the front of the house, the kitchen was dark.

David stepped out of the car and headed up the walkway.

The front door was unlocked. He went inside. "Hello?" His voice travelled into the early-evening dusk and fell away.

No answer.

"Kara? You here?" David walked farther into the house. No sign of anyone. He did a lap through the first floor, returning to the foot of the stairs. Nothing.

He ascended.

The doors that lined the hallway all opened into still rooms, except for the last one on the right—the bathroom. That one was shut, no light emanating from its edges, as he imagined it might if it were occupied. "Kara? You up here?"

Still no answer.

David walked down the hall, peering inside each room and finding no one. When he came to his daughter's bedroom, he leaned in. Her bed was made but wrinkled and depressed, as though someone had slept on top of the covers. The little purse she carried everywhere, the blue one with silver buttons, sat on her nightstand, and on the floor next to that, her backpack. He exited, turned, and popped his head into his and Ellie's bedroom. Another empty room.

Where was she? A fresh wave of nerves washed over him. Maybe she'd gone to a friend's house after school. But all her stuff was here.

The only door he hadn't checked yet was the bathroom. But why wouldn't she answer him if she was in there? His mind would not—or could not—comprehend.

"Kara?" David placed his hand on the doorknob and turned. It was locked. He knocked. "You in there? Kara? Can you answer me?" He jiggled the knob and placed an ear against the door. Silence. "Kara, it's Dad. You there?" No answer. Panic was building quickly, his gut tightening.

The telephone began to ring downstairs. But it was not a phone at all. In this moment, it was an alarm. That was how David heard it, anyway. Something was wrong.

He pressed a hand against the thick edge of the door and pushed, turning the doorknob simultaneously. It wouldn't budge. "Kara, open up, c'mon, sweetie, it's Dad."

The hope he had so briefly felt down in his car drained from him. Now it was a sickening dread. "C'mon, Kara. This isn't funny." He used his shoulder—a gentle shove, then a forceful one. The solid door barely moved in its frame. The slider lock must've been latched, too. "Kara, please, if you're in there, open the door. Everything is going to be okay. I'm here now. It's over." But of course she was in there. He wasn't trying to break the door down with the expectation of finding the room empty.

The phone clattered on, screaming in the background. Who the hell was calling? Didn't they know that his daughter might be...

David backed away from the door. He would have to kick it in. But, dear God, what would he find?

"Kara, please!" He yelled, sending his weight forward again.

At the last second, there came the sound of the door unlocking. Then, just like that, she stood in the doorway, an angel appearing from nowhere. It was as if David's final scream had fallen on the ears of heaven and God had instantly answered. He stopped in his tracks as the door swung open, almost toppling forward with momentum. There she was, standing in the doorway, soaking wet in all her clothes. It didn't matter why, because there was his daughter—alive. That was all that registered. Their eyes met, and for a moment there was only silence between the two. There were no words capable of capturing what was being communicated. But they both knew what was being said.

At last, David took a step toward his daughter, still finding his breath. "Kara, what were you—" he tried, but before he could get any further, his daughter bridged the distance and wrapped her arms around him. She squeezed tight, her frigid body finding safety in the warmth of her father. For a moment he could only stand stiff, caught off guard.

Over Kara's shoulder the scene framed in the bathroom doorway confirmed his fear. He had almost forgotten about that razor, but now, he supposed, he would never be able to shake its image. In a future he had already begun to paint in his mind, he would forever see its rusty blade sitting there on that porcelain ledge when he closed his eyes. What it had almost been used for would be a constant reminder of how frighteningly thin the membrane that separates life and death actually was. How fragile.

"It's okay. It's going to be okay now." David lifted his arms and embraced his daughter as she began to cry. "It's over. They got him... they got him, honey."

Kara didn't ask to know more. It was enough now. She lifted her head away from her father's chest. The look on her face wasn't happiness or sadness or anything easily decoded. But it might've been the look of a person finally at peace. And that was a start. "I love you, Dad. I love you. I'm so sorry," she said, refusing to let go.

The words warmed his heart. "I know, sweetie... I know. It's not your fault. I'm here now." He kissed the crown of his daughter's head. She smelled of wildflowers. And for that moment, she was the little girl in the purple sundress, the girl who had chased fireflies in the twilight fields of long ago memories.

Through the bathroom window, the orange glow of the falling sun kissed the tops of the trees on the faraway horizon. Fiery colors painted the sky heavenly shades behind pastel clouds. And from here, a beautiful awareness came into view: somewhere, beyond that sunset, a good life waited for Kara, a life filled with joy and love and laughter. That she would find it someday would be his promise to her. It always had been.

Kara squeezed tighter, and David held her. He would hold on until she let go, forever if he had to. And that was all right with him.

That was all right.

CHAPTER 41

Machines beeped at steady paces. Nurses came and went, drawing blood and hanging IVs. Doctors hovered at the end of his bed, speaking in ominous tones. "Just nicked his aorta," he remembered hearing while in and out of consciousness. He was lifted, rolled, scrubbed, and then lifted and rolled again. Bandages were changed and then re-changed what felt like every few hours; he couldn't be sure. His arm was pricked and poked. His blood pressure was taken at unknown intervals. All of this went along without his consent, not that he could've given it anyway. For the first forty-eight hours, the staff of Massachusetts General Hospital made all his decisions for him while he floated out there in some gray area between dreaming and awake. But on the third day, Calvin Gaines opened his eyes and retook the reins.

At first, his head had been a slurry of out-of-focus memories, a spliced-together B-reel of pain and procedures. But slowly, pieces fell together as his mind gained footing. He had been shot. A cautious self-inspection of his chest revealed a calamity of tubes and dressings as well as a relentless throbbing. His wife had been waiting there beside his bed, too, attempting to sleep in a half-upright position on a small vinyl couch that had been moved into the room. Staff had tried to tell her she could not stay overnight—*visiting hours only*—but Linn had laughed in their faces, and now there was a couch.

It had been night when Gaines finally came around, and awaking to find himself in a dark room was reassuring, in a strange way. It felt real. Not too perfect. Had his eyes opened upon a scene of bright white hospital fluorescents, everything clean and pristine, he might've assumed he had moved on to the Upper Room. So in a way, the darkness had allowed for a gentler return. And there was something profoundly enlightening about that. Maybe he was connecting dots where there were none—his blood had still been rich with morphine at the time—but he couldn't help but think being able to see a silver lining inside darkness was a significant thing.

His mind still set in the moment of his last conscious memory, Gaines's first words upon rejoining the world, croaked through a cracked-leather throat, had been: "Is Catherine okay?" There was much he did not know. The previous chapter of his life had abruptly ended with a cliffhanger, and his mind reached, panic-stricken, for the resolution.

Linn had thrown her blanket off and rushed to the side of his bed. A nurse was called in. Gaines was inspected. Tubes were adjusted. Vitals taken. But still his question lingered out there unanswered and overshadowed by the relief for his awakening. He had to repeat himself after demanding a sip of water, brushing aside the concern directed toward him, to finally get an answer. "What happened? Tell me, Linn. Is she okay?" Gaines stared up at her—worried, terrified.

Linn had placed her hand on his shoulder. "Catherine's just

fine, Calvin. Tough gal. Harry Bennett is dead. Do you remember anything? He was going to kill you—both of you, because of those pictures. She says you saved her life."

That was all Gaines needed to hear—that he hadn't lost another deputy, another friend. Everything after that could be taken in at a casual pace as his mind continued to re-center. For the next twenty minutes, Linn filled him in on all that he had missed. She told him what had transpired in that second floor hallway of Town Hall after he had lost consciousness: The shootout (the newspaper's account, anyway). How the aftermath of those photos was still slowly unfolding. How stories of Harry's violent past were starting to emerge as the media began digging into who Harry Bennett really was. She warned him about how the story was already in all the papers and how more and more angle-hungry reporters were showing up every day in their vans, many of which were camped outside the hospital. Catherine had done her share of interviews, relayed the facts, and given statements. But mostly they wanted to speak to Sheriff Gaines, the man who had been shot and was fighting to stay alive against all odds. The dramatic edge, that was what America wanted, a hero injured in the line of duty, serving his public, whether it was true or not. That was the last thing Gaines could think about, though, and he had expressed that fact by suggesting exactly where the media could stick their cameras and microphones. And on that note, Linn had laughed and recommended he get some rest. Then she left to call Maddie at her aunt's to let her know her father was awake and acting like himself.

The moment his wife had left the room, Gaines closed his eyes and was out, back into a dreamless sleep.

The next morning his daughter had come into his room bright and early, and soon after there were tears and love and nervous smiles that gave way to more tears and gentle one-armed hugs. He was told how lucky he was and how he had almost died on the operating table, a small detail his daughter had revealed proudly, which Linn had conveniently left out the night before. "Didn't want to scare you," she'd said, shrugging it off lightly. He asked if the doctors had saved the bullets they had taken out of him. They had. And that was good because he wanted a souvenir. But behind all this love and these small tension-cutting stabs at lighthearted humor, Gaines continued to feel the cold edge of terror lurking in the shadows of his mind. Hiding this from his family just seemed like the only option.

His family stayed a while longer, Linn adjusting his pillow every so often, Maddie rolling around lazily in a spare wheelchair she had discovered in the back of the room. It was the anxious energy of a kid trying to hide just how terrified she really was. After about an hour, a nurse showed up and topped off his morphine, and his eyes began to grow heavy again. Before the drugs completely took hold, he urged his wife to take Maddie and go home and get some real sleep. He would be fine on his own for a bit.

Reluctantly Linn had agreed with a kiss to his forehead and said, "I'll be back tonight."

Then his daughter planted one on his cheek.

He was a man surrounded by love.

"Don't you dare come back tonight. I'll have them throw you out." He had laughed weakly, staying under the radar of his pain. "Get some sleep. I love you—both of you," he'd said, watching with one eye starting to close as his wife and daughter exited the room. Then his eyelids grew heavier still, and sleep came for him again. There was no fighting it, so he went along peacefully into the darkness.

When he awoke, the room was dark again. Instinctively, he glanced at the couch where his wife had been before. Empty. A crippling loneliness rippled through him. He had told Linn to go, but the truth was he liked knowing someone was there, even while—especially while—he slept. It was like having someone stand guard to keep him tethered to the world while he dreamed, lest he should drift off and never wake up.

Then a familiar voice cut the silence of the room.

"A lot of people are mighty pissed, Cal. Had to postpone the festival. They wish you'd waited a few more days to find those photographs." Catherine's face emerged from a dark corner of the room, a humble grin set across her face.

"Good. Let 'em be pissed," Gaines said, and smiled. "How long you been there?"

"Not too long. Fifteen minutes or so." She took a seat on the couch beside his bed. "How you holding up? You look like hell."

"Yeah, well, getting shot a couple times will do that. But I'm okay. I'll be here a little while, I guess. They want to wait until my staples heal a bit. Worried about infections or something. That's what the doctors tell me, at least." Gaines looked down and adjusted his covers, pulling them farther up his lap.

"That's good." Catherine put her hat on the seat beside her. "So I gotta know. I haven't been able to figure it out. Where did you find those pictures? Where the hell did they come from?"

Gaines smirked. "Right to the point. A girl who knows what she wants." He scratched the scruff of his chin. "You won't believe it. It was a damn accident. Remember that ammunition box Millis had, the one full of cigarettes?"

"Yeah, I remember. But Millis? How was he involved in all this?"

"Dumb luck, I think. I figure he must've stumbled upon Harry assaulting Kara and snapped a few pictures, not quite sure what or who he'd seen. Who knows what he was planning on doing with those pictures? But it's good for us he saved them."

"I thought you searched that box. It was nothing but cigarette packs."

"I did, and it was. But the box had a false bottom."

"How'd you figure that out?"

"I didn't really. I knocked it onto the floor by accident and the bottom came loose."

Catherine sniffed and slapped her leg. "Talk about cracking the case. Jesus, what're the odds? I won't lie, I was imagining something a little more…"

"Exciting? Yeah, me too," Gaines said. "I told you, it was an accident. I'm no great detective or anything."

"No, I guess not," Catherine said lightheartedly.

They looked at each other, admiring the sheer coincidence of the situation until the moment faded.

Catherine leaned over to the window behind her, pushed aside a shade, and looked out into the parking lot. "Boy, those cameras can't wait to get a hold of you."

Gaines shook his head. "I heard. I have no idea what they want with me."

"You're a hero, don't you know that?" Catherine smiled.

He couldn't tell if she was being serious. There was an ambiguity in her voice. Gaines looked up at the ceiling as if searching for help. "Gotta be kidding me," he muttered. "How many're out there?"

"Half dozen or so." She turned away from the window. "I'll tell 'em not to wait up."

"That's putting it mildly," Gaines said. "But thank you."

Catherine spread her arms out over the back of the couch and started absently tapping her fingers. "Heard one of those bullets barely missed your heart. You got lucky. I figure someone must've been looking out for you."

"Yeah, real lucky," Gaines said sarcastically, gesturing to all the tubes in his chest. "So how about you? How're you doing with all this? Sounds like you have your hands full."

Catherine rubbed a hand over the back of her neck, glancing around the room. "Me? I'm fine. Been so busy with everything, I haven't really had time to think about it."

Gaines doubted that was true. "That's good," he said.

"Yeah, I suppose it is." Catherine nodded.

Their conversation stalled, and they both stared down at their hands. Slowly a pocket of silence grew between them. Gaines sensed the inevitable thing hanging out there, the thing thickening the atmosphere between them. It needed to be gotten out of the way. It was coming.

Catherine sat forward, the vinyl couch letting out a squelch. "Listen, I just want to get this out there. I know what you did. I saw you step in front of—"

Gaines waved a hand. "We don't need to do this. I was only doing what anyone would do. Hell, from what I hear, you're the real hero in all this, not me. You should be the one the reporters talk to. So please don't thank me. I honestly don't deserve it." He believed that too. This might've never even happened had he done his job with a little courage from the outset. Her gratitude was like a knife twisting in his side, reminding him of that fact.

Catherine exhaled the breath she had reserved for her thank-you speech, her face grimacing into a veteran look of annoyance. "Dammit, don't be a stubborn idiot. Just let me say thank you. Maybe you don't care, but I do. You saved my life. You can't just step in front of a gun for me and expect me not to say something. Jesus, you can be a pain, you know that?"

Gaines snorted an agreeable laugh. "And *I'm* the stubborn one? Says the girl who can't take no for an answer."

"I mean it, Cal. When I came around that corner, I was already dead in Harry's sights. If you hadn't done what you did, I don't think I'd be here right now. At the very least I'd be laid up in a bed beside you. And I don't know about you, but *I* think that deserves some show of appreciation."

Gaines searched the room for something else to focus on, but eventually he surrendered to her gesture, his smile fading. "I'm sorry. I don't mean to be a jerk."

"You're not being a jerk. There isn't really any right way to react to all this, I guess. Neither of us have ever dealt with anything like this before. I just wanted you to know that I'm very grateful for what you did."

"I do know that." Gaines hesitated. "And if you weren't I'd be mighty pissed. It hasn't exactly been fun being here."

They laughed, lifting the tension from the sentimental moment.

She leaned farther off the couch and patted him firmly on the shoulder. "I have no doubt about that. Just glad I didn't have to find out the hard way."

Gaines winced, grabbing his arm. "Easy, still a little sore."

"Sorry." She quickly removed her hand.

"And I suppose I owe you a bit of gratitude, too," Gaines said. "Don't think I don't know I wouldn't have made it outta there if it wasn't for you. I doubt Harry would've called me an ambulance. Probably would've finished me off if you hadn't—" He stopped himself before entering the unchartered territory of her killing Harry Bennett.

Catherine looked away briefly, and then just as quickly her gaze returned. "What? Shot him? It's okay, you can say it. I'm not as fragile as you think."

"I don't think that. Trust me. And it has nothing to do with being fragile." Gaines used his good arm to push himself up the bed. "I know I can't speak from experience, but I don't imagine taking a man's life is as easy as squashing a fly and getting on with your day."

Catherine's face darkened. "You're probably right. I don't doubt that. But I wouldn't know anything about taking a man's life."

"How do you mean? You killed him, didn't you?" Gaines said, slightly confused.

"Maybe Harry lived and breathed like you and me, but that doesn't mean he was anything close to being a man. He was something much less, believe me. I saw those pictures—hell, I didn't even need to see them to know he was guilty, I always knew—and anyone who could do that deserves far worse than the quick exit he got. Part of me wishes he were still alive. Some time in prison, taking what he was giving, would've been better suited for him." There was no remorse in her eyes. Nothing that even resembled it. "So like I said, I don't know what it's like to take a man's life. Squash a bug, sure."

"Seems like maybe you've thought about this more than you let on."

"Enough, I guess." Catherine relaxed some. She'd brought herself to the edge of her seat again, and now she eased back. "Enough to know that I shouldn't lose any sleep over it."

"No, I suppose you shouldn't. I can't say as I see it like you, but that doesn't mean I don't understand what you mean or that I think you're wrong," Gaines said.

Catherine nodded, the corners of her mouth twitching ever so slightly.

A nurse entered holding an assortment of bandages in her hands. "Time to change your dressings, doll," she announced.

Gaines held up a hand. "Could you actually give us a few minutes?"

The nurse stopped and looked at Catherine. The two smiled politely at each other.

"No, it's fine," Catherine said. "Let her do what she needs to do. We can chat some more later. I need to get back—"

"I need to talk to you about something," Gaines said. "It won't take long."

"I'll come back in ten, but after that, you're all mine. Need to keep that clean," the nurse said.

"Ten it is." Gaines gave her a thumbs-up. "You have my word."

The nurse walked out.

"What do you need to talk about?" Catherine leaned forward, her hands planted on her knees.

Gaines regarded her earnestly. "How're things going for you at the station? You're pretty much running the show now, aren't you?"

"Pretty good, all things considered. I feel a little strange telling people what to do. I get the idea some of the guys don't think I should be in the position I am. No one's said anything, but I can tell. And I don't know how seriously the locals take me. To them, I'm still the little girl they all knew growing up." Catherine folded her arms and looked sideways. "I mean, it isn't like an official thing that I'm in charge or anything. It kind of just happened that way."

"You don't think that says something?" Gaines said.

"What're you talkin' about?" Catherine narrowed her eyes.

"That you stepped into the role without being told to," Gaines said. "In my experience, leaders are hardly ever chosen at random. They're either elected, like I was, or they emerge out of necessity, and that's you. The ones that come about in your fashion are the best kind. It's a truer leadership. Anyone can get elected under the right circumstances, but that doesn't make them a leader. Don't believe it, look at me."

"Cal—"

"Let me finish. I ran for sheriff because at the time there was an empty seat in Heartsridge County when Billy Surret died— that and I had a kid, and Linn thought it'd be a good pay bump. Christ, I barely had any experience. I was still wet behind the ears. The only reason I was elected was because no one opposed me. All the other deputies were either too close to retirement and had no interest, or they were morons, so it seemed like a no-brainer. Sometimes the timing is just right. It was an easy choice, not necessarily the *best* choice, though. But you, you did what had to be done when it needed to be done, and that's admirable, that's baptism by fire. You've already proved to yourself you can handle the job. You can't learn that kind of courage, it's just who you are. The same way I was born a man and you were born a woman. You don't get to choose."

Catherine raised her eyebrows. "I don't know that I'd call myself a leader. I mean sure, I'm keeping things going while you're in here, but that won't last. This is a temporary thing. Believe me, people will be glad to see you come back. *I'll* be glad."

"And what if it wasn't temporary?" Gaines asked.

Catherine's lips parted and her eyes widened. "Look, maybe you're just a little shaken right now, but—"

"I'm not shaken. I've thought about this a lot, mostly before this all happened. This"—he pointed to his chest—"me getting shot, and you killing Harry, was just what it took for me know I wasn't crazy for thinking it. I'm not cut out for this. I never was. Maybe collaring drunks and settling disputes and petty stuff like that, sure. But girls getting raped, murder, all this self-serving darkness in people, I just don't have the stomach for that. And until last week, I honestly was naïve enough to think Heartsridge was spared all that miserable stuff. But it isn't. No place is, I suppose. Even if it's not right out in the open, if you know where to look, it's always there."

Catherine stood, running a hand through her hair and beginning to pace slowly. "You sure they haven't cranked your meds up a bit too high? You're talking a little loopy." She pretended to check his IV. It was a joke, but her face wouldn't lie; she knew he was serious. Or at the very least, that he believed the words he was saying.

"I'm sure. I don't want this burden anymore. That's what it feels like now, you know that? A burden. You're more suited for this than I ever was. You knew from the get-go that Harry was guilty. You had no doubt." Gaines shook his head, staring down at his lap, ashamed. "The worst part is that I think I did, too, but was just too foolish to do anything about it. And that's really what matters. I saw what I wanted to see. I should've let you run with it. I should've trusted you. Who knows, maybe I wouldn't be laid up in this bed right now, and you wouldn't have had to shoot someone and almost get yourself killed."

"You can't beat yourself up for that," Catherine said. "I was a little hotheaded about the whole thing at first. I had my own agenda. And besides, you were only doing your job."

"No, I wasn't," Gaines said abruptly, looking her hard in the eyes. "*You* were doing my job. I was doing what was safe. And Kara Price deserved better than safe. You knew that, but I couldn't see it."

"So you're just going to step down—quit?"

"If that's how you want to see it. Or you could look at it as I'm turning the job over to someone more qualified."

Catherine scoffed. "I don't think you can just give me the job like that. I mean, it's a nice gesture and all, but—"

"No, but the county advisors will need an interim sheriff, and I have enough influence to make sure they choose who I say for my remaining term. After that, it's outta my hands. If you want to keep the position, you'll have to earn it. You got a little while until the next election, so show the people what you're capable of. Prove to them what you've already proven to me."

"I don't even know where to begin."

Gaines's face lightened. "Maybe I can point you in the right direction. Consider this a gift for saving my life."

"What gift? What're you talking about?"

"You heard back about the ballistics on Millis's gun yet?" Gaines asked.

"No. They said a few weeks on the results."

"Good. Once they figure it out, you'll have lost your chance."

"Figure what out? I don't follow," Catherine said.

"There was something else in the bottom of that ammunition box. Some driver's licenses Millis was… collecting, I guess you could say. They should still be in there."

"What? Whose licenses?"

"You'll figure it out. Gotta earn it, remember? But when you do connect the dots—and I know you will—those news cameras aren't gonna want me. So do us both this favor."

Catherine's eyes were bright with curiosity but undercut by confusion. "I don't really know what to say. I wasn't expecting this."

"Say you'll do it," Gaines said. "It's time for me to move on to something else. You're the right person for the job. I never was."

"Yes," she said with little hesitation. "I'll do it. I can't say I have any clue what I'm doing, but I'll do it."

Gaines grinned. "You'll do just fine, I have no doubt. I'll place a call tomorrow and make it official. Just look into the licenses in that box and you'll have no problem earning people's respect."

"I will, I promise. The second I leave here." Catherine came closer and stood beside his bed. "What'll you do? You can't retire, you're too young—hole in your chest or not."

"Flattery will get you nowhere," Gaines joked. "To tell you the truth, I don't know what I'll do. I haven't really thought about that yet. But I'm not worried. In my experience, the next thing is always right around the corner." He glanced beyond Catherine briefly. "Now before I get in trouble, I think I need to let this nurse do her job. I'm getting the evil eye. Last thing I want is an angry woman taking care of me."

Catherine looked behind her.

The nurse was standing in the back of the room. "Time's up," she said pleasantly.

"So it is," Gaines said, looking at Catherine. "So it is."

Catherine nodded at Gaines and stuck out her hand. They shook. "I'll tell those reporters not to wait up," she said.

"Thanks, Catherine. Oh, and maybe you want this." He opened a small drawer in his bedside table and pulled out his sheriff's badge. He tossed it to Catherine, and she caught it. "Anyone gives you any trouble, this should shut 'em up. I don't need it anymore."

Catherine eyed the badge thoughtfully for a moment. "So this is really what you want, huh?"

"It is," Gaines said. "It's for the best."

"I hope you know what you're doing." Catherine sighed.

"Does anyone ever? Just take the leap and hope for the best. The bets we dare to make when the odds are against us are what define us. Sometimes you win and sometimes you lose. But that's life. We can't always protect ourselves. And as long as you do your honest best with what you have, everything else is just noise."

"I think you're probably right." Catherine slid the badge into her pocket and looked at him without saying a word for a few moments. Then she smiled. "Take care, Cal." She grabbed her hat off the couch, set it atop her head, and walked out, her stride sure and steady.

With a heavy heart, Gaines watched her go, until she disappeared around the corner, taking in her pocket the last decade of his life. It wasn't easy, but the most important things never were.

The nurse approached and set a small plastic bin down beside him. It was full of pads and wipes and gauze and sterile things. "Hope I didn't interrupt anything too important," the nurse said.

"Not at all. I'm ready when you are." Gaines smiled wanly.

The nurse pushed another dose of morphine into his IV. It would take the edge off, and he didn't mind that right now.

Gaines turned his head to the side and looked out the window as the nurse began removing his bandages. Divine warmth rushed through his body. His eyes fell heavy again. The stars were just beginning to poke through the early night sky and twinkle like a million tiny eyes of God. All the while, Catherine's question lingered in the back of his mind: *What would he do now?* It was a legitimate question, one for which he did not have an answer. But that was okay. He was certain an opportunity would present itself, if it hadn't already. After all, a position had just opened up down at Town Hall, and Gaines was sure that somewhere inside him he had at least one more blind leap into the unknown left.

He closed his eyes and allowed himself to drift off into the stars. He would rest now. Tomorrow there would be much to do.

About the Author

Christian Galacar is a writer of many things—bad checks, self-proclaimed hilarious Facebook updates, angry fast-food Yelp reviews—but mostly he enjoys writing fiction of all genres. The lovechild of Tabasco Sauce and Ayn Rand, he lives in Massachusetts with his couch and a poor selection of spices.

Follow on Twitter @Christian_Lang
Or reach out through email at cgalacar@gmail.com
www.christiangalacar.blogspot.com

ONE LAST THING

So you've made it this far. Congratulations! You're awesome and I already think you deserve a lifetime without ever having to visit a dentist again. Unless, of course, you like that sort of thing, in which case I cannot help you. Just kidding—I am forever grateful, regardless of your bizarre behavior. All I ask is that you take a moment to write an honest review. The power of your opinion is greater than you may know and helps bring my work to the attention of others. Thank you for any consideration you give this, dear reader, and I hope you continue to read what I write. Drive safe.

Made in the USA
Middletown, DE
07 November 2019